ONE TIN SOLDIER

ALSO BY CHRIS TULLBANE

<u>The Murder of Crows</u>

See These Bones
Red Right Hand
One Tin Soldier

<u>Stories from a Post-Break World</u>

The Stars That Sing
The Storm in Her Smile
A Sure Thing
Fire of Unknown Origin *

<u>The Many Travails of John Smith</u>

Investigation, Mediation, Vindication
Blood is Thicker Than Lots of Stuff
Ghost of a Chance
The Italian Screwjob *
A Dead Man's Favor *
Godswar *
John Smith Doesn't Work Here Anymore *

*Forthcoming

ONE TIN SOLDIER

CHRIS TULLBANE

GHOST FALLS PRESS

NEVADA

First published by Ghost Falls Press 2021
One Tin Soldier. Copyright © 2021 by Chris Tullbane.

GHOST FALLS PRESS

Publisher's Cataloging-in-Publication Data
provided by Five Rainbows Cataloging Services

Names: Tullbane, Chris, author.
Title: One tin soldier / Chris Tullbane.
Description: Henderson, NV : Ghost Falls Press, 2021. | Series: Murder of crows, bk. 3. | Also available in audiobook format.
Identifiers: ISBN 978-1-955081-05-4 (paperback) | 978-1-955081-03-0 (ebook)
Subjects: LCSH: Superheroes--Fiction. | Heroes--Fiction. | Self-actualization (Psychology)--Fiction. | Fate and fatalism--Fiction. | Bildungsromans. | Fantasy fiction. | Science fiction. | BISAC: FICTION / Superheroes. | FICTION / Coming of Age. | FICTION / Fantasy / General. | FICTION / Science Fiction / General. | GSAFD: Fantasy fiction. | Science fiction. | Bildungsromans.
Classification: LCC PS3620.U45 O54 2021(print) | LCC PS3620.U45 (ebook) | DDC 813/.6--dc23.

Book cover design by ebooklaunch.com

FIRST EDITION

For Nami,
the reason for everything

ACKNOWLEDGMENTS

Thank you to everyone who helped make this book a reality:

My angel-wife, Nami.

The usual suspects: Jamie, Johanna, Keith, Kerri, Mark, Sam, Shawn, Simon, and my parents.

The talented newcomers: Claudia, Cory, Mitch, Tom, and Ziggy.

This book (and series) would not be what it is without their aid, support, and input.

The Class of 76

Given Name	Cape Name	Power Class
Alan Jackson	The Manimal	Beast Shifter
Caleb Mikkazi	Supersonic	Jitterbug/Flyboy
Damian Banach	Walker	Crow
Erik Thorsson	The Viking	Titan
Erin Pearson	Cyclone	Wind Dancer
Evelyn Mandelhoff	Wormhole	Teleporter
Jeremiah Jones	Stonewall	Mineral Shifter
Johannes Callum	Prince	Siren
Kayleigh Watai	Vibe	Empath
London Sullivan	Ember	Pyromancer
Matthew Strich	Paladin	Stalwart
Nadia Kahale	Orca	Stalwart
Olympia Kennedy	Spectra	Lightbringer
Orson Douglas	Oscuro	Shadecaster
Patricia O'Connor	Makara	Hydromancer
Penelope Von Pell	Winter	Weather Witch/Wind Dancer
Santiago Tomayo	El Bosque	Druid
Sofia Black	Silt	Earthshaker
Tessa McShane	Poltergeist	Telekinetic

Former members:

Given Name	Power Class	Status
Frederic Ficus	Switch	Transfer
Ishmae Naser	Pyromancer	Missing
Jason Abara	Hydromancer	Transfer
Rebecca Wells	Spark	Transfer
Shane Stevenson	Healer	Dead

PROLOGUE

In a suit and tie, Dominion looked old, worn, and shockingly normal. Just another civilian, come to watch the ceremony taking place in the auditorium below, wearing a rumpled suit, dark face etched with lines. It was hard to believe he was the most powerful man in the world.

It was far less difficult to believe he was dying.

The woman formally known as Midnight wove her way through the observation room's small crowd to stand next to the old Power, breaching his perpetual bubble of space.

"Alexa." Dominion's voice was deep and gravelly, more suited for battlefields than quiet conversation.

"Sir." She was a head taller than him, even in flats. "It's good to see you. Jonathan wasn't sure if you would be coming this year."

"This is one of the Academy's two ceremonies that I try never to miss. The other is graduation." He nodded to the stage below. "You're in time for Mammoth's recruitment speech."

"I'm surprised he even bothered this year."

Dominion shrugged shoulders that had always looked too wide on his frame. "There's something to be said for tradition. Mammoth always gets first crack at selling the third-years on the Mission's work. They do a lot of good out in the Badlands, and it gives third-years who might not be getting an internship the chance to save face. Better to volunteer for field work with the Mission than to be forced to go because no Cape team wanted them."

"Still. This year, of all years... he has to know every student down there will be getting an invitation."

"He knows it. And while it's also tradition to keep the students in the dark, some of them have probably run the numbers and figured it out too. Nevertheless, the man believes in what he does, and—" Dominion's smile was a flash of white, almost lost in the greying wrinkles of his face. "—he does love to give a speech."

Nineteen students sat in costume in the first two rows of the auditorium. Behind them were their instructors, along with representatives from every Cape team in the country. Of them all, only Nikolai, the Academy's close-combat professor, came close to matching the size of the man on the stage. *Mammoth* was as much a descriptor as it was a Cape name.

"Speaking of those students," continued Dominion, "how is your patient?"

As if of their own accord, Alexa's eyes came to rest on one student in the second row. His costume was black with green accents, and he wore a full mask with a white skull on its front. To his left was a sharp-eyed, dark-haired woman in a matching color scheme. To his right, a stocky woman in shades of brown.

"Is this the part where I pretend ignorance as to which patient you're referring to?"

"I'd rather you didn't. Mammoth's speech hasn't changed in twelve years, so we have the time to talk in circles if you wish. But neither of us is getting any younger."

Alexa winced. "Damian is… resilient. He's had to be, given his childhood and his mother's murder. And he's survived everything the world threw at him these past eighteen months—his father's death, the battle at the Hole, and even his own kidnapping and the loss of his hand. His instructors will all tell you he's ready to be a Cape."

"And what does his therapist say?"

"Damian has always been hard to read. On the surface, everything is fine, but the mind mirrors the body in some ways. Repetitive trauma causes damage that is invisible to the naked eye… and we don't have the luxury of x-rays or MRIs when dealing with an individual's psyche."

"You think he's damaged goods?"

"I think we're *all* damaged goods. It comes with the territory. Damian has passed every test with a determination that puts even some professional Capes to shame, but…" She shook her head. "Professional distance is both harder to maintain and all the more necessary when making life or death decisions on behalf of your patient. I may be compromised when it comes to Damian Banach."

Dominion said nothing.

Alexa sighed. "All things being equal, I think he would make an exceptional Cape and deserves the opportunity, but as we are both aware, all things are *not* equal."

"Because of his power."

"Yes. It always comes back to the necromancy. Despite all that he has achieved, no Cape team wants the risk of taking on a Crow. What if he goes full Crimson Death in the middle of an operation? Or worse?"

"*Or worse?* Have the results of his new Test leaked already?"

"Not yet. But the Academy's students aren't the only ones who can do the math. Other Capes look at the Black Hats he's killed and the situations he's survived, and they know damn well he's not a Low-

Three. If they knew the truth, that the Academy's only Crow was a Full-Five…" She shook her head again. "When Paladin found out—Paladin senior, that is—he called Walker a *walking bomb* and wanted him sent as far away from the Free States as possible. That man's an unmitigated asshole, but he's also as media-savvy as they come. He knows there are only a handful of teams who could weather the public relations storm of even having a Crow join their roster. What team could actually survive Walker if he breaks bad?"

"I can think of one."

That set Alexa back on her heels. For the first time, she tore her eyes from the students below to look Dominion in the face.

"Stormwatch hasn't recruited in years."

"We lost Tempest and Moth at the Hole." The Cape's voice was empty, failing to disguise emotional wounds a long way from healed. "Undertow is retiring to spend time with his grandchildren, and God bless him for that. Meanwhile, the doctors give me another eighteen months of active service, at best. We need new blood and—"

"And if Damian snaps while on his internship, you'll be in position to stop him and minimize the damage," she finished. "Shit."

"Excuse me?"

"I'd convinced Zeus to offer Damian an internship."

"The Hammers of God are looking for members?"

"Not exactly. But they're out on the borders and cover a lot of territory. Nobody would ever realize Damian was actually still here in California, training with my agency."

"As a government shadow."

"Rough edges notwithstanding, he's shown all the requisite skills. And since we don't officially exist, public relations aren't a concern. I should have known it was coming together too smoothly."

"You don't think he'll choose the Hammers of God once he realizes their offer is a smokescreen on your behalf?"

"According to Jonathan, he *quoted you* in his own expulsion hearing, Dominion. There's no way he's turning down an opportunity to join your team, even if it's just a six-month internship."

Mammoth was nearing the end of his speech, the almost ritualistic request for any third-year who had been moved by his words to stand and accept the call. Alexa would have felt sorry for the Shifter, whose recruiting trip to Los Angeles had been a lost cause from the beginning, if she didn't know he'd be leaving again with a mountain of supplies and charitable donations.

"I won't deny the value your agency provides," said Dominion, "but the country needs its symbols. As someone who wore the cape, you understand that. Sooner or later, word about my condition will leak, and when it does, the Free States will need to know that a new generation stands ready to serve as its shield."

"And you want *Damian* to be the face of that generation?"

"One of them, yes. Like you said, he deserves the opportunity. What he's already done earns him that much."

"Carnage?"

"I was thinking of the people he rescued in Reno. Killing is easy. Putting your own life at risk to save others is considerably less so."

"As much as I think he'd flourish as an agent, I'm really happy to hear you say—"

Her words trailed off as a murmur swept the observation room. Mammoth had finished his speech, one enormous hand stretched out to the student audience in supplication. And against all expectations, one student—one of the nineteen who had made it this far—had risen to his feet.

The third-year's left hand was clenched in a fist at his side, lumpy scar tissue stretched tight across white knuckles. His right arm was tucked behind his back as if to hide that it ended in a stump, and the voice that came from behind the skull mask was hoarse, worn thin by hours screaming in the ghost town of Reno.

"I volunteer," said Walker.

It was the only time Alexa ever heard Dominion swear.

CHAPTER 1

When I was five, my father murdered my mom.

Shit only got worse from there.

Thirteen years in the Bakersfield orphanage, then two and a half more at the Academy, learning to defend the country as a Cape. A month trapped in the belly of the beast of Reno, where I lost my hand but learned the truth of what I was.

Just an experiment.

One of many attempts to breed a new crop of necromancers, to see if any of us would escape the madness of our power. To the man responsible, Mr. Grey to some, Tyrant to the rest, we were all just disposable vessels... temporary carriers of one of the powers he'd yet to claim as his own. We were tools to be leveraged in a war he had not yet begun to fight.

There's always a fucker who wants to take over the world, isn't there? Just our luck that the Free States got two: Tyrant and Tezcatlipoca, mastermind and self-proclaimed god. Pick your poison and hope like hell you survive.

I survived Reno. Freed a handful of people Tyrant had kidnapped. Killed the shit out of some others who had it coming and burned the whole god-damned building down, but I didn't do it alone. And the help I got didn't come for free.

One favor.

Can't say it changed *everything*, because I probably would have ended down here eventually anyway, talking to all of you, telling you my tale. Can't even say that favor was *the* reason things went the way they did, but it was *a* reason.

The past is the past. All that matters is what you do with it.

The people of the Free States will call me a murderer. The Capes and Black Hats call me Walker. A long time ago—so long that I can't even remember her voice—my mom called me Damian.

This is the story of how I died.

ooo

"You didn't climb the wall this time, Bakersfield?"

In the shadow of the alleyway, Her Majesty was darkness in the shape of a woman. As she stepped into the light, the details became apparent: a long-legged body sheathed in leather, her head and face hidden beneath the ever-present motorcycle helmet. The yellow smiley face decal on that helmet's visor looked a little more tired than normal, but I could've just been projecting.

I looked back to where the Academy rose above the surrounding streets and waved the stump of my wrist. "Climbing's not really my thing these days."

"I thought your little school's Healers would have taken care of that."

"It takes more than a Two to regenerate limbs." I wasn't sure even Unicorn would have been able to do it, and he would have been the best Healer the Free States had seen in decades. "I've got a prosthetic but it's more trouble than it's worth, most days. Anyway, Bard's loosened my leash this year. I'm allowed the occasional trip off campus."

I *was* supposed to notify people of my destination in advance, in case Tyrant was lurking outside waiting to snatch me again… but telling the guards that I was off to meet the wanted mercenary known as the Queen of Smiles had seemed like a dumb fucking idea. And a good way to get a bunch of well-meaning guards killed, for that matter.

Besides, Tyrant was public enemy number one in the Free States right now, hunted by Cape teams *and* Alexa's black-ops agency. Nobody had seen him in months, and the sociopath certainly wasn't stupid enough to show up outside the Academy. Especially not with the way the school's defenses had been bolstered after Fallout's attack.

"I wasn't sure you'd even show."

"We made a deal," I said, "and you saved my ass. I'm not going to forget that."

"Actually, I saved your ass and *then* we made a deal." As usual, her voice was a snarl of metal, barbed wire dragged over the teeth of a chainsaw, a crowbar jammed into the gears of some Technomancer's creation. That didn't bother me anymore. It was the times her voice went all liquid and soft that still fucked with my brain. "Even so, I'm glad you came. Guess that school hasn't totally broken you yet."

"Guess not. What can I do for you, Your Majesty?"

"Just like that? No foreplay? No small talk? Just wham, bam, thank you ma'am? Baby Crow gets a girlfriend and suddenly the rest of the world is chopped liver."

I'd had chopped liver a few times at the Academy cafeteria, and it wasn't bad. Beat the hell out of the synth-rations we'd grown up on at the orphanage. But I got what she was saying. I reached for the emptiness at my core, let it spill out of that hole inside of me to smother my frustration and nerves.

"Sorry. I didn't sleep at all last night and we've got our internship assembly tomorrow. The Mission and all those Cape reps.

Our whole fucking class has been on edge for the past week. It's nothing personal."

"And the walker stashed around the corner? Is *that* personal?"

"That's just insurance." There weren't any corpses in or around the Academy, now that my zombie cat had finally met its maker again, but I'd been off campus twice for power-related experiments, and the last such trip had been to one of Los Angeles' cemeteries. I'd snuck this guy back the following night and stashed him in one of the city's many abandoned homes. "Even in the daytime, L.A.'s not the safest place to wander. All sorts of bad elements, they tell me."

She barked a laugh. "Fair enough. Anyway, I won't keep you in suspense. I'm here to call in my favor. And in a roundabout way, it has to do with that assembly tomorrow."

"I don't do assassinations," I told her.

"That makes precisely one of us," came the reply, the smiley face briefly maniacal in the alley's dim light. "I want you to find someone, not kill them."

"*At* the Assembly?"

Her sigh echoed within the confines of the motorcycle helmet. "If they were at the Assembly, I wouldn't need you to find them, would I? The person I'm looking for is out in the Badlands, near as I can tell. I want you to go there and find him. Or her."

"By interning with the Mission for the next six months."

"Got it in one."

"How?"

"By volunteering?"

"No, I mean how am I supposed to find one person that could be anywhere in the Badlands? I'm happy to keep my eyes open, assuming you have a description or a name, but—"

"No name. Not a real one anyway. No description either."

"So then…"

"You talked to Sally Cemetery, right? Her ghost?"

"Yeah."

"And your mom and the little girl at the orphanage too?"

"Nyah." The emotions that name generated skated across the emptiness, leaving me to wonder how the hell Her Majesty knew it. Or the fact that I had a girlfriend, for that matter. "But in those cases, it was less talking, and more them showing me how they died."

"Bingo. I want you to do the same thing. Travel the Badlands. Talk to the dead. Find the person I'm looking for."

I put two and two together and got three and a half. "So, I'm going to have to seek out ghosts whose deaths were linked to the guy you're hunting."

"That's the easy part." She rolled her shoulders, but her helmet remained steady. "This person is responsible for more deaths than anyone in the fucking world. More than that pretend god south of us, even."

Tezcatlipoca had taken over the vast majority of Mexico, turning the surviving inhabitants into little more than drones, and was now extending his domain into San Diego. Who the hell could have killed more people than that?

In the end, there was only one possible answer.

"Thing I like about you, Bakersfield," said Her Majesty, somehow divining where my thoughts had taken me, "is that you've got brains to go along with that sweet little ass. I want you to find Dr. Nowhere."

CHAPTER 2

I loathe being the center of attention. Maybe things were different back when my mom was still breathing, but if so, growing up in an orphanage had beaten the attention-seeker right out of me. Do what you have to, fight for what matters, and don't back down from anyone, sure enough… but public speaking? Stepping out from the crowd, drawing every eye and sudden hushed whisper?

Not my idea of a party.

The whispers had started even before I stood to volunteer for Mammoth's Mission, for a six-month trip into the God-forsaken Badlands to spread peace and joy and whatever the fuck else it was we'd be doing. Truth was, I'd felt the weight of eyes on me the moment I trooped into the auditorium with the rest of my classmates.

Wish I could say it was because my costume was just *that* cool.

That's the problem with fame. It follows you, marks you like a stain that's never coming out. Makes anonymity a pipe dream, mask be damned. I was the Academy's only Crow. The kid who killed Carnage out at the Hole. Who got his ass kidnapped on Christmas Eve and showed up more than a month later in the dead city of Reno. Everyone there, from parents to faculty to Cape team reps, knew my name and nobody knew quite what to do with me.

Fuck if I was going to back down from that though.

Fuck if I was going to let anyone see me sweat.

Even if volunteering hadn't been *my* idea.

Mammoth was a huge guy, all muscles and hair, but that wasn't what impressed me about him. In a world of Titans and Shifters, size wasn't all that rare. Conviction was something else entirely. You could hear the belief in his words. See it in his eyes. This was a man who spent his days in the shit, far from the cameras and the Free States' safety net, who only came back to civilization when it was time to fundraise, to solicit donations, and to convince third-years that his cause mattered.

Half the draw of being a Cape—maybe more than half for some of us—was what came with the role. Fame. Endorsements. Money. Groupies. Hell, El Bosque *already* had groupies, with graduation still seven months away. And here was a man asking us to put all that aside to focus on service and anonymous charity out in the dozens of small towns that had managed to hang on in the Badlands?

That anyone paid attention at all should tell you something. People recognize sincerity when they hear it, even know-it-all twenty-year-olds. It's hard not to respect genuine passion, especially when it's tied to something selfless.

Not that his speech had a damn thing to do with my decision, of course, but you already know that.

Tessa squeezed my hand—my left hand, my only hand—as I stood, as the whispers rose in volume, and our classmates in the front row turned to see what was going on. Halfway through our last year at the Academy, and Poltergeist and I were somehow still together. I gave her all of the credit for that; it hadn't been easy going, especially since Reno.

I'd known better than to spring me volunteering for the Mission on her there at the assembly. Instead, I'd filled her in as soon as I came back from my clandestine meeting with Her Majesty. Hell, I'd even told her about *that* meeting ahead of time.

Never piss off a Telekinetic.

Not when they know where you sleep.

And *especially* not when it's in the same damn room.

I locked eyes with Mammoth across the auditorium, ignoring the murmurs and the stares. If the big Shifter was surprised, he didn't show it.

"I volunteer," I said.

That much was part of the plan.

"Me too," said Silt, to my right.

That sure as hell wasn't.

"Hell yeah," said the spiky-haired asshole in the front row, blurring to his feet the way only someone part Flyboy and part Jitterbug could. Caleb turned and shot me a victorious grin. "No way I'm missing out on the action this time!"

ooo

With the auditorium now filled with family members and team representatives, it took me a while to find my Earthshaker friend. I'd left Tessa back with her beaming parents. Hard to fault them for their pride. First third-year invited to intern with Stormwatch in almost a decade, and it was *their* daughter? That shit was front-page news.

I was every bit as proud. Poltergeist was going to be one hell of a Cape. Being away from each other for six months was going to suck, but we'd known that would be the case even before Her Majesty called in her favor. Chances of me getting an internship at all were close to zero, and the chances of us ending up on the *same* team were even worse than that.

She *could* have volunteered for the Mission with me—had even floated it as an idea—but I'd shot down that plan like a Stalwart with a sniper rifle. And then, after the inevitable blowup, we'd settled down long enough to look at the facts.

Fact 1: There was no way in hell Tessa *wasn't* getting an internship. Given how much ass she'd kicked as a third-year, we could assume she'd be getting several.

Fact 2: Even if Her Majesty hadn't called in my debt, my chances of getting an internship were miniscule. Despite all I'd done to prove myself, Cape teams were still just a bit wary about a Crow's propensity to go crazy and possibly murder anyone around them. Go figure.

Fact 3: That same problem would haunt me on graduation, *unless* at least one Cape team had been convinced that Damian Banach, Baby Crow and one-time kidnappee, wasn't all bad.

Fact 4: The woman I'd briefly shared a blanket with—until my dreams forced us back into separate beds—was uniquely positioned to advocate on my behalf.

Now that she'd be interning with Stormwatch, that plan had gone tits up—no way the pre-eminent Cape team in the country would want someone like me—but at least the argument had convinced her to stay in the Free States. That meant she'd spend the next six months being supported by a full team and the country's greatest hero, instead of traipsing through the Gods-fucked Badlands with her boyfriend, looking for someone who might not even exist.

I called that a win.

And then my best friend had to go and volunteer to join me.

"Silt... what the fuck?" Sofia was over by the food table, looking like a tree stump, if that tree stump was ninety percent muscle and thirty percent attitude. She had distant family in Phoenix, but travel post-Break wasn't something people did lightly without a

Teleporter, so there'd been nobody around to stop her from making a beeline for the food.

"What the fuck what?" She looked up at me over a plate piled high with barbecue—real beef, which I was still getting used to after two-plus years.

"Why did you volunteer? I thought you were hoping for an internship with the Thunderbirds?"

"I figured I'd leave that spot open for someone else." She shrugged and finished chewing. "It's not like I'm going to be on a team long-term anyway. Once we graduate, I'll serve my time, and then—"

"Brownsville?"

"Damn straight."

Brownsville was a town in the war-torn region of Texas, just across the river from what had once been Mexico. Silt had grown up there before she and a few others fled through what was left of New Mexico and into Arizona. I wasn't sure what or who she had left behind, but Sofia was dead set on returning, and returning in force.

"Still… the Mission? Hiking all over the Badlands can't be your idea of a good time."

"All that dirt out there… what's not to love?" The grin slid off her face, and her brown eyes went hard. "You may have talked Poltergeist out of joining you, but I'm a tougher nut to crack, Boneboy."

Damn it, Tessa. "She told you."

"Sure did. Kinda makes me wonder why *you* didn't, but we'll have plenty of months on the road to talk all about that."

"You know you don't have to do this for me. Or for Tessa."

"Shit, I'm doing this for me. Every time you go off on your lonesome, a little less of you comes back. Hell if I'm letting that happen again." Her grin made a triumphant return. "Now, eat some tri-tip. It's a hell of a lot better than whatever garbage we'll get on the road."

She wasn't wrong about that. I was halfway through my own heaping plate of meat when another thought occurred to me.

"What about Supersonic? Did you or Tessa talk him into going too?" *And if so, why?* was the unspoken question. Next to Wormhole, Caleb Mikkazi was my biggest critic in our class. And an asshole, as I may have mentioned a few dozen times in this long, rambling tale.

"Hell no," said the Earthshaker. "Far as I can tell, he just decided, all spur of the moment. Guess he's serious about wanting some action."

"What an idiot."

"Says the one-handed man headed into the Badlands to hunt down the world's only Cat Six Power," said Silt, eyes sparkling. "Maybe you boys are more alike than you thought."

CHAPTER 3

We had a week to get things together before Mammoth and the Mission left town. I spent most of it with Tessa, of course, each of us coming to grips with the reality that the next time we saw each other would be damn near Christmas.

Given how my last two Christmases had gone, it would be nice to have something *good* to look forward to, but it wouldn't make up for all that lost time in between. Supposedly, long-distance relationships had been the best kind of relationship, pre-Break, but that was then and this was now. I'd be well off the grid in the Badlands, with no way to stay in contact. Meanwhile, Tessa would be getting her first taste of the high life of being a Cape: fancy events, promotional shoots, and... worst of all... groupies.

I trusted Poltergeist plenty; I just didn't trust the men of the Free States. After all, I was one of them. We were a shifty fucking lot. The good thing about dating a Power was that anyone who crossed a line would find out just what she could do... but even so, our relationship was barely six months old. I don't know if either of us was totally confident it would survive the coming separation.

We each did our best to pretend though.

Wish I could say that whole week was good times and making out, but we had our share of arguments. That was kind of how things went for us. Given how we got started, it shouldn't have been a surprise. I thought I might almost love her, and that she might even love me back, but it didn't keep us from getting on each other's nerves.

Big part of that was my fault again. Ever since Reno, my dreams had gotten worse. That was saying something; my dreams had always been shit with a side order of awful. But after Reno, it was anyone's bet whether I'd have nightmares of my captivity and torture—nightmares that sure as hell didn't end with Her Majesty rescuing me on Sally Cemetery's dime—or... the other dream.

You remember the one. Nothing but dead people around me, watching me, waiting on me, worshipping me.

It was that dream, the dream all Crows eventually experienced, that had caused us to switch back to separate beds. Even before that, we hadn't been fucking—the close call with my one and only groupie as a second-year had put an end to that—but Tessa had taught me that sharing a bed was about more than just sex.

And then I woke up one night, mid dream, and found I'd accessed my power subconsciously; emptiness flooding my body, every sense primed, death pooled in my fingertips. If Poltergeist and I had been touching... if she'd been a snuggler like Silt's latest girlfriend...

I didn't even want to think about it.

After that, we'd swapped out our queen for two twin beds, and the only thing Tessa had to worry about was being woken up every other goddamn night by my nightmares. Which was at least half the reason we were both perpetually tired and irritable. Hell, she was probably looking forward to our separation just so she could get a decent night of sleep.

Like I said, I gave her all the credit for us still being a thing.

Fighting and making up and trying to hold onto every dwindling minute with Tessa wasn't all I did that week, of course. My usual Academy greys would make me a target in the Badlands, so I took a trip off campus with Silt to get some clothes for the trip: a few pairs of jeans, fresh underwear, and some shirts. I even got a jacket, because our trip through the Badlands would take us into the north, and winter didn't fucking play up there.

I didn't have to pay for any of it, or the backpack that I packed those clothes into, along with my toiletries and the device Her Majesty had given me to contact her with. Apparently, the Academy was providing a small per diem for third-years while we were off campus saving the world.

Got to be honest… it made shopping a hell of a lot more fun.

There were a few parties too on the second floor of the Liquid Hero. With the new second-years stuck running the place, we made a bit of a nuisance of ourselves, I'm sure. Still, it was good to hear where everyone else would be headed. Vibe and Paladin were interning in Los Angeles with the Defenders and Matthew's dad, while Stonewall had managed to get a slot with the Society, who had just lost Mistral a month earlier. The rest of the class was divvied up between the remaining Cape teams, from the North Star all the way down to the Bayside Brawlers, who had been responsible for the infamous fight in the Liquid Hero when we were first-years. Fifteen third-years, spread out amongst almost as many teams.

Muse wasn't one of them. The little Switch hadn't come back to the Academy, and from what I knew, it had been as much Freddie's decision as the school's. Last I'd heard, he was doing contract work with the city's local teams, serving as support staff alongside the usual cadre of Normals. It let him boost Capes before they went into action while staying far away from that action himself, and was a compromise everyone seemed happy about.

No word on whether he'd quit drinking as part of that deal, but I kind of doubted it.

○○○

On Thursday, I got called into Bard's office. Two days until I left town and by that point, I was honestly ready to go. Maybe some people enjoy anticipation—sick fucks, one and all—but for me, I've always preferred getting to the action. Sooner we left, sooner we'd be back, and that's all that mattered. I hadn't spared the actual Mission—or my small-m 'mission' for Her Majesty—more than a moment's thought.

Guess I was the only one.

Bard wasn't alone in his office. Alexa was there too, all in black, as still as a broken vid screen, and looking strangely out of place in an office that wasn't hers. By contrast, Bard looked rumpled and tired, suit jacket hanging on the back of his chair, eyes slightly bloodshot behind the glasses he'd started wearing. I recognized that look: some Cape student was giving him heart palpitations. I didn't know many of the new first-years, but several of my former mentees were now serving as mentors themselves, and they said the new class was a handful.

Nobody had died yet though, so they couldn't be too bad.

"Mr. Banach," said Bard, that famous voice of his every bit as tired as his face, "I wish you would have warned us that you'd be volunteering for the Mission."

Or maybe *I* was the reason he looked like something King Rex's walker had just stomped all over.

"Why's that?"

"So we could have talked you out of it."

"Let's not pretend I was going to get an internship, Bard." I shook my head. "A half-year in the Badlands sounds like it'll be just my speed."

"Are you saying this decision had nothing to do with you meeting the Queen of Smiles last week?"

Without conscious effort on my part, the emptiness filled me. "Are you having me followed now, Alexa?"

It was Bard who answered. "In light of the attack on my Academy last year, we have expanded our passive security layers out to the surrounding areas. You and the mercenary were spotted on camera."

"I hope you didn't send anyone to try to stop her." Her Majesty was a Shifter of a type I'd never seen, a woman who turned into a snarling storm of shrapnel. She'd taken Fallout's best shot and come back hungry for more. The Academy guards wouldn't have stood a chance.

"We are in the business of training Capes and their support teams. I leave the pursuit of dangerous felons to the professional Capes and law enforcement."

"Given her role in the rescue of almost two dozen civilians, the Queen of Smiles is not at the top of anyone's priority lists," added Alexa. "Which does not change the fact that she is extremely dangerous. I know you have a history with her, Damian, but further involvement is not recommended."

"I'm already involved." I shrugged, letting the emptiness retreat to my core. "But it's not a big deal, and it's nothing illegal either. She heard I was going out into the Badlands and wanted me to do some research while I was there."

"Research?"

I waggled my fingers. "Ghost research. Like I did for you and Door in Bakersfield."

"I see."

"So… is that all you needed?" I looked between the two adults. "I still need to finish packing."

That was a lie. It had taken me barely ten minutes to pack, for obvious reasons. But I wasn't a big fan of being ambushed with surveillance footage, even by two of the few adults I actually kind of liked.

"Internship offers notwithstanding—" For some reason, Bard shot Alexa a look as he said that. "—we can't forget that you were kidnapped from these premises last Christmas, and that the Black Hat ultimately responsible remains at large."

"At large and nowhere to be found," I said. "Nobody's even seen Tyrant since I burned down his base, and I doubt we will until he's good and ready. If there's anything that asshole made clear to me, it's that he plays the long game."

"He also made it clear that you are a part of that long game," said Bard. "You will be more vulnerable out in the Badlands than you would have been with one of the Cape teams here in the Free States."

Which meant fuck-all given that none of those Cape teams had been planning to offer me an internship.

"Are you saying I *can't* go on the Mission?"

"If we did, would it stop you?" asked Alexa.

I shook my head. "I gave my word."

Her half-smile came and went and she gave Bard a look.

The older man rolled his eyes. "We figured as much. More importantly, you are an adult in the eyes of the Free States, and we are not in the business of holding our own students prisoner."

I didn't point out that I hadn't been allowed off campus for most of my first two years. Bard was getting to his point and pissing him off wouldn't make this go any faster.

"That said, we've made some adjustments, with your security—and the security of everyone else on the Mission—in mind."

"Oh." It was hard to bitch about that. "Like what?"

"Like hiding your participation entirely. It took me several days and more favors than I wanted to spend, but the family members and Capes who were present for Mammoth's speech have been sworn to silence."

I was starting to understand why Bard looked so tired.

"That secrecy will only last until someone from the press realizes you haven't showed up as an intern on one of the existing teams—and they *will* realize it—but it should give you and the Mission at least a month of grace time."

"When you do leave," added Alexa, "you will be traveling with a larger security presence than normal and along a different route than the one that the papers and news vids will be posting."

I honestly didn't know much about the geography of the Badlands, but I knew it was a lot of territory. Not knowing our route would make finding us damn near impossible.

"I bet Mammoth was thrilled about that."

Bard winced. "He will be speaking to you, no doubt."

"Okay. Anything else?"

"We told him you were a Full-Five."

"You did *what?*" After Tyrant's revelations... after facing down Sally Cemetery in that dream that wasn't a dream... one of the first things I'd done when finding myself back at the Academy was to retake my Test. I'd had to get Bard and Alexa's help to make it happen, but the results were supposed to be a secret.

"He'll be responsible for your safety over the next half year, Damian. He needed to know."

"And I don't get any say in the matter?"

"No more than you'll get one when you join your permanent team. As soon as you go professional, this all becomes part of your record."

Which… made sense too, even if I didn't like it. "And he was still okay with me coming?"

"The Mission needs all the help it can get. A Full-Five Crow is more than Mammoth or anyone would expect, obviously, and I'm sure he'll speak with you about that as well, but he's not going to turn down a volunteer." Bard's voice softened. "He is a good man. I think you, Ms. Black, and Mr. Mikkazi will learn a lot from him."

I hoped so. And if I did well enough, maybe Tessa wouldn't be the only one putting in a good word for me with the real Cape teams. Still. I scowled.

"More security, different route, and dozens of people sworn to secrecy. Why is everything always such a pain in the ass?"

"Welcome to life as a Cape." Bard's smile didn't quite reach his eyes. "I'd ask you to stay out of trouble, but where you're going already makes that an impossibility. Instead, all I ask is that you keep your classmates safe, come back in one piece, and do this school proud in the process."

"Not a problem," I said.

By the end of the Mission, I'd have managed only one of the three, and that one by sheer luck… but that's the post-Break world for you, isn't it? That's not just *dust* collecting in every corner, creeping into your house no matter how regularly you clean.

It's age and it's regret, but mostly, it's all that's left of our good intentions.

CHAPTER 4

The last two days passed in a blur. Holding Tessa. Meditating out on the bench overlooking the Pacific. Eating the cupcakes Winter had made for Silt, Supersonic, and me, as if we were headed to our own funerals, already lost forever in the wind-stricken plains of the Badlands.

My former teammate had gotten an internship with the Emerald Legion, up in Seattle, and she'd woven a few suitably green ribbons into her waist-length white hair. She only mentioned the team, the city, and how happy she was to be going to both eighteen times in the ten-minute process of giving me my brownies. For Winter, that was remarkable restraint.

None of us were teenagers anymore, and we'd all come a long way from the kids who had walked through the Academy gates just two and a half years earlier. Even so, I didn't envy the other members of the Emerald Legion. Penelope may have always been *our* pain in the ass, but it didn't change the fact that she was one.

And then it was Saturday, and we were saying our final goodbyes. Usually, the Mission left town first, so the poor, sad-sack third-years who'd been drafted didn't have to watch their classmates head off to their bright and shiny teams. This year, all the third-years gathered back in that same auditorium with our suitcases or bags, saying goodbye to classmates and family and those Normals we'd developed relationships with. El Bosque had a crowd of soon to be graduating seniors and more than a few juniors around him. All of them women, because of course they would be.

I hadn't started building my own support staff yet—hadn't even tried, despite suffering through a semester-long class on recruitment strategy and team synergy—but I had my own small group of people to say goodbye to.

Every damn one of the first-years I'd mentored had made it to second-year. Not sure how much credit I deserved for that, but they were all there to see me off, from giant Lucy all the way down to little Lynn. Reid shook my hand—my only hand—and patted me on the shoulder, saying he couldn't wait to watch me on the vids. Jacinda, followed as always by her twin brother, Shawn, swung by just long enough to make sure I knew her shirt size if I wanted to bring back some merch from my Cape team. Lucy just beamed at me, a far cry from the young woman who'd ended up in the med ward because of an asshole student.

And then there were two. Lynn and Paco. Technomancer and Summoner, respectively, and the two second-years who had decided to follow my example by becoming mentors for the incoming first-years.

Lynn gave me a hug and stepped back, her eyes drifting down to the stump of my right arm. "You're not wearing the hand I made you?"

"I made the mistake of sparring with Orca this week," I said. "The Healers put me back together, but the prosthetic wasn't quite that lucky."

"That's okay. By the time you get back, the new model should be done. Assuming I can get the energy core working properly."

I hid my wince. Lynn had come a long way as a Technomancer since the days of cube-shaped lighters, but she *was* still just a student.

"Don't worry," she told me. "It will be awesome." She cleared her throat and looked away for a second, and Paco and I both pretended not to see the wetness in her eyes. "Just... make sure you come back okay? Whatever team you're headed to, make sure they keep you out of trouble."

"I don't think that's how the Cape thing works," murmured Paco, in the understatement of the century.

"You know what I mean, Francisco!"

"It's okay, Lynn." I gave her another hug. It felt like I'd been doing nothing *but* hugging people all week. "You know I'm a survivor." I looked over her head at Paco, who was visibly uncomfortable with all the touchy-feely stuff going on. "You two look after each other and the others. And if anything goes wrong with your first-years..."

"We know, Dad," said the Summoner. "We should go talk to Bard *before* we decide to break into someone's dorm room and threaten them with a dead cat."

"Yeah. That." I shook my head. "Give your rats my regards."

"Who's to say Woodrow and Hazel aren't in here with us?" He grinned.

"The auditorium is still standing, for one. You know how Silt feels about them." I reached past Lynn to shake his hand. "Seriously, good luck."

"I think you might need it more than we do. You're the one going off to fight crime, after all."

"Yeah." I didn't correct him, even though Lynn and Paco were as trustworthy as anyone I knew. "But I'm not the one stuck with another semester of Ethics classes taught by Isabel Ferra."

The cocky grin disappeared from the Summoner's face like a Wind Dancer had sent it flying.

○○○

I'd already said my goodbyes to Tessa and Kayleigh both, but they swung by for one last hug—*more* hugs—before friends and family filtered out and we all aligned ourselves with the team reps who had chosen us.

Or, in the case of Silt, Supersonic, and I, the team rep we had chosen.

Vibe's hug damn near broke a rib and then she was dashing over to take Matthew's arm. The Stalwart gave me a nod across the room as the Defenders rep came to join them.

Kind of weird that, with all the problems Matthew had with his dad, he and Kayleigh were still interning with the old man's team. I spared a moment to wonder how that was going to work. Especially with both men using the same Cape name.

Then Tessa was in my arms, and my world was her warmth pressed against me, curly hair tickling my face, and the delicate fragrance of the body lotion she wore when not out in the field. My old orphanage 'friends' would have had something to say about little Damian clinging to a girl like she was the only thing that mattered. Dingus would have called me a pussy, but Dingus was a shithead who ended up in juvie after he tried to rob his own foster family.

Fuck what he or anybody else thought.

"Six months," said Tessa, stepping back to look me in the eye. "You better be back here at the end of it."

"I'll be back. This is home."

"The Academy?" She nodded. "For now, anyway."

That wasn't what I'd meant, but the team reps were calling for their recruits to fall in, and I didn't get the chance to correct her. I

watched her run back across the auditorium and went to find Silt and
the Mission.

Up close, Mammoth was every bit as large as our combat
instructor, Nikolai Tsarnaev, if lacking the other man's serial killer
smile. His hair was brown and close cropped, but a full beard, streaked
with grey, came halfway down his massive chest.

As I came up beside Silt, Mammoth's eyes fell on me, stayed for
a few seconds, and then flicked over to Supersonic.

"Normally, I give this speech when we reach base camp," he
said, his words a quiet rumble, "but we're pretty far down the list this
morning. It'll be a while before the Teleporter gets to us."

His gaze swept over us again. "Forget everything you think you
know about the Badlands. The maps you've looked at and the stories
you've read. I've spent most of my life out there, and it still finds ways
to surprise me. The Badlands are not just a buffer region between the
Free States and this continent's other burgeoning empires, or a fly-over
zone for Wind Dancers and Flyboys to soar past and ignore. Much like
the Pacific, the land we'll be traversing has changed in ways that science
cannot explain. Many of those changes can and will kill you."

"That's a hell of a recruitment speech," griped Supersonic.

"This isn't about recruitment anymore," said the other man.
"This is about keeping you alive. My team is mostly Normals, but every
one of them has years in the Badlands. Listen to them and learn from
them. The Mission is not a Cape team, but we have a chain of
command that will be followed at all times."

For some reason, he was looking at me for that last part instead
of Supersonic. Like I hadn't spent most of second-year following
Tessa's orders. Learning the truth about my powers, realizing that I was
a Full Five, hadn't changed my lack of ambition on that front. I had no
interest in leading and no problems following someone else's orders.

As long as those orders made sense, anyway.

"What exactly will we be doing?" asked Silt.

"Mostly what I talked about in my speech. There are small communities spread throughout the Badlands and we'll be bringing them supplies and medicine. Doing what we can to keep them going."

"Why?" Caleb frowned. "If they don't want to move to the Free States where it's safe, why should we go out of our way to help them?"

"Because they need it," came the reply. "They're people, just like us. Some good, some bad. We do our part to assist the good so the bad don't take over and turn that territory into another Dirty South or something even worse."

"I thought you said the Badlands *weren't* a buffer region?"

"I said they weren't *just* a buffer region. Ours is a humanitarian mission, but at least half of our funding comes from political and social concerns inside the Free States. The government would prefer that stories of the Badlands remain just that...stories. The longer some semblance of civilization exists out there, the safer our country's citizens will be."

The auditorium was slowly emptying as he spoke, teams and their interns stepping through an exterior door that opened and closed on a different location each time. Next to that door, I saw a familiar figure in a fedora and trench coat.

"We'll have a more thorough briefing when we arrive," continued Mammoth, "and we'll spend a few weeks with my team getting ready and going over our travel route."

"I looked at the route last night." Caleb sounded proud of himself. "A few Net sites posted it early this year."

"Things have changed." The Shifter's eyes fell on me again. "We'll be taking a different route than previously announced. There are a few towns we'll still be hitting—towns our donors expect their contributions to reach—but otherwise, we're going off book this year."

Another team vanished through the portal.

"Get your gear together and line up," said Mammoth, "Unless Door needs to take a breather, we'll be heading out in less than five."

As if he'd heard, the fedora-wearing Power turned and looked our way. The past few months hadn't changed Door at all; face like an anvil in the shadow of that fedora, stubby fingers seeming even more so with the pinky that ended at its first knuckle. He looked past Mammoth to me and gave a small nod.

If anyone was going to send us out to the Badlands, I was glad it would be Door. And not just because Wormhole, the only other Teleporter I personally knew, would be just as likely to dump me in the Pacific. Door had been the reason Alexa made it to Reno in time to save my life. As far as I was concerned, he was my favorite Defender, Matthew's dad be damned.

"Walker." While I'd been watching Door, Silt and Supersonic had been following Mammoth's directions, leaving the Shifter and I alone for a moment. The big man took one long step in my direction, and I was suddenly looking up just to meet his gaze. "We need to talk."

"Yeah. I guess we do." After meeting with Bard and Alexa, I'd been expecting something like this.

What I hadn't expected was the enormous hand that was extended in my direction. After a moment's pause, I reached out and shook it.

"I really appreciate you volunteering," said the other man. "Given the shortages every Cape team is facing, I didn't expect we'd have any students coming with us this year. Thanks to you, we have three. Every Power is a force multiplier. I'm excited to see what sort of things we can accomplish together."

"Even though you're having to change your whole plan because of me?"

It was like watching a bear shrug. "Switching to an alternate route will ruffle some feathers, but we'll deal with it. And if the government wants to send some of their people along as security, I can live with that too. That's two more sets of hands that can be put to work. As for the rest? Who and what you are?"

I tensed, but the big man kept on talking.

"You and I will have to sit down and review your abilities before we know how best to utilize them. There are a lot of stories being told, but I'm not sure how accurate they are."

"I raise walkers," I told him. "I can even puppet myself like one. And I kill with a touch."

"Not sure how much good that last one will do unless we get attacked. Which we probably will at some point." He chewed that over for a bit, lips buried somewhere beneath that greying beard. "How are your walkers at manual tasks?"

"I'm sorry?"

"Like building things. Or even just lifting."

"Depends on the state of the walker when I raise it, but I think they should be fine. They don't feel pain or get tired."

"That could be handy." He scanned the auditorium. "Are you bringing any with you?"

"Uhm." I'd severed the link with my only walker on the way back from meeting with Her Majesty. It had never occurred to me that the Academy would allow it on school grounds… or that the Mission would be in favor of me bringing it along. "There aren't any corpses on campus, but if you give me fifteen minutes, I can go get one."

"No need." He clapped me on the shoulder and my arm instantly went numb. "If there's one thing the Badlands have, it's bodies."

CHAPTER 5

Door's portal took us to a dirt courtyard surrounded by a stone wall at least twice Mammoth's height, with guard towers spaced out around its length. Squat buildings of the same stone filled the courtyard. The largest of those buildings faced us, its interior exposed and divided into wooden stalls. Most of those stalls were empty, but inside a few...

"Are those *horses?*" asked Supersonic.

Mammoth nodded. "There's no grid this far out of the Free States, so we have to do things manually. Have any of you ever ridden before?"

"When I was knee high to a grasshopper, but never since," said Silt.

"Seems like you'll still have a leg up on your classmates." Mammoth smiled. "We're here for the next few weeks, getting our donations sorted and loaded and nailing down the details of our route."

"I thought you knew where we were going already." That was Caleb again.

"I do, but it was, as you know, not the route we had originally planned for. Which means my team and I need to make sure I didn't miss anything and that we can adjust our loadout to accommodate that change. You three will be a part of that; try to listen and pick up as much information as you can. We'll also set aside time in the mornings and afternoons for riding lessons. Supplies necessitate wagons, and we'll need people driving those wagons, but you'll all be spending time in the saddle over the next six months. Best get used to it now."

I eyeballed the brown and white horse that had stuck its head out of the stall, as if listening to our conversation. I'd seen horses on vids, of course, but they were a lot weirder looking in real life.

"Derek will show you to your bunks," said Mammoth, nodding to a smaller man in fatigues and a floppy hat who had appeared out of the general chaos like magic. "Drop your gear off and then I'll introduce you to the rest of the team."

Derek looked like he'd seen ten years of bad road, stopped for a beer, and then turned and done those ten years all over again, just to prove he could, so I was surprised when he opened his mouth and sounded only a few years older than the rest of us.

"*Three* Powers? Damn. That's better than any of us were expecting. Is it true you all volunteered? I know Old Mammoth's got a silver tongue, but still." Despite the torrent of words coming out of his mouth, Derek's movements were economical. He led us to the far side of the courtyard and one of the smaller stone buildings. Inside, several cots had been assembled. "Privy's over there," he added, waving to another building. "We've got actual plumbing too, but don't get too used to the creature comforts. Once we head out, it'll be tents and bushes whenever we stop between towns. If you're nice to Emma, she'll make sure there's toilet paper packed at least."

"Have you been part of the Mission long?" asked Silt.

"Almost three years. Joined up in what used to be Colorado when the Mission rolled through."

"Wanted to see the world?"

"Kind of."

"Wanted to meet girls," guessed Caleb.

Derek's blush looked odd on his young-old face.

I hadn't said a word yet, and I didn't break that streak as I carried my bag over to one of the unused cots. There were no lockers to store our valuables, which made me nervous. I'd only just bought my new clothes. Per diem or not, we were a long way from any stores out here. I couldn't afford to have someone steal them.

Nobody else seemed to share my concerns. Nor did Silt bat an eye about sharing sleeping space with the rest of us. We'd gotten over that sort of thing in our mixed gender second-year dorms. As long as I didn't have to deal with Winter's stray hairs ending up on absolutely everything, I'd be happy.

"Come on," said Derek once the others had chosen their cots. "I'll take you to meet the rest of our team. Word to the wise; don't say anything about Stark's face. Guy's hell on wheels in a firefight but he holds a grudge."

We crossed the courtyard yet again, this time to a large building near the stables. It was cloudier than it had been in Los Angeles, but the sun beat down like a hammer. I hoped the Mission had extra hats available because I hadn't even thought about bringing one.

I blinked my eyes to adjust as we moved back from sunlight into shade. The new building had bunks along the far wall, along with a door that led to a kitchen and another that I assumed was a private bathroom, but the main area was dominated by a large table and a bunch of chairs. In front of that table, Mammoth stood with almost a dozen men and three women, all dressed in the same worn fatigues Derek had on.

I spotted Stark right-off, thanks to the scar that cut across his face, narrowly missing an eye, and dragging the corner of his mouth down in a perpetual scowl.

"Team," said Mammoth, turning to us. "Meet the Powers who volunteered to join this year's Mission. Silt, Supersonic, and Walker."

"Now *there's* a cursed name if I ever heard it," muttered a man with a shaved head and swirls of ink in red and blue along his temples.

"Everything's a bad omen to you, Reese," teased the woman next to him. She was small and dark, jet-black hair pulled back in braids.

"And most of the time, things go to shit," retorted the other man. "Seems to me like you could learn from my example."

"These two are Reese and Cagney," said Mammoth. "Next to them are Stark, Emma, Gage, and James."

"Dagger," said the last man. Unlike Derek, he looked every bit as young as he sounded.

"Nobody's calling you Dagger just because you think it sounds cool," said Reese. "Not until your third Mission anyway."

"James is a fine name," agreed Emma, a deeply tanned woman with hair so blonde it was almost white. "Someone named James wrote a Bible and everything, back before the Break."

"The rest," continued Mammoth, "are Lady, Cob, Joe, and Denali. Don't worry if you can't remember anyone's names. You'll be working with them a lot over the next few weeks before we head out."

"You're all part of the Mission?" asked Silt.

"Ayup," said the man Mammoth had called Cob, even darker than Cagney. "Drivers, riders, shooters, doctors, and even an engineer, right Lady?"

Lady was tall and rangy, with long, brown hair that could have given Winter's a run for its money if it wasn't braided within an inch of its life. "One of these days, you're going to learn that mechanic and engineer are two different things, Cob."

"I wouldn't bet on it," said Reese.

"Walker…" said the scarred man known as Stark. "Why is that name familiar?"

"Maybe because it's what we call the shambling dead things that are a pain in our ass every time we cross the Rockies over in Montana?" said Reese.

"You have walkers out here?" I couldn't help but ask.

"Yeah, leavings from an asshole Crow who died some time ago. Things are less dangerous when they aren't being controlled, but it feels like we have to put down a few every year."

"That's not it." Stark shook his head, and then his eyes went wide, the right one more so than the other thanks to all that scar tissue around his left eye. "You're the kid who killed Carnage and Red Dragon."

Technically untrue. Alexa had killed Red Dragon about twenty seconds before he would have melted the flesh from my bones.

"Wait," said Emma. "I thought the news we got out of the Free States said they were killed by a—"

"Yes," cut in Mammoth. "Walker here is a Crow."

The closest people—Reese, Emma, and James—all took small steps back, making sure they were out of my reach. Stark didn't budge, but the glare he split between Mammoth and me spoke volumes. None of them saw the ghosts that had crowded into the building around them, my dad near the front, my mom off far to the left, swaying back and forth.

"Uh, can we have a sidebar, boss?" That was either Joe or Denali… I couldn't honestly remember which was which, even though they looked nothing alike; one of them balding, with a face like cracked leather, the other dark-skinned, with hair in braids down to his waist. "Won't take but a moment, I'm sure."

"I already know what you have to say, Joe. But the Mission takes all the help it can get."

"How do you think Reese got on the team," joked Cagney. "It sure as shit wasn't his personality or singing voice."

There was a general rumble of agreement.

"Glad you feel that way, Cagney," said Mammoth. "You're first up for teaching our newcomers how to ride."

"Just these three or should I rope in the others as well?"

"Might as well grab them all. I know they said they already knew how to ride, but you can take this as an opportunity to make sure of it."

"We're not the only recent arrivals?" asked Silt.

"No, the Free States has seen fit to send a couple of security guards along to bolster our firepower."

"For the first time in for-fucking-ever," said one of the men whose name I couldn't keep straight.

"You can thank Walker for that too," said Mammoth.

I got some more looks for that. A few were almost friendly.

"Three Powers fresh from Cape school and two government fixers," said Cagney, ushering us out the door. "Won't this be fun?"

CHAPTER 6

Learning to ride was *not* fun, and not just because my horse, the innocuously named Cloud, was part demon and anxious to drag me down to hell with it. With *him*, I guess; it was hard to miss the proof of his sex. If someone had removed my testicles, I'd probably be ninety-percent homicidal rage too… but any sympathy I had went right out the metaphorical window the third time he tried to kill me.

The actual mechanics of riding a horse were difficult enough to grasp on their own. Even mounting was more of a pain than it should have been, thanks to my missing hand. Once I was up, getting my posture right, with my feet under my hips and my ass positioned just right, took more time and practice. And every time I got it wrong, it felt like I was one bad bounce away from crushing my own balls.

Presley and Jacobs, the government's security team, hadn't been lying about their riding experience, but they still sat through lesson after lesson as Cagney and then Gage and finally Denali—who I'd learned was the dark-skinned guy with a nose like mine and beads in his long black hair—all took us through our paces. While Presley was black and Jacobs was white, they both kept their hair cropped close, said very little, and seemed to be watching everything around them at once. It seemed like a quick road to a splitting headache, and nothing at all like what Jessica Strich had taught us, but I was too busy trying not to fall off Cloud (at which point the damn horse would inevitably try to put a hoof through my skull) to care.

Riding lessons weren't the only thing that occupied us for those long few weeks. Mammoth and Stark gave the team breakdowns on some of the towns we'd be visiting, and the dangers that we might encounter on the way, everything from freak blizzards to mosquitoes as big as a man's head to some sort of wolf-bear hybrid called a howler. We weren't expected to remember everything they told us—and thank fuck for that, because the sheer number of names and places was enough to cause a brain bleed—but they wanted to give us a foundation so that we knew what to expect.

Dr. Nowhere's dream had done a whole lot more than just bringing superpowers into the world. As Mammoth had told us, the Badlands had changed in ways that we hadn't really seen in the Free States. Topography had shifted. Distances had altered. They didn't have the weird alien lizard things that had come out of the Pacific to attack the Academy, but that was the only good news. That much became clear when Jacobs asked what cities we'd be visiting on the Mission.

Stark leaned back in his chair and fixed the other man with a look of scorn. "There aren't many cities left in the Badlands."

"Because of Powers?" I'd seen what Crimson Death had done to Reno. Multiple Powers going at it could take out whole blocks in a matter of minutes.

"In part." Stark shrugged. As far as I could tell, he was Mammoth's second-in-command. The rest of the Mission visibly deferred to his judgment. "Of the cities that survived the dream, Kansas City lasted the longest, but it fell almost ten years ago."

"What do you mean *cities that survived the dream?*" asked Supersonic.

"Just that. Records show there were a lot more cities out here, pre-Break, but good luck finding any of them, or the people who lived there. Hundreds of thousands of people gone, maybe millions, as cities devolved into towns overnight. It's like Dr. Nowhere turned back the clock on this part of the world by centuries."

"There are a few larger communities," added Mammoth. "Wichita absorbed some of the people who fled Kansas City after its fall. We have base camps like this one in Colorado and Arizona, and the nearby towns have populations in the high five figures. But the Badlands is mostly wilderness, dotted by an increasingly small number of towns. We're here to keep those towns from falling into anarchy... or disappearing entirely."

"No pressure," joked Silt.

Stark didn't even crack a smile.

The rest of our time was spent eating and sleeping. As the two-week training period came to a close, we also helped load the wagons with the supplies that Emma and James, the team quartermasters, had itemized and organized. Three wagons, each carrying a roughly equal split in terms of weight and their contents.

"If one of them gets damaged beyond Lady's abilities to fix, we'll want to reallocate, based on need and priority," admitted Emma as we all paused for a water break in the shade. Her white-blonde hair was tied back in a thick ponytail today, and she was as sweaty and tired as the rest of us. "But if we have to leave a wagon behind, at least we'll still have some of everything we need in the remaining two."

"Why would we ever choose to abandon a wagon?"

She looked at Supersonic, eyes hard. "Because there's worse things than howlers out there, kid."

ooo

"She's totally into me," announced Caleb, as we slumped back to the visitors' dorm following our evening riding lesson.

"Who is?" Denali was teaching our lessons now, and he would never be mistaken for a woman. He was quieter than Cagney and more serious than Gage, but he rode like the fucking wind.

"Emma, obviously."

"She's like ten years older than you are, Supersonic, and way out of your league." Silt rolled her eyes. "Stop letting your little head do all your thinking."

"I don't mind a woman with some experience," he argued. "And you know what they say... once you fly, you'll never say bye."

"I have no idea what that even means."

"It means—"

"Could you just give it a rest, Caleb?" I was tired, hungry, and after just two weeks, sick to fucking death of his non-stop attitude. "Use your hand like the rest of us and stop the bullshit."

"Or what?"

"Or I'm going to fill your cot with undead rattlesnakes and order them to have a party." I hadn't ever raised a rattlesnake before, but Derek said there were plenty of live ones in the general area, and my experience with my dearly departed zombie cat suggested it was at least possible.

"That was a threat on my life! You heard it, Silt!"

"All I heard is two boys getting on my last nerve. If you want to party with Emma, tell her, not us."

"That's exactly what I'm going to do." He shot me a glare and headed toward the main bunkhouse where the other members of the Mission tended to gather.

"I can't believe you're encouraging him."

"Is that what you think I'm doing?" Silt shook her head. "There's no way in hell that woman is interested in Caleb. I doubt he'll even find her in the bunkhouse."

"How can you be sure?"

"Because I'm meeting her for a drink at the mess hall in five minutes." She nodded in the opposite direction and sent me a shit-eating grin. "Sleep tight, Skeletor, and don't wait up."

○○○

The next morning, Silt was a no-show at breakfast and for our first riding lesson. During our break, I found her still in her cot, a pillow and arm thrown across her face to block out the light.

"You doing okay, Sofia?"

She shrank back from my voice, her response a faded whisper. "The next time I say I'm going to go drink with that woman, fucking stop me."

A full year of dealing with Muse's alcoholic excess had eradicated any sense of consideration where hangovers were concerned. I leaned in close and spoke directly to the pillow in a loud voice. "You don't like alcohol anymore? No shots? No mixed drinks? Should I just drink this *whole bottle* by myself?"

The hand clutching the pillow shifted position, one finger extended skyward. "That wasn't just alcohol last night. It was liquid fire."

"Scotch?" Just like that, sympathy made a comeback. I'd had my own bad experience with whisky.

"Worse. Tequila."

"Tequila's not so—"

"*Pre-Break* tequila. There was a worm and everything."

I had no idea what a worm had to do with tequila. "So that's a big no on pre-Break alcohol then."

"Never again."

"And Emma?"

"Shit, Skeletor." The pillow shifted just enough so I could see how bloodshot her brown eyes were. "I think I'm in love."

CHAPTER 7

It was two weeks to the day after our arrival in the Mission's base camp that we finally headed out. Three wagons, seventeen people, and a whole string of horses; it felt like we were in a fucking parade.

The people that had come out to watch us leave added to that. The Mission had three main outposts, all of them along the western border between the Badlands and the Free States, and each had their own permanent small population. Farmers and ranchers who grew or looked after the food we'd been eating. Carpenters and roofers who kept the buildings livable. A handful of guards who would walk the walls in our absence. Most were retired members of the Mission and their families, but there were a few families in the process of migrating to the Free States, using the outpost as a waypoint in their journey.

They seemed sad to see us go, which told me most of them hadn't spent any real time with Supersonic. Lucky bastards.

I was on Cloud, riding at the rear of the train with Silt. The last wagon was directly ahead of us, its string of horses kicking up dirt and dust. Stark had told us we'd be taking rear guard for the day, but I'd already noticed Cagney and Gage making careful sweeps behind us and out on the perimeter. No doubt Denali was doing the same up ahead. Those three would see any threats long before we did.

I spat out another mouthful of dust and tried to guide Cloud around a steaming offering the horses ahead had left us. "Any chance you could do something about all this dust, Silt?"

"Like what?"

"I don't know. You're the Earthshaker. Maybe tell it to keep out of our faces?"

"I don't have that kind of control, and I'm not sure I could keep it up for hours at a time even if I did." Our packs were on the wagon, but she reached into a pocket and pulled out a red bandana, tossing it my way. "Try wrapping this around your face like a vid bandito?"

Wonder of wonders, Cloud stayed steady enough that I caught the bandana without falling off. Having one hand made absolutely everything more difficult. The bandana didn't help at all with the smell, but it at least kept the dust out of my mouth. "You don't want one for yourself?"

"It's just dirt. Nothing wrong with that." Silt's horse had yet to try to kill her, which made me think it might be defective. "Anyway, I was half asleep during briefing. Did they say how many hours we're going to spend on the road today?"

"I think the plan is to go until sunset and then make camp." We were still weeks away from our first town, so we'd be sleeping under the stars for a while.

"Shit. I was hoping I'd heard that wrong. I'm already tired."

I nodded in understanding. This was the longest either of us had spent in the saddle, and it was a lot more exhausting than the others made it look.

"Maybe you and Emma should cool it a bit so you both can get some sleep." Although I hadn't noticed the blonde quartermaster showing any signs of weariness. Then again, *she* was riding on one of the wagons.

"Way ahead of you on that front. Stark gave her an earful yesterday. Man's wound tighter than you were as a first-year."

"So, the summer romance is already over?"

"Hardly, but it's safe to say we're going to have to pick and choose our moments from here on out. Not that I'll have the energy to do much but eat and sleep by the end of today."

"What about Anita?" I asked, naming Silt's most recent Academy girlfriend. "Are you two done for good, or just on break?"

Silt sighed. "I had to let her go."

"That sucks. I liked her."

"So did I. Too much to ask her to wait six months for me when she should be building connections with someone who'll be a career Cape."

"She could have joined you for your year of service after graduation."

"I guess so. But then what? Brownsville? I'm not dragging someone I love into that hellhole."

I coughed. After all, Silt had already gotten several of our class members, me included, to commit to going to Brownsville with her.

"You're different," she said. "Anita's a Normal and has every reason to be scared of Texas."

"And I don't?"

"Hell, Boneboy," she drawled, "Texas should be scared of you."

○○○

We made camp at sundown. In pre-Break history, the pioneers had circled their wagons whenever they camped. Don't ask me why... pre-Break people were weird. Maybe it was a declaration of togetherness, or maybe they all worshipped pie and it was a religious commandment to replicate its shape whenever possible. That would certainly fit with a people who raced rats and jumped out of airplanes for a living.

With only three wagons, we couldn't really form a circle, and the small clearing we stopped at wasn't wide enough to even try. Instead, Cob and Derek unhitched the horses from their harnesses and led them and the rest of our mounts over to the knee-high grass. I wasn't sure how they would keep the horses from running away—or how I would prevent Cloud from sneaking over in the dead of night to kill me in my sleep—but nobody seemed worried about it but me.

After a quick but filling dinner of stew that Reese whipped up in a pot over a fire, most of the group went to sleep. Silt had used her powers to create a raised dirt platform, smooth and hard-packed, with a small wall around it to keep out the worst of the crawling bugs, and most of the Mission, including me, had laid our bedrolls on top. Thankfully, the platform was on the opposite side of the clearing—and upwind—from the non-stop shit factory that was our herd of horses.

I was tired, but too restless to sleep. I wandered the perimeter of the camp, looking up at the multitude of stars in the sky above us, and trying not to be too obvious as I scanned the surrounding trees for jaguars.

As I turned back to the camp, a huge shape materialized out of the darkness. I was already stepping back, waves of emptiness spilling out from my core, when that shape resolved itself into Mammoth.

I let my killing hand slip back down to my side.

"Feeling jumpy, Walker?" If Mammoth knew how close I'd come to turning him into a giant pile of dust, he didn't seem to care, his deep voice a quiet rumble.

"Camping in the middle of nowhere isn't really a thing, where I come from," I told him. "I'm just trying to stay aware."

"I'm surprised you're upright at all. Normally, that first full day of riding is enough to wipe anyone out."

"It wasn't fun, especially with my demon horse, but..." I shrugged. "I don't know. I feel like I haven't actually *done* anything today."

In the darkness, I could barely see whatever face Mammoth had made when I mentioned Cloud, but I assumed it was full of sympathy and regret.

"We try to give our Cape students a few days on the road before we add them to the work rotation, but if you're bored, I can move that timeline up a bit. Cooking, gathering firewood, caring for the horses." His cough sounded suspiciously like a laugh. "Maybe not that last one, but there's always something to do."

"Sounds good." I didn't *like* doing work but being bored out of my mind was even worse. "I feel useless."

"Like you said, you're all new to this. My team knows what it's doing, and we're largely self-sufficient on the road. Having you three along is a bonus that will pay off when we reach town. Or when we get attacked."

"When? Not if?"

"Yeah. We're fine this far west; that's why there are only two of us on duty per guard shift tonight. It's once we pass through the Rockies and Montana that we'll have to worry. The supplies in these wagons are a treasure trove, and a dozen or so people on the road make for a more tempting target than an entrenched town of several hundred."

"Bandits?"

His nod was mostly just a sound in the darkness. "Bandits, cannibals... there was even a sect of demon worshippers out there, though I think the Thunderbirds may have finally wiped them out five years back. The Badlands—the true Badlands, not the fringe countryside we've been riding through—have a way of sneaking into a man's soul to whisper sick little nothings. Doesn't take all that much to drive a man bad."

Given the madness that had brought down every Crow before me, that cut deep. "How do we make sure that doesn't happen to us?"

"I wouldn't worry about it. It takes years of being out here, not months, and most of the townsfolk I've met weren't affected at all. Community and social bonds have their own sort of magic, I guess."

On any other day, I would have laughed at the thought, but I'd been missing my friends back at the Academy all day. Tessa and Kayleigh. Paco and Lynn. Alexa and her steadfast refusal to blink. Hell, I even missed Matthew and Jeremiah. Somehow, over the course of two and a half years at the Academy, I'd found a community of my own.

Thank God Silt had come. Six months out here with just Supersonic really would drive me mad.

"Every person in the Mission can fight," continued Mammoth, "but according to Dean Bard, you're an army all on your own."

"Once I gather some walkers, yeah." It was weird to have a conversation about my powers with someone I barely knew that *didn't* end in fear and horror.

"Good. I hope we won't need it, but better to be prepared than dead. But worry about that after Billings. For now, you should get some sleep if you can. I'll add you to the worklist when we camp tomorrow."

"Thank you."

"Like I said at the beginning, I can't afford to turn down help when it's offered. We'll start you off on night watch, paired up with Lady so she can show you the ropes. Anything she should know?"

"Yeah. If I need to be woken up, call my name. Don't shake me awake, and especially don't touch my skin."

"Derek said something about that back at the outpost, although he didn't know why."

"Sometimes, I access my power subconsciously."

"In your sleep?"

"Yeah. I'm not going to raise walkers or anything, but I'm not always safe to touch."

"Stark's the same way, although he's more liable to just stab a person. I'll spread the word." He headed away into the night but called back over one enormous shoulder. "We're breaking camp a bit later than usual tomorrow. Want to give you newcomers a bit of time to recover."

"Recover? From what?"

"Today."

I had no idea what that meant, but knowing I'd have something to do soon was enough to sate my restlessness. I headed for my borrowed bedroll.

CHAPTER 8

The next day showed me exactly what Mammoth had been talking about. *Everything* hurt: my back, my knees, my thighs, my shoulders. Even the hand I'd lost in Reno hurt. Somehow. I called on the emptiness to muffle that pain and got to my feet. For the first time in forever, I almost felt bad for Sofia and Caleb. Neither of their powers would do anything to help make the day less obnoxious.

Then again, neither of their powers was going to potentially drive them insane either.

I finished packing up my bedroll and helped Silt stagger over to the campfire. Last night's stew was a distant memory, replaced by tin thermoses of coffee and some sort of bread that seemed determined to destroy my teeth. I tried dipping pieces into the coffee to soften them, but they still took a lot of chewing before I could swallow.

Meals at the Academy had spoiled me, of course, but this was ridiculous. Frankly, I'd have preferred synth-rations. Fake pork isn't all that bad if you eat it cold.

Silt was moving better when she finally emerged from the nearby woods after handling her business. She had another tin with her, this one flat and roughly the size of her palm, and tossed it over.

"Gift from Emma," she said, "for the chafing. I'm assuming your thighs are as torn up as mine? Pass it on to Supersonic when you're done."

I took my own trip into the woods, checked for snakes, and then took a leak as quickly as possible. Before I pulled my jeans back up, I spread the tin's ointment on the inside of my legs. Wrapped in the emptiness as I was, I couldn't tell if it helped, but it sure as hell wouldn't hurt.

Without tents or much in the way of belongings, breaking camp was just a matter of putting out the fire with a shovelful of dirt, saddling the horses or hitching them to their respective wagons, and packing away the cooking pots and dishware we'd used for dinner and breakfast. There were no nearby sources of running water, so we refilled our canteens from the fifty-gallon jugs in the wagons. We'd cleaned up as much as we could after first making camp, but I was sure I still looked like something feral.

Thankfully, Derek said our next camp site would be near a stream, and we'd all get a chance to wash up there. Even better? Silt and I weren't stuck at the back of the wagon train this time, eating the dust of everyone else's passage as we played pretend rear-guard.

ooo

That night, I pulled new clothes on over my freshly scrubbed and clean body. I'd never used to care about being dirty. I wasn't sure if my time at the Academy had changed that too, or if it was just a factor of getting older. Either way, I felt like a new man by the end of my bath in the ice-cold stream. Hell, I probably smelled like one too.

I was in the middle of one of my usual horrible dreams when something bounced off my forehead. I sleepily frowned and turned away, and took another hit, this one right next to my ear. Nobody had warned me about the damn bugs. I waved my hand around in the air above my head, but when something bounced off that hand, I finally realized I wasn't being attacked by insects.

Lady was crouched nearby, carefully outside my reach, with a handful of pebbles in her hand and a mischievous smile on her face. Before I could say anything, she flicked another pebble in my direction.

"I'm up," I hissed, coming over to join her away from the other sleeping bodies.

"Had to be sure. Mammoth said you don't like to be touched."

"It's not that I don't like—" I waved it off. "It's time for our watch?"

"Yeah. We don't normally have three guards to a shift until we're further east, but since you and I are working as a training team, James and Gage are up too."

"Cool." I hadn't spent much time with the Mission's mechanic so far, but she seemed nice enough. Not counting the whole pebbles in the face bit anyway. And standing watch with her meant I wouldn't have to hear another dozen of Gage's truly awful knock knock jokes. "I've stood watch on the Academy walls. What's different about this that I should know?"

"I've never been to your Academy, but I know Los Angeles—"

"You do?"

"Yeah. I was born there. So was Gage, for that matter, though we didn't meet until after we'd joined the Mission. Anyway, the city has lights and walls and grid access to power security networks. Out here, we don't have any of that. It's all on you."

"Meaning?"

"Gage is walking the perimeter, which means the rest of us are on static watch duty. Find a spot away from the campfire over in this direction. A tree would be best, to help mask your silhouette. Face away from the camp so the light from the fire doesn't kill your night vision… not that you're going to be seeing much in the darkness anyway. Hearing is your most important tool."

"And if I do hear something?" We'd already left the wagons behind, and the night forest was black and probably crawling with snakes.

"Oh, you will. There's not a lot to worry about this far west, but this is a live forest, so it's got its share of birds and squirrels and deer. Occasionally, we'll run across black bears or grizzlies, and there's a pack of timber wolves that roams about forty miles to our south. When you hear something, just relax. Try to figure out how big it might be. If it seems to be coming our way, alert your fellow sentry and they'll know what to do, but it's unlikely anything will want to mess with us until after we cross the mountains."

"Pay attention to the horses too," she added. "Their senses are better than ours, and they might react to a potential predator before you even hear it. If the horses start making noise, the whole camp will be up in a hurry. The bigger concern is human predators or creatures smart enough to use the wind to mask their scent. But don't worry about that tonight, with the rest of us out here helping. Did you get all that?"

"Find a tree away from the campfire. Don't look at the light. Listen for noises and pay attention to the horses."

"And come get one of us if you hear something that concerns you… or tell Gage when he comes by if you think it can wait that long. Any questions?"

"I think I'm good." I wasn't scared, but it was a different sort of feeling to be surrounded by potentially savage wildlife. I'd almost rather deal with bandits; at least they didn't have claws or a habit of leaping out of trees or anything.

"You'll be fine. I'll come collect you in a few hours and we'll wake the next shift together."

And just like that, she was gone. Wish I could say I saw her leave. Or heard her. All I knew was she suddenly wasn't there. The crescent moon was enough for me to identify the shapes of trees in front of me, and I felt my way over to one that seemed large enough.

Was I supposed to climb the tree? No, that didn't make any sense if the tree was supposed to mask my silhouette. Instead, I crept around the trunk, made sure there was clear space at the base, and sank down, knees tucked up into my chest, bark rough against my back. All I could see in front of me was darkness, occasionally graced by moonlight.

After what felt like an hour, I finally started to hear the forest around me. The hoot of an owl that froze whatever small creature had been scurrying up a distant tree. The soft, untroubled sounds of the horses well behind me. A surprisingly cool breeze that snaked its way through the branches, setting them rustling.

A pebble bounced off my forehead, and a shadow detached itself from the blur of trees in front of me.

"You're supposed to be listening," chided Lady.

"I fucking was!"

"I stepped in a dry leaf bed twenty feet back. Scraped against a tree not long after. Didn't you hear the squirrel stop?"

"I thought that was because of the owl. And how the hell does a mechanic learn to sneak through the woods like that?"

"I wasn't always a mechanic." I could hear the grin in her voice. "Keep trying, rookie. You'll get the hang of it."

Ten or twenty minutes later, it was that same cold wind that had me calling on my power, distancing myself from my body's reaction to the chill. With my power filling me, I should have the edge in speed against anything I heard coming. Like Lady with a handful of pebbles. And if I didn't hear her coming—

I paused. After I killed my half-brother on the streets of Reno, before Alexa showed up and saved my ass from Red Dragon, there had been a... moment. I didn't like to think about it, but that moment had been as much of a reason for me to volunteer for the Mission as Her Majesty's favor.

Part of me—maybe it was my power, maybe it was just me— had looked at the fleeing prisoners, people I had used my favor to help save, and wanted them dead. Wanted to scour the earth of their living presence. Wanted to extinguish them one by one, like so many candle flames in the night.

That's not the sort of shit you tell your shrink. It's not even the sort of shit you tell your girlfriend of almost seven months. Nobody knew about that moment but me, and I'd spent countless hours in the time since trying to figure out what had caused it, and how I could restrain myself if it happened again. The Mission seemed a safer place to be—for me and others—than a Cape team in the heart of some populated city of the Free States.

But my apparently latent homicidal tendencies weren't what had stopped me in mid-thought. What I was thinking of was how I had sensed those prisoners. The living had been lights in an ocean of darkness, and I hadn't even had to look at them to find them.

Maybe hearing *wasn't* my most important tool, after all.

It took a while to figure it out. It was kind of like how I'd learned to summon my power, that I needed to step outside myself and let the emptiness fill what was left. With that power already summoned, I instead needed to let go of my senses: the sight that wasn't helping at all and the hearing that was mostly just confusing me. I didn't turn those senses off—fuck knew how I'd do that, or whether I'd be able to ever turn them back on again—but I stopped paying attention to them. What I saw, what I heard... it was all just more extraneous static skating off the surface of the void.

And for the third time in my life, the world became an ocean of lightness and dark.

The trees around me were dim toothpicks pointed to the sky, the animal life brighter still. I was looking away from the camp, but my power saw the sleeping forms of the Mission's team, saw all that life energy that was bound up in our horses, saw past them to where someone—presumably James, since they were stationary—had adopted a similar position to mine, looking in my strange vision like a bright barnacle affixed to the side of a tree's dim trunk.

See was the wrong word, really. I sensed them with a Crow's eye, felt them with a power that had nothing to do with vision. I closed my regular eyes, and nothing changed. For a hundred feet, maybe more, in every direction, I felt the life that infested this wood… tiny wisps of light in the earth that must have been worms or beetles, the owl I'd heard earlier, now sweeping soundlessly overhead, the fish that swam the nearby stream, and the creatures that lived deep within its bed. I could sense the candle flame that was Gage, walking the far perimeter, and closer to me, creeping in from the left…

I scooped up the pebble that had hit me twenty minutes earlier and waited. When Lady slipped out from behind the tree line, my pebble was already in the air.

"Ow." She stopped dead, surprise leaking into her voice. "Now you're using your ears! I won't have to be so obvious on my next approach."

But of course, I wasn't using my ears at all. And when she crept in again, almost an hour later, this time as soundless as one of my ghosts, I was waiting.

CHAPTER 9

Lady's seal of approval was all Mammoth had been waiting for. After that, I was part of the watch almost every night. It meant less sleep, but came with its own perks, like not having to help set up camp on the nights I had early watch, or break camp on the nights I was still up to greet the dawn.

Unfortunately, my sudden utility didn't keep Cloud from continuing to be an asshole, but after three weeks of knowing the hooved demon, I was pretty sure that was just his normal state of being. I fed him a withered apple, dodged his latest attempt to remove fingers from my only remaining hand, and looked to the mountains clawing at the skies to our east.

Derek said those were the Rockies, and while whoever had named them was never going to win any awards for originality, it fit. The forest line petered out about three quarters of the way up those forbidding crags, and even in summer, there was still snow at the very top. The trail we'd been following would skirt around those peaks, and after another week or two, we'd end up in what had once been Montana. Or maybe Wyoming. The old state lines were hard to verify.

That's what Derek said anyway; I'd heard bald old Joe call this the Madison range instead, so maybe Derek was talking out of his ass. Meanwhile, Silt had heard Denali talk about the Teton mountains to the south, and she was pretty sure *teton* meant tit in Spanish... so it was possible everyone was just fucking with us rookies. For all I knew, we were in northern California.

Standing watch, making camp, eating meals whose quality depended entirely on whose night it was to cook, and trying to avoid Cloud's assassination attempts wasn't all I did in those first eight days of travel. Our lessons on the Badlands continued each night, the five of us—three baby Capes and the security people sent to keep us safe—seated near the campfire as one or more of the Mission expounded on the dangers we might run into.

As Emma had said, howlers weren't the worst of it. The Weaver's territory was still far to our north, a careful six or more hours from anywhere we were headed, but there would be plenty of shit willing to kill us once we were through the mountains, from a breed of crow that preferred their meat alive to mountain lions the size of small cars. The worst predators of all, however, were almost invariably human.

Bandits were a fact of life, and probably the most frequent challenge the small towns we'd visit faced. Above and beyond living in a territory literally called the Badlands, anyway. But while bandits were the most common threat, they were a long way from the worst. As Mammoth had said, there'd been a band of demon worshippers a few years back, and he was pretty sure there were still cannibals out there too. Marauders were considered different from bandits because they did more than just steal—they pillaged and raped and left nothing but destruction in their wake.

And then there were the slavers.

If you were born post-Break in some part of the world that still had schooling, you probably heard the story of slavery. Centuries of human subjugation, finally ended when the great wartime president, Abraham Lincoln, rode down out of the clouds on his red, white, and blue Pegasus, and set the land's slaveowners on fire with a single, terrible match, declaring the country that was then the United States of America to be a free land for everyone.

It was a great day for everyone but the slave owners. And the turkeys, I guess. Apparently, there was some sort of feast afterwards, and that was how Thanksgiving had gotten started. A yearly reminder that we were all free, regardless of the color of our skin or the content of our character.

And then Dr. Nowhere went and broke the world. After that, strong men and women took over and did what assholes in power too often do. It wasn't a question of race anymore, but of dominance, and with Powers on top, there were too many places where Normals were treated like chattel, from Steel and his band of neo-Nazis in the far northeast to the tribal warlords of the dirty south. Slavery had made a hell of a comeback, and that meant human life was once again a source of potential profit.

There weren't any big cities in the Badlands, but there were still a fair number of people, all spread out in towns, and the lack of a unified military presence meant there was nothing to keep slavers from coming to kidnap people they'd then sell to more established regimes.

Of us all, Silt seemed the least surprised by that news. Texas was its own strange beast, but I knew she'd seen shit that would make even Winter's long hair curl.

Maybe someday, the Free States would expand into the Badlands. Maybe there would be more than one team of mostly Normals responsible for thousands of square miles of space. Maybe the next generation of Capes after us... or the next generation after them...

would be able to stamp out the fuckers who thought a lack of powers made a person subhuman.

I wanted to think so, but the truth I'd learned in Reno was that even my own country was barely hanging on. Our great protector, Dominion, was dying. Tezcatlipoca was expanding northward into San Diego, and I couldn't decide if the mindless drones he made from people were worse or better or just different than the slavery seen elsewhere. And then there was Tyrant, who was hell-bent on taking over the world, using the powers he'd already harvested from other Capes and Black Hats, and the necromancy he'd bred me and others to provide him.

The Free States weren't in any position to wage war against the empires to our east—not now and maybe not ever—but looking at the grim faces around the campfire, feeling the scar tissue on my left hand stretch as I clenched my fist... I had no doubt we'd kill the fuck out of any slavers we ran into.

Sometimes, you take your wins wherever you can.

○○○

As the elevation changed, the distance we traveled each day shrank, and what Supersonic swore would have taken him only a few days in the air took us a week. The streams we passed were practically overflowing their beds, fed by the snow melting high above us, and there were a few times where Mammoth chose alternate routes because the main trail was too dangerous for the wagons. The more we climbed, the thinner the air got and the colder the nights were. I wasn't surprised at all when Cagney said these mountains were impassable several months out of the year. On the colder nights, the one campfire became several, and those of us that didn't squeeze into the still-full wagons made our bunks as close to the fires as possible.

All those days kind of blurred together, but one morning, I realized the road ahead of us was starting to dip back down in the distance. We were still a long way from being out of the mountains, but we'd crested the top and everything was downhill from there to Montana.

It didn't *quite* work out that way, of course... turns out mountains have a way of breeding *more* mountains, so our descent turned back into a brief climb a day later, and so on for almost a week. Even so, we were clearly descending, and the road was a hell of a lot easier for it. My thighs didn't even hurt anymore, thanks to Emma's ointment and some pointed suggestions on my riding form from Denali.

I took a swallow of water from my canteen, and for the first time let myself enjoy the natural beauty around us. Supersonic was riding at the rear with Reese, the two of them kindred spirits in being pains in everyone else's asses. The river to our right was distant enough to be pretty without worrying about whatever mutant fish it probably contained. Even Cloud's usual horsey bitching seemed a little bit less strident than normal.

Montana, or Wyoming, or wherever we were, wasn't half bad.

So, of course, that's when the walkers showed up.

ooo

Being the only Crow in this year's Mission, and most likely the most powerful Crow in the world, you'd think I would have been the one who noticed the walkers first.

Nope. I was focusing on my horse and admiring the world around me and completely fucking unprepared when the cry went out up front. In fact, I thought Gage was calling my name at first, and had urged Cloud up front to see what he wanted.

Take that as a lesson, if you find yourself as a Power in your next life; don't pick a codename that's also used to describe the shambling undead things that might one day sweep down on your unsuspecting wagon train.

It'll just confuse the shit out of you. Trust me.

By the time I reached the front, the wagons had stopped, and Joe, Denali, and Cagney all were off their horses and down in firing positions, long rifles out and pointed to the road's left. I risked a glance over at the river, verified nothing was crawling out of it and up our asses, and turned to see what they were waiting for.

Gage came out of the tree line first, bent low over his horse's back, hat in one hand instead of on his head for once. Seconds later, the first walker charged out from the trees after him.

Walkers stopped decomposing after being created—part of the same mind-fuckery that let full-on skeletons move without any muscles or tendons—but they didn't regenerate what they'd already lost... or any damage they suffered after their creation. This walker's arms and legs were mostly bone, the flesh likely torn away by the environment it had been discarded in, but the face and torso were nearly intact.

It didn't make it any prettier.

As the wind shifted, Cloud chose that moment to prance sideways in sudden terror. Two weeks earlier, that would have put me on my ass in the dirt, but now, I had enough experience to stay in my saddle for the moment it took me to voluntarily dismount.

"I've got the two on the left," said Cagney, all playfulness gone from her voice.

"I'll take the two on the right," said Joe, the sun gleaming on his bald head.

Denali just grunted. That left him three in the middle, including the very lead walker, but he didn't seem to mind.

Problem was, it took a shit ton of bullets to bring down a walker. A small-w walker, anyway; I was pretty sure a bullet to my brain would put me down like anyone else short of a Titan or high-ranked Shifter. Point was, there were better ways to handle a sudden undead invasion than by throwing lots of small pieces of lead in its direction.

"I've got this," I said.

None of the three acknowledged me at all, but maybe that's because Gage was still thundering our way, trying to curve to the side to give our shooters an angle without letting the walkers behind him catch up. Or maybe, in the heat of the moment, all three Mission members had forgotten what I was. Maybe the last few weeks of peaceful travel had lulled them into thinking I was just another Cape student.

Wouldn't that have been nice?

I unchained the emptiness at my core, let the part of me that was death itself spread out past my body, past the sparks of light crouched directly in front of me and the two sparks that were Gage and his horse, Buttercup. I let my senses find the vacant spaces behind him, tiny pools compared to the ocean I carried with me, and I pushed my power into them.

The last time I'd done this, I'd been fighting against my half-brother, trying to take his walkers and make them mine. The Crow who had raised these walkers was long-dead and his creations were like puppets running free. All I had to do was take up their strings.

It was almost too easy.

"What the fuck just happened?" murmured Joe.

Gage made it to the wagons, still riding like hell was chasing after him, but the walkers had come to a halt, halfway between the tree line and road, and now stood stock-still, every eye or socket trained in my direction.

"Walker," said Mammoth, joining our group. "Is this you?"

"Yeah."

"What did you do?" asked Cagney, looking away from her rifle's sights for the first time.

"They're walkers. I'm a Crow. I made them mine." I looked to Mammoth. "If you need an army, here's our start. Where do you want them?"

He answered my question with one of his own. "How total is your control and for how long can you control them?"

"Absolute and until I die or a stronger Crow takes them from me." I hadn't just spent the first semester of third-year playing at being a Cape. Several of my approved and supervised field trips had been off campus to practice raising and using walkers. These seven barely even registered as a drain on my power. "When not charging, their pace is probably about the same speed as our wagons, so—"

A shot rang out and I felt as much as saw one of my walkers stagger. Smoke curled lazily upward from the barrel of Joe's rifle.

"Joe?" Mammoth gave the old man a look.

"Just making sure," he said. "Not that I don't trust Walker here or nothing when he says his control is perfect, but it seemed like shooting one was a good way to test it."

"Boss." Stark didn't say much, and when he did, it was usually to point out something stupid that we had done, but his rough voice was respectful as he addressed Mammoth. I hadn't even noticed him ride up. "The path up ahead is going to be rough enough without those things spooking the horses. And people in the towns we visit will waste a whole lot more than one bullet when they see zombies coming down the road."

"You think we should hide what Walker is?" Something about the way Mammoth said it made me think the two of them had had this discussion before. Only now, I got to hear it for the first time.

Lucky me.

"As long as we can, yes," said Stark. "I think it makes sense. Leading a pack of walkers all over the Badlands isn't going to encourage towns to open their doors to us."

"I can have them follow behind," I said. "Way behind. Avoid towns and stuff. Once the connection is made, distance isn't as big a factor as you'd think. As far as I can tell."

Stark shot me a look. "You don't actually know?"

"The furthest I've been from one of my walkers was about a mile," I admitted. "But it wasn't any harder to control than when it was right next to me."

"And what happens if that stops being true after a mile and a foot? Or two miles? Or five?"

"Stark is right." Mammoth shook his massive head. "We can't risk it."

"So... what do you want me to do with them?"

"Just hold them still," said Joe, "we'll shoot 'em down."

"Set a fire and walk them into it," argued Cagney. "No point in wasting bullets."

It was my turn to shake my head. With a thought, I severed my link to the seven walkers and took their death energy—the emptiness I'd pushed into them to make them mine—back into myself.

In the field, seven bodies sagged to the earth.

"There goes your tireless work force," I told Mammoth.

○○○

"Why did the walkers keep roaming after their original Crow died?" asked Silt, several miles after we'd left my potential army to rot in the fields. "Shouldn't they all have fallen down when the necromancer did?"

"If Tezcatlipoca dies, do you think all of his drones will just keel over?"

"I sure as shit hope so, yeah. Scientists say there's nothing left of their personality or higher thought processes, so death would seem like the next logical step."

"Maybe. It doesn't work that way for Crows. There are two steps to raising a walker. I put some of my energy into them to animate them and then I create a link to control them. Kill the Crow and you break the link, but the seed of energy is still there. Once they've been raised, they're mobile until someone else destroys them or I do."

"And when the Crow who raised them dies, they become whatever those were? A hunting pack?"

"I think they keep following whatever their last established set of behaviors was."

"So, the last Crow had them hunting people."

"Sounds on-brand, doesn't it?" I swirled the sip of water around in my mouth and spat it out to the side of the road. "And now the whole Mission has been reminded that I've got the one power nobody wants. Did you see how careful Reese was not to touch me when he was ladling out soup?"

"He'll get over it," said Silt. "They all will. If they knew you like I did, they wouldn't worry a second."

"Because I'm harmless?"

She snorted. "You're the scariest person I know. But who have you ever done in that didn't deserve it? The only people who have to worry are the real monsters out there."

"And they've got it coming," I agreed.

"Every damn one of them."

CHAPTER 10

It turned out Silt was right. By the time we'd reached our first town, most of the Mission had gotten over my minor display of power. Not all of them, but the few I interacted with on a regular basis—Lady, Derek, Denali, and Cagney—settled back into the professional relationship we'd developed on the road. Once I stopped being pissed at Mammoth, I realized the lack of walkers probably had something to do with that. A constant reminder of what I was, trailing along behind our caravan, wouldn't have done anything for the missionaries' nerves. Or my fragile new friendships.

Still, unless the Badlands were a cupcake parade, I was *going* to be using my powers again over the remaining five or so months. It felt like we were kicking the can of consequences down the road instead of just dealing with shit then and there. I'm a big fan of facing problems head on—if you've been here for this whole tale, you know that as well as I do—but I wasn't the person in charge. And when Lady started teasing me again for the way I'd set up my portion of camp, I couldn't argue with the results of Mammoth's decision.

Anyway, far as I could tell, the whole southwestern portion of Montana was mountains, but as we made our way down out of the hills, we found our first sign of civilization in weeks. And it bore no resemblance to the tiny towns I'd been told spotted the Badlands.

"How many people live here?" I asked James, as he and I pulled our horses up. A stone wall—with rock taken from the surrounding hills, no doubt—rose almost a dozen feet into the air, encompassing dozens of multi-story buildings and an unknown number of single-story structures. The gate we were stopped at was half again as wide as one of our wagons, and I was betting there was another gate just like it, facing east.

"Not sure, really." The man who wanted to be called Dagger was even younger than I was, and this was only his second outing with the Mission. His story wasn't all that different from Derek's: native Badlander who grew up seeing the Mission come through and decided to join when he was old enough. Except James was upfront with the fact that women had had a lot to do with that decision. "Maybe ten thousand, if you include the surrounding farmlands? It was bigger before the Break, but a lot of folks moved west and a lot more died."

"Ten thousand isn't all that much smaller than Bakersfield."

"What's that?"

"Place I grew up in. It's a day or so north of Los Angeles."

"Cool. Maybe once I've found a wife, we'll start our family there."

"Don't. It's a shithole. You can't even see the ocean."

"Do they have Net access and electricity from a grid instead of decades-old, piece of shit generators?" He read the answer in my face. "Then it sounds like heaven to me. I might spend the rest of my life just watching those vids you keep talking about."

"You should go to Los Angeles instead. Maybe accompany Mammoth when he makes his next sales pitch to the Academy?"

"That's the plan, although he only brings a handful of us each year." He grinned, twisting in the saddle to stretch out his lower back.

"Hell, maybe I'll meet my future wife there instead? I've heard all about Free States women."

"They don't suck," I admitted.

Some of them anyway.

Up ahead, the gate doors were swinging wide open, and the wagon train was starting to move.

○○○

Population aside, Billings wasn't anything like Bakersfield, starting with that stone wall and working inwards. No faded billboards. No failed tourism pushes. There were no cars out here, none left running anyway, and what once must have been asphalt roads had been replaced with a mix of cobblestone pavers on the main thoroughfares and gravel on the side streets.

After passing the gate, we veered right, following the inside of the southern wall until we found ourselves in an open square large enough to fit a dozen wagons and their accompanying teams of horses. There was one other covered wagon present, half the size of any of ours, and with space in front for only one horse.

"Traveling merchant," said Emma when I pointed it out to her. "Nobody covers the entirety of the Badlands like we do, but larger towns like Billings here serve as hubs for their communities, and there's always profit to be made for those willing to take a risk."

"What do they need us for then?"

"The Mission is the first link of that chain," said the quartermaster. "Some of our donated supplies go to the town for its use, and some of them are redistributed through merchants like that one to towns we don't have time to visit ourselves."

"Doesn't that mean they're making money off of our charity?"

"Off the charity of the Free States, yeah. Although outside of larger towns like this one, it's more about barter than currency." She looked up from her careful inventory long enough to note the look on my face. "I know. It seems like we're being taken advantage of, right?"

"Yeah."

"Remember, the Mission's role isn't to make money. Our goal is to serve the Badlands—to make people's lives better, and to keep the greater territory from descending into total anarchy."

"And to maintain a buffer between the Free States and other nations."

"If you want to be mercenary about it, yeah."

"How does this town profiting from our work help with that?"

"A regular influx of goods maintains Billings' position as a hub for the area. Trade between it and smaller outlying villages makes for a sense of cohesion and unity, again without us having to visit those other villages. Mercantilism keeps the lines of communication open when we're not here, and our occasional visits help keep that mercantilism flowing smoothly."

Mammoth waved to Emma, and she left with him to go talk to the mayor and town council, leaving the rest of us to watch over the wagons or move our bedrolls into one of the designated buildings around the square.

Truth was, I still didn't really get what Emma had been trying to tell me. Maybe that was the orphan in me again. As a second-year, I'd struggled with the idea of defending a populace of potential assholes once I became a professional Cape. The idea of giving a town free stuff so they could turn around and profit from it made even less sense.

It was a question of time and resources, I finally decided. It had taken us weeks to reach Billings. If we visited every town and village around us, we might not even make it out of Montana before winter. I didn't like the idea of merchants reselling charitable donations, but if there wasn't any profit involved, there wouldn't be any merchants at all, and that meant those smaller villages would be shit out of luck. And over the decades, those villages would probably fade away, leaving even fewer pockets of civilization in the Badlands.

But even so…

"Boneboy!" Silt had already taken her horse into the nearby stable, removed its gear, and was now poking her head back out of the bunkhouse. "What are you still doing out here? This place has actual showers! And hot water!"

That was enough to get me moving. I'd leave the big picture thinking to someone else. After two weeks of bathing in ice cold streams, a hot shower sounded like heaven.

ooo

I'd love to tell you all about Billings, Montana. The people who lived there and their customs. The lives they led. The mayor and town council who kept things running smoothly. Even the militia that helped keep everyone safe.

Problem is, I didn't see *any* of that. We spent two days in Billings, but almost all of it was in the town square that had been set aside for travelers.

When Mammoth and Emma had returned from meeting with the council on that first day, it was almost dark. We had a home-cooked meal—our first in weeks—but the townsfolk who brought it out to us kept quiet as they set up tables and covered them with dishes full of locally grown fruit, freshly made bread, and fish. And by the time we'd all finished eating, the sun was down and the full day on the road was making itself felt. I don't even remember setting my plate aside as I wandered off to bed.

The next morning, Emma and James had us unpacking supplies from the wagon based on what the town council had identified as necessities. With the inventory already evenly spread between three wagons, we were able to pull from each wagon as needed, but Emma still had us shift things around when we were done, ensuring the wagons were once again equally balanced.

Silt's summer-time girlfriend was kind of a taskmaster, but she also knew what she was doing. I put things where she told me and tried not to think about the seven discarded walkers that would have made all this manual labor that much easier.

Then again, a good number of our crates of supplies were food staples, and zombie flesh was a long way from sanitary. Maybe the walkers wouldn't have been that much help after all.

While Silt, Derek, Supersonic, and I were unloading and then reloading the wagons under Emma and James' supervision, the rest of the Mission was similarly busy. Lady and Joe had gone to investigate problems with one of the local generators, while Mammoth and Reese were out lending their muscle to help raise a barn that had collapsed a half-day's ride out of town. Meanwhile, Cob and Denali had made their way to the town's hospital with the requested boxes of medical equipment and books… and then stuck around afterward to help out where they could. I already knew Denali was something of a healer—he'd made the ointment Emma had given us after those first days out riding—but Cob was a surprise. The way the guy talked, it sounded like he had maybe three brain cells to rub together, but he'd spent a year in the Free States getting emergency medical training and was the closest thing to a full doctor the Mission had. And then there were Cagney, Stark, and Gage, who, after making sure we'd adequately cared for our own horses, left to visit the town's other stables and offer their services.

"I thought we'd be a lot busier than this," said Supersonic, as he half napped in the shadow of one our repacked wagons. "Being on the road sucked, but this isn't so bad."

"Billings' size means they don't need us for much other than the supplies we bring," said Derek. "As we get deeper into the

Badlands, the work gets tougher. A town of a few hundred might have us there for a week, whereas we're leaving here tomorrow."

"Tomorrow? Shit." Without access to whatever product he used back at the Academy, Caleb's hair had gone floppy, but he'd been careful to comb it after shaving that morning. "I was hoping I'd have some time to talk to that girl who keeps bringing the bread every meal. The cute one with the—"

"That's Casey," said Derek, a mournful tone entering his voice. "She's married. All the women tasked with feeding us are. Council doesn't want us luring their young women away... or getting them knocked up and leaving them behind to fend for themselves."

"I'd think a town would welcome new blood, just to keep the population going." I'd been doing my best to block out Caleb's voice as I meditated but couldn't help joining in the conversation.

"Some of the other towns we visit will be like that," said Emma, her voice drifting lazily over from where she and Silt were seated together, "but Billings has all the people it can support right now. Much bigger and they'd have to expand beyond the wall, and that's not something the council is ready for just yet."

"But we're Powers," protested Caleb. "I am, anyway. I'd think that would count for something."

"Regretting not taking an internship, Supersonic?" drawled Silt.

"Nice try; I know shit's going to go down eventually. It's like Reese said," he added, pointing in my direction, "Walker over there is a living, breathing, bad omen. Sooner or later, he'll wander right into another war and this time, I won't miss out on the action."

I tried to remember just how many Flyboys I'd seen die at the battle of the Hole. Supersonic didn't have a fucking clue how good he had it.

"Is that how you lost your hand?" Derek asked me. "In a war?"

"No. He's making shit up, as usual. The closest I came to a war was out at the Hole—that's the prison the Free States have for Powers that go bad. This happened a long time after that."

"So, how *did* you lose it?"

"Derek, if Walker doesn't want to talk about it, you need to respect that," said Emma. Silt had gone stiff under the other woman's arm.

"It's fine," I said, turning to lock eyes with the young-old missionary. "My half-brother cut it off with a cleaver, about a month into my capture and subsequent torture by his boss. And I paid him back by breaking out, burning down the building, killing a fuck-ton of other Powers, and stabbing him through the eye with his own knife. Any other questions?"

There weren't any, shockingly enough.

I'd spent the last month tiptoeing around who and what I was with the rest of the Mission, playing nice and doing my best to fit in, but even I had my fucking limits.

ooo

Later that night, after a goodbye dinner where we finally got to meet some of the townsfolk we'd been helping, I was lying on my back, eyes closed, trying to find that peace that had always come so easily on my bench overlooking the ocean. Before we'd gone to bed, I'd tried communing with Billings' ghosts to see if any of them could point me towards Dr. Nowhere. Lot of dead people in that town over the years, and not a one of the spirits left behind had been able to resist my call, but if they'd had any information, it had stayed locked away. Maybe I was doing something wrong, because there had been no visions. No flashes of their own death, cued up like a vid, just waiting for me to watch it.

Not like with my mom, two Christmases ago.

Not like with Nyah.

Even now, ghosts gathered around me in the darkness of my Crow's eye, brief shadows against the black-watered ocean and the bright little sparks of the rest of the Mission. Many of those ghosts—the ones I'd brought with me from Bakersfield, from the Hole, and from Reno—existed because of Tyrant. The bandits he'd hired on a suicide mission against Her Majesty and me as we made our way to the Academy. The Capes, Black Hats, soldiers, and inmates who had been killed in the prison break he had helped orchestrate. The Powers and mercenaries working for him in Reno, and the prisoner who'd died helping us make our escape. Mama Rawlins and her entire house of unwanted brats, from club-footed John to little Nyah. And then there was my mom, killed by her own husband, a low-level Crow she'd been unknowingly paired with in part of a breeding scheme as monstrous as it was successful.

So many ghosts, so many dead people. And the only one Tyrant *wasn't* in some way responsible for was my friend, Unicorn. Part of me was glad that the Free States' Cape teams hadn't found the Black Hat in all the months since my escape, glad that Alexa's agency was still coming up empty. I owed Tyrant a debt of pain and death, and once I had become a real Cape, once I had a team standing behind me, I was going to see that debt paid.

And then, maybe all these ghosts would finally be put to rest.

It took less than a thought to send them away. If Sally had been there, it might have been a different story, but I hadn't seen the dead Crow since Reno, hadn't seen the monsters that were her own ghosts either. The spirits that followed me were just empty vessels; a trickle of power scattered them like dry leaves. They'd be back by the next night, or maybe even the morning, but their temporary absence made it easier to sleep.

And to see that one of the sparks of light in our bunkhouse was moving closer, creeping past the sleeping forms of Silt and Emma toward me.

I kept my eyes closed and watched the spark approach, emptiness pooling in my limbs. If whoever it was had a weapon, I'd need to roll to the side... just enough to dodge their strike, but not so far to put myself out of arm's reach. Apparently, Mammoth hadn't told everyone I could kill with a touch—and Stark hadn't shared whatever stories he'd heard—or my would-be attacker would have shot me from a distance.

The spark crouched over me, and I readied myself to show them just how big a fucking mistake they had made.

"Damian, are you awake?"

Or... maybe I wasn't being assassinated after all. I let my power go, and cracked one eye open, looking up at the shadow above me.

"What do you need, Derek?"

His voice was a whisper. "I just wanted to say sorry. I shouldn't have been nosy. Supersonic can make all the jokes he wants about girls, but the real reason I left home was curiosity. Sometimes, I let it get the best of me."

"It's not a big deal," I said, voice gaining color as the emptiness drained out of me. "It's just a sore subject, I guess."

"I can see why." I heard a rustle of clothes as he shook his head. "Out here, people tell all kinds of stories about the Free States. Make it seem like it's some kind of paradise, but I guess it's got its own problems, huh?"

"Whatever the village, the town, or the country, we're all part of one world," I told him. "And it hasn't had any place for paradise since Dr. Nowhere broke it."

CHAPTER 11

By morning, we were on the trail again, cobblestone giving way to gravel and then dirt. The land flattened out the further we went east until you could see towns on the horizon as we passed them.

We didn't make any stops for those first few days, and I was reminded of what Emma had said about Billings being a hub for the surrounding region. As we rode out, local merchants were no doubt getting ready to do the same, taking the goods they'd just purchased from the council out to the villages that would pay for the convenience.

On our third day, we came across a handful of homes just off the remnants of a road, and this time, we did stop. The place was a far cry from Billings—maybe a few dozen people instead of ten thousand—and I never did get its name, but for a night, we had a roof over our heads, and when we left, we'd swapped out more supplies from the wagons for fresh grain for the horses and water from the village's well.

The people had seemed excited to see us, and even more excited when they realized a few of us were Powers, and that was just enough to incite a fresh round of complaints from Supersonic when we left the next morning, before he could make any headway with one of the prettier girls in the village.

"I'm going to wait until we make camp and then fly back," he said, several hours into the ride. "Lou said she'd wait up."

"Why are you telling me this?" Caleb and I had been civil since leaving the Academy, which was something of a minor miracle, but we were a long way from being friends.

His head shot up and he looked over from under the brim of the floppy hat he'd borrowed from Reese. "Shit. Where did you come from? Where's Reese?"

"I've been here. And he's up ahead, where you used to be before you and your horse lagged back. Are you sleeping in the saddle again?"

"You didn't hear me say a word," he said, ignoring my question. "Don't cockblock me, Damian."

"If you want to go for a midnight flight in the Badlands, that's your business. When you get eaten by one of those giant bat things Stark told us about, I won't say a word."

"Emma says we're going to spend a week at the next town," said Silt, riding up. "Maybe you can find someone there?"

Caleb sniffed, tapped his heels to his horse's flanks, and sped up to join Reese.

"He's still pissy about me and Emma?"

I shrugged. "Who knows? He talks to me even less than he does you. Except when he falls asleep and thinks I'm someone else, apparently. Did Emma say when we'll reach this next town?" I knew Mammoth or Stark would probably give us the necessary information over the campfire that night, but advance notice never hurt.

"Should be tomorrow, I think." Silt shifted in her saddle. "Either I'm getting used to riding or my ass is developing calluses. The road since Billings has been pretty easy."

"Yeah. I know we're still on the western edge of the true Badlands, but I'm starting to wonder if this place really deserves its reputation."

"Now you've done it." She shivered. "What have I told you about poking the bear?"

"What do *bears* have to do with anything?"

"You don't ever want to do it," she continued, ignoring my question, "or it will take your damn head off."

"I'll keep that in mind if we see one. Although something tells me Cagney would just shoot it."

We rode in silence for a bit, or as much silence as there could be with three wagons, two dozen horses, and seventeen people. I didn't dare sleep in the saddle like Supersonic had been doing—Cloud would sense it and the next thing I knew, I'd be down in the dirt with a hoof coming for my skull—but I was getting used to what our second-year Control instructor had called *moving meditation.* It helped me keep my power at the ready, senses spread across the land around us.

It also helped the time go by faster. That didn't suck.

"Are you doing okay?" asked Silt, a few minutes later.

"What do you mean?"

"It's a simple question, Skeletor."

"I'm tired and I'm bored. Why?"

"I don't think I've heard you swear once today. Whenever that happens, I know something's wrong."

"Maybe I turned over a new leaf. Damian Banach, pure of heart, mind, and tongue."

"Won't Tessa be surprised," joked Silt. "Although it seems like a shame. From what I hear, that tongue of yours has had *her* cussing plenty."

It wasn't until she leered in my direction that I got what she was saying, and if Cloud had tried to buck me off then and there, I'd have been eating dirt.

"Jesus. Did she tell you all about our sex life before or after she told you I was going on the Mission?"

"Tessa and I don't have that kind of relationship, Boneboy. But she and Olympia don't keep their voices down as much as they should, especially when chatting on their way to class. When I hear about someone who knows what they're doing down there, I can't help but listen." She shook her head. "Of course, then it turned out they were talking about you, and that just made me queasy."

"And you decided to share the nausea with me?"

"Why not? It was your girlfriend's fault, so you might as well pay the price." Her grin came and went. "How do you think she's doing?"

"I'm sure she's kicking ass."

"Do you miss her?"

"It's only been a month or so. We were apart almost as long over the end-of-year break, if you don't count the few days I spent at her parents' house."

"Cool story, Damian. And?"

I sighed. "Yeah, I guess I do. With us sharing an apartment this year, we were together almost constantly. It's weird to wake up and not see her there."

"That's what I thought."

"Is that why you came over? To see if my not swearing was because I missed Tessa?"

"Nah, that was just about satisfying my curiosity." She paused and lowered her voice. "I wanted to see how the *other thing* was going."

"The other thing?"

"You know, the reason we're out here at all."

"I'd be out here, regardless, since no team wants me, but if you're talking about Her Majesty…?"

"Yeah. Still can't believe you never told me about her. Hot babe in biker leathers? Hell, I'd hire *her* to accompany us to Brownsville."

"There wouldn't be much left of the place when she was done," I said. "And I didn't tell you before because…"

"Yeah, yeah. Plausible deniability and you were trying to keep me safe. I've heard it all before, and it's bullshit, but as long as it's the last time it ever happens, we're cool. But we've hit two towns now, and Billings had to have a ton of dead people. Any progress on finding you-know-who?"

"No. I told Her Majesty it would be a long shot. Finding ghosts is easy. Finding one with knowledge of—" I made sure we were alone. "—Dr. Nowhere's whereabouts is a lot harder. And getting that ghost to talk to me? I don't know."

"So, you're just going to… what? Commune with the dead at every stop?"

"If you have any better ideas, I'm here for them."

"I don't do spooky, Boneboy. You know that." She took a swallow of water from her own canteen. "Maybe the whole *talks-to-you* thing only works when it's someone you knew?"

"Maybe."

I almost hoped so, to be honest. If Dr. Nowhere really did exist, finding him might be the last thing I ever did.

Still, a favor's a favor. I'd do whatever it took.

ooo

Another night on watch was followed by another early morning. If Supersonic had flown back to that unnamed town, Lou hadn't been waiting for him after all, because he seemed in an even fouler mood than usual. Or maybe he was pissed that Stark had assigned him rear guard for the day's travel. It wasn't my problem, and I was happy to avoid him.

We were far enough out from Billings that the road was more suggestion than reality; whatever traffic came this way was too infrequent to do more than beat down the fireweed and beargrass. I hoped someone knew where we were going because I was totally lost.

Around mid-afternoon, the town we'd be visiting came into view, still at least an hour away. About thirty minutes after that, Denali rode back to the wagon train like he was being chased. He made a beeline for where Mammoth was walking—the Shifter too big for any horse—and leaned down to murmur something in the other man's ear.

Between the noise of the wagons and the horses, I couldn't hear what he said, but the Shifter turned to the rest of us. "I need five of you to stay with the wagons. The rest of us need to reach Baker before there's nothing left of it." As he looked back to the town, the form of the man fell away, replaced by a four-legged, brown-coated beast that towered over the wagons. Long bone tusks curved upward, flanking his trunk. And then Mammoth charged down the road toward whatever trouble awaited us.

Apparently, someone had poked Silt's mythical bear.

It wasn't me. Honest.

CHAPTER 12

Riding Cloud at a full gallop wasn't as terrifying as I'd expected. Part of that was the emptiness, of course, muffling my emotions and letting my thoughts operate in a cold vacuum, but the horse seemed to genuinely enjoy going full-out. For a few short minutes, we were almost in sync.

Behind us, Mammoth's heavy footsteps quickly fell behind. Even shifted into his hairy elephant-like form, the older man couldn't keep up with those of us on horses. Still, it was a relief to know that we had multiple tons of Beast Shifter following behind us.

By the looks of it, we'd need him.

What I'd first taken for clouds above Baker were crows… and not the small crows we'd occasionally see pinwheeling above Free States cities, but birds the size of eagles or even condors. Every now and then, one would swoop down like it was an actual bird of prey, striking at the streets below, but most were content to wait for the carnage to finish below.

Because Baker wasn't just being attacked by crows.

I'd seen enough Cape vids starring Timber to recognize wolves when I saw them, and these were every bit as oversized as the Beast

Shifter's form had been, leaping over the town's short wall and darting through the streets beyond.

That same wall meant we couldn't just charge in after them. Stark was out of his saddle before his horse had even come to a stop, and the rest of us tried to follow his example.

"Cagney." His voice snapped like a whip. "Take the horses up the trail and wait for the wagons. Keep your rifle out for any wolves or crows that might circle back around for easy prey. Silt, get us over this wall. Supersonic, as soon as you have a path, get in there and start raising hell. But keep your feet on the ground. Those crows will swarm you if you take to the sky. Everyone else, move in pairs through the town's streets. Our priority is the townspeople but check the animal pens too. Kill any wolves or crows you come across."

Silt was already at the wall. Rather than bring it down in true Earthshaker fashion, she pantomimed like she was lifting something and the earth outside the wall responded to her call, forming a crude but sturdy ramp. It wasn't fully complete before Supersonic blurred up it, using his flight powers to leap the gap and disappear into the streets on the other side.

Stark followed soon after, gun in one hand, bowie knife in the other. Then Denali and Joe, James and Reese, and the two Free States' guards, Jacobs and Presley. Finally, it was my turn to charge up the ramp, dropping over the wall into a town that had become pure chaos.

The others had already split up, heading down different streets in pairs as pony-sized wolves darted out of alleyways and came at their flanks, but Silt was still reinforcing the ramp for Mammoth, so I had a moment. I let my power drift out around me and found the dead waiting for its call. By the time Sofia joined me, we had an escort of four dead wolves.

The Earthshaker blinked at the unexpected reinforcements. "Now, that's something you don't see every day." She pulled her shotgun out of its holster and nodded. "Let's go hunting."

ooo

We'd learned city fighting at the Academy, clearing buildings and taking back territory block by block. In some ways, this was easier. No snipers up on the rooftops. No armored vehicles serving as barricades. Most of all, no enemy Powers there to make it a really bad fucking day.

But without the net, we didn't have comms. Thanks to the crows keeping Caleb out of the sky, we didn't have overwatch. And between smashed windows and doors, at least one fire that had gotten out of control, and what had to be fifty wolves and twice that many birds, we didn't have anything approaching organized resistance.

I charged into a hut and found a wolf crouched over bloody human remains. It growled and lunged at me, but I was already dodging aside, bringing down my spiked weapon in a vicious arc that crushed the creature's oversized skull.

I'd had to abandon my staff after Reno—two-handed weapons, by their nature, relied on the user having two hands—but I was pretty damn happy with its replacement, a mace with a titanium head the size of my fist. The staff had been more versatile, giving me better reach and the option to go non-lethal, but there was something deeply satisfying about blasting monster brains all over the wall.

Silt's shotgun boomed outside, and I ducked back through the door to find a dozen wolves loping down the street toward us. Either they'd been driven off by other members of the Mission, or they'd cleared whatever resistance had kept them bottled up.

I sent my walkers to meet them, including the wolf I'd just bludgeoned to death, and focused on my other senses, hunting for the sparks of light that felt human. When I found some nearby, I tapped Silt's shoulder.

"Let's go, Sofia!"

She was pumping buckshot into the mass of wolves, some living, some undead, some dying and soon to be undead. "You go. I'll hold these off!"

"They're already done for," I shouted. One of my walkers had been torn apart beyond hope of recovery, but I'd replaced it with the four wolves who had fallen in the process, and there were now more walkers in that tangle of fur and fang than living creatures to fight. "Let's save who we can!"

It went like that for I don't know how long. A loud trumpeting had announced Mammoth's arrival some time earlier, but Silt and I were busy clearing houses, seeking out the living and moving them to a more defensible location. And all the while, my walkers stalked the streets on four legs, guarding our flanks and burying the enemy in waves of undead fur.

Until the real crows decided it was time to get involved.

With smoke masking the sun, there was no shadow to warn me. No cry, no call, just the sound of something streaking through the air from above and behind me. I threw myself down to the dirt road but couldn't entirely avoid the talons that tore a bloody furrow up my back and shoulder. One of my wolves leapt for the attacking bird but was too slow.

I ignored the blood pouring down my back and climbed to my feet. All across the town, crows were diving down to take the meals they'd now realized might otherwise be denied them. Outside the wall, I could hear a fresh round of gunfire, but didn't know if it was someone defending the wagon train or Cagney trying to keep the winged things away from our horses. It didn't matter, either way, because there were already another five eagle-sized predators coming my way.

A Crow fighting crows.

Guessing that was someone's idea of a joke.

This time, I was ready for the birds' incredible speed. I had my mace in hand and a pack of walkers crouched and ready to leap. Most importantly, I was standing in a dirt road next to a friend who could control the earth.

"Silt," I called out, as the crows swooped below the roofline. "Now!"

The buildings about us shook as the dirt of the road reshaped itself into a wall six feet high and at least a foot thick. As big as the crows were, they were still birds, hollow bones and all, and the first two hit the wall so hard they pulverized. The second pair had more time to react, to desperately pull out of their dive, but the loss of speed and easily anticipated trajectory meant my wolves were there to end their lives with a crunch of oversized jaws. From the height of Silt's wall, another two wolves leapt down onto the last of their winged prey.

I reached out and grabbed the crow bodies still in any shape to fly and sent them back into the sky. I don't know if it was having their own kind turned against them or the arrival of the wagon train and five additional shooters, but the murder of crows finally broke off its attack and fled, harried by my flying walkers and an angry Supersonic. The staccato cacophony of guns trailed off, no longer drowning out the screams of pain and anguish.

Silt took up a guard position, protecting the villagers we'd herded together, and my walkers and I headed off to find Mammoth and see what came next.

ooo

What came next was worse than the battle that had preceded it. We didn't have any Healers and the entire town had two doctors.

Three, if you included Cob and his EMT training. Still, we had ample medical supplies once the wagons reached the gate, and Cob quickly set up triage in the village's main square. Denali, Cagney, and a handful of others helped provide first aid.

As for me, I'd been assigned to bandage duty until I told Mammoth that I could literally sense life sources. Then, I was dispatched with my wolf walkers to prowl the street, killing off any live wolves who thought to hide and locating villagers too injured to come for help.

There were a lot of the latter.

An hour or two later, Silt and I were at the source of the fire we'd spotted. As far as we could tell, it had started from someone smashing a kerosene lantern across a wolf, and even though it had burned out on its own, the blaze had left several buildings in shambles. Silt helped prop up those buildings as we dug for the sparks of life I felt buried somewhere inside.

I'd like to say all the people we located in that endless afternoon made it, but many were dying by the time we reached them, and a lot more seemed liable to follow their family members and neighbors into the grave. Still, we saved as many as we could, my senses leading us to sparks of life before they could fade entirely.

The sun was already going down when I scooped a little girl out of the arms of her dead mother and passed her off to the people Mammoth had following us to transport survivors to the makeshift hospital. The belt tied about the girl's thigh had kept her alive, but there was nothing left of her leg from the knee down. She screamed for her mother as they carried her away.

I don't cry. Haven't since I was six, since I learned tears just meant a beating from the older kids. Still, that little girl, soot-stained, missing her leg, and crying for the mother who'd shielded her and died in the process, made something clench deep inside me that not even the emptiness could mask.

Crows as big as eagles. Wolves the size of ponies roaming in packs of fifty. Cannibals, slavers, and devil worshippers. And a whole goddamn world of orphans because of one man's fucking dream. If I ever did find Dr. Nowhere, he'd have a hell of lot to answer for.

CHAPTER 13

Mammoth found me just after I'd gotten my own wound stitched up and bandaged. Back in his human form, he sat beside me with a grunt. Across the square, Supersonic was surrounded by admirers. To hear the townsfolk tell it, the Jitterbug Flyboy had been everywhere at once; I'd lost count of the number of people who had come up to personally thank him for saving their lives.

Baker wasn't anywhere as big as Billings had been, but it wasn't small either. Emma thought there'd been just under five hundred people before the attack, and the wolves and crows had put only a small dent in the city's population. The butchers were already working on the dead wolf carcasses, ensuring the town would have meat for months.

In other words, shit could have been a lot worse. *Would* have been worse if we hadn't shown up. Problem was, it could also have been a hell of a lot better, and that was eating away at me.

"Why the fuck does a town this size not have a bigger wall when there are horse-sized wolves running around?"

Mammoth's deep voice was calm and considering. "Until today, the biggest threats Baker faced were bandits and the occasional mountain lion. Eight-foot walls have served them well since they were built just after the Break. These wolves… Denali says their natural territory is a hundred or more miles north of us."

"What were they doing down here then?"

"That is the question," he agreed. "As soon as dawn comes, Joe and Denali are headed north to make sure there's nothing else we have to worry about."

"I'll go with them," I immediately volunteered.

"I need you here. I'd send Supersonic if I didn't think his head would explode at the thought of leaving his admirers."

"Caleb's a dick," I said, "and spends a lot of time thinking with his, but he came through when it counted."

"You all did. Don't think the people of Baker missed you and Silt clearing multiple streets by yourselves… or the number of people you saved afterwards."

"Yeah." I looked at the circle of space around us. "Their enthusiasm has been overwhelming."

"It's nothing personal—"

"I get it. This is nothing fucking new, I promise. I don't do any of this shit for the adoration."

"You do it because it's the right thing to do."

Actually, I did it because I hated bullies… and if I didn't stop them, I wasn't confident anyone else would, but I just nodded along. I was too damn tired for philosophical debates.

"If you don't want me joining Joe and Denali tomorrow, I'm guessing you need me to do something?"

"Yeah." He paused. "From what I hear, you only raised *wolves* in the fight?"

"And a few crows. Why?"

"Is there a reason you didn't raise the dead townsfolk too?"

"Two reasons, I guess. One's high-minded. The other one... not so much."

"Let's hear them."

"I didn't think the townsfolk needed to see their dead relatives repurposed as cannon fodder."

"And the less high-minded reason?"

"Wolves have a hell of a lot more in the way of natural weapons than humans. If you're going to raise a walker, go for the best material available."

"Smart. So, you don't have any moral issues with raising people? As opposed to just taking control of walkers that someone else already made?"

Clearly, the government had done a better job squashing the details of my battle in Reno than they had that mess out at the Hole. "No. What do you need?"

"You helped recover the living. Now I want you to recover the dead. We can put a crew together, but it would be a lot easier and a lot faster if someone just went around and ordered the dead people to come out on their own."

"Someone."

"It's not glamorous work, I know."

Until Caleb got swarmed by single women, I would have laughed at the idea of there being any glamorous work at all out here in the Badlands. "Not a problem. Is there a morgue I should walk them over to?"

"There is, but it can't handle numbers on this scale. The town cemetery is outside the wall, and the mayor has decided burial preparations will be made there instead."

"Makes sense," I said, climbing to my feet. "I'll go gather them up. Just let the gate guards know so they don't shoot me."

"It can wait until tomorrow, Walker. You've done enough for one day."

I shrugged. "I don't have to see the dead to raise them. Better that I do it in the dark than march them past all their loved ones in broad daylight."

"You're a good man."

"Wouldn't that be nice?" I looked over at the Shifter. Even seated, his eyes were almost on a level with mine. "But Mammoth?"

"Yeah?"

"I don't give a shit what the townsfolk think. I'm keeping my wolves."

"Just make sure they're away from Baker. We're going to be here longer than expected, and the people don't need a reminder of what we just saved them from."

"Deal." Six of my wolf walkers had survived, but only four were still in a state worth keeping. I ate the death of the other two and sent the survivors down the road from Baker to a copse of trees we'd passed on our way in.

My two eagle-sized crows were already perched there waiting.

Fuck if I was ever going into battle again with just one hand and a weapon when I could have an undead platoon clearing the way.

○○○

It took me several hours to walk out all the dead bodies, and by the time I woke the next day, Joe and Denali were already gone. I wasn't too upset about that though. As much as I wanted to see what could have caused the wolf pack to migrate south, spending yet another day in Cloud's saddle—at faster than wagon speeds, no less—sounded like hell.

In the light of day, Baker was bigger than I'd thought. The town wrapped around a small lake at its center, and the wolves' assault had been focused on the western half. On the other side of the lake, large swaths of town remained entirely untouched.

With the smoke still heavy in the air near the west gate, we'd bunked down in a market square on the east side of town, but Stark had us up almost as soon as the sun was. Not even Supersonic bitched about that; he'd gotten his taste of action... and a taste of one of the locals, from the way she followed him around, cheeks blazing red. Now, it was time to do the work we'd signed up for.

Much like in Billings, Mammoth and Emma handled the trade aspects, but given the damage Baker had suffered, the rest of us didn't have the luxury of waiting by the wagons. Those with medical expertise saw to their patients, bringing in the town's herbalist to help, and the rest of us cleaned up the debris and gore. Several of the houses were complete losses, including those that had borne the brunt of the small fire, but there was no shortage of broken windows to board up, sagging walls to add supports to, and shattered doors that... well, there wasn't a lot we could do about the doors, to be honest. Lady was a mechanic, not a carpenter, so we just noted down their locations on a list of damages she'd turn in to Mammoth and the mayor that evening.

Cleaning up the gore was nasty business. If our class Hydromancer, Makara, had come along with us, she could've just washed all the filth right out of town, sweeping it through the gate we hadn't had time to locate in our initial frenzied charge. Without her, there were buckets of water, shovels of dirt, and a smell so foul it made me almost miss the aftereffects of one of Muse's benders at the Liquid Hero.

Finally, Stark freed us for the day. With easy access to the nearby lake, Baker had ample water supply, and I spent close to an hour in the shower, until even the nub of my wrist was pink and shiny clean. The west side of the town still reeked if you got too close to it, but it already smelled significantly better than it had that morning. And thank fuck for that.

Supersonic was off with his newfound girlfriend and Silt had said she'd had something to do, so I was left with a few hours to myself in the late afternoon. For a time, I watched Lady work with one of the town's mechanics as they investigated a recent source of sporadically occurring electrical brownouts. Without access to the Free States' grid, Baker was run entirely on a combination of solar and wind, with most of the pivotal components having been donated on previous Missions.

That was cool, but also not particularly exciting, so I moved on, wandering the streets. It was hard to go more than a few blocks without stumbling across someone from the Mission. Everyone was busy helping where they could, but nobody seemed to need my help.

Then I found Cob and the hospital where they'd relocated the victims of the wolf attack.

CHAPTER 14

As much time as I'd spent being treated by Gladys in the Academy's med ward, you'd think I would have been prepared to pitch in taking care of the injured. Problem was, the two places couldn't have been more different. With a Healer, fixing things was just a matter of time, power, and skill, and the patients were mostly asleep while it happened. In what was left of Montana, with mundane doctors whose training had come from books or apprenticeships, the hospital was pure bedlam.

The waiting room was full of cots and those cots were full of patients that couldn't be squeezed into the hospital's half-dozen long-term care rooms. Few of them were asleep, almost all were entertaining visits from friends or family, and the sheer level of noise, even before a saw started whirring from one of the place's two operating rooms, hit me like a physical force.

A moment later, I was stepping back out into the street, but before I could make my escape, Derek spotted me. His old man's face somehow seemed more appropriate than ever in the midst of all that suffering.

"Walker! Are you here to help?"

"I don't have any training—"

"You don't need it." He waved at the mix of men and women navigating the haphazard aisles with cups of water and towels. None of them were in white uniforms like vids had taught me to expect, but I still knew nurses when I saw them. "Cob included, there are only three people in this whole town with medical training. Six, if you add in the apprentices and the town herbalist."

"So, what do you need me to do?"

"Help me look after the patients in the back rooms. Bring them water, talk to them if they're lonely, try to make sure they're as comfortable as they can be… that sort of thing."

Right. Because bedside manner was something I was *so* well known for.

Derek ushered me through the overstuffed waiting room to a hallway with long-term care rooms on both sides. Two battered steel carts had been loaded with cups of water and blankets. "I'll take the left side if you take the right. More water and blankets can be found in the supply room around the corner, but we're already running low on the latter, so don't go overboard. If anything serious happens, come get me and I'll grab a doctor." The saw continued its grinding and he winced. "Once one of them is free anyway."

The back rooms were a mixed bag. There were fewer patients and therefore fewer people, even accounting for the family that had come to see them, but those patients were all worse off than the ones filling the cots in the waiting room. Every person I visited bore visible injuries from the wolf attack: broken limbs, concussions, bites, claw marks, and worse. One wall of the first room held nothing but burn patients from the small fire that had taken out half of a city block, each person doped up to the eyeballs and yet somehow still visibly in pain.

There wasn't anything I could do for those people, so I passed off cups of water to their family members and kept moving.

At first, nobody paid much attention to me, other than to maybe give a nod of thanks or ask for another blanket, or—in the case of those patients who were totally alone—grab for my hand and ask questions I didn't have answers for.

In the second of my three rooms, however, that all changed. One woman's eyes widened as soon as she saw me enter, and she turned to talk to her companions in hushed whispers. Thing about squeezing a dozen people and their families into a single small room is that there is no such thing as privacy. Those whispers were overheard by those around her, repeated by the next row over, and soon, the entire room—the conscious portion of it anyway—was staring at me, worn faces pinched in fear.

One guess what that woman had just told everyone.

Maybe Ricky, my second-year public relations consultant, had been right. Maybe I *should* have chosen Captain Kahuna as my Cape name. Of course, then I'd have killed myself out of embarrassment and never even made it to the Badlands to save some of these assholes' lives.

I ignored their reactions and kept passing out water. In general, the wounded were too caught up in their own pain, or too hopped up on whatever drugs the doctors had dumping into them via IVs, to care that the water they were being given or the blanket being awkwardly wrapped about them came from a Crow. It was their lucid family members who treated me like a rattlesnake ready to bite.

But fuck those people. Like I'd told Mammoth, I wasn't doing this for the adulation. I wasn't even doing it for the groupies anymore, unless I wanted Tessa to shotput me into the Pacific.

I let the emptiness fill me—not enough to make me dangerous, just enough to muffle things—and did my damn job.

In the third room, that got harder.

ooo

At first, there was little to distinguish the third long-term care room from the first two. There were a few empty beds, likely waiting for whoever the doctors were currently operating on, but that was counterbalanced by a slightly larger number of people visiting patients. No burn victims, but that had been true of the second room as well. The men and women on cots were—

And that was when I saw the key difference, and likely the reason this room had more visitors. Not all of the patients were men and women. Half a dozen cots held smaller figures, swaddled in bandages, and whimpering in pain.

This room held the children who'd been hurt in the attack.

Either everyone in the room recognized me or word had spread while I was moving through the second room, because the same fearful expressions greeted me as I pushed my cart of water and blankets inside. If I'd been a Pyromancer, capable of roasting them all from the inside out, they'd probably have thought I walked on water. Figuratively speaking, obviously, unless they didn't know the difference between Pyros and Hydros. But because I could raise the dead, kill with a touch, and might possibly be doomed to go insane—

I thought of my dead half-brother Jimmy. Of Nyah's final day at Mama Rawlins' in Bakersfield and the walkers that had rushed the orphanage to kill its inhabitants. Thought of Sally Cemetery and her years-long parade of terror up and down the coast as the Free States' most productive serial killer. Thought of Crimson Death's march into Reno at Sally's urging and the sheer number of dead who had followed.

I thought of that fleeting desire I'd had to extinguish the lives of the prisoners I'd saved in Reno, all those years after Crimson Death was gone.

Maybe... maybe I could understand their fear.

I opened myself up to the emptiness even more, let it swell inside me, pouring in through that crack in my soul, and ignored the way people flinched as I drew near. Water for every patient and the older members of the visiting families. Blankets upon request and then on to the next patient, the next family, the next blood-soaked bandage that, for the ten or fifteen seconds I was nearby, was no longer the family's primary source of concern.

It was worse with the children. Few of them were conscious enough to even notice me, but their families' protective instincts were already roused. Throw a Crow into the mix and none of them even wanted me near their injured offspring. I couldn't really blame them for that either... so for four of the five children, I just parked my cart and let the family members take what they needed.

But the fifth child... she was conscious.

What's more, I recognized her.

ooo

The spindly, gray-haired woman seated by the cot had a clear familial resemblance, but I knew she wasn't the little girl's mother. I'd already seen the little girl's mother, dead in a collapsed building, wrapped around her daughter, as if to shield her from harm.

The doctors had taken off the rest of the girl's leg below the knee, wrapped what was left in bandages almost as thick as she was, and given her a cocktail of drugs that should have left her senseless, if not entirely unconscious, but somehow she was still awake. Somehow, she remembered me. Her small arm reached up toward me, intercepted by the woman who wasn't her mother, as the rest of the family pushed forward to stand between me and the cot.

I couldn't hear what the girl whispered into the gray-haired woman's ear. Given her youth and all the drugs in her system, I probably wouldn't have understood the words anyway. But I watched emotions chase themselves across the older woman's face. Finally, she nudged one of her male relatives aside and stood to greet me.

"I understand we have you to thank for my granddaughter's life." Next to her, the girl's eyes, cloudy and unfocused, turned back in my direction.

"She was touched by him?" The man's face went white.

"How long will she have?" asked the second man, alike enough to the first to be brothers.

I frowned. "Until what?"

"Until the madness takes her."

I blinked. "What?"

"The madness of Crows," clarified the old woman.

Oh, for fuck's sake.

"Being a Crow isn't contagious," I told them.

"Of course not," said the first man. "But the madness…"

"That's not contagious either."

I was a long way from being able to read people like Alexa could, but their disbelief was so obvious a blind man would have seen it.

"A Crow's insanity is caused by their power," I explained. "Without that power, neither she nor anyone else I dragged to safety has anything to worry about."

I saw something change in the faces around me… and not just the family I was speaking to either. At least a few were people that Silt and I had saved.

"And you?" challenged the old woman. "Are you mad?"

I looked around the pain-filled room, looked at the cots with gravely injured children, looked down at the little girl who'd lost her leg, and pushed the emptiness away so that emotion leaked into my voice. "I am definitely mad," I said. "I'm just not crazy."

Maybe it was that emotion that convinced them. Maybe it was knowing I wasn't contagious. Either way, some of the hostility seeped out of the grandmother's expression.

"What's her name?" I asked.

"Daisy." She swallowed. "Her parents were Marigold and Peter. I'm Bea."

"Marigold saved Daisy's life. I found her curled up around the little girl, protecting her even at the end."

Bea's thin lips quivered. "My daughter played her part, but you did too. Dr. Edwards says she would have bled out if you had found her even twenty minutes later. She owes you her life."

"What's left of it," muttered the last of the three men. He shrank back as the two brothers turned on him. "I'm just saying. Hard to work the fields with only one leg."

"Then she'll do something else, Cedric." Bea's voice was hard enough to drive rail spikes into solid concrete. "And as her family, we will do whatever we can to help."

I wasn't sure how much of the conversation Daisy was tracking, but her unfocused eyes flicked back and forth between speakers. I turned back to Bea. "Can I show Daisy something?"

Even now, the old woman had to think about it, as if I was asking for permission to unveil some fresh eldritch horror right there in the hospital room. Finally, she gave me an uncertain nod.

I rested my right arm on my cart's surface and used my left hand to roll back the sleeve and reveal the stub of my wrist. I held it out so Daisy could see it.

"Some of us," I told her, pitching my voice so Bea and Cedric and the other two could hear me clearly, "are so big and so brave that the world knows we can handle situations that would make everyone else give up. It's going to be hard, and there are things you're going to have to learn all over again, but this—" I waved my arm and then gestured down to her amputated limb. "—and this are badges of honor. Life took its shot, but we're still here."

Can't say if she understood what I was saying. Can't say if she even really heard the words, or if the drugs made my voice sound like birds chirping. But Daisy saw the stump that was my arm. She looked down the cot to the mountain of bandages around her leg. And while she didn't smile or speak at all, I felt a moment of understanding pass between us.

I don't know. It kind of sounds like bullshit when I say it now. Maybe I'm remembering things the way I wanted them to be. Maybe I'm trying to amplify every light left behind to make up for the darkness that came after.

All I know is that Daisy's family, from Bea all the way down to asshole Uncle Cedric, had better treat that little girl right… or madness will be the least of their concerns.

And also the biggest.

CHAPTER 15

It was evening by the time I left the hospital, a whole lot more tired, but also feeling like I'd maybe accomplished something of value. Surgeries had been completed, and the real doctors were out checking on the patients. Derek and Cob had thanked me for my help and gone off to get dinner. I went in search of Silt.

Eventually, Emma pointed me in the Earthshaker's direction. My power was great for finding the living (or the dead), but not so great on the identification aspect; one spark looked much the same as another.

Only, as I stepped through the western gate, and started following the wall around Baker, I realized that wasn't entirely true. When I'd seen Carnage out at the Hole, when I first slipped into the space between life and death, and right before I turned the fucker into a pile of ash, he'd been a towering inferno of energy. When I'd nearly lost it in Reno, some of the fleeing sparks had been a tiny bit brighter than others.

And as I finally neared Silt, I realized she too was easily brighter than the lives I sensed on the other side of the wall.

It seemed like Powers registered differently to my senses than Normals… and going off the three different experiences I'd had, I was betting the actual magnitude of the person's abilities played a part. Carnage had been a High-Four in multiple power categories. Of the people I freed in Reno, only a few had been Powers, and none higher than a Two. And Silt, as a Mid-Three, fell somewhere in between.

If I was right, I might be able to rely on more than just ghosts to find Dr. Nowhere. As a Cat Six, he would probably shine like a second sun.

Of course, my new sense didn't stretch much further than my actual eyesight, so I'd still need to find some ghosts who could help me at least narrow down what portion of the Badlands the infamous Power might be in. We'd been on the road for over a month and had only seen two former states so far. There was an awful lot of land still to cover.

I scanned my surroundings, just to make sure I hadn't missed a supernova spark hiding somewhere in Baker, and then turned to Silt. The Earthshaker was leaning against the town's exterior wall, and now that I let my other sense fade, I could see her brown hair was plastered to her forehead, sweat dripping down her equally brown face.

"You okay, Sofia?"

"This is more work than I expected it to be," she said. "Guess I'll have to finish it tomorrow."

"Finish what?" I followed her pointing hand and realized she'd cleared a channel of earth next to the wall, at least eight feet wide and deep enough for me to stand in without seeing out. That channel ended where she stood, making it clear she was working backwards towards the gate.

"I spoke to Mammoth and Mayor Elspeth this morning. Town's wall has served them well, but it was too low to stop the wolves. They were hoping I could raise it some, but I work in dirt, not stone. So, I'm doing the next best thing."

"You've dug a moat around the entire town?"

"Not quite. Haven't made it back to the gate yet, as I'm sure you've noticed. Also, with the lake in the middle of the town, it provides its own barrier, so I stopped there."

"Fucking hell. And I thought I was being helpful at the hospital."

"You went to the hospital?"

"Yeah." The sun was already going down, but I saw something in her expression. "What?"

"Nothing. It's just your bedside manner—"

"I know; it's better suited to scaring the monsters hiding under the bed." I rolled my eyes. It wasn't the first time Silt had said that. "Anyway, if you've been using your power all day, you need dinner even more than I do."

"I guess so." Despite her words, she didn't budge.

I'd mentored my first-years enough to know when something wasn't right. Okay, I'd *mostly* relied on Paco or Lynn to alert me—I'd had plenty of shit on my plate as it was—but still... between mentorship and having a girlfriend, I wasn't quite as clueless as I'd been when I started at the Academy.

"What's bugging you?"

"Sorry?"

"Stark said we're going to be here for at least a week. As much as a taller wall will help, you didn't have to try to do it all in one day."

"I've still got—"

"Yeah yeah. Three hundred more yards or whatever. Which means you've been using your power non-stop since we split up just after lunchtime. No wonder you can barely stand."

"We're not all juggernauts of endless power like you, Boneboy."

Yeah, Silt knew I was a Full-Five too. She and Tessa had been the two people I told as soon as my Test finished.

"All the more reason not to bleed yourself dry. Right?" She didn't say anything, and I sighed, grabbing a seat along the chasm she'd created with her abilities. "Seriously, Sofia… what's going on?"

"All that time in Nikolai's pits. In the Training Grounds." She shook her head and dropped down next to me with a tired grunt. "I thought I'd be better prepared for my first real battle."

"What are you talking about? You kicked ass. We both did."

"All that training, all those classes, and I spent the whole time following you around the streets with a shotgun. I think I used my power once in actual combat. I might as well have been a Normal."

"And the one time you used your power, it saved me from a half-dozen giant-sized crows… *and* ended up giving us some aerial troops. What am I missing?"

"I just… need to be better. That shit might cut it against wolves and birds, but against people? Against other Powers?" She flicked a pebble into the moat. "How do you do it?"

"Do what?" For the three years I'd known her, Sofia Black had been the most confident person I'd ever met. Seeing her like this was fucking weird.

"Just charge into a fight. String everything together and make it work?"

"Practice." She snorted and I shook my head. "I'm serious. Some of it is training, a lot of it is real world experience. I just… focus on what needs to be done."

"What about when that task is impossible?"

"Then I try something else. And if that doesn't work, I try something else again. Fuck giving up, right? I'm not going to give them that satisfaction of seeing me quit."

"Who?"

That brought me up short. "I have no idea. Dr. Nowhere maybe? Everyone? The world, in general?"

"Is that something you learned at the orphanage?"

"I guess so. When you scratch and claw for everything, it becomes a mindset as much as a strategy."

"And you're never afraid?"

"Shit, I'm always afraid. Always angry too, for that matter. When bullets start flying, I just sort of… lock all of that away so I can focus on what matters. Is that what you're upset about? Being afraid?"

"I was terrified. As many times as I've fought and killed and died in the Training Grounds, all I could think as I climbed over the wall was 'this is real.' If you hadn't been waiting in the street for me… shit, I don't know if I'd have made it over at all."

"Did I ever tell you about my talk with Freddie last year?"

"Muse? No… why?"

"Tessa wanted me to get him to tone down his drinking, so I had a heart-to-heart with him one night. Turns out our former classmate had a reason for drinking so much."

"He was an alcoholic?" guessed Sofia.

"No. Well, probably, yeah… but really, the alcohol gave him a way to hide."

"From what?"

"From the Academy and everything that came with it. Our classes. Our training. Muse never wanted to be a Cape, except to give his little brother something to be happy about. Every aspect of it terrified him."

"So, you think I'm like Muse? Fantastic."

"That's not what I'm saying. Everybody is scared. What matters is how we respond to it. Freddie ran like a coward when the Academy was attacked, leaving me to die. I get it… I even understand it, sort of… but when push came to shove, he fucking ran. In *your* first real battle, you tried to hold off an entire street of wolves with nothing but a shotgun."

"I could have done so much more."

"Then do more next time. These are the Badlands. You know we're going to run into more than just oversized animals."

"Just like that?"

"You didn't freeze. You didn't get anyone killed. You probably saved my life at least twice. And you didn't end up with your guts spread across the Mojave either, like I did in *my* first fight as a Power."

"Well, there's a *reason* I'm higher in the class rankings."

"Because you're Silt and being awesome is just what you do?"

"Hell, Boneboy. You *have* been listening." There was no trace of melancholy in her shit-eating grin.

"I think it just seeped in over time. Like osmosis or whatever. Now, can we go get some dinner? I'm starving."

"*You're* starving?" She climbed back to her feet, her grunt a perfect echo of the one she'd made sitting down. "I'm the one who just used her power for five hours straight. I could eat a damn horse!"

"Cloud's available," I offered.

Silt's laugh filled the night like the smell of the home-cooked meal we were finally going to have.

CHAPTER 16

Joe and Denali made it back the next day, tired and dirty, but otherwise none the worse for wear. Mammoth called a meeting of the Mission shortly after and everyone, even Cob, stopped what they were doing to attend.

We were still on the east side of the lake, away from the destruction. Most of us had been sleeping in a large warehouse with the wagons, but Mammoth and Stark had rooms in the nearby house that doubled as an inn when visitors came to town. It wasn't big enough for all of us, even just to meet in, so Mammoth and Stark came to the warehouse instead.

"We're going to be staying in Baker a little bit longer than expected," said Mammoth. "Mayor Elspeth has asked us to do what we can to bolster their town's defenses."

"I take it you didn't bring back good news?" Cagney asked Joe.

"Not so much," said the old man. "That wolf pack isn't the only group that's shifted south since we last came through."

"It's good hunting territory up there." Cagney seemed worried, which told me I probably should be too, but honestly, my knowledge of Montana could fit on a napkin.

"Yeah. Either something's changed or a new predator's moved in and scared everything else off," said Joe.

"Could be both," added Denali.

"You guys didn't go scout to see what it was?"

"Anything that can drive an entire pack out of their land—not to mention a mountain lion and a mama grizzly with four cubs—isn't something we want to stumble across," said Joe. "Besides, Mammoth didn't want us gone for more than a day."

"Too easy for something to go wrong," agreed Denali, as quiet as ever.

"When we get to Wichita, I'll see if someone from Red Flight can do a flyover and figure out what's going on," said Mammoth.

Supersonic cleared his throat loudly.

"Nobody goes anywhere without a buddy, Supersonic. And since you're our only Flyboy, that means we'll have to offload the work to a Cape team instead."

"I thought Red Flight was in Arizona," I said.

"They are."

"Then what does Wichita have to do with anything?"

"It's the closest thing to a city left in the Badlands, and they have a microwave radio tower high enough for its signal to reach the repeater chain that runs through New Mexico up to Flagstaff. Red Flight doesn't have the time or inclination to police the Badlands, but Aftermath is an old friend. I'm sure he'll agree to have some of his crew do a fly-over."

I looked at Mammoth with a new sense of appreciation. It hadn't occurred to me that he'd have contacts with people on actual Cape teams. Maybe a letter of reference from him would help land me a spot on one of those teams when I graduated.

"Wichita is more than a month away though," said Lady. "What are we doing for Baker in the meantime?"

"Like I said, we'll be improving their defenses." He looked to Sofia. "Is your moat almost done?"

"Yeah… it's not much, but both people and wolves will have a much harder time even reaching the town wall… let alone jumping it."

"Well done. We'll have you tie it into the lake in a few days, so it's more than just a dry bed. In the meantime, we'll all be building some watchtowers inside the walls. One by each gate, and one a piece to the north and south."

"We should have done that years ago," griped Reese.

"If this had been Kansas, Oklahoma, or even Nebraska, we would have." Mammoth's voice was a low rumble. "Montana's been quiet a long time, and Baker's far enough from everything that there's not much in the way of human threats. The existing defenses have gotten this town through the handful of bandit attacks it's seen. They didn't see the point in wasting time, lumber, and manpower on defending against just the possibility of something worse."

I thought of the sheer number of wounded I'd seen in the hospital and the two dozen bodies I'd marched over to the town cemetery and fought to repress a scowl. It seemed the Badlands and Free States had one thing in common: people were fucking idiots.

"I know Lady has some ideas for the gates and for some simple traps that could make a difference at the walls," said Mammoth, "and we'll get to those as soon as the watchtowers are done. In the meantime, how are the wounded looking, Cob?"

"Ours or theirs?"

"Let's start with ours."

"James took the worst hit and should probably sit out the fun to avoid tearing his stitches. Stark took a bite on the leg but scared the possible infection away just by glaring at it. Jacobs needs to keep off his ankle until it heals all the way, but we can use him keeping records at the hospital. And Walker—"

"I'm fine," I said.

"James isn't the only one with stitches."

"I'll be fine," I said. "Find me something to kill and I'll be more than fine."

"Well, *that's* a little bloodthirsty," muttered Derek.

"If I kill with my power, I can absorb some of their energy," I said. "And that energy heals me."

Maybe I should have kept that information to myself, given the general attitude about me being a Crow, but the Mission had been plenty willing to leverage my power to avoid the dirty work like corpse removal. I figured we might as well get it all out in the open then and there.

"I don't think there's much left around these parts that needs killing," said Cob, talking over the silence that had fallen in the warehouse.

"There's always Cloud," I volunteered again.

"What is it with you and that horse?" asked Cagney.

"Other than him being part demon and part serial killer? Which of you named him Cloud anyway? That's a sick damn joke if I've ever heard one."

"I gave him the name," said Cagney, "because he's just about the sweetest, most easy-going gelding anyone is ever going to meet, and riding him is kind of like riding a cloud."

"Actually," said Supersonic, "clouds are wet and gloomy and kind of gross."

"Maybe you should try to make peace with him, Walker," said Emma, not even trying to hide her grin as she nestled under Silt's arm. "Have you fed him any apples?"

I had, and more than once, but when the meeting broke up, I tried again, bringing a couple of apples with me to the town's stables.

Damn horse tried to take off my fingers. Again.

"You may have the others fooled," I told him, tossing the second apple down into the hay at his feet, "but I'm on to your bullshit. Make one wrong move and I swear you'll be worm food."

Cloud whisked his tail around and ducked his head down to eat the second apple, but as I left, his whicker sounded an awful lot like a laugh.

Stupid horse.

ooo

When Mammoth had mentioned watch towers, I'd envisioned the sort of massive stone or steel structures you saw in the fenced-off yards of aboveground Free States prisons and wondered how the fuck we were going to make one of those, let alone four.

Turns out, the answer was simple; we weren't. The towers that went up were primitive as hell; wooden and roofless, with a single viewing box surrounded on three sides by chest-high wooden walls. Four posts held that box up almost fourteen feet in the air just inside the wall, and a rope ladder dangled from the box to the ground, providing the only means of entry and egress.

I was pretty sure a Wind Dancer could blow any of those towers over with enough effort—and a Titan could do the same just by shattering the legs—but for the first time ever, Baker's small guard force had a clear view of the surrounding territory. The bells mounted in each tower gave them an easy way to sound the alarm, and the crate of ammo we'd offloaded from the wagon meant they'd be ready to shoot down over the walls at any attackers.

It wouldn't do much to stop an army... but against a pack of wolves? Or even bandits? Suddenly, Baker was a much tougher nut to crack.

Because of my wound, I wasn't part of the tower raising, but Stark had the rest of us gathering smaller bits of wood for a different project—branches from the surrounding forest and beams from the few homes that had collapsed beyond saving. When our wood pile turned out to be insufficient for the task, Mayor Elspeth had her lumberjacks fell almost a dozen thin trees.

A few days later, woodworkers returned all that lumber to us as hundreds of crude wooden spears, each roughly four to five feet long and sharpened on one end. With Silt's help, we planted those spears at strategic spots along the base of the town wall, facing outward like a hedgehog's quills. There weren't nearly enough to surround the town, but between the spears and the moat, attackers would hopefully be funneled into better prepared kill zones.

Can't say I ever planned to have my Cape base out on the frontier but learning some of the basics on how to design one was kind of fun. Pity we'd be long gone before we got a chance to see how well our defenses worked.

With the towers up, the moat dug, and spears in place, that left only the gates to worry about, and Lady had a plan for them. First, she had Silt extend the moat past each of the gates, completing its semicircle and removing all access to the town outside of the lake and its river. Given that our wagons couldn't float, I wasn't sure how we'd be getting back out of Baker, but a few days later, we were laying down beams that crossed the moat, and sheets of thinner wood atop those beams.

"The bridge is short enough that we don't need pilings," explained Lady, "and the two rods we've inserted through the wooden sheets on the town-side should keep the bridge from moving laterally even with a wagon's load. But if the guards spot attackers coming, it will be easy enough to pull the rods and retract the beams. It's not as efficient as a good drawbridge, but we don't have the materials or time to install those. Maybe next year."

I looked at the flat, destructible bridge we'd just built and back to the rangy woman. "Are you sure you're not an engineer?"

"Out here, every mechanic has a little bit of engineer in them, and vice versa." She tucked her hair behind an ear, clearly pleased with the day's efforts. "Why don't you all go and get lunch. I've got a crew of townsfolk coming out soon to learn how to dismantle and reassemble one of these."

"Can I bring you back anything?"

"Cookies, if they have them."

I was pretty sure they would. One of the town's bakers had a hell of a sweet tooth. "Any preference on type?"

"Delivery boy's choice." She sent me off with a wink and a laugh.

"You know," said Silt, as we made our way back through the town, "I don't recall you ever bringing *Tessa* cookies."

"We went to the mess hall together."

"Uh huh."

"I'm just being friendly, Silt. We still have four-plus months to spend out here with the Mission."

"Ah, friendliness. *Definitely* one of your most celebrated qualities," she agreed, voice mild as the summer rains.

That brought me to a halt. I shot my friend a glare. "When all of this is done, I'm going back to the Academy and a life with Tessa. I'm not going to screw that up."

"Glad to hear it. Only... maybe make sure Lady knows it too?"

"What?"

"Between Vibe and Poltergeist, you have a history of missing signals." Silt tucked one of her own brown curls behind an ear and sent me an exaggerated wink, giggling flirtatiously in an over-the-top rendition of Lady's parting farewell. "And it inevitably blows up in your face."

CHAPTER 17

Before we left Baker, I made one last trip out to their cemetery, weaving my way past all the freshly filled graves. The town predated the Break, and its cemetery did too. Many of the headstones had long since fallen, the graves little more than slight mounds in a field of wild grass, but I headed for the oldest graves I could reliably identify. And then, like I'd done in Billings earlier that month, like I'd done in Bakersfield almost a year prior, I called on my power.

If I pushed the emptiness into the earth beneath me, it would find the decayed bodies of Baker's former residents. Enough power and they'd become walkers, ready to dig themselves out of their rotted coffins on my command. But I already had my wolves and crows and raising the town's dead wasn't going to do much but piss off the living. Instead, I let the emptiness trickle out of me, like a whisper on the wind.

Come, I commanded the lost souls of Baker. *Be seen.*

And they came, tattered and translucent, specters of men, women, and children, gathering in uneven ranks before me, shifting back and forth, swaying through headstones and grass and each other's bodies without awareness.

There were a lot fewer ghosts than there were bodies buried. That had been true in Billings too, and I wasn't entirely sure why. Maybe it took something for ghosts to form. A violent death? Unfinished business? Or maybe it was just random chance, like so much else; a chaotic swirl of events that left a fragment of a person behind, like a signpost that nobody could see but me.

I doubted even the dead knew for sure.

All told, roughly forty ghosts had answered my whispered call. I asked them a half-dozen questions about Dr. Nowhere to no avail. But I'd given the matter some thought in the weeks since Billings. Truth was, Dr. Nowhere was just the name a journalist had given whoever caused the Break. If such a person existed at all, there was no reason the dead of Montana, people who had died even as my country was still being formed, would necessarily know that name.

It was time to approach things from a different angle.

If you were alive during the Break, during the time when people first started developing powers and everything went to shit, step forward.

To be honest, I still didn't expect anything to happen. Mom and little Nyah were the only two ghosts who had ever responded to anything I said, and even they had forgotten my existence as soon as they'd passed on the visions of their own deaths. But I'd told Her Majesty I would try, so here I was, infusing my silent commands with all the power I could, on the off chance anything would happen.

To my shock, something did.

Four ghosts stepped forward. Their sightless eyes remained focused on anything but me, their swaying never slowed, but suddenly, there was a space between them and the rest of the spirits I'd summoned.

I'm looking for the person responsible, I told them.

No response.

I tried again. *If you were asleep when it happened, your dreams may have touched theirs. If you heard a voice in your dreams or saw something that matched the new reality you later woke up to, I need to know.*

Still nothing. A wind blew through the cemetery, rustling the long blades of grass, but the ghosts remained silent.

"Okay then." I sighed and let that sigh disperse the power I'd sent out into the night sky and the ghosts that power had summoned. "On to the next fucking town."

ooo

The *next fucking town* was little more than a pre-Break rest stop turned into an outpost a day east of Baker. We stopped overnight, long enough for Lady to look at their generators and for Cob to give medical checkups, and were on our way again the next morning, wagons headed deeper into what had once been North Dakota.

I didn't know much about North Dakota, except that it apparently was where the term *Badlands* had first originated, pre-Break. Can't say that gave me a rosy feeling about the place, even if I wasn't sure how it had earned the designation. Maybe there'd been a bunch of Black Hats there? Or whatever existed before Black Hats were a thing. Pirates?

The trail we followed took us through a region of canyons and hills that lacked the elevation of the mountain passes in Montana but more than made up for it with the number of switchbacks and turns. Denali said those canyons had been formed by wind and rain and thousands of years, but it looked to me more like a snake Shifter whose size would put even King Rex to shame had slithered its way through, digging passages right through the fucking earth.

As we rode through those canyons, I had my wolves patrolling almost half a mile in either direction. Unlike a Summoner, I couldn't see *through* my walkers, but if something destroyed them, it would at least give us advance warning.

How we'd then escape a snake that had to be at least five hundred feet long and a hundred wide was another question entirely.

Thankfully, either the monster snake was gone or Denali's story had some semblance of truth, because we made it through the canyons unscathed. There, the rest of North Dakota spread out before us...

It looked a lot like eastern Montana, if I was being honest.

A few days later, Denali came back with word of a wagon up ahead. Within an hour, it came into sight, growing closer with every passing minute because that wagon wasn't moving at all. In fact, it was leaning over to one side like it was drunk. Stark and the outriders Mammoth dispatched were almost on top of the few people milling about that wagon before they even noticed.

Ten minutes later, Stark gave the all-clear and we drove our own wagons up the trail. I nudged Cloud to the front so I could hear what was going on.

"Traders from Eagle Butte headed to Regent," the scar-faced man told Mammoth. "Horses got spooked by something and the wagon broke an axle."

"Eagle Butte? How'd they get past the nomads?"

"Same way you're planning to, I assume, sir," said the small man in a floppy hat who'd come over with Stark. "Trade goods and some bargains decidedly in their favor. We make this circuit once or twice a summer. I think they're used to my ugly mug by now."

"You're headed to Regent?"

"Ayup. Then on to Dickinson, over to Belfield—if it's still there anyway—and back down. I'm Carl. Carl Jenkins. We've got a smith in Eagle Butte that can put out some quality work. Sells well up here, as you can imagine. Anyway, I sent a man up to Regent for help on one of our two horses this morning before I realized the Mission was on its way."

"How did you know we were the Mission?" I asked.

Carl sent me a friendly smile and nodded to Stark. "Fellow over there introduced you as all as such. And there's not a lot of folk out here like your boss."

Given that Mammoth was twice the size of the rest of us, he kind of had a point.

"Axle's shattered," said Lady, sliding out from under the wagon. "And that back wheel is bent all to hell. What did you say spooked your horses?"

"Never saw it, actually," said Carl. "Whatever it was came up on the side of the trail, and next thing you know, our horses were bolting in the wrong direction. Off the trail, then back on it, and we hit one hell of a rock somewhere in between. Lucky none of us were hurt, to be honest."

"Lucky?" Cob shook his head. "Given the state of your wagon, I'd say it was a miracle."

"My family and I would be indebted to you folks if you could help us get our goods to town. Once we have a new axle and wheel, we can come back and get the wagon."

"Regent's just up the road. I'd say we have the time to spare if you're willing," Stark told Mammoth.

"It's what we're here for," answered the big man, calling Emma over. "Can you get their goods loaded into one of our wagons?"

"You got it, boss."

o o o

An hour later, we were on our way. Carl's wife, Alice, a hard-faced woman half a foot taller than her husband, rode up front in one of the wagons, while Carl and his teenage son, Billy, rode with us.

"What's life like as a merchant?" Silt asked the teenager.

"What?" He visibly started. "Oh. Not bad, I guess. Lots of travel. And selling. You know."

"Seems kind of dangerous."

Billy frowned. "What makes you say that?"

"When we were unloading your wagon, it looked like it had taken some fire at some point. Bullet holes and everything."

"Oh. That." He shrugged. "The nomads aren't always as friendly as we'd like."

One horse behind them, it was my turn to frown. That didn't really mesh with what his father had told Mammoth. Granted, if they made this trip multiple times a summer, the son could've been talking about an attack in the past, but... wouldn't they have patched the holes, if so?

Three years at the Academy hadn't changed the fact that I was a suspicious little bastard. Probably because I'd learned my whole life was a lie along the way. I let Cloud drop back until I was riding alongside Derek. "Do you guys run into traveling merchants a lot?"

"Maybe once or twice a year. Why?"

"Have you ever seen these three?"

"Nope, but that's not so strange. The Badlands are a big place, and we've only come this way once since I joined the Mission. Why?"

"I don't know. Something about this seems odd. The wagon shows signs of being in a gunfight."

"If they came from down south, that's not really a surprise. The Badlands started when we crossed the mountains, but the northern lands are peaceful by comparison."

"Except for the Weaver."

He shivered. "There's a reason there are no towns anywhere near her territory. Anyway, the further south you go, the more people there are, and that's when things get dicey. What's left of Kansas

City…" He shook his head. "That place is something else. Good and bad both. You'll see if we go there."

Given that I'd spent the last three years of my life in the city of so-called angels, I kind of doubted *Kansas City* would be enough to blow my mind, but I just nodded. So far, except for the horse-sized wolves, the Badlands had been nothing at all like I expected. Maybe the city would be another surprise.

I was half-asleep in the saddle when the link to one of my walkers disappeared. I straightened up, scanning the area around us. We'd entered a stretch of forest, and my wolves were way out on our flanks, ghosting through the trees, but if something *had* attacked, I still should have been heard the noise of their fight.

Mammoth was riding rear guard, so I hurried up to Stark.

"I think we have a problem," I told him. "One of my walkers just disappeared."

"Wolf or crow?"

"Wolf." I shook my head. "There was no warning at all… it was there and then it wasn't."

"Might be a grizzly or something," said Stark, "but…"

"But?"

"Joe was supposed to come back to be relieved by Denali almost ten minutes ago. And the forest is quieter than I'd expect it to be."

"Something's wrong."

"I think you're right." He turned his horse to call back to Mammoth, and something streaked through the space he'd just vacated. I looked down to find an arrow quivering in a stump on the side of the road.

"Shit!" I threw myself out of my saddle. All those times I'd fallen off Cloud finally paid off, as I had ample practice hitting the dirt and avoiding his dancing hooves.

Stark was still on his mount but hunched low, using the horse as a shield. He had his gun out and was firing back in the direction the arrow had come from. I don't think he hit anything, but the boom of his revolver was enough to alert everyone in our wagon train that something was wrong.

As if to reinforce that thought, there was a scream of pain as someone behind us caught an arrow. Then, guns opened up on us from both sides of the trail.

CHAPTER 18

Stark's shot had shocked everyone into motion, so we weren't the sitting ducks we might otherwise have been. Still, by the time everyone was firing back into the forest at people they couldn't quite see, at least two of the Mission were face down in the dirt outside the wall Silt was swiftly building.

One of those bodies was Mammoth's.

I let my power loose, like I should have done way back when my first walker died and immediately sensed twenty sparks of light on either side of the trail. We'd ridden right into their crossfire, and the wagons and Silt's little wall were our only protection.

Good thing the attackers weren't the only things in the woods.

I heard a loud scream of pain, somewhere to my left, and smiled, even as Cloud tried to yank his reins from my hands. My three remaining wolves slipped toward the shooters on my command, ambushing them from the rear. Another scream, this one ending in a gurgle, but a second walker vanished from my senses soon after.

I frowned. Whoever had just destroyed one of my wolves wasn't a spark to my senses. They were a fucking torch. And that meant—

I moved away from Cloud and past the first wagon to where Silt was kneeling in the earth. She had two walls up now, filling the space between the front two wagons, and half the Mission was taking advantage of that cover. Cagney had her rifle out and kept peeking over the wall to return fire on one side, while Derek did the same on the other. Lady was up on the second wagon with James, both lying flat but keeping their eyes peeled. Cob was tending to Presley, who'd taken a round to the knee, but Jacobs was kneeling next to Derek, sending carefully controlled bursts into the woods opposite him with what looked like military hardware.

Too bad he hadn't brought enough toys to share with the rest of us. My little club wasn't going to do much good from fifteen feet away.

"We've got problems," I told Silt.

"You think? I count nineteen people out there." She paused, one palm still flat against the earth so she could sense what was moving across it. "Eighteen now. Your walkers at work?"

"For however much longer they last." I'd dumped energy into the bandits my wolves had killed, but whoever was out there was bringing them down almost as soon as I raised them, and there was only one wolf running free. "They've got at least one Power with them."

"Well, shit." She eyed me. "That must be the particularly heavy asshole. Titan?"

"Or Shifter, yeah. Makes sense."

"Can you take him?"

Maybe a year ago, I'd have hesitated. Then again, maybe not. Aggression had always kind of been my thing. "If I can reach him, he's dead." Truth was, I was hoping I could kill him the normal way, because a Titan walker would be damn near unstoppable. But we already had casualties. If I had to death touch the asshole, then so be it. "Can you get the shooters off their feet?"

"Yeah, but not for long. Earth doesn't like to stay in motion and even if there were any fault lines nearby, I'm not strong enough to trigger them."

"Just get me to the trees."

"I think we should all just stay right here," came a voice from the lead wagon. We looked up to find Alice, the traveling merchant's wife looming above us. I don't know where she'd gotten the gun, but she had it pointed at the back of Supersonic's head.

"I couldn't have said it better myself, my lovely bride," said Carl, coming around the second wagon. He was off his horse now and marched a struggling Emma in front of him.

"Fuck off, Elmore," spat Alice. "That's the last time I'm ever pretending to be your wife."

"Last time you'll have to," said the man, "thanks to the Mission here." All life drained out of his eyes, leaving them cold and hard. "Throw down your weapons, folks, or we'll kill you all where you stand, starting with Emma, the boy, and the asshole my fake son has cornered back there."

"You're going to kill us all anyway—" Emma's words cut off as the merchant kicked out her legs, dropping her to her knees in the dirt. Much like Supersonic, she now had a gun leveled at her head.

"Nonsense. As the proud new owners of our own town, we'll need servants—"

Another loud scream came from the forest, and Carl—or Elmore, I guess—scowled. "What the hell is going on out there?"

"Wolves, boss!" came back a deep-voiced reply.

"Well, fucking kill them and get over here. Do I have to do everything myself?"

"Sorry, boss!" A chatter of gunfire came from within the woods and I lost connection with the last of my wolf walkers. Moments later, a giant of a man came out of the forest, trailed by the half-dozen remaining shooters on that side. I heard the woods rustle behind us as more bandits emerged from the other side of the forest, but kept my eyes focused on Elmore and his powered henchman. Shockingly, the Titan seemed unwilling to meet the much, much smaller man's eyes, dropping his gaze as he approached. A blood-spattered club the size of a fire hydrant told me what had been used to end at least two of my walkers.

"Where's the rest of our crew?" Elmore scanned the trail, keeping Emma carefully in front as a shield. "And the rest of the Mission for that matter? We've got three of these fools down at the back of the train and a couple of deaders to feed the dogs when we get back to Regent, but where's the guy with the scar... or the Indian?"

That set off a fresh round of spirited debate among the bandits, but I wasn't paying them any attention anymore. I twisted just enough to lock eyes with Supersonic, high on the wagon above us, and then slowly rolled my head back and to the right. It took a second, and enough repetition that if Alice had been looking down, she'd have known something was going on, but eventually he understood I wanted him to help Emma.

At least I hoped he did. Silt would never forgive me if I got her girlfriend killed.

Supersonic's eyes met mine again. He clearly didn't have a clue what I had planned, or how he'd avoid the bullet with his name on it, but he gave me a slow eyeblink of acknowledgment anyway.

I don't like Caleb. Never have, never will, but that was the moment I started seeing him as a Cape and not the spiky-haired shithead who'd sucker punched me at Unicorn's funeral. When it mattered, he was ready to throw down.

A moment later, my crows came streaking out of the sky.

The first flew *through* the covered wagon, bringing its wings in tight to its body, and hit Alice from behind, talons outstretched.

Even a normal bird would've made an impact, but this crow was the size of an eagle and undead besides, and it was clawing and driving its beak into the woman's skull even as its hollow bones broke. The second the bandit staggered, Supersonic was in motion, tearing away from her before she could squeeze the trigger, and making a Jitterbug-fast dash for Carl and Emma.

As quick as Caleb was, it takes a High-Four or a Five to outrun a speeding bullet; Carl was already squeezing the trigger.

My second crow hit the bandit's gun hand like a feathered missile. The roar of the gun sounded, but its bullet buried itself harmlessly in the earth, followed by the gun and the hand holding it. A fraction of a second later, Emma was a dozen yards away in Supersonic's arms.

And then all hell *really* broke loose.

ooo

A sharp rumble of earth tossed the bandits in front of us to the ground, and by the time they were back on their feet, our shooters were firing again from behind Silt's barricade. One of the bandits in my line of sight dropped, hit at least three times by Jacobs' automatic.

I was already moving, leaping over Silt's wall. Behind me, one crow left the wagon in a flurry of barely functional wings, followed by the walker that had recently been Alice. Ahead of me, the other crow died as Elmore's giant-sized minion crushed it into paste. The bandit leader himself was screaming, clutching his savaged arm to his chest, but that noise was distant, just like the gunfire, muffled by emptiness as I pushed my body to its limit.

Bullets passed by, close enough to kiss, but there was no space for fear in the heart of my power. I was five feet out into the open, then ten, and then Elmore was spinning to the ground, skull fragments and brain matter spraying the Titan behind him.

I ducked under and past the big Power's reactionary swing in a dive roll that had my recently healed back screaming, but pain was secondary too. I came out of that roll and spun back toward the Titan, whipping my now-bloody mace about in a vicious arc toward the back of his knee.

I'd tried something similar out at the Hole, and watched my weapon slide right off, but this Titan wasn't on Maul's level, and my weapon wasn't a partially melted table leg.

Even so, the results were less than inspiring.

The spikes on my mace failed to penetrate the Titan's armored skin, and what I'd hoped would be a crippling blow instead just caused the Power to stagger and drop his club.

Before I could press the advantage, I felt more than saw a second bandit charge me from behind. I threw myself to the left to avoid what my detached mind informed me was a fucking tomahawk aimed at my head.

Apparently, the tomahawk-wielding bandit had missed Jessica Strich's classes on not overextending yourself when attacking, and he was every bit as vulnerable to a mace in the face as Elmore had been. I paused to push power into his body, raising it as it fell… and the Titan's massive fist caught me from behind, launching me over the bandit I'd just killed.

Bones snapped—my right arm… why was it *always* my right arm?—when I landed at the surprised feet of a bandit firing from the cover of the tree line. He fumbled for the knife at his belt, but I was already reaching out, ignoring the flash of white-hot pain from cracked ribs and the humerus that had broken my fall.

My hand grazed bare skin.

I let some of the emptiness inside me go.

The bandit's rifle fell to the ground, followed by unwashed clothing and a man-sized pile of dust.

Whatever energy I'd gained from death touching him wasn't nearly enough to heal my right arm—or even my ribs—but it got me to my feet. Not much had changed in the thirty seconds since I'd first attacked. Silt and the others were pinned down behind their barricade by the bandits' superior numbers, Derek still firing even though an arrow had sprouted from his back. My last crow had been shot down, but the Alice-walker was charging the bandits positioned on the other side of the trail.

On the near side, Supersonic had engaged the Titan, darting through the air like a drunken hummingbird, but the bullets from his two guns—because *of course* Caleb would dual wield semi-automatics against the advice of our professors—weren't any more effective than my mace had been. As I watched, he barely avoided being swatted aside.

I looked back at my feet, at the pile of what had once been a man. With only one hand available, the bandit's rifle was useless to me except as a potentially even less effective weapon than the mace I'd lost being thrown twenty feet through the air. I grabbed his knife instead and buried it in the back of a second bandit as I raced back down the hill, every step a spear of pain that my power couldn't quite hide.

Given how quickly my wolf and Normal walkers were dying, I had really, really wanted a Titan walker of my very own, but enough was fucking enough.

As I ran, I pushed my power into Elmore's body and raised him at the Titan's feet. The big man had shown no hesitation at all in swatting down the other walkers, but this time, he stumbled backwards from the bloody shell of his leader, a look of horror on his broad features.

"Boss—?"

And then I was on him, and my hopes for a superpowered walker vanished again in another shower of dust.

I felt my ribs knit themselves back together as the Titan's energy poured into me, but a nearby rifle barked and it was my turn to be spun about, feeling like Cloud had just kicked me in the arm.

It was my left arm this time. Apparently, Dr. Nowhere had heard my bitching.

I let myself pinwheel to the ground, focusing instead on sending the walkers of Elmore and the bandit I'd knifed against the asshole who'd just shot me.

Unfortunately, the man knew he'd only winged me, and seemed set on ignoring my charging walkers long enough to rectify that issue. I was scrambling to my feet, but there was nothing approaching cover around me. Time ground to a halt as I tried to eke every bit of speed I could out of a body that was, in the end, only human. I watched a cold smile make its way onto the bandit's face, finger tightening on the trigger.

And then his face blew outward like the world's ugliest piñata, and Denali emerged from the forest behind him, smoking pistol in one hand, bloody knife in the other.

I sent my walkers after a new target, gave the scout a nod of thanks, and reconsidered the wisdom of being out there in the fucking open when I wasn't anything close to bulletproof.

ooo

"Welcome back," shouted Silt, as I vaulted the barricade. She looked like she'd gone on one of Nikolai's ten-mile 'training sprints', sweat dripping from her face, but even as she greeted me, she squeezed one hand into a fist, and I heard a bandit scream as the earth swallowed his feet. "Tired of punching people?"

"It just doesn't have that thrill anymore!" I pulled myself up into the lead wagon, ignoring the puddle of gore that one of my now-destroyed crows had made of the woman I'd raised as my now also-destroyed walker. "And it's hard to direct traffic while I'm getting my ass shot off!"

Denali emerging from the forest had saved my life, but it had also told me that not all the sparks of life I was sensing out there were bandits. Stark was missing too, and he was either hiding or flanking the enemy. I was betting on the latter. Allies in the woods meant I couldn't just send my walkers out to indiscriminately kill anything out there, and *that* meant I needed a better vantage point than I'd had out in the field... or even huddled next to Silt.

With phase one of that plan complete, I pushed the emptiness back out of me, seeking the corpses that surrounded us. The bandit Denali had defaced was too gone for even zombiedom, but our shooters had brought bandits down on either side of us, and I raised them all, one after the other. I raised whoever *our* dead guy was too, because this wasn't the time for fucking sensibilities.

I know what you're thinking: you're thinking *didn't you and Carl both say that* two *of the Mission were down?*

And the answer to that is: *yes, yes I did.* But there's a big fucking difference between down and dead—if anyone knows that, it's me—and one of the two bodies I'd seen out there was Mammoth.

From the Weaver to King Rex all the way down to the nightmarish whatever-the-hell-*that*-is of Alan-Fucking-Jackson, all Beast Shifters have one thing in common.

They heal a hell of a lot faster than the rest of us.

As my walkers surged to their feet, something massive mirrored the motion on the other side of the rear wagon. The battered shape of Elmore's pretend-son repeated my epic flight through the air. Unlike me, this asshole landed on his neck, in a snap I somehow heard over the gunfire.

As a fully shifted—and enraged—Mammoth waded into battle, I raised his most recent victim too.

CHAPTER 19

From beginning to end—or soup to nuts, as Amos used to say in one of his many phrasings that made not even a little bit of sense—the ambush and subsequent battle took less than five minutes. As my walkers engaged the enemy, Stark finally made his presence—and his bowie knife—felt, cutting throats and slashing hamstrings as he staged a one-man ambush all his own. In his bestial form, Mammoth was every bit as unstoppable as the enemy Titan had been, trampling bandits and trees alike in his charge. And without a deadly crossfire to worry about, our shooters went to work.

In the end, I had seven walkers in good enough shape to travel. One of them, I was sad to see, was Gage, whose lessons in how to fall off a horse had likely saved my life when the shooting started. I walked him over to one of the wagons, laid him down in what I hoped was a respectful manner, and reclaimed that seed of energy. Six walkers now, including the fake merchant and his equally fake son. I parked them all near the lead wagon and went to check in with Stark and Mammoth.

Denali had just left with Supersonic to recover those horses that had smartly fled as soon as the shooting started. Cloud wasn't one of them; my dumbass demon horse was waiting calmly in front of the wagon, making me wonder if he was deaf in addition to being possessed. That left Stark and Mammoth alone to talk with Cob, while Cagney walked around making sure any of the bandits who had fallen weren't going to get back up again.

I waited for her to move on and then added another walker to my squad.

"How bad is it?" Mammoth asked Cob.

"It's a mess," said our resident doctor. "Gage is dead. I'm assuming Joe is too since he never made it back. Presley's knee is shattered from the same bullet that killed his horse. Derek took an arrow that grazed his lung, and I have him in the second wagon, with Emma watching. James, Lady, and Jacobs…" He shook his head. "They all got shot but are varying degrees of stable. I've got temporary seals on the wounds and will stitch them up when we get somewhere safer. As for Walker, I don't even know—" He paused as I joined them. "How the hell are you upright? That Titan hit you so hard I didn't think you'd ever come back down to earth… and that was before you got shot."

"Like I said in Baker, if I can kill something, I'll generally be okay. Ashing that Titan took care of my broken ribs and arm." Wrapped in my power, I'd completely forgotten about being shot. I'd been so busy directing my walkers that I never found another kill of my own, and the wound was still bleeding down my arm and all over yet another of my apparently insufficient changes of clothing. As I let my power go, bottling back up the emptiness that *still* seemed ready to overflow my core—I had to lock my knees to keep from falling. "Okay, that does hurt a bit."

"I'll get it wrapped and—" Cob paused with one hand stretched out, fingers inches away from my bare skin. "Uh… assuming it's safe to touch you?"

"As long as I'm conscious and aware, touching me is fine," I told him. "I haven't accidentally killed someone all year."

Nobody else seemed to find that funny.

Cagney came back from checking the enemy bodies. "Denali said he saw a temporary camp in the woods nearby, but none of the dead have any supplies or rations on them. I'm guessing they're operating out of Regent, and just set up camp here to ambush anyone that came this way."

"It fits what Carl… or whatever his name was… was saying about them having their own town," said Cob,

"The question is," said Stark, "do we keep going north to Regent, knowing that it's occupied, or do we turn back to our original route?"

"Some of our wounded need beds," said the doctor.

"I'm not leaving bandits in control of a town anyway," agreed Mammoth, "but my carelessness already got two of ours killed."

"Denali and I can scout it out while you all bring the wagons in behind," said Stark. "We just killed almost two dozen bandits. Can't imagine there will be all that many left back in town."

"Take more than just Denali with you," decided the Shifter. "We've already lost one scout. Until we know the bandits are all dead, I want us traveling in force."

"You need people to drive the wagons and shooters to defend them." Stark shook his head. "Add in the injured, and there's not much left."

"Keep Silt with the wagons," I suggested. "Her power is pretty versatile, and now that everyone's on alert, I assume she and Mammoth can handle any stragglers that show up."

"Does that mean you want to come along?" asked Stark.

"Yeah. Mammoth said to travel in force, and—" I motioned to my band of walkers. "—I'm kind of a one-person force."

"Bring Supersonic too," came a new voice. We turned to find Silt standing there, strong arms crossed in front of her chest, and a scowl directed at me. "Felt my ears burning and came over to hear I was being volunteered to stay behind."

"You're way more useful defending the train than I would be," I told her.

"Uh huh." Her lack of a rebuttal told me she couldn't muster a compelling argument, but her tone said she damn sure wasn't happy about it. "Gonna be hard to watch your back from miles away, Skeletor."

"Why Supersonic?" Cob wanted to know.

"Flyboy can make it back to the wagon train faster than anything on two legs or four, letting the rest of us know whatever it is you find."

"Makes sense," said Stark, his tone slightly warmer than its usual arctic chill. "Seems like that Academy is teaching the right sort of stuff."

"Silt's better at it than I am," I admitted. "Mostly, I just kill things and hope everything else works out."

"And so far, it has," added my friend, still scowling. "So far."

"Get your gear together," Stark told me. "As soon as Denali is back with the rest of the horses, we're heading out."

∘∘∘

Regent was a small town, quaint and picturesque in a forest that Denali said had been farmland before the Break. In place of a wall, the town had just a water tower, red and rusted, that was used to spot people before they arrived.

Given how heavily forested the area was… and the total lack of kill field to make spotting people even vaguely feasible, I wasn't sure the tower did any good.

Given the bandits we found lording it over the town, I was one-hundred percent sure it didn't.

"I count nine," said Stark. "Most of them concentrated in or around the inn."

"Ten with the one up in the tower," said Denali.

"I can get him before he even knows I'm coming." Supersonic's second battle—and having a gun held to his head—hadn't dampened his enthusiasm even a little bit.

"Soon as they see us, they'll retreat into the building." Denali shook his head. "Fortifications and ready-made hostages are a bad combination."

"Can we draw them out somehow?" I hadn't been lying when I said Silt was better at tactics than me—and Tessa was honestly probably even better than Silt—but we'd had enough team exercises at the Academy that I felt comfortable making suggestions.

"No fire," said Denali. "Rain came through here not long ago and everything's still wet."

"Maybe we can pretend to be the bandits we killed?" volunteered Supersonic.

"I don't know. Elmore feels like the kind of asshole who would've instituted pass phrases." I shook my head.

"Only one way to find out, isn't there?"

I didn't even dignify that with a reply. Some of us couldn't dodge bullets.

Stark was busy ignoring our bickering when his eyes fell on the walkers behind me. The grin that spread across his scarred face was nothing short of evil.

To be honest, I was impressed.

"Gentlemen," he decided, tone every bit as malevolent as that smile, "I think Regent is about to suffer its first undead apocalypse."

CHAPTER 20

Stark's plan worked perfectly.

Once he and Denali had taken position on the far edge of the town, creeping through the surrounding forest like ghosts I could sense but not quite see, I sent my walkers wandering down the hill in a disorganized fashion. The bandits still in Regent took the bait, spilling out of the tavern to defend themselves against what appeared to be a random incursion. Without a living enemy in sight, the idea of leveraging their hostages never even entered the picture.

I waited until I saw Denali slip into the building that was the inn, followed soon after by Stark, and then kicked my walkers—the four who had so far survived the bandits' salvos anyway—up from a shamble to a sprint. The results were satisfying; the first line of bandits went down in a wave of undead flesh, and even from a good three hundred yards away, I had no problem raising the casualties as reinforcements.

The guard up on the water tower was leaning over, shooting down into the town, when a blur hit him from above, tossing him off the tower and all the way down to the street. Supersonic didn't have the inherent coolness of my eagle-sized crows, but I decided he'd do in a pinch, especially when he spun and immediately started taking out the bandits who had climbed onto rooftops to get better defensive positions against my walkers.

Five minutes later, it was over, and ten minutes after that, we'd tracked down and killed the last of the bandits hiding in town.

Given how small Regent was, I was surprised it even took that long, honestly. It seemed like the further we got from Billings, the smaller the human outposts became; Regent had maybe fifty buildings in total, including the inn.

A town that had started out with a population of just over a hundred was now down to thirty after the bandits' occupation. *All* the survivors were women, and the way they flinched away from us made me want to kill the bandits' asses all over again. Instead, I sent my now-oversized squad of twelve walkers out into the forest around the town where the townsfolk wouldn't have to see them.

The original mayor had been killed when the bandits first took over, and Stark was talking to Eleanor, the grey-haired woman who had assumed the vacant position. Supersonic had been dispatched back to the wagon train as soon as the fight was over, and before we'd even finished cleaning up the carnage, Cob was emerging from the woods at the vanguard of the wagon train.

After that, we fell into a routine. The one thing life at the Academy had never prepared us for was how much of a Cape's life was dealing with the aftermath of battles: the wounded and the dying, the detritus and the destruction. Maybe the real Cape teams had it different, back in the Free States, with access to emergency services and, if they were lucky, an actual Healer.

Out in the Badlands, things weren't so clean.

Over the next day, the inn became a makeshift hospital, with Cob and Cagney doing what they could for our own injured while also treating the town's survivors. We'd come through the fight back in

Baker practically unscathed, but the bandits' ambush had left the Mission a wreck. Denali had found Joe's body out in the woods, bringing our total number of dead up to two, both long-time veterans. Five more were wounded, and I wasn't sure how Derek or Presley would be able to accompany us when we left.

Part of me wanted to second-guess Mammoth's decision making. If he hadn't chosen to help the fake merchants in their broken-down wagon—

I shook my head. Truth was, I'd have done the same damn thing. The whole reason we were out here was to help people, and none of us had realized we were being suckered into a trap until it was too late.

With the addition of my walkers, we were actually stronger than we'd started, but fewer live people meant fewer able hands and watchful eyes. And while I hadn't spent much time with either Gage or Joe, I could tell their loss had hit everyone hard.

The only good news was that we had plenty of food to eat. Eleanor, the only woman in Regent over forty, turned out to be a Druid. This far from the Free States, she'd never been tested, but I was pretty sure she'd have been ranked as a Two at best, strong enough to help things grow, but without any real control over what those things would be. Still, it meant that, if you weren't too picky, there was always some variety of fresh fruit or vegetable to be eaten.

Fresh anything had been a rarity for me before the Academy, and the rest of the Mission seemed just as pleased to supplement their usual rations with Eleanor's fare.

We had three days of downtime. By the end of it, Lady, James, and Jacobs were up and about, and Derek and Presley were both stable, if not roadworthy. Three days to do what we could around Regent, burying their dead and ours, cleaning things up, helping Eleanor with her out-of-season harvest and some badly needed repairs. Three days clearing out some of the growth around the town, giving them the view and killing fields they'd lacked before.

Denali and Cagney were even teaching some of the remaining women how to shoot with the bandits' leftover guns, and while the haunted look hadn't left those women's eyes—would maybe never leave—it was joined by a grim satisfaction when their bullets hit the targets that had been erected.

Three days wasn't enough to teach them what they needed to know. It wasn't even enough for the less severely injured members of our party to fully recover.

Unfortunately, three days was all we had.

○○○

"You okay, Sofia?"

Silt and I were on watch together for the first time since freeing Regent. Three days in, and we'd barely seen each other, and while I knew some of that was because her power had been in heavy demand for the town's reconstruction, and part of it was that she was still irritated I had left her behind, it seemed like there was something more going on.

"When am I ever *not* okay, Boneboy?" came the reply.

We were up on the rooftop of one of the vacant buildings along Regent's north side, the town's light at our backs. Up this high, Silt couldn't use her earth sense, but my... whatever the fuck it was I did... more than compensated.

"You've just been quiet since we got here." My shrug went unseen in the darkness. "You know I'm plenty happy to stare into the darkness all night. Wish there was an ocean out there, but a bunch of trees will do, I guess. But a friend of mine once told me it helps to talk things over with someone."

"Kayleigh?"

"No... you."

"Seriously?"

"Yeah. Back when we started second-year."

"How the hell do you remember that?"

"There haven't been a ton of people in my life who gave a shit. When someone does, it makes an impression." I shrugged again. "If you're just pissed about staying behind with the wagon train, that's one thing. But if something else is bothering you… well, I'm here to listen."

"Shouldn't we be focused on keeping watch?"

"I'll sense anyone coming long before we hear them."

"Ugh. I didn't think you being a Full-Five would be so damn annoying."

I didn't say anything. Truth was, even after six months with an honest-to-fucking-God girlfriend—seven months if you counted my time in the Badlands—I still sucked at the emotional stuff. If Silt didn't want to talk about it, I sure as hell wasn't going to make—

"I killed one of the bandits during the ambush. When I tossed them off their feet, he went down, broke his head open on a tree root, and that was all she wrote."

I nodded, even though I wasn't sure who the *she* was that was writing things. Madame Fate, maybe? Word was, she was every bit as much a bitch as Mother Nature had been, pre-Break.

"I'm *glad* he's dead," she continued. "Every one of them deserved what they got, but…"

"But?"

"I've never killed anyone before, except in the Training Grounds. I thought it would feel the same, but it doesn't. At all."

"It gets easier," I told her.

"Does it?"

I winced. "Honestly? I don't know. Killing has never really bothered me."

She turned my way, a broad patch of darkness to my eyes, and a lantern of energy to my senses. "Not even that first time? When you killed Carnage?"

"He wasn't the first person I killed."

"Wait, what?"

"There was a Technomancer down in the Hole that I shot with a Legion tech gun. Firewall. That's how the alarm got triggered in the first place."

"And what did you feel when you killed him?"

"Nothing." I shrugged again. "I was too busy trying to stay alive. After the Hole, I kept waiting for it to hit me, but it never did. I had nightmares, yeah, but they were more about the people I didn't manage to kill. Or the ones who died because I was too weak. My dad. Tempest. The White Knight. But Carnage and Firewall? I'm glad they're dead. Fuck them both for all the harm they caused. Same holds true for the bandits I killed this week."

"Well, shit. That doesn't help me at all."

"It's okay to feel something when you take a life."

"Is it? What if that feeling doesn't go away? I have—"

"Unfinished business," I finished for her.

"—people to kill," she corrected. "I can't afford to let regret or fear or whatever the fuck this is slow me down."

"Maybe focus on the reason you're doing it?" I suggested. "Set your goal and then do what you have to." It had gotten me through the Hole and Reno. Hell, it had gotten me through most of life.

"Huh." She chewed on that a bit. "You really never felt anything?"

"Not with Firewall or Carnage or Jimmy or—" I shook my head. "You're worried because killing bothers you? Pretty sure that just means you have a soul. I don't even know how many people I've killed at this point. What does that make me?"

"A survivor."

"I guess so. That's the one skill I seem to have in spades. And if all else fails, you'll have a Crow in your corner to do the killing for you. There's no reason you should have to carry that load."

"That's one of the nicest things you've ever said to me," she said. "How fucked up is that?"

"I beg to differ; I offered to steal one of Winter's brownies for you last year."

"Yeah, but you never carried through on the promise."

"Because I was kidnapped and tortured in Reno!"

She sniffed. "Excuses for everything." I felt as much as heard her reach out, but she was on the wrong side of me for holding hands, and she kind of flailed about where my hand should have been before she remembered that little fact. "Shit."

"Got to sit on my left if you want to get all handsy—" I started to tell her, only to trail off, mid-sentence.

A spark of light had just entered my area of awareness to the north, moving fast.

And it was distinctly human sized.

CHAPTER 21

His name was Aidan. He was maybe a decade older than I was, from a town called Gladstone, and judging by the dirt on his face and the state of his clothes, he'd traveled all day and some of the night to reach Regent. Mammoth and Stark took him into the inn to talk, leaving the rest of us—those who were still awake anyway—to return to our watch.

Got to be honest… I was getting more than a little bit tired about being kept out of the loop. Yeah, I was new to the Badlands, and didn't know shit about shit, but hadn't the past month proven I had something to offer? If anything, Silt was even more annoyed than I was. She was used to being a team leader at the Academy and being part of every planning meeting.

She could also have used a distraction from thinking about the battle and the bandit she'd killed. As I'd learned with Muse—and with Alexa before that—there's a limit to what can be solved through discussion. Some things take time. Some things never heal; they just kind of scab over and you move on with your life, only to be surprised on dark, quiet nights, when a word, a sound, or a thought tears away the scab and brings all that shit back again.

There's your human experience in a nutshell.

Stick that in a theme song.

An hour later, Mammoth emerged and made his way over to where we sat on our now-familiar roof. He hadn't looked well since Joe and Gage's deaths. "Walker. Silt. Can you join us in the inn? We've got some decisions to make."

We entered the inn, the only light from a lantern on the badly worn bar top and the fire roaring in the hearth. Aidan was seated on one of the benches, a steaming mug in his hands. Stark had unrolled an old map across the table, and he and Reese were looking it over. Jacobs was a quiet presence in the corner. Reese looked angry, Jacobs and Stark as impassive as always.

"Aidan here is from Gladstone, about a day's ride north of us," said Mammoth, voice a low rumble. "They've got a problem. Some of their livestock's gone missing recently, and the town sent him down to see if Regent's ranger could help trap whatever's been doing the killing."

"More bandits?"

"Bandits don't come this far north," said Aidan. On hearing his voice, I had to adjust my estimation of his age downward. If he was my age, I'd be surprised. Something about growing up in the Badlands made people look older than they were. "Or at least they didn't, I guess."

"It could be bandits," agreed Stark. "Or a mountain lion or even a howler, though they normally stick to the south too. Unfortunately, Regent's ranger died when the bandits took the town."

"And we're the next best option?" asked Silt.

"We're the only option. Every year, there are fewer towns in these parts." Mammoth shook his head. "We have wounded, and work still to do here in Regent, but Stark and Reese are going to go up to

Gladstone to lend their expertise. I wanted to ask if you three would join them."

"Why us?" I asked.

"Whatever is disappearing cows up there isn't something I want to take chances with. Twelve walkers are practically an army all on their own, especially with your ability to make more as needed. And Silt—"

"Is going anywhere Damian goes," said the Earthshaker.

"Exactly. Not to mention how useful your power is in a pinch." He turned to the Free States' security officer in the corner. "Are you going with them?"

Jacobs nodded. "That's the job. Especially with Presley down for the foreseeable future."

"So, five people—six including Aidan—two Powers, and a whole heap of walkers. That should be enough to roll right over whatever you run into."

It was hard to argue with that.

"What about Supersonic?" Silt wanted to know.

"I'm keeping him here, so we have an eye in the sky to spot anyone else coming. We have injured and noncombatants to protect."

"Any worries about the Weaver where we're headed?" asked Jacobs.

Stark answered that one, drawing a line on the map. "Her territory is a lot further north, up here near the border of what used to be Canada. That's several days past Gladstone, and there's the Little Missouri and the Killdeer mountains in between."

And thank fuck for that. Visiting a giant spider Shifter was not on my list of things to do while out in the Badlands.

Actually, I didn't even have a list. More than a month into my time with the Mission, that was starting to feel like a mistake.

"It's got to be mountain lions," said Reese, eyes fixed on the map. "Maybe a big one, like the wolves in Baker. Make sure you all bring rifles. The bigger the caliber the better."

"Whatever it is, deal with it and come on back." For some reason, Mammoth shot Stark a look over Aidan's downturned head. The scarred man nodded.

Better believe I was going to find out what the fuck *that* was about. I'd learned a long time ago that what you don't know really *can* hurt you.

"In the meantime," the older Power continued, "get some sleep. Silt, you and Walker are off watch early. Aidan, the mayor has prepared a cot for you upstairs. You'll all be leaving bright and early tomorrow. If something is prowling the woods around Gladstone, I don't want you encountering it after sundown."

ooo

The next morning, we left Regent and the rest of the Mission behind. Cagney gave us a half-hearted wave from her vantage point at the town's northern edge before she and the town were swallowed up by trees. She had taken Gage's loss particularly hard; the two had joined the Mission around the same time and been as close as siblings ever since.

According to Lady, this whole state had once been prairies, but the forest we rode through towered above our heads. Either those trees had been growing since the Break or Dr. Nowhere had dreamed them into existence full-size. Or maybe both. I wasn't sure if we'd ever know the full extent to what had changed with his gods-fucked dream.

Got to be honest… snakes and jaguars notwithstanding, I had almost enjoyed riding in the forest back when we started out in Idaho, but the recent bandit ambush had me on edge. Now, I rode with my power extended around us, looking for any spark of life larger than a squirrel or songbird.

Naturally, Cloud picked up on my inattention, but before he could get it in his malevolent little horse mind to toss me off, I leaned forward to whisper into his ear.

"Don't even think about it. Only reason I haven't turned you into a walker is because you're a loaner from the Mission… but accidents do happen."

"Do you and Cloud need a moment together?" Reese snickered. He was one of the Mission members who had never warmed to my presence. Part of that was probably that he and Supersonic were as thick as thieves. Part of it was probably the troop of walking dead following along behind us. Part of it might even have been that Lady and I spent a lot of time together. I'd seen the way he watched her when he thought nobody else was looking.

"I'm just making sure he knows what's up."

"He's just a horse, Damian." Silt sounded amused. "He can't understand you."

"Keep telling yourself that." *Her* horse had shown no signs of homicidal urges. Even Aidan, whose riding experience to that point had been limited to a single old plow horse, seemed to be having an easy enough time of things on his borrowed mount.

Apparently, *I* was the lucky one.

We ate in the saddle, trail rations and fresh fruit, the latter provided by Eleanor's erratic green thumb. I'd never had passion fruit before, but it wasn't half bad. Kind of sweet but also tart, and it went a long way to making the rest of the meal almost palatable.

The trail we followed was even more overgrown than the one up to Regent had been. If merchants came this way, it wasn't often enough to tramp down the wild grass. I kept my walkers behind us, far enough back to not spook the horses but close enough to defend us when needed.

Human walkers, I was finding, were different than wolves or crows. Some things had seemed to come instinctively to my bestial minions: stalking prey, navigating the forest in silence, even flying, in the case of the birds. But the ex-bandit corpses just shuffled along under my direction. I'd tried to send a couple out into the woods to flank us, but they'd plowed right through whatever was in their path, making the sort of racket that had Stark turning around in his saddle to give me the eye.

Clearly, I needed a higher class of walker.

CHAPTER 22

Gladstone made Regent look like a thriving metropolis. What had once been several hundred people had dwindled since the Break to roughly twenty-five. The unlikely forest we'd been traveling through had finally given way to the plains that had typified North Dakota, pre-Break, and the town's houses spread out in an uncertain sprawl to our right along what had probably once been roads. Beyond those few buildings were plowed fields and, even further, a fenced-in pasture, where sheep and cows grazed together.

At some point, the town had started building a wall around the town's center, but the builder had run out of energy or motivation or maybe even just stone about halfway through. Compared to Regent and now Gladstone, Baker had been a fucking fortress, even before our modifications.

Cows and sheep. Intact buildings and houses that had succumbed to time and the elements. A half-finished wall and an acre or two of carefully cultivated fields.

What I didn't see were any people. There were sparks of life in many houses, adult-sized and kid-sized both, but even with all the noise we'd made riding up, nobody came out to see us.

Aidan had opened up to Silt and me in the course of our full day of travel. He was the youngest of five brothers, three of whom were still alive, and the first sheep that had disappeared had been from his family's flock. I knew he even had a girl, Seraphina, that he was hoping to marry. To hear him tell it, all of Gladstone was depending on us. The fact that he'd found more than just a ranger would be a cause for celebration.

So, why did it feel like we were riding into a ghost town?

I turned to Stark. "There are people in the houses."

"Hiding?"

"I don't know. Maybe?" I'd left my walkers just outside of town, but Stark looked every bit the vid villain, and Reese wasn't all that far behind, with his shaved head and the full armory he'd brought with him. And after what we'd been through at Regent, even Silt and I looked at least half as dangerous as we were.

"What is this, Aidan? Was there something you didn't tell us?" Stark's voice was mild—or as mild as his voice ever got—but his right hand was caressing the handle of his knife.

"What? No! Of course not!" Aidan cleared his throat and called out. "Everybody! It's Aidan! I'm back with help! The Mission and two Powers!"

Nothing. Some of the human-sized sparks stirred in nearby houses, but nobody ventured out into the street.

"Something's wrong," said Jacobs, stating the obvious.

"I don't know what's going on," said Aidan. I wasn't an expert on people—didn't even like them, for the most part—but his confusion seemed genuine.

"We'll check the closest house that Walker senses people in," decided Stark. "Silt, you watch our six. Jacobs and Reese, take up spots across the way with a good firing angle. Whatever this is, we're not losing any more of ours."

Every person but me had brought a gun. Hell, Reese had three: two pistols and a long rifle. Silt pulled her shotgun out of the loop at the back of her saddle, and we all dismounted, following Stark's instructions. I reached out to my walkers, calling them into town. Whatever the fuck was going on, almost two thousand pounds of zombies would help sort it out.

As we moved toward the nearest house, the older man looked at my mace with a scowl. "Why don't you carry iron?"

"I only have one hand," I reminded him, "and this one wasn't my dominant one. I've had to relearn how to shoot and I'm a long way from accurate."

"Shit. We should have had you practicing with the women of Regent."

I didn't bother telling him that I'd literally been training every day at the Academy after Reno. Making the switch to my left hand had been a pain in the ass even for everyday things—there was a reason my shoes stayed pretty much permanently tied—but for some reason, shooting was a whole different level of problematic. Truth was, Stark was right. I *should've* been practicing in Regent. It was the only way I'd ever get better.

Assuming I ever did get better.

The house we approached was all stone, its roof recently patched, with two front-facing windows open to the street. There was no reason the people I detected inside wouldn't have heard us, but while I could feel a couple of them moving about, they were still staying inside.

"The Barretts," said Aidan. "Jennie and Abel. She makes great pies at harvest time."

That caught my attention. "Only two people live here?"

"Yeah. Why?"

I waved to Stark, who stopped in his tracks maybe ten feet from the house's front porch. "I sense four people inside. Two adults and two kids."

In fact… I turned my attention to the rest of the town. Every occupied house had a few people in it, which hadn't been weird enough to trigger my paranoia. But if you added them all up…

"There are a shit ton more than twenty-four other people here." And the majority were children. What the fuck was going on?

Stark already had his gun out but now it was leveled and pointing at Aidan. He raised his voice so it echoed through the town. "Gig's up, people. I've got your man in my sights, and we're all loaded for bear."

"Don't shoot me," squeaked Aidan. "I don't know what's going on, but I promise, this isn't a trap!"

Which was, of course, when the trap finally sprang.

○○○

Turns out, my power to sense people by their life energy had one glaring weakness. All I could see was their size and, if they were a Power, some indication as to their strength. But a human-sized spark didn't necessarily mean what I was sensing was a human.

And Gladstone didn't have thirty-plus children.

What it *did* have was one hell of a spider problem.

The creatures that poured out from the buildings around us were enormous: hairy bodies the size of dogs, with spindly legs that gave them a reach almost as wide as I was tall. Those legs weren't just for show either; the two crawling out of the Barretts' house immediately launched themselves from the windowsills, easily crossing the open gap between us.

The first one took two bullets in the midsection from Stark's forty-five and practically exploded in a shower of guts and goo. The second caught my mace in the face. As large as the spiders were, they weren't all that heavy… my blow sent it spinning back to the street, its many legs writhing as it fell.

Behind us, Silt's shotgun boomed, Reese's two pistols played a musical accompaniment, and Jacobs' automatic chattered like a nervous Jitterbug, but the streets were overflowing with giant spiders, and I couldn't spare a glance in their direction. My walkers waded into battle, tearing apart arachnids, even as they were stabbed by legs the size of spears.

It wasn't just the legs that we had to watch out for. I found that out the hard way when a spider dodged most of my blow and sank its knife-sized fangs into my shoulder.

My left shoulder. Apparently, *that* particular joke was still in play.

The arm immediately went limp, and if I hadn't sent my power into it, I might have dropped my mace. Instead, I used my power to swing my arm back up, driving the mace's head into the spider's underbody like it was a particularly blunt dagger. The spider fell away, and I looked down to make sure my arm was still there. I couldn't feel it at all. In fact, I could feel a chill creeping into the entire left side of my body.

"They've got some sort of paralytic venom," I shouted, my words lost in the gunfire. "Don't let them bite you!"

And then, I gave the emptiness inside of me free rein.

Silt called it going full walker. I hadn't ever read about another Crow who could use their power on themselves at all, but going full walker was another step entirely. Instead of just muffling the pain or the emotions, pushing myself to the limits of what a purely human body could do, I could actually take that body over entirely, controlling myself like I was one of my own minions.

Actual walkers—old ones anyway—don't have the muscles or tendons to move on their own. Sometimes, they don't even have flesh at all. The mechanics of undeath don't make any sense, but they don't need to make sense in Dr. Nowhere's world. All they need is a Crow's power and enough limbs to stay upright.

My body was coursing with a venom that explained why the people of Gladstone were still lying in their homes. I *should* have fallen to the dirt, myself, but my power kept me upright. My power kept numb muscles moving, kept my mace whistling through the air, covered in gore.

Stark wasn't so lucky. He went down in a pile of spider flesh, and while one of those spiders jerked and died in a flash of gunfire, Stark's body went limp right after, the second spider's fangs buried in his leg.

I took two steps and punted the spider off him. It smacked into another house's wall, and by the time it had made it back onto its eight legs, I was there, mace splattering its spider brains across the dirt.

Another spider tried to jump me from above, and I shoved my right stump into its maw, ignoring both its bite and the leg that tore through my shirt to leave a bloody furrow across my chest. I smashed the spider to the ground and stomped on its body.

Out of the corner of my eye, I saw Aidan go down, the rifle he'd brought with him to Regent and then all the way back to Gladstone falling out of limp fingers.

Enough was fucking enough.

Only eight of my walkers were still on their feet, but we had killed almost twenty spiders. I tapped the well of emptiness inside of me, a source that seemed bottomless the more I drew upon it, and pushed it into the corpses around us.

Nine of the spiders were in a good enough shape to respond, and I sent them into the fray. And then, taking a stand between Stark and Aidan's paralyzed forms, I went to work.

CHAPTER 23

Time has a way of stretching out in combat. It's even worse when I've gone full walker. Every movement is a careful ballet of choice and consequence, playing out in slow motion as I watch from outside myself. I don't know how long we fought in the streets of Gladstone, but the chatter of gunfire had long since faded by the time the last few spiders broke and ran. My own spider walkers hadn't proved much more durable than the living stock I'd created them from, but with all the corpses littering the street, I'd finished with fourteen spiders and three of my original human walkers left over.

Seventeen wasn't any harder to control than the original twelve, but I'd known that would be the case. First thing I'd done after being released from the Academy's med ward following Reno was taking Tessa to the Remembrance Day dance. Second thing had been retaking my powers test. And the third thing?

That had been a field trip to Sunnyside Cemetery, with Alexa, the adult Paladin, and Door all in tow to see just what a Full-Five Crow could do. I'd started raising walkers, and kept raising them, and kept raising them. When I stopped at fifty, it wasn't because I was feeling strained… it's because the Capes with me were no longer confident in their ability to contain the outbreak if I lost control.

That was the first time I ever saw anything but disinterest on the face of Matthew's father. Behind the chiseled jaw that had earned him a king's ransom in endorsements, behind the crystal blue eyes that had graced a dozen movie posters, and the flawless good looks that, if the rumors were to be believed, had earned him mistresses in every city in the Free States, I saw only one thing:

Fear.

By the time Alexa and I returned to the Academy that night, I'd known for sure I wouldn't be getting an internship with the Defenders… even with the younger Paladin *and* Vibe speaking on my behalf. Even with Door a rock of silent support.

Paladin—the legend, the original Stalwart, the man whose branded t-shirt I still owned—didn't want me anywhere near him.

I guess I learned two truths that day. But it was the one about my power that really mattered. Whatever my limits might be, I hadn't found them yet. Seventeen walkers, some of them with eight legs, others with only two? That was nothing at all.

When the last spiders fled, I stopped where I was, hearing my own pants in the sudden silence. Blood coated my body from the cuts and punctures and bites I'd taken, and I was pretty sure I'd broken two of my own fingers instructing my hand to grip tightly to the mace's handle, but I'd ashed the last three spiders I'd faced, healing myself in the process. I was alive and I was mostly whole and that's what mattered.

Stark and Aidan were both alive too, spider guts charting a circle around their bodies from where I'd first stood guard. Truth was, the spiders had ignored them as soon as they went down. Instead, every spider in the town had come after those of us still standing.

I turned to look for the others and found Jacobs collapsed against the house where he'd taken up his firing position. He too was alive, eyes open and tracking my movements as I crouched over him, but he'd taken at least three bites, and his body was completely immobilized. Worse, a spider had speared him through the leg. It was a minor miracle he hadn't bled out while I was fighting. I removed his belt, tied a makeshift tourniquet around his thigh that reminded me of Daisy back in Baker, and kept moving.

Reese had retreated inside another house but had fared no better than Jacobs, face-down in the dirt next to his discarded pistols, his rifle unfired. I rolled him onto his back and checked his vitals. Yet again, it seemed like the spiders had been content to paralyze the opposition and move on.

But Silt…

Her shotgun was in the street, next to several spiders that had been impaled on hardened spikes of earth, but the Earthshaker herself wasn't there.

I switched to my other sense and counted the sparks of light left in the town. There were *still* a few child-sized sparks, but they were motionless in the houses with adults, and I was willing to bet they were Gladstone's few actual children. All told, there were twenty-six sparks instead of the thirty there should have been. Gladstone had lost some of their people, but that wasn't what sparked a panic I felt even through the emptiness.

Not a single light in that town glowed any more brightly than the standard level I'd come to expect from Normals.

Silt was gone.

ooo

I walked the streets of Gladstone for another twenty minutes, hunting for any sign of my friend, and coming up empty. I'd have thought her and the three missing townsfolk dead except there weren't any corpses left in the town. Not to mention I'd raised every dead thing I found during the battle.

Four people, and they were all just… gone.

By the time I made it back to Stark, everyone who had been bitten only once was starting to recover, from the Mission members lying in the streets to some of Gladstone's citizens. I'd taken so many bites that I had little choice but to keep piloting myself with my own power, so I kept a tight rein on the emptiness as I helped Stark to a seated position.

"We have a problem," I told him. "Silt and some of the townsfolk are missing."

Probably should've waited for him to recover before I hit him with that, but time was wasting.

Stark twitched. "You can't sense them anywhere with your—"

"No. And they're not dead either or I'd have raised them as walkers to defend the town. I think the spiders took them."

"Shit." He shook his head and looked me dead in the eyes. "I'm sorry. I know you and she were close."

"What? I just told you she's *not* dead. We need to go get her back. *Them* back, I mean."

"Walker… I know you're new to the Badlands—"

"What the fuck does that have to do—"

"—but creatures of that size, with paralytic venom, who capture rather than kill? Those weren't just spiders. They were her children."

"Whose children," I asked, ignoring that part of me that already knew what his answer would be.

"The Weaver's." He shook his head again. "Silt might not be dead yet, but she will be soon enough, and there's not a damn thing you or I can do about it."

ooo

I let that sit for all of a second. "Fuck that."

"Excuse me?"

"I killed most of the spiders that were here in Gladstone. I can finish off the ones who took Silt and the others."

"This wasn't even a single hatching. The Weaver has thousands of children."

"But the Weaver herself is up north, you said?"

"Yeah… and?"

"And that means most of her children are too. We still have time to catch the ones who fled. But we have to leave right fucking now."

"Look around you, Walker. This entire town needs our help." Aidan was struggling to his feet, and the cries of confused townsfolk were starting to swell.

"Reese and Jacobs can stay behind to help here," I said, ignoring the fact that Jacobs couldn't even walk. "I'm going after Silt, but I need your help. I don't know the first thing about tracking."

"I'm sorry. The needs of the many—"

"Help! Please!" A dirt-streaked, blonde-haired woman threw herself at our feet. "Please! My son is missing. I think they took him!"

"Where is Cassie? Has anyone seen my daughter?" cried out a man, emerging from the nearest hut.

"Eric? Eric?!?" called another couple.

"Whatever it was Mammoth wanted you to ask of the town of Gladstone," I told Stark, remembering the glance those two had shared before we left, "I bet they'd be a lot more receptive if you helped me rescue their missing sons and daughters."

Stark looked from me to the distraught parents.

"Fuck."

ooo

It wasn't as easy as all that, of course. It never is where people are involved. Still, we were on our way in less than an hour, and I tried not to let the delay eat at me. Stark and I had been joined by the father of the missing Cassie, and while I didn't think he'd be much good in a fight, he knew the surrounding area a hell of a lot better than we did.

It didn't take long to pick up the trail, or for Stark to announce that the indentations left by the spiders' legs in the dirt were heavier than most of those we'd seen around Gladstone. I didn't know how they'd gotten their burdens up on to their backs, but it was clear that the fleeing spiders were carrying the captives with them.

"Looks like maybe seven," said Stark. "We'll have numbers if we can catch them."

That was thanks to the walkers I'd brought along.

"They're making a beeline for the north," said the townie, whose name I'd quickly forgotten. "Moving fast, but if our... uhm... escort is any indication, our horses should be faster."

Half of the delay had been us having to gather up the horses that had scattered when the attack started. All the horses except Cloud, who had watched the whole battle like it was theater. The townie was riding Reese's horse and doing a much better job of it than Aidan had.

"The question is," continued Stark, "do we take advantage of our mounts' speed, or do we keep pace with the walkers?"

"There's another forest about fifteen miles up north," said the townie. "Tracking them will be harder once they reach it."

"I can handle seven spiders," I said.

"No fucking kidding," muttered Stark, who'd seen the gore I'd left through Gladstone. "Alright then. Have your walkers follow behind, but we'll speed up to catch them before they reach the woods."

The scar-faced man urged his horse into a ground-devouring canter that Cloud matched of his own volition. I did my best just to hang the fuck on.

ooo

In less than an hour, the woods the townie had mentioned were visible on the horizon. Even better, so were the spiders.

Or *a* spider, anyway, scurrying forward with a limp bundle wrapped in silk on its back. We caught it two hundred yards from the tree line, and I saw immediately why it had lagged behind the others; three of its legs were missing their lower segments, apparent battle injuries from Gladstone.

Stark circled in front to cut the spider off, but there was no way for him to get a clear shot with the bundle that was almost definitely a child on its back. Instead, it was up to me and the mace he had thought so little of. With the townie and Stark boxing in the spider, it was almost easy to slip past those questing mandibles and smash my weapon into its face.

The townie jumped from his horse and used his own knife to cut away the webbing, revealing a little girl whose small features were the spitting image of his.

"Cassie!"

I was already back on Cloud, following Stark to the forest's edge. As we neared the tree line, the other man pulled up short.

"What are you stopping for?" I asked him. "The rest of them can't be too far ahead."

"What do you see, Walker?"

"Trees?" I frowned and looked closer. Past those first rows of trees, rays of sunlight caught on something that almost shimmered in the illumination. "Wait. Are those—?"

"Webs. Yes."

"And?"

Instead of answering me, he turned to the townie, who rode up with his daughter draped across the saddle in front of him. "How far does this forest go?"

"We haven't come this way in years. But my father's father fancied himself an explorer and said it stretched all the way past the Killdeer mountains and the Missouri beyond. I'm guessing it goes just as far west? Weather patterns here aren't what our ancestors said they were, pre-Break."

"Why does it matter?" I asked Stark.

"Because I think we just found the threat that pushed that wolf pack out of its territory back in Baker." His scowl was a thing to see. "The Weaver's extended her domain down south."

"You got all of that from some webs in the trees?"

"The Weaver's children don't operate like normal spiders. They're almost a hive, and the further they get from their mother, the more rudimentary their programming. Outside of hunting parties, they stay as close to her as they can. And," he added, "they have to be within a hundred miles of her to regain their web spinning instincts."

"How do you know that?"

"It's my job to know these things, and yours to fucking listen," said the older man. "If I'd seen webs back in Gladstone, you'd have never talked me into coming out here." He glanced over at Cassie. "But you were right to take the chance. At least we saved one."

The townie's eyes were wide. "Does that mean this past week's attacks will keep happening?"

"Yeah. Gladstone is part of the hunting territory now. You and the rest of the town need to move somewhere defensible."

"Like Regent?" I challenged. "That was the plan from the beginning, wasn't it? Consolidate the two towns?"

Stark shrugged. "Regent doesn't have enough people anymore, particularly men, but it should at least be defensible by the time we're done with it. Mammoth thought maybe some of Gladstone's residents would want to come back down with us. Moving a whole town was definitely *not* the plan, but hell if I'll leave them behind to become spider food after we take off."

"And Silt? And the other two? Eric and—"

"Stephen," filled in the townie.

"They're out of our reach." Stark shook his head again. "Nobody goes into the Weaver's land and walks back out."

"He's right," said Cassie's father. The man looked almost embarrassed as he held the daughter I'd helped save, but I could see the relief in his eyes.

"Fuck that," I told them both. "I'm going in there and I'm getting Silt. And the others too if I can." I turned to Stark. "I could still use your help."

"We've already lost too many people... on this year's Mission and today," said the scar-faced man. "I'm not throwing my life away and I'm not going to let you throw yours away either."

I gave him a smile as dry as sun-bleached bone. "What makes you think you can stop me?"

He rested a hand on the grip of his revolver. "Your walkers are still two miles back. Right now, you're just a boy with a club."

"That's the thing about Crows," I said, sending emptiness into the corpse of the spider I'd just killed. It rose onto its five remaining legs, silent and still. "We're never truly alone."

Stark swallowed, his horse prancing about as it picked up on its rider's nervousness. I couldn't help but notice that, for once, Cloud was solid and steady under me.

"Walker... look. I get it. I know you and Silt were close, but this is suicide, even for you. Mammoth says you have big things ahead of you. Important people waiting for you back in the Free States. For all we know, you could save the world one day. Please don't throw that away for just one person."

"That one person is my friend." I bit the words off and fired them into the growing space between us. "And I don't give a fuck about the world if my friends aren't in it."

CHAPTER 24

I left Cloud with Stark. I wouldn't be able to take advantage of his speed in that web-strewn forest, and likelihood was, I wouldn't be able to protect him from the spiders either. Also? Cloud had been a loaner and fuck if I was adding horse thief to my growing list of titles. I patted the horse on his nose, dodged an attempt at my fingers, and entered the forest.

Stark and Cassie's still nameless father watched me go. And if they'd had anything they wanted to say, the presence of my seventeen other walkers, freshly arrived, convinced them not to fucking bother.

Yes, I waited for the walkers to come before I went into the spider-infested woods. I'm not an idiot, all the details of this story I've been telling you notwithstanding. My power might protect me from the spiders' venom, but as I'd proven with my half-brother, Jimmy, a knife through the eye put a Crow down just as easily as anyone else. And those spider legs were a hell of a lot longer than knives. I needed my walkers to do the killing—and dying—on my behalf.

After all, every dead enemy was another conscript for my cause.

As for the Weaver herself? If she was as far north as everyone said, I wouldn't even have to meet her. And thank fuck for that, because I had no idea what I would do about a Spider Shifter the size of a damn house.

ooo

When I first arrived at the Academy, I'd known shit about shit. My entrance exams had proven that much. Math, Science, Literature... I was a walking black mark against Bakersfield's home-schooling initiatives. The one portion of those exams I aced—the only portion— was the history of Powers. Turns out watching hero vids since I was a baby, long before Sally Cemetery reminded Dad of what had been done to him and who I was, had some benefits.

There was still some shit I hadn't known, of course... the sort of details that didn't make it into publicly broadcasted edutainment programs, but most of that same information didn't make it into our textbooks or tests either. After all, Capes are contractors, not slaves... they have agreements with both the government and the press that preserve some measure of privacy.

Unless something goes horribly wrong, in which case they get sent to the Hole like any other Power found guilty of criminal behavior. Or they march off to disappear into the Badlands, like Evan Earthquake did back in the day.

Still, even before I made it into the Academy, I'd been something of an expert on Powers. But there are some names *everyone* in the Free States knows enough to fear.

Tezcatlipoca. Grannypocalypse. Legion. The Voidsinger. The now-dead members of the Legion of Blood, fuck all four of them very much. And last but never least, the Weaver.

Stories had it that she and her husband had been preppers, up in what was Canada at the time of the Break. For those of you who never had to hear Alan-fucking-Jackson's monotone presentation on the subject as a second-year, I'll just say preppers were people convinced the world was going to collapse into anarchy, who spent their lives stockpiling goods and weapons to ensure they survived that collapse.

In other words, they were geniuses.

Unfortunately, sociopolitical unrest is easier to prepare for than people waking up with superpowers overnight. A concrete bunker keeps the starving mob at bay, but it does shit-all to protect you when your husband or your child or your best friend since you were eight suddenly goes supernova and cooks you, your family, and those one-hundred-and-fifty cans of beans you've carefully stockpiled.

Or when your long-time wife, moments after a little naked midnight madness, transforms into a spider the size of that bunker and eats you.

Got to imagine that did something to the woman who would become known as the Weaver, once she'd recovered and turned back to human. Did something more to her husband, of course, but there wasn't anything left of him to complain. And then, legends have it, the prepper woman turned right back into a spider, took her husband's semen and fertilized her eggs with it.

Her *spider* eggs. Because nothing in Dr. Nowhere's world is normal or right or even minimally disgusting.

Not sure how human sperm could fertilize spider eggs—maybe shifting transformed the sperm as well?—but soon enough, the Weaver was laying her first egg sac, and not long after that, the first of her many, many children were born.

Since then, she'd carved out space for herself somewhere in the wilds of Canada, her spawn finding food for themselves and their mother. Humans… animals… it takes a lot to feed that kind of legion, and the hunting never stopped. And given the fact that the number of spider children kept growing, it was a sure thing that the men who were taken were being used for more than just food.

Aren't many more fates I can imagine more horrible than that, and I can't say it wasn't on my mind as I took my first steps into the Weaver's domain. Rape wasn't something I had to worry about, given that just touching me during the act was deadly, but I didn't want to die either. Not with debts unpaid to Her Majesty and Tyrant both.

Tessa. Sofia. Kayleigh. Alexa. Paco. Lynn. The only six names in the world that could have convinced me to enter those woods. I didn't have many friends, and like I told Stark, I'd be damned if I lost any more of them.

Besides, they'd have done the same for me.

○○○

Twenty minutes into the forest, and I was good and lost. The canopy of branches and webs made it impossible to see the sky or the sun, and a month or two on the move with the Mission was nowhere near enough to make me some sort of expert tracker. I looked for spider trail, and found it, but it told me nothing at all, as far as direction. Worse, now that we were in a forest and not in the flat plains outside of Gladstone, the trees provided the spiders a highway of their own.

I kept pushing forward, hoping I was maintaining a steady heading north even as I constantly had to adjust my course to accommodate the trees or underbrush or even just webbed walls in my way, but after a few hours, any hopes I'd had of following Silt, let alone catching up to her, were gone. Without Cloud, I was slower than the spiders, and *they* knew where they were going.

Chasing them wasn't going to get me anywhere except even more lost.

Luckily, that was when I walked right into a trap.

The web spun between the trees in front of us was gossamer; thin and light and impossible to see in the forest's perpetual twilight. My spider walkers didn't even notice it, skittering underneath in that disquieting way that they'd kept even in death.

The human walker I had up front, though? He smacked right into it and stopped, legs churning as he tried to continue on the path I had sent him. The two trees that formed the ends of the clotheslines started to bow before the webbing finally tore free. But of course, by then, the spiders who had been lying in wait were on us. And then, a dozen of my walkers were dropping onto our attackers from those same trees, as I sprang a trap of my own.

I'd known the Weaver's children were there, of course. It's pretty damn hard to surprise someone who can sense life energy. Truth was, there'd been spiders in the trees above me from the moment I entered the forest, but none of them had Silt or the townsfolk with them, and when I'd sent my spiders after them, they'd fled instead of fighting, scattering in all directions. So as I'd been walking... as I'd been doing my shitty best at following any sort of trail... I'd also been looking for a cluster of spiders that would give me a fight.

Some spiders spiraled down on webs of their own. Others simply leapt from the branches, to be met by my own walkers, or, if they made it past the wall of undead flesh, by my mace. One particularly large spider tore through my defensive line, only to be killed by the spider at its back... a spider who itself had been killed by one of mine and raised just as quickly.

Raising spiders, commanding walkers, and puppeting my own body all had a cost. I felt a little bit more of the emptiness drain out of me, but by the time this hunting pack broke and ran, we had killed almost eighty percent of their number, and I had thirty-one walkers under my control.

I'd never wanted to be a Crow. Most sane people want to be anything but. Even not being a Power at all is preferable.

But fuck if I wasn't glad about it just then.

I marshalled my forces and we headed in the direction the survivors had fled.

See, every spider out here was one of the Weaver's children, and when faced with hardship, children seek out their mother.

Unless she's dead because your dad is—

I spared a glance for my father's ghost, almost lost in the woods nearby, and killed that thought. I wasn't sure what I thought about him. Was sure as fuck never going to forgive him, but truth was, he'd been a victim too.

Anyway. Give a child a spanking and it runs to its mom, and I was betting these weren't any different for being spiders. And given that the spiders who had hit Gladstone were no doubt bringing their captives—Silt and the two teenage boys—back to mommy dearest, it meant I had a trail even I could follow.

Until they sped out of range of my senses, of course, which took about an hour. Thankfully, I was deep into the woods by then, and a new hunting pack wasn't far off. When the survivors of the new pack fled in the same direction as the first one, I knew my plan was paying off.

Now, I just had to reach the Gladstone spiders before they reached the Weaver.

ooo

Two days.

Near as I could tell, I spent two days in the woods, killing spiders, raising them as my own, and following the survivors ever deeper into the Weaver's domain. I'd long since lost all my human walkers, who were as ill-suited as I was for the environment, but the spider walkers I'd raised more than compensated for that loss.

On the first full day in the forest, I'd proven that fifty walkers weren't my limit. By the second day, I was over a hundred. The walkers around me were legion, and there was still more emptiness inside of me. I hadn't been bitten or even touched in hours, and the few spider attacks we'd suffered recently had been little more than annoyances.

That was part of the problem. The closer we got to the Weaver, the smarter her children were, and at some point in the past few hours, they'd figured out the general range of my ability to sense them. I knew they were out there, but other than the occasional straggler, we'd lost our unwitting guides.

The other problem I had was that I was exhausted. I hadn't slept since Gladstone, using my power to keep myself going even after the venom had faded from my body. The only food I'd had was the leftover bread in my pack, and I'd run out of water by the second day. I'd found a stream to refill my canteen, but that had cost more time, and more energy, and while my power seemed almost endless, my ability to wield it sure as fuck wasn't.

As yet another hunting pack fled, vanishing over the low hills of what I assumed were the Killdeer mountains Stark had mentioned, I had to finally stop and take stock. I'd been pushing myself, trying to catch up to Silt as quickly as I could, but there'd still been no sign of my friend. At some point, I was going to have to sleep. Would it be better to do so now, and risk having Silt and the others make it all the way to the Weaver before I caught them... or to start making mistakes because I was too tired to think?

Worse, I wasn't sure if I'd already passed that point. With the spiders no longer behaving like mindless drones, I didn't know if they were still fleeing to mother or if they'd instead figured out what I was doing and were leading me somewhere that they wanted me to go.

As it turns out, they were doing both.

I was at the bottom of the latest hill, still pushing onward despite my better judgment, in what Jessica Strich, my tactics professor, would have surely called an *amateur decision*, when the life sparks of spiders appeared to my senses. And not just in front of me, but on all sides. Any question I had to their intelligence was answered when they massed at the very borders of my awareness. The distance masked their numbers, but the noise of their presence, of hairy legs rasping together in a warding sound I hadn't heard until now, told me my own little army was outnumbered. Badly outnumbered.

I tossed my pack aside and readied my mace.

And then, they were on us.

If you've never been in a deep-forest war with a thousand spiders, no backup, and two days of exhaustion wearing on you, let me just say: it sucks. My first rank of walkers were torn apart in seconds, and the handful of spiders I was able to raise in the process didn't in any way make up for the ones I'd lost.

I pulled the rest back in a circle around me, five or six walkers deep, and there the difference between the living and the dead began to tell. My walkers thought nothing of hurling themselves into the venom-dripping fangs of the opposition, but the newly intelligent spiders saw the wall of legs and blank, staring eyes, and paused.

And by the time they overcame their own hesitation, I had dropped to a knee, put my mace aside, and placed my one remaining hand flat on the earth in a poor man's rendition of when Silt used her earth sense.

Forests are an ecosystem. I never took science, so I don't really know what that means, other than that it's a mix of things and their environment. Energy from the sun reaches plants, plants are eaten by prey, prey is hunted by predators, who themselves die and become soil for the plants. There's a continuous cycle of eat and be eaten and even though the spiders had driven out many of this forest's normal predators, that cycle had been going long before the spiders' arrival, and would no doubt continue long after we were all gone.

Predator and prey. Hunter and hunted. Life and death.

And where there's death, I'm your fucking king.

I sent my emptiness out into the ground beneath me, into the hilly slopes of the spiders' latest trap, and found pockets of the dead, waiting for my call. Worms, bears, birds, even a person or two, dead before the Break... Inside my cocoon of spiders, I couldn't see what I was raising, could only judge by the size of the empty space and the amount of power it took to raise it, but over the course of years, or decades, or however long it took for even the bones to be entirely scattered past any hope of repair, this forest had seen its share of death, and it shared that bounty with me.

If you've never been in a deep-forest war with a thousand spiders, you probably also don't realize the one bright side to that scenario: there's no shortage of targets.

I didn't so much direct my newly raised walkers as unleash them; a hundred more undead beasts attacking the unsuspecting spiders from behind or beneath, giving me fresh spider fodder to raise. By that time, I was so fucking tired I could barely see my defensive circle, but as the spiders around me killed my minions and were killed by them, rising to take their place, I knew I was smiling; sparks of life extinguishing around me like someone was attacking a birthday cake with a fire extinguisher.

I ate those deaths, took the energy, sent it right back out into the fresh round of corpses.

And it still wasn't enough.

There was a moment of peace as the spiders pulled back. Space enough for me to spread my senses once again, ten feet, then fifty feet past what had been my maximum less than twenty minutes before... and to sense the sheer number of spiders that had gathered.

Not counting all the packs I'd slaughtered over the past few days, we'd just ended at least four hundred of the initial one thousand spiders. From their numbers, I'd added another hundred-and-fifty walkers, giving me almost three hundred of the dead still standing.

Three hundred versus six hundred? Those odds wouldn't be so bad, especially when I'd be able to raise some portion of the enemy's casualties. Unfortunately, while we'd been fighting, more spiders had come to join the party.

There were too many to count. At least twice as many as had initially attacked, and all I could think was that every spider for hundreds of miles must have been making their way here almost since the beginning, coming to crush the interloper in their midst even as they led me deeper and deeper. And yet, even that didn't explain the numbers, this far south, away from the Weaver and her endless hatchlings.

Somewhere in the middle of my tired rumination, I realized the new spiders still hadn't attacked. I took the moment to pull my own walkers—the freshly raised spiders and the tattered remnants of the long-dead creatures I'd raised from the earth—into ranks around my defensive spider wall and then took back my energy from the few walkers too decrepit to join us.

And then I felt it.

I felt *her.*

A bonfire of energy, swaying through old trees that had been mere saplings when she was born. Silent for all that mass, for a thorax and abdomen longer than one of the shuttle cars I'd ridden in on my way out to the Hole.

The spiders around me made their hissing noises again, but this time, the timbre of that sound was different. I'd had *the* dream enough, with its endless ranks of swaying dead, that I recognized adulation when I saw it, even in this alien form.

She had come.

The Weaver had come.

Fuck my fucking life.

CHAPTER 25

Some things just don't make sense at a certain size. I know the Weaver was a spider, the world-fucking version of all her little children, but I don't remember her that way. There was something so alien about her that my mind took her image and shattered it, leaving only the individual pieces; legs as thick around as I was even at their most tapered end; black, bottomless eyes high enough above the trees' canopy to catch the light of the dying sun; fangs longer than Mammoth was tall.

Maybe Tezcatlipoca's like that. Maybe what Tyrant thinks of as mind control is just sheer otherworldly presence and all the lava god's drones in Old Mexico simply gave up their lives to worship him as was his due. After meeting the Weaver, I could almost believe it, could feel the look of awe and maybe terror on my face as she came into view.

Tyrant had said my power is what protected me from mind control. Not sure I believe that either. Truth is, I'm just that fucking stubborn—ornery, as Amos would have said. Fuck bending the knee to anyone. Especially the creature whose children had taken my friend. I used the emptiness to force myself upright, spine stiff, face blank of expression, and waited for what was coming. I doubted I could even reach her through her own army, doubted I could snuff that bonfire in my mind even if I did, but I was going to bring as many of her children down with me as I could.

And then the Weaver did something I didn't expect.

She shifted.

It was oddly difficult to find the woman who had appeared in the shadow of that now-departed spider form. By the time I located her—an old, hard-faced woman with steel-grey hair down to her thighs, hiding her leathery-skinned nakedness—she was already walking out of the tree line.

The spiders poured in after her, but instead of attacking they formed a carpet that covered the vale. The Weaver stopped walking and was instead carried from spider to spider, passed along until she reached a spot some twenty-five feet from my walkers. There, spiders swarmed on top of each other to form a chair, and then lifted her into that chair.

"Lord of death." Her human form looked normal, but her voice was anything but, undertones of something alien coloring her words, even as the spiders swept their legs against each other in a loud murmur of approval. "Why have you come to our forest?"

"Since when is this your forest?" I challenged. "Everyone knows the Weaver makes her home in the north."

She studied me with eyes every bit as black and bottomless as her spider form's, and if my answering her question with my own had pissed her off, she didn't show it. "There is a sickness," she finally said, that alien voice cracked and dry, "spreading inch by inch on the tundra that even those such as we must heed."

If I hadn't been controlling my body with my power, I would have blinked. Someone or something had driven the Weaver south? "You and all your children?"

"Yes."

"What could possibly—"

"Lord of death, heir to bone," she interrupted, eyes fixed on me, "why have you come to *our* forest?"

The sea of spiders swayed back and forth, but her throne remained perfectly still.

"One of your hunting packs attacked a town."

"What do such as we care about towns?" Before I could respond to that, she continued. "What do such as you care about towns? The stars bleed across the cosmos, dreams drift like bloodied sand, and all that remains is the breeding and the dying."

I honestly didn't know what the fuck any of that meant, so I just stuck to the facts.

"Your children took my friend."

"Death has no friends."

"This death does."

Another long pause, during which her children made their noise, while *my* children stood in silent ranks, as still as the grave. Finally, she stirred, those black eyes meeting mine.

"And if we take our prey as food and pleasure fairly gotten? Will the king of the grave go to war?"

The fact that she thought all the killing I'd already done didn't qualify as a war would've shaken me badly if the emptiness hadn't been there to keep my emotions distant.

"Yes," I said instead.

"You are outnumbered," she mused.

"I walked into these woods with seventeen," I told her. "Now, I have three hundred. I'd say the numbers are on my side."

Something dark crept into her expression. "We would fuck you and eat you. Our hatchlings would be glorious."

"Your hatchlings would be dead," I told her. "There is no life in me to give."

Damn it. Now, I was talking like her.

Her scowl disappeared and she nodded. "Death."

"Death," I agreed, "but I'm here for just one person. Or... three people, I guess. The three taken from the southern town two days ago. Give them over, let us walk away, and you and your children will live. Fight and those stars will watch us all die."

And then, remembering the last time I'd bluffed this badly, as a first-year in a much different forest, facing down a pair of Beast Shifters that didn't even hold the shadow of a candle to the Weaver, I met the Weaver's eyes again, and smiled.

Maybe it was that smile that convinced her. Maybe a lifetime alone had left her unable to see I was on my last legs, and she truly doubted her chances against me. Or maybe she just didn't want to have to replace the even more hundreds of children my army and I would take with us as we died.

Either way, she nodded again, and turned to the spiders at her side. "Bring us the prizes of which he speaks."

A dozen spiders scurried away to do her bidding.

"They understand you?"

"Of course," she said, tone now as mild as milk, even with the alien sounds creeping into every consonant. "We are their mother, after all."

○○○

If you've never sat in a vale literally covered in man-sized spiders, talking to one of the great horrors of the world, as her children scurry to fetch one of your only remaining friends—

Fuck it. You know where I'm going with this. I'd have almost preferred the battle.

Very little of what the Weaver said made sense, but I couldn't decide if that was because she was crazy or if she just knew things that I did not.

"The town I came from is packing up," I told her, hoping dearly that was true, "but if you go much further south or west, you're going to run into larger towns and cities. You'll get your war."

She sniffed, the movement curiously delicate for a naked old woman who looked like she could beat up Supersonic even without her powers. "What care we for such vermin?"

"Push hard enough, and you'll get more than just vermin coming at you," I said, still bluffing. "Dominion won't stand for an incursion into the Free States."

I don't think she had any idea what the Free States were, but somehow, the name Dominion got her attention. Which was weird, because she shouldn't have even heard of him, alone in her woods, with only spiders for company.

"The Sky Lord?" She asked, interest finally piqued. "He will not leave his domain any more than we will leave ours."

"What?"

"Those such as he, and we, and you," she said, a sly grin that I didn't trust making its way onto her face, "find our kingdoms and go no further. When you claim your throne, you will know, just as he. Just as we."

"But your domain didn't extend past the mountains—"

"We have told you of the tundra and the sickness! We have redefined our domain's border, but its size remains the same."

That almost made sense. Not the part about Dominion, who was the furthest thing from a king of the Free States... and not the part about me, given that I was headed back to Los Angeles as soon as this fucking Mission was over... but the part about the Weaver and her domain.

"So, if this sickness doesn't spread any further south?"

"We will be as we have been since the beginning."

"And if it does spread?"

"The stars will keep bleeding," she said, "and we will get on with the breeding and the dying."

CHAPTER 26

Eventually, the spiders returned with three human-sized bundles of silk. Two of those bundles were wriggling as the paralytic venom started to wear off. I went directly to the only one that glowed like a Power and had one of my walkers tear the webbing free to reveal Silt. The Earthshaker's deep brown eyes were wide and terrified, then wide and confused as my face swam into view.

"I'm getting you out of here," I said quietly, as my walker cut her arms and legs free. "Can you stand?"

"I… don't know." Her voice was hoarse, her face drawn with obvious dehydration.

"Give it a try while I take care of the others," I said, passing her my canteen.

"Others?"

"One second." I wanted to answer all her questions, but I could feel myself only minutes from crashing and we needed to be way the hell away from this vale by the time I did.

I cut free the second bundle of webbing, revealing a young teenage boy. "Eric?"

He just lay there and shook. Something told me asking him to stand wasn't going to get me anywhere, so instead I went to the third webbed figure.

The lack of movement and any semblance of a spark already told me what to expect, but I had to be sure. My spider walker shredded the webbing, revealing another young man, this one's eyes staring sightlessly past me into an afterlife I was pretty sure didn't exist.

Fuck.

I left the dead teenager mostly cocooned, ignoring the rage that was growing somewhere outside my emptiness. Two people alive was better than none, and I could at least get this one… whatever his name was… back to his family for burial.

Silt had made it to a seated position, color returning to her face with every sip of water, but Eric was still lying on his back, shaking. I crouched over him again.

"My name is Walker. I'm with the Mission. We're going to get you back to your family, but we need to go now. I'm going to load you onto the back of… well, a mount, of sorts. As soon as we're somewhere safe, we'll give you some time to recover, okay?"

Still no response. I hoped it was just shock, but hell if I could tell for sure. Maybe Cob, with his EMT training, would know what to do. For now, all I could do was load him onto one of my dead spiders.

Then, it was back over to Silt, helping her to her feet. She was shaking her head like she was trying to dislodge something in her brain, eyes still wide as she took in the array of walkers at my back.

"Boneboy, what the fuck is going on? And what's that noise—" She stopped dead, her eyes going to the legion of live spiders still waiting in the vale. "Why is there a naked old woman sitting on a chair of fucking spiders?"

"I'll tell you later. How do you feel about getting out of here?"

"Something tells me it's a good idea." She stomped feeling back into her feet, and took a cautious step forward, then another. "What happened to Gladstone?"

"It's two or three days south of here. We're headed there as soon as you all are ready."

"We were taken," she said, voice still sluggish as she puzzled things through.

"Yeah." With Eric and the dead boy loaded onto walkers, I started walking Silt to a mount of her own.

The hissing of thousands of legs rose in volume.

"We would request that Death return our fallen children. Flesh to feed us, flesh to keep us strong."

Silt shuddered at the discordant tones of that alien voice.

I turned back to the Weaver. Leaving my spider army behind meant we'd be unprotected from the Spider Shifter and her children, but the truth was, we were badly outnumbered even *with* the dead spiders. Worse, I was damn near passing out, and I wasn't convinced I'd be able to hold on to this many walkers once I did. And if the mother and her children were busy devouring the remains of their own...

"And if I do? You will give us passage out of these woods?"

"We will stay here until you are out of our woods," she said, "so that our children who hunt know you are not prey."

"And then?"

"We will return to our nest in the mountains, and the fucking and the feasting, the bleeding and the breeding, will continue until what was broken becomes whole."

That was about as close to assurance as I was going to get. "Okay. But I need some of your dead children to transport and defend these three. The rest will be left for you."

She hissed in a way no human ever had and then sat in silence. Finally, she nodded.

"We find this acceptable, a compact made between such as we and such as you. Go, heir to bone. Leave our forest. Find your throne. This will be one more dream in a world too full of them."

I paused, struck both by the oddness of her tone and the words she'd used. "You've been alive since the beginning, right? Since everything changed?"

"We are the mother," she told me. "And the destroyer."

"And the dreamer? Did you hear him? Or her?"

"*His* domain is the whole of reality," she said, and her children's many, many legs had gone quiet and still, causing a hush to fall over the vale. "His throne reaches toward the void and the bloody stars are his crown."

And then, the naked old woman covered in hair was gone, and a nightmare that towered over the trees around us was in her place. Again, my mind tried to put the pieces I saw into a coherent picture, but a gasp from the woman I was supporting had me turning away.

"That's—" Silt managed.

"Yeah." I brought one of my larger spider walkers over. "How do you feel about riding something I killed less than two hours ago?"

"Maybe by tomorrow, I'll be freaked out by the idea, but I'm not up to walking yet. If it gets me the fuck out of here…"

We left the vale, Silt riding behind me on a dead spider, Eric draped over another, the corpse of his fellow townie bundled onto a third, and the corpses of the long-dead trailing after. The Weaver's children parted for us, and the silence that had fallen was replaced again by the hissing of thousands of legs rubbing against each other.

I stopped at the top of that hill and looked back. The Weaver's body was lost among the treetops, her legs oddly shaped trees amidst the forest, but her children still covered the clearing like a living, twitching carpet. I reached out to the hundreds of spider walkers I'd left behind and took back the pieces of emptiness I'd buried in them, letting their corpses collapse to the earth.

Spiders streamed past us down into the vale, and I left the Weaver and her children to their cannibalistic feast.

ooo

Riding an undead spider was nothing at all like riding a horse. The thorax and abdomen of my walker was wider than Cloud, and its skittering was nothing at all like the horse's gait. Without a saddle, stirrups, or reins, it was a long way from comfortable.

About a half-hour after we'd left the vale, Silt stirred.

"That was the Weaver, wasn't it?"

"Yeah." I kept my voice low, but our walkers moved in silence. "A story to tell everyone when we get back to the Academy."

"Like anyone will believe it." Her strong arms, wrapped around my waist from behind, trembled for a moment, and we both pretended not to notice. "How are we still alive?"

"I convinced her that any war between us would lead to our mutual destruction."

Silt sucked in another breath. When her voice came, it was quiet and maybe a little bit scared. "And would it have?"

"Fuck no. Did you see the size of her? And the sheer number of spiders she had with her?" I shook my head. "I have a policy against fighting anything bigger than a house. There's no future in getting smashed into paste."

Silt's arms tightened around me. "*Goddamn*, Boneboy. I've said it before, and I'll say it again. When you bluff, you bluff hard."

"I wasn't leaving without you."

"And I appreciate that, even if I'm still a bit woozy on what the hell happened. Where are we? Where are the others?"

I wanted to tell her, but I could feel the reins I had on my power loosening. The Earthshaker wasn't touching my flesh, but I broke free of her grip anyway and slid off the walker, my legs suddenly wobbly beneath me.

"Damian…?"

I tried to say something, tried to reassure her, but more than two days of travel, of combat, and of power usage hit me like one of Orca's punches. I felt the world around me go indistinct, had only a moment to send commands to my walkers, and then I fell into a darkness as bottomless as the Weaver's ancient eyes.

CHAPTER 27

I woke from a dream, *the* dream, to a different kind of darkness, the sound of multiple people breathing in an enclosed space, and the knowledge that most of my walkers were gone. I could feel the three spiders we'd been using as mounts, but the rest—the forest's long-dead beasts I'd raised in that last desperate defense—were once again just empty vessels, scattered around us.

"Silt?" I kept my voice low, but it was still overly loud in whatever space we'd found ourselves in. My head pounded like I'd just come off a three-day whisky bender. Almost on reflex, I reached for the emptiness to muffle that pain, but for the first time in more than a year, the void within me was slow to come, the dark waters refusing to rise.

I'd wondered what my limits were, and two days of constant battle, of raising literally hundreds of walkers, and of facing down another Full-Five in her own domain had finally shown me.

"Damian." I could hear the relief in Silt's voice, even if I couldn't see her. "Thank God you're awake."

"Where are we?"

"Right where you fell off the spider, fourteen or so hours ago. I wasn't sure you were safe to move, and before most of your undead minions fell apart, they didn't seem keen on letting me near you anyway."

I blinked. "Then why can't I see anything?"

"Oh. That's me." I heard a sound, like sand running through an oversized hourglass. A hole appeared above us and to the right, light streaming through. As I watched that hole spread downward until it formed a doorway out of the dome we'd apparently been sleeping inside.

A dome formed entirely of hard-packed earth.

Silt was shielding her eyes from the sudden glare. "I figured even if the Weaver gave you safe passage, there might be other predators out here that would see three humans lying in the open as prey."

"Smart. Eric's still okay?"

"Eric?"

"The kid we rescued. He's from Gladstone too. They both are."

"Oh." She shrugged. "He's having a hard time, I think, but he's alive."

"Okay." I pinched the bridge of my nose.

"Are you doing alright?"

"Yeah. I think so. Just fighting the first headache I've had to actually pay attention to in more than a year."

"If you want, we can find something scary for you to death touch on our way out of here," she said. "Speaking of which, where the hell are we?"

"We're about two and a half days north of the town," I said. "At least I think so."

"You think so?"

"The Academy didn't teach us to navigate through forests that didn't even exist, pre-Break," I reminded her. "I've just been heading in the general direction of north, hoping something would lead me to you."

"I'd say something about how terrible a plan that was if I wasn't living proof that it had worked." She frowned. "Denali can track a mosquito through a swamp, and Stark's not much worse. It's hard to believe he couldn't follow a few spiders. Where the hell are he and the rest of the Mission anyway? Did they not survive the ambush in Gladstone?"

"Oh, they survived. And Stark helped track the three of you right to the edge of the Weaver's woods—which, by the way, are now way further south than anyone knew. And then..."

She read the truth in my face. "Then they gave us up for dead."

"Yeah. Stark tried to stop me from coming after you but fuck that. As far as I know, the Mission is still in Regent. We can catch up with them there, if you want, or we can try touring the Badlands on our own. Although," I admitted, as my stomach made itself heard, "they do have food. And water."

I looked about for my canteen, suddenly parched, and found it lying within arm's reach. Surprisingly, it was full again.

"There's an underground stream about a hundred yards in that direction," said Silt, motioning to the back wall of her dome. "I bored a channel to it and made a makeshift well. The water's not the cleanest, but it's drinkable."

"Defensive walls, protective domes, and now wells on demand?" I shook my head. "Earthshakers are ridiculously useful."

"Oh yeah, we're fucking fantastic. Except maybe for the whole *getting kidnapped by spiders* thing." She frowned. "If the Mission didn't come with you, how *have* you been eating? Or sleeping?"

"I had some rations in my pack. Still do, if you and the kid are hungry," I said, nodding to the recumbent form of the townie I'd saved. "As for sleeping? I didn't. These woods are crawling with the Weaver's children, and I was trying to kill my way to you before—"

"Before they could take us back to Mother."

"Yeah." I swallowed. "It didn't occur to me that she might leave her nest and come to me instead."

Silt was looking at me strangely. "You left the Mission, went into spider-infested woods by yourself, fought the Weaver's children for two days without sleep, and then bluffed a creature older than the Break into letting me go?"

"Yeah." I shrugged. "What other choice did I have?"

Instead of answering me, she just shook her head, giving me a look that I'd never seen from her before.

"What?"

"Why did you have to be born with a dick?"

I frowned and went with it. "Because it gives me an excuse to act like one?"

Silt snorted, and then that snort turned into a laugh, and then for the second time since I'd known her, Sofia Black was crying, quiet tears charting a path down her round face. "You know I love you, right?"

"Like you said when I came back from Bakersfield, we're family. Two years ago, that wouldn't have meant shit to me, but between you and Vibe and Tessa ... I guess I've learned some things."

"Don't get all weepy on me now, Skeletor," she said, steadfastly ignoring her own tears. She reached out to me, and then paused, hand a safe distance away from mine. "Is it safe?"

"Yeah," I told her, reaching over to squeeze her hand in mine. "I don't have enough power in me to ash a mouse."

"Ugh. You just had to bring up rodents." She shivered, warm, callused fingers squeezing mine in return. "Thank you for saving my life."

"You're welcome. You'd do the same for me."

"Damn straight I would." She ran her other hand across her face, wiping away any unshed tears, and sent me a grin that was classic Silt. "What do you say we get this kid back to his family, and then go surprise Mammoth and the others with our miraculous resurrection?"

ooo

The journey out of the woods was a lot easier than it had been going in. Part of that was that there weren't a thousand spiders trying to stop me. Part of it was that I had Silt with me. But the biggest part was that we had mounts of our own. A quick climb up a tree showed us the sun's position in the sky, and that was enough to point us south. By the end of the day, we were nearing the edge of the woods. Not an edge I particularly recognized, but still… the plains just past the forest seemed a match for the general area I'd seen around Gladstone.

Our still-living townie had remained unconscious for most of that trip, awake only long enough for Silt to get some water into him from our single, rapidly emptying canteen. We weren't sure if he had internal injuries or was just seeking refuge in sleep, but as we started to exit the forest, he finally stirred again.

This time, he actually woke up.

Only to see the dead spider he'd been draped over.

With a loud scream, he jerked away and fell off the walker entirely, scuttling backwards on his hands and feet like he was a spider himself.

"It's okay," said Silt, but Eric's eyes went from his mount to ours and his screams went up in volume by at least another decibel. In his panic, he climbed to his feet, and would have run away from us if Silt hadn't caught him with a half-wall of dirt.

The Earthshaker dropped from our spider mount and made her way to Eric, hands held out before her like she was trying to calm a scared animal. I couldn't hear what she was saying. Finally, she turned around and called back to me.

"Damian, can you get rid of your walkers? I don't think we're going anywhere as long as they're around."

"How are we supposed to get Stephen's body back to Gladstone?" It had taken me a while, but I'd finally remembered the name of the second missing townie.

Eric twitched at my words for some reason.

"This *is* Stephen," said Silt, coming closer, "and he says we should only be a few hours away. Maybe you can, you know… make Eric follow behind us?"

"He's okay with me raising his neighbor, but not with us riding back to Gladstone?"

"I think he's an arachnophobe. And after the last few days, I'm not sure I can blame him."

"Let's just knock him out again until we reach town."

"If you're that sure there's no internal bleeding going on, then be my guest."

I sighed. "Fuck."

"*Can* you raise Eric?"

I didn't answer for a second. The well of my power had slowly been refilling throughout the day. Slower than it should have been. At first, I'd worried I had broken something by overextending myself, but as the hours passed, I'd realized that wasn't it at all. As far as I could tell, the emptiness was pouring back into me at the same rate as ever… maybe even a bit faster than before. It only *seemed* slower because the well itself was broader and deeper.

Two years earlier, Sally had told me Crows reached their full potential through death. I was starting to think she was right… and I'd just killed fucking hundreds of spiders.

I was still a long way from being full, or even from what would have qualified as such before I entered the Weaver's woods, but raising one recently dead townie?

That I could do.

"Yeah." I reached out to the bundle of webbing, flesh, and bones on our last spider, and let emptiness seep into its form. "But if we're hiking all the way back to Gladstone, there'd better be a damn feast waiting for us."

CHAPTER 28

There was no feast waiting in Gladstone.

In fact, there were no people at all, except for one old man who nearly shot us because he couldn't tell even at a hundred paces that we were human. After a whole lot of shouting and explanations, he put aside his rifle and we entered what was left of Gladstone. Turned out, Stark and Cassie's dad had convinced the rest of the town to move down to Regent, where they'd hopefully be safe from the Weaver's children.

"You didn't go with them?" asked Silt.

"Nah." Old Man Ricket, as Stephen had roused just enough to name him, was in his seventies, blind in one eye, and with only four teeth left to his name, but his reedy voice had no give to it. "Told that scarred boy I was born here, and I was gonna die here."

"Not if the Weaver's children paralyze you and carry you away to be eaten in the woods," I pointed out. "And they will."

"Pssssh." He cleared his throat and spat a wad of phlegm past me and into the street. "It's my choice, young fella. Ain't a lot of choices someone my age has left. And you don't have to worry about them spiders. Got me a fine bottle of moonshine in my house and a date with Bessie tonight."

Bessie, it turned out, was the rifle he'd almost shot us with.

"Only stuck around this long," the old man continued, "to say goodbye to the town my mom and pop grew up in... the house I buried my angel and two dogs behind. If you folks had come tomorrow instead, there'd have been nothing left to see."

"Mr. Ricket..." Apparently, that had been enough to break through Stephen's ongoing funk.

"Don't you worry about me," said the old man after a long bout of coughing. "My granddaddy's granddaddy served in the navy, and I always liked the idea of going down with the ship."

We were a thousand-plus miles from the ocean, but I understood what he was saying. Truth was, I kind of agreed with him too. Lot of decisions in life get taken away from us. Maybe how we die shouldn't be one of them.

"You and that Duke boy take care," he told Stephen, nodding to Eric's shambling corpse. "And if you don't mind taking Bessie Junior with you down to Regent when you go, I'd appreciate it."

Bessie Junior turned out to be his plow horse. No, I have no idea how or why the rifle had seniority. Old Man Ricket had kept the horse to maintain the pretense that he was going to keep farming his little plot of land. With his date with Bessie coming up, the nag was no longer a necessary part of that fiction.

"Do we just leave him here?" asked Silt, as we were bringing Bessie Junior in from the rundown corral. "Or drag him down to Regent?"

"Old Man Ricket?" I got a nod in return. "I don't know. I kind of think it's his right to die when and where he wants to."

"You think the people of Gladstone would have left him if they knew he was just going to—"

"He's dying anyway," said Stephen. "Something in his lungs. Everyone knows it."

I traded glances with Silt and she just nodded again, and the subject of Old Man Ricket was over and done with. The horse didn't come with a saddle, but we put a thick blanket on her back, and Stephen on that blanket. We refilled our canteen at the town's well, did a quick pass looking for Silt's pack and shotgun, both of which must have been gathered up and taken south ahead of us, said goodbye, and then left for Regent.

I don't know how the old man's date went, or even if it went at all. By the time night fell, we were way down the trail. I thought I heard a single gunshot, but at that distance, it could just as easily have been a tree branch cracking in the wind. Either way, his was one ghost that didn't come to join my eternal parade.

We slept in the woods, inside another of Silt's dirt domes. Between Stephen and I, we only had four nightmares, so I'm thinking that was a pretty good night. When morning came again, I parceled out the few remaining clean clothes from my pack. We weren't going to win any fashion awards, especially with how poorly my clothes fit Silt and Stephen, but just wearing something halfway clean went a long way to improving morale. By the time we headed out, Silt was almost her usual rock-solid self, and Stephen had mustered up enough enthusiasm to eat some of the food Old Man Ricket had forced upon us.

By mid-day, Regent came into view.

The town had changed in the four or five days we'd been gone. The forest had been cut back for a solid hundred yards from the nearest house, in a demolition job I knew only Mammoth could have accomplished so quickly. A wall was going up around the town itself, constructed from that fallen wood, and though it was a long way from being completed, what was already there gave the town at least some small protection against anything coming from the north.

Given how high the Weaver's children could jump, I wasn't sure that protection would do much, but it was something. More than the construction, the first thing I noticed was the people. With the former residents of Gladstone mixed in now with the residents of Regent, the town was almost bustling.

Someone on the water tower called down a warning less than a minute after we'd come into view, and we were still a dozen feet or more from the newly constructed wall when we were greeted with a half-dozen rifles, pointed straight at us.

"I'm getting really tired of guns," I told Silt.

"I'm getting really tired of not having mine."

We both raised our hands and waited.

"Is that... is that Stephen?" came a voice.

"Dad?" For the second time since the previous day's spider incident, our rescued townie showed signs of life, his head whipping up as he scanned the faces peering down at us from behind those rifles. "Dad!"

I finally recognized one of those faces... Cassie's dad, the guy who had come with Stark and I out to the edge of the woods. His eyes went wide as he looked from Stephen to Silt to me.

"They saved Eric too," he yelled. "They're all back and alive!"

ooo

That's right; I'd gotten so used to Eric stumbling along behind us as a walker that it hadn't occurred to me to cut his strings as we came into town with Bessie Junior. I did so as soon as Cassie's dad called out, of course, which just incited its own firestorm of panic from people seeing Eric collapse before their eyes.

I was in the middle of trying to explain that fuckup when a huge shape made its way down the street toward us. Mammoth.

"Walker. Silt." He closed his eyes for a moment, and his relieved sigh was a warm wind that reached us from three feet away. "Thank God."

"God had nothing to do with it," I told him. "And neither did your man."

"Yeah. I heard." He shook his head and sighed again. "Can't say I agree with him on that, but as field leader, it was his choice to make."

"Choosing to abandon a teammate?"

"Focusing on the needs of the many." He finally spared a glance for the rest of the people around us. A pale-faced Stephen was being mobbed by his family, mother, father, and sister all crying even as they hugged him. On the other side of the street, a different sort of reunion was taking place, as Eric's parents were held back from rushing to the body of their dead son. "You found the missing boys?"

"Yeah. One was already dead, although I'm not sure from what."

"I'll have Cob look and find out. You two, get some food and water. Silt, Emma has your pack and your shotgun. If you're up for it, I think people will want to hear your story once you've had a moment to recover."

"I was paralyzed or unconscious for half of it," said Silt.

"I need a shower," I told Mammoth. "And then to do some laundry. If I'm still awake after that, I'm all yours."

"You got it," the older Power said, stepping out of our path. "And Walker?"

"Yeah?"

"Thank you."

I shrugged. I hadn't done it for thanks.

CHAPTER 29

I'd never been much of a fruit or vegetable guy, but there was something about freshly grown Druid food that was every bit as refreshing as the shower I stood in so long that my fingers and toes went wrinkly. When I came out into the men's changing room of the town's communal facilities, I found a plate of food and a fresh set of clothing set aside for me, my old clothes already whisked away by someone to be cleaned.

My borrowed outfit didn't quite fit, too short in the legs, and too broad in the waist. Our classmates back home were probably getting parades and finalizing their post-graduation endorsement deals in between stopping the occasional burglary. I'd just faced down the Weaver and was getting a shower, some fruit, and someone else's clothes.

Crazy thing was, I was okay with that. I'd seen the faces of Stephen's family. I'd been to enough funerals now to know that Eric's parents would find some closure in at least having a body to bury. And I'd gotten Silt back, alive and kicking, and currently in the women's facilities being made much of by Emma.

That was worth a dozen endorsement deals.

Besides, you'd better believe I was going to have my agent sell vid rights to my encounter with the Weaver. Once I had an agent, anyway. The idea of some kid watching my exploits on vid, like I'd watched Tempest and Paladin? Honestly, that wouldn't suck at all.

I was running a comb through hair growing long enough to be annoying when James stuck his head through the door.

"Walker? You decent?"

"Depends on who you ask."

"Mammoth needs you."

I should have stayed in the shower longer. Problem was, I'd probably burned through five people's daily allotments of water already.

"Okay. Where can I find him?"

"In the inn with Eleanor, Gladstone's mayor, and their respective councils, where he's been stuck the last three days." The guy who hoped to one day call himself Dagger lowered his voice. "If you want to accidentally terrify them all into working together, I don't think anyone would mind. Emma says we're not going to be here forever."

"I'll do what I can."

I followed James over to the inn, which was more difficult than it should have been. The bustle I'd seen from outside the wall was even more pronounced in the streets, and everywhere we went, someone from Gladstone was stopping us to thank me for bringing back *their boys*. The fact that one of those boys was a corpse didn't seem to change anything.

I hadn't gone into the woods for anyone's gratitude—I hadn't really been focused on Stephen and Eric at all—but damn if that gratitude didn't feel nice.

We passed Lady and a handful of townies, working on the scaffolding for another guard tower, and the Mission's mechanic stopped what she was doing to almost tackle me with a hug that came close to cracking the ribs I'd only just healed a week earlier. She pulled back, went up onto her tiptoes to brush her lips against mine, and then fled back to her scaffolding without a word.

That whole encounter told me two things.

First, Lady felt disturbingly good in my arms.

Second, Silt was right. Lady and I needed to have a talk.

I know: you're all crying into your spectral beer mugs for me. Guy gets a girlfriend at home and then has to deal with an attractive older woman showing interest out on the road. Boo fucking hoo, right?

Well, fuck off. I don't like many people, but I liked Lady. But I still wasn't going to mess up what I had with Tessa. Maybe I'd get back to Los Angeles to find she'd rethought our whole relationship, maybe I'd end up regretting spending six months as a choir boy, but a man who can't stay true to his own convictions... what good is that sort of asshole?

Didn't mean I was looking forward to that talk with Lady though. Especially with the feel of her lips still lingering on mine.

James coughed to get my attention, pretending he hadn't seen anything, and we finally crossed over to the town's inn. Even from outside, I could hear the argument happening within.

"Mammoth said to just go on in," said James.

"You're not coming?"

"Oh hell no. I'm staying out here like the junior worker bee I so happily am." He cleared his throat. "We had the funerals for Joe and Gage while you were gone, but now that everyone is back, a bunch of us are having drinks tonight. Kind of a wake of sorts, I guess."

"You waited for us?"

"Mammoth insisted. He was convinced you'd make it back. Less so as the days went on, but..." James shook his head. "I guess that's why he's the boss."

"I guess so."

I turned and made my way into the inn.

ooo

When I'd last been in Regent, the inn had had five tables spread out through its common room. Those tables were now all in the center of that room, forming a lopsided circle. On the far side of that circle were Mammoth, Stark, and Cagney. I met Mammoth's eyes as I came through the door, but Stark kept his eyes on the heavyset man currently on his feet and speaking. I vaguely recognized that man as one of the people of Gladstone, flanked by two others who must have been their town's council.

To their left was Eleanor, Regent's grey-haired mayor, sitting with her own two councilmembers. Both were women, on account of the bandits having killed all of Regent's men. By the look on Eleanor's face, she was deeply regretting that those same bandits hadn't hit Gladstone first.

"—telling you," said the standing man, "we can't just stay here. How do we know that what happened to Gladstone won't happen to Regent?"

"We're building defenses," said Eleanor, voice hard. "They would be finished more quickly if you and your family would actually lift a finger to help."

"What's a wall going to do to stop the Weaver's children?" the man demanded.

"It'll at least slow them down," I said from the doorway. "Give you targets to shoot at."

"Who the hell are you?" He paused as the woman who had been seated next to him whispered into his ear, and his voice softened considerably. "I see. I appreciate what you did, finding Cassie, Stephen, and Eric for us, but maybe you should stay out of a conversation that has nothing to do with you."

"We're almost a full day's ride south of your town," said Eleanor. "There is no reason for the Weaver to move this far south."

"That's what we thought, and the next thing we knew, we were waking up to three missing children, and a mess of corpses in our streets. We don't even know why she moved in the first place!"

I coughed, feeling absolutely no shame about interrupting again. It had been a long fucking week, and this asshole was ruining the reunion. Even if I kind of agreed with him.

"You have something to say, kid?"

"Call me Walker. And the Weaver moved south because of some sort of sickness in the north. Unless it spreads further, you shouldn't have anything to worry about. And if it does, you should have plenty of warning, as long as you pay attention to your defenses and keep scouts deployed."

There was a long moment of silence as everyone in the inn turned to stare at me.

"What?"

"I said she moved south because of a sickness in the north—"

"How do you know this?" asked Eleanor, grey eyes intent on my face.

"It's what she told me."

Another pause, and then the asshole man burst into laughter. "Of course. *You* met the Weaver. And I'm the Singer's son."

"I asked Walker here," said Mammoth, "to share his story. As the only person to willingly go into the Weaver's woods and come back out, I suspect his insight will help you all finally come to a decision."

"Of course, Mammoth," said the other man, voice respectful as he responded to the enormous Power. "But there's a difference between insight and tall tales."

"What's your name?" I asked, ignoring the way Mammoth blanched at the tone in my voice.

"This is Bob Wallace," said Eleanor. "Former mayor of Gladstone."

"Bob, I don't know you, I don't care about you, and I don't give a fuck if you believe me or not. But I was the only person standing in Gladstone when the spiders broke and ran. Every damn one of you would have been taken into the woods if it wasn't for me. So, you can at least do me the fucking courtesy of listening."

"He's not lying," said a quiet voice from the door. Stephen, leaning against the woman who could only be his mom.

Stephen's white-faced presence drained the anger out of the room. Bob softened even further. "You shouldn't be up and about, lad. Not after what you've been through."

"He isn't lying," Stephen insisted. "I was in and out of it, thanks to the venom, but I heard her voice. I still hear it every time I close my eyes. Every time I try to sleep."

"If you encountered the Weaver," asked Eleanor, her tone respectful, her words chosen with care, "why didn't she kill you?"

I paused, not entirely sure what I wanted to say. The fact that Stephen had been conscious for at least some of it, to overhear my conversations with Silt, meant I stuck to the truth.

"She wasn't sure if she could," I finally said.

CHAPTER 30

It took a surprisingly long time to tell the story, and Stephen had to leave again about halfway through when some of those details triggered another panic attack. When I finished, there was a silence so deep I could swim in it.

You know, if I knew how to swim.

"Who *are* you?" Bob finally breathed. All the fight had gone out of him right around the time he slumped back into his chair.

"Walker is one of our Cape students, on loan from the Academy of Heroes in Los Angeles for this year's Mission," said Mammoth.

"Are all the Free States' Capes this—"

"No," said the older Power. "Walker is a bit of a special case."

"First Crow Cape ever," I said, not wanting to get into my power classification when even Cagney was looking at me like I had three heads. "And still sane, shockingly enough."

Weirdly, that didn't do anything to reassure anyone.

"So, you actually met the Weaver," said Eleanor. "And she's not coming any further south?"

"She's not planning to. I don't know what this sickness she's talking about is, but she's moved her nest into the mountains, and from what I could understand, she's there to stay."

The old woman turned to give Bob a triumphant look.

"The whole reason she moved her nest is because the sickness *did* spread," argued the other man. "We can't just bury our heads in the sand and pretend it might not happen again."

"The people of my town have been through hell in the past month," said Eleanor. "Your town is a day's ride away and on the very outskirts of the Weaver's new hunting grounds. I'm not going to abandon this town on the off chance that some mysterious sickness displaces the Weaver for only the second time in a century!"

"I didn't move *my* people down here just so they could be spider food," roared Bob.

"Then feel free to keep on moving down the road," barked the older woman. "Nobody's forcing you to stay!"

Mammoth surged to his feet, and that big of a man moving suddenly was an argument all on its own.

"The Mission will be leaving Regent in two days. We do not have the horses, the wagons, or the supplies to take more than a handful of you with us. You need to come to an agreement."

"Two days?" asked Eleanor.

"That's not a lot of time," said Bob, at almost the same time.

"We have spent all the time we could spare," said the Shifter. "Regent wasn't even on our original route, and there are other towns we have to reach."

"How big are the hunting packs, Walker?" asked Cagney. The slim black woman had stayed quiet through my story and the arguments before and after. "On average?"

"I'd say about twenty to forty spiders."

"And do you think they'd attack a fortified town? One with walls and guards, unlike Gladstone?"

I met her eyes across the room, knowing nobody would like my answer. "Yeah, they would—"

"Then we're leaving," declared Bob.

"—but they'd go for the easy prey first," I added, ignoring his interruption. "This far from the Weaver, they'd be operating purely on animal instinct."

"So, they'd clear out the forest," said Cagney.

"Yeah. Whatever they could catch and kill. They have to eat too. If it's not human, I don't think they'll necessarily drag it all the way back to the Weaver, but I'm not positive of that."

"So... keep an eye on the northern forest," she reasoned. "Send out scouting patrols like we've been doing with Supersonic. Obviously, none of your people can fly, but still... Regent should have plenty of warning, and if the town is alerted, the defenses we've started should be enough to hold off a hunting pack."

"And what then?" demanded Bob, turning on Eleanor.

"Then we'll know that the Weaver *has* moved again," she said, her voice tired but strong. "And we'll all travel south together to find a new town together. You have my word on that."

"We should make sure we have stockpiled supplies," suggested Gladstone's former mayor. "And wagons of our own at the ready. It took a full day to pack up and move from Gladstone, and you all have a lot more in the way of stuff worth holding onto."

"I can agree with that. A contingency plan that we will hopefully never have to use. We even have some iron from back when there was a working mine to reinforce the axles and hounds." She turned to Mammoth. "If that meets your approval?"

"You know I'm not here to make your decisions for you," the big man rumbled. "Not on my own behalf and certainly not on behalf of the Free States."

"Well said." All the anger was gone from Bob's voice. "If we wanted to be told what to do, we'd have gone west ages ago." He turned to me, face suddenly apologetic. "No offense intended, of course."

I shrugged away his apology. I didn't understand the allure of living away from the grid, the net, and some modicum of safety, but truth was, the Free States had plenty of assholes.

The last thing we needed was another one.

○○○

A few hours later, we were back in the inn, but this time, it was mostly just people from the Mission; Emma and Silt in a corner looking lazy and content; Presley with his leg extended across a bench, his knee wrapped. Stark, Denali, and Mammoth were at one table, while Lady, Derek, James, and I were at another, and Cagney brought out a fresh round of home-brewed beer to cheers from her table of Supersonic, Reese, and Jacobs.

Cob was the only one missing, attending to Stephen after having finished looking over Eric's body, and the medic showed up not soon after, greeted at the doorway by Cagney and something that didn't look like beer.

"Eleanor's husband, rest his soul, had a still and a brewery out back," said Lady, shouting over the general noise. "It was one of the first things I got working once everyone was safe."

"Drinks before defenses?" I asked back.

"People work harder when they know there's a reward waiting for them at the end of the day!"

It made sense, but I'd been nursing the same mug since we started. The emptiness at my core was a long, long way from whatever the new measure of *full* would end up being, so I wasn't worried about losing control or anything like that, but it had been a hell of a week. I was drained and ready to sleep.

Finally, Mammoth rose from his chair, and the common room went quiet.

"I grew up in Kansas City," he said, voice filling the space. "My family and I fled, like so many others, after the city fell, fled all the way to the Free States, but a part of me has always seen the Badlands as home. I started the Mission to give back to that home, to make sure that other towns wouldn't suffer the same fate as mine... or that the refugees would have a helping hand when the worst did happen. I've been doing it now for longer than I can remember—"

"Because you're old!" shouted a very drunk Derek.

"Yes, thank you, Derek. And thank you even more for volunteering for last watch tonight," said Mammoth, to laughter. "Anyway, the Mission has never been a summer vacation. It's not a ticket to explore the Badlands at your leisure. It's grime and sweat and hard work, but it's necessary. People need us."

He took a swig from his own beer mug and set it back down on the table. "Sometimes, it's not enough. There are dozens of Gladstones in the Badlands, disappearing with each passing decade, and nothing we do will fully stem that tide. Sometimes, we lose. Sometimes, even victory costs us some of our own. Does that mean we give up?"

"Shit no!" shouted Lady.

"That's right. The truth is, there's no winning against entropy. One day, we'll all be dead. This world will be dust. But the more we fight, the more we delay that day. The more we ensure something and someone remains when we are gone. That is the Mission. Without us, this town wouldn't be free. The people of Gladstone would be gone without a trace." He nodded to me. "And parents would be missing their children. That, too, is the Mission. It's hard but we do it anyway because it needs to be done. Joe knew that. Gage did too. Tonight, we honor our fallen brothers with drink. Tomorrow, we honor them by continuing the work they devoted their lives to." He lifted his mug. "To Joe and to Gage!"

The responding roar shook the inn's rafters.

As Mammoth sat, Denali rose to take his place. "I met Joe when I was sixteen. He was a white man from Missouri, but he rode as well as any member of the nomad clans. He taught me about the world we didn't roam through, I taught him how to speak in proper tongues, and—" He paused, a rare smile making its way onto his face. "—and we both got our asses chewed out when we missed trail sign our elders thought blindingly obvious. He was my brother, and now he rides free across the sky. To Joe."

"To Joe," came the chorus, as everyone downed some more beer or alcohol.

It went like that for hours, people standing up and toasting their fallen companions. By the time Derek had to leave on wobbly legs for the guard duty he'd talked his way into, most of the Mission was gone, drunkenly headed off to their beds or tents. Mammoth cradled another full mug of beer in his hands as he stared into the crackling fire, Reese was lying flat on his back in the middle of the floor, loud snores coming from the hole in his face, and I didn't envy Eleanor's assistants for the work they'd have cleaning up after us tomorrow.

As for me? Against all odds, I was still there, Lady asleep against my side, my still half-finished beer on the table in front of me. During the rounds of toasting, my ghosts had filtered in to share space with the living, and I hadn't had the energy or the willpower to send them away. Not my parents, not Unicorn, not little Nyah or any of the dozens of people whose deaths I'd been witness to. And as for Joe or Gage, who had stood in the middle of that bar, hearing not a word their companions had said?

I let them be too.
Hell of a wake.
Glad I'd missed the funerals.

CHAPTER 31

Two days later, we left Regent behind. Not *just* Regent either. Between Presley's knee and Derek's still-healing chest wound, neither one was in a state to travel. Mammoth had promised that once we got to Wichita, he'd reach out to his contacts in Red Flight and send someone to get Derek back to one of the Mission outposts and Presley to a Free States Healer, but the two of them would be spending the next month or so stuck in Regent, waiting for that ride.

Honestly, given the way Derek had been getting on with one of the women in town, I wasn't entirely sure he'd take that ride when it came. He may have originally joined the Mission to travel but finding a girl could very well replace that desire with another. And frankly, Regent could do with another solid gun.

It was odd being on the road again. It felt like we'd been hanging around town for months, but really, it had only been a week and a half since the initial bandit ambush. Now, here we were, back on our horses or in the wagons, with only thirteen of us left of the original seventeen.

Of course, if we'd just left Supersonic behind too, we wouldn't have had to hear his continued bitching as we rode.

To his credit, one of the first things Caleb had done on the day after the wake was to find Silt and me. Or, Silt, Emma, and me, really... the quartermaster hadn't let our Earthshaker out of her sight since we made it back.

"I'm glad you're safe, Sofia," he said.

"That makes two of us," drawled Silt.

"Three," corrected Emma.

They all turned to me and I rolled my eyes.

"I'm the one who got her. Obviously, I'm glad!"

"You know, there are all kinds of rumors going around about that," said Caleb. "Are any of them true?"

"Did they involve two thousand spiders, a naked old lady and a monster bigger than King Rex?" asked Silt, lazily chewing a piece of grass. "Because if so, they're true."

"Unbelievable." Supersonic threw up his hands. "One trip! One fucking side trip that I'm not on and suddenly you're meeting the damn Weaver while I'm stuck providing overwatch for a town where we already killed all the bandits!"

"Next time we almost die to a Full Five, I'll make sure you're around," I told him, rolling my eyes.

"I'm holding you to that. Although if I'd been along, I could have caught the spiders before they even made it *to* the woods." He shook his head. "Maybe I'm just too powerful for my own good? But how are *you* still alive after all that?"

"I'm not really big on biology," I said, "but I'm pretty sure it has something to do with my heart pushing blood and oxygen through my body."

"You know what I mean. You're a Low-Three for fuck's sake! Why didn't the Weaver just squash you like a bug?"

"People can't help but like me, I guess."

"Bullshit."

I acknowledged that truth. "Guess I'm just *that* good."

Could've told him the truth, I guess. That the tall, skinny kid he'd sucker-punched at Unicorn's funeral was a Full-Five. Might have been fun to see his reaction. But honestly, I kind of liked how frustrated *not* knowing made him.

○○○

Within the day, we passed the broken-down wagon where we'd picked up those three bandit assholes. Mammoth had given Eleanor its location, figuring they'd be able to repair the vehicle and be one wagon up on their whole contingency plan, but they hadn't sent out a recovery team yet. As we came upon its discarded shell, I tried not to think about whoever's wagon it had been before the bandits took them out. Clearly, the whole runaway wagon thing had been bullshit, just like everything else. If we'd searched the area when we had first come here, would we have found the corpses of the wagon driver and their family?

I guess I could have checked myself. Could have opened myself to the emptiness and seen what was waiting out there for me to call on it, but we were already riding past, I was a long way from top form, and...

Honestly, I didn't want to know.

A day or two later, we turned south. Denali said this had been South Dakota, before the Break. No clue how he could tell; we'd left the post-Break forests behind us and one endless plain looked like another to me.

We stopped briefly at a trading post to share news and replace some of the supplies we'd left with the people of Regent, and then crossed over a river that was nowhere near as grand as its name, but for the most part those days were quiet. No pony-sized wolves or spiders larger than biology should have allowed. No bandits proving all over again that humanity could always, always take a bad situation and make it worse. Just open country, a hot late-summer sun, and our wagon train, crawling across the earth.

Whatever Supersonic thought about it, I found that stretch peaceful. I kept Cloud pointed in the right direction, avoided his inevitable attempts to bite my fingers, and indulged in more of that moving meditation. And all the while, the emptiness poured into me through the crack in my soul.

I was pretty sure Stark had been avoiding me, so I was surprised when he appeared beside me on his horse during the middle of one of my meditations.

"Walker."

"Stark. What do you need?" I kept my tone even, though part of me wanted to punch him right off his horse. Maybe everything had worked out with Silt—and Stephen, if not Eric—but I couldn't forget that the fucker had written her life off like she was already dead.

"Wanted to see if you're ready to be put back on guard rotation. With four fewer people, we need bodies."

"More than ready," I said. Mammoth had wanted to give me time to rest and recover, but honestly, I was bored again. Not sure what that says about my life. Free time had been all I wanted—and so rarely could get—at the Academy, and now, I was finding the lack of constant drama almost dull.

"Okay." He started to ride away, then paused. "You understand why I made the decision I did, don't you? Back in Gladstone?"

"The needs of the many," I said, quoting Mammoth.

"Yeah." The scarred man nodded. "That's what the Mission is about, after all. Doing what we can to help the greatest number of people possible."

"I get it," I said. "I doubt I would have been able to keep you alive if you *had* come with me. But the fact is, they took Silt, and you wrote her off like she was just a statistic. I understand what you did and why, but don't ever fucking expect me to do the same."

He took that in silence, then nodded. "Fair enough. But think about this: you might have the power to survive whatever you throw yourself into, but the people around you won't always be that lucky. I'm glad you rescued Silt, but what if you had just pissed off the Weaver instead? How many others might have paid the price for your actions?"

"People always have reasons for not doing things." I shrugged. "Seems to me our world would be better off with fewer excuses."

"I'm not talking about—" He cut himself off and sighed. "Never mind. I'll add you back in for tonight's watch."

I watched him ride off, rejoining Jacobs at the front of the train.

"What was that about?" asked Silt, riding up beside me.

"I think Stark is trying to get me to think before I do shit."

"He really doesn't know you at all, does he?"

"He really, really doesn't."

○○○

Apparently, it was a day for weird conversations, because that night, I was paired with Lady on watch duty. I hadn't seen much of the mechanic since her unexpected kiss. Gage and Joe had been two of the Mission's scouts, and with them both dead, she and a few others had been filling in as outriders to spell Cagney and Denali.

I wasn't entirely surprised when, an hour into our shift, I felt the spark of her presence drawing closer.

"How's everything going?" she asked, taking a seat next to me.

"Pretty quiet," I said back. "But aren't you supposed to be watching the other side of camp?"

"Are you telling me your senses don't extend that far?" She nudged me with an elbow. "Reese told everyone how you somehow could feel the people in Gladstone... and the spiders."

"Life energy," I said.

"Well, that's kind of spooky." Her laugh took any sting out of the words. "And here I thought I was just that good of an instructor. You didn't hear me at all that first night, did you?"

"No... but I'm not sure I would have thought to use my power like this if you hadn't kept plinking me in the head with pebbles."

"Annoyance is a great motivator," she agreed. "Anyway, I think the only reason Stark bothered assigning a second person to your watch shift was to make sure you stayed awake. So, here I am. Water?"

"Please." I took a sip from her canteen and passed it back. "Actually, I'm glad you came over."

"Oh yeah?" I could hear the smile that warmed Lady's voice. "Why's that?"

"I wanted to talk."

"Oh. Fair enough. What about?"

"When I made it back to Regent... you kissed me."

"The hero gets a reward," she said easily. "Isn't that how the stories go? Honestly, I've been wanting to do that for a while. I know it's usually the man who makes the first move, but I got tired of waiting. If you want to take things further though, it'll have to be when we're not on watch. Unless you're *really* good at multi-tasking."

"I'm not." I swallowed. "And I don't."

"Don't what?"

"Want to take things further. Not that you're not cool and hot and—" I sighed. "I have a girlfriend. Another Cape student like me."

"And she let you come out on the Mission for six months by your lonesome?" Lady's voice had sharpened just a bit.

"She's taking an internship with the premier team in the country."

"Dominion's Stormwatch."

"Yeah." I sometimes forgot she'd grown up in Los Angeles.

"So, she took a fancy position, and you came out into the muck with the rest of us? That doesn't seem fair."

"She wanted to come with me. I convinced her not to."

"Well, I'm not here to judge your girlfriend," said Lady, "or to cause trouble either, but expecting someone to go *six months* without any action seems a little beyond the pale. At the end of the Mission, I know you'll head back to the Free States to be a rich celebrity and media darling. I'm not looking for something long term, or even a real relationship. But a summer fling, like Emma and your friend Silt are having? Take it from an old woman: we need to find pleasure when and where we can."

"You're not that old. You're what… thirty?"

"Ouch. I'll try not to bleed all over the grass from that little dagger. I'm twenty-eight, thank you very much."

I winced. "I'm sorry."

"I can think of a few ways for you to make it up to me." She filled the ensuing silence with an uncomfortable laugh. "Or not. Do you love her, this girlfriend of yours?"

"I think so."

"You only *think* so?"

"I'm not entirely sure what love is," I finally said.

"Sweet Jesus and his little lamb, that might be the saddest thing I've ever heard." She patted my knee, hand warm even through my jeans. "So… just friends then?"

"Yeah. Sorry."

"Don't be. She's lucky to have you. Besides, it's not like the Badlands aren't full of impressionable young men looking for a roll in the hay."

CHAPTER 32

We rode along for another week or two without seeing a soul, and as hot, and dusty, and tiring as it was, I think it was exactly what everyone needed. Or at least what I needed. Hard work and no drama, with the tension of being alone in those woods, of what had felt like non-stop bloodshed, finally slipping away. It wasn't formal therapy, but with all respect to Alexa, it felt every bit as effective.

South Dakota was different. Nothing like the mountains or the forests we'd passed through; just rolling plains and hills and the occasional steep, flat-topped mound Denali called a butte. We forded more than a few streams and rivers and saw nothing but wildlife—most of it normal—as we went.

For me, heaven would always be somewhere next to an ocean, but damn if that quiet, empty countryside didn't come in a close second.

And then, one night as we were setting up camp, Denali came riding in with words for Mammoth. Minutes later, the big Power was sharing the news with us all around the campfire.

"Denali's seen signs of recent passage."

"Nomads?" asked Stark.

"Nomads," said the tracker. "Great Plains clan."

"Likelihood is we'll run into them tomorrow," said Mammoth. "If they haven't already seen our smoke. As those of you who have been this way before know, the nomads are a reasonable enough people, but they have their traditions and taboos and we cannot afford to get on their bad side. So, I've asked Denali to give us all a rundown. A refresher for some of you, a necessary lesson for the rest."

The Mission's tracker rose to his feet, features harsh in the flickering campfire, and began to talk.

A long time ago, before the Break, before the sainted Abraham Lincoln and his Pegasus, or even the birth of the United States of America at all, there had been another people living in these lands. Over the centuries, they'd been pushed back, displaced, and sometimes just plain exterminated, leaving only small regions under their control, islands of sovereignty in the wide sea of the nation that had committed genocide against them.

When the Break hit, the world descended into years of anarchy and upheaval. By the end of it, there were an awful lot of dead people, and old boundaries and laws had fallen by the wayside. The nomad clans had started out as those ancient tribes, returning to a life where they roamed the open wilderness. As time went on, they flourished and grew, joined by people of other races and cultures, people fleeing the madness of fallen cities and seeking safety in a return to nature. What evolved was a blend of cultures and beliefs like nothing that had preceded it. And now, all these years later, the nomads' territory covered hundreds of miles of what had once been the mid-western United States of America.

Denali had, as we'd learned in Regent, been born a nomad, and he talked us through the taboos for the Great Plains clan. In all likelihood, the nomads would just let us pass on through, but there was a chance we would instead be invited to a sit-down with their people, and knowing what was considered respectful behavior and what was not could be the difference between moving on or being turned back entirely.

I was left off guard duty that night. So was Lady, for that matter. Only the old hands stood watch—Stark and Denali, Cob and Mammoth himself—as if they didn't quite trust the rest of us to keep our cool if nomads showed up out of nowhere. I didn't sleep much anyway, bothered first by dreams and then by my own senses telling me we had company watching us from outside the camp.

When I found and told Mammoth, he just nodded. "I figured as much. Tomorrow, they'll either introduce themselves or quietly escort us through their lands."

Sure enough, the next day, there were three men on horseback waiting in our path, with another half dozen hidden in the surrounding grasslands, despite my eyes insisting those fields were utterly absent of life. Denali went to speak with them and when he came back, Mammoth turned to the rest of us.

"We've been invited to their camp. Remember what we discussed last night."

ooo

The nomad camp was a town in its own right, larger than anything we'd seen since Baker, and sprawled out across a stretch of fields. Instead of buildings, they had peaked tents made of some sort of hide that had been painted with varying scenes. Those tents were laid out in a series of circles, with their sides rolled up to aid air flow. The camp was busy but not hostile, and few people spared us more than a glance as our wagon train parked on the outskirts. The scouts who'd found us walked us past tent after tent.

I'd love to tell you what the clan chief was like and what he and his council had to say to the Mission, but most of us weren't invited to that meeting. Instead, Denali and Mammoth were led away into a larger tent, and the rest of us were diverted to one of the many communal campfires nearby. It was still early in the morning, but we were in late summer by then, and the day was promising to be a hot one. I kept to the outer fringe of the circle around that campfire, finding a spot on the ground to sit near Emma and Silt, and tried to take in everyone around me.

True to Denali's lessons, the nomads around us were as diverse as a Free States city, people of all colors and cultures and ages. Despite that, there was a uniformity to their appearance; the men mostly long-haired and bare-chested, wearing pants made from animal skin; the women in deerskin dresses decorated with bits of fur. Wild bison had reportedly been wiped out long before the Break, but Dr. Nowhere's dream had brought the animals back overnight, and we'd been told that it was those great beasts that supported the nomad lifestyle.

Children ran through the camp, chasing each other in noisy excitement, and everywhere I looked, there were pockets of people working; cooking, cleaning, dancing, or training with spear, bow, or axe. Several of the nearby men and women glowed brighter to my Crow's eye than the rest, a few moving with that grace unique to Stalwarts. Either the nomads had an outsized number of Powers, or those Powers had been directed to keep an eye on the travelers in their midst. We kept our heads down as instructed by Mammoth, responding courteously to the few friendly comments given, but otherwise doing our best to remain inconspicuous and inoffensive.

Guess you can figure out how well that turned out.

And who was, as always, at the center of the action.

○○○

I was looking up at the endless sky, at the birds pinwheeling through a crisp blue canvas free of clouds, when a boy, as dark-skinned as Denali, tugged on my sleeve. Like the men, he was bare chested, and although he couldn't have been much older than twelve, he had a short spear in his other hand.

"Mister, Grandfather wishes to speak with you. He asks that I bring you to his fire."

I glanced at Emma and Silt, who seemed as confused as I was. "Is that allowed? We were told to stay here."

"Grandfather is *Wičaśa Wakan*," he told me, as if I would understand what that meant. "It is permitted."

"Skeletor," murmured Silt, as I climbed to my feet. "Don't do anything too... you know... you."

"I'll do my best, but—"

"Yeah."

I followed the boy to another campfire. Unlike the circles we'd passed, there was only one person seated by the low flames, an old man in a horned hat, grey braids long enough to almost brush the earth. A brightly colored blanket was wrapped about him, and he was so close to the fire that I at first had thought he was sitting in it. At the boy's urging, I took a seat across from the old man, the fire spitting and crackling between us.

He wasn't the oldest person I'd ever seen—that would be Old Man Ricket, if you didn't include Powers-based longevity, or Amos, if you did—but there was a weight to his presence, dark eyes black and unblinking in a forest of bronze wrinkles. He looked at me, then around me, then back again, like he was peeling away the layers of my soul.

For my part, I sat there and tried not to do something that would piss him off. Grandfather or no, the fact that he'd been allowed to summon me from where we were being held suggested he was someone important. The horned hat probably had some significance too.

After a few awkward minutes, he nodded, waved a hand at the boy I'd followed over, and began to speak. I didn't understand a word of it, but as those first few words hung in the air, the boy was already translating.

"He says he has never seen a man with so many spirits following him. He asks if you are a *Wičasa Wakan* for your own people."

"I don't know what those words mean," I said carefully. Denali had told us that many of the clans had differing beliefs about the dead, and I suspected my being a necromancer would go over poorly.

Instead of translating my response, the boy thought it over. "It is something like *holy man* or *man with sight*. Grandfather interprets the dreams we experience on our quests and guides the clan."

The old man spoke again, not waiting for my reply, and again the boy translated.

"He asks when the spirits first came to you."

That was something I would never forget.

"I was nine," I replied, as the boy became part of the background, the intermediary through which we talked.

The old man nodded. "And have they ever spoken to you?"

"Twice," I told him, my eyes finding my mother and Nyah in the ever-growing crowd of the dead surrounding me.

"And was their message heard?"

I didn't quite understand that either, but I gave it some thought. My mom's vision had led to me going to the Hole, where I learned there was more to her murder than I'd thought. Nyah's vision had shown me who was responsible for the Bakersfield massacre, and I'd paid him back with a knife through the eye.

In both cases, the actual murderer was dead, but the man behind it all remained. Tyrant.

"It was heard," I finally said, "but I don't think the work is done yet."

He nodded again, and something softened in his gaze. "'It is often that way,' he says," translated the boy. "Grandfather asks that you join him on the plains tonight, under the *mahpíya*."

Context suggested that last word had something to do with the sky. Or maybe the moon or stars. "We might not be here that long."

"You will," replied the old man through his grandson. "The clan chief has much to speak of with your war chief and there are deals that will be struck."

Again, I had no idea what that meant, and again, I nodded. "Okay. I'm not sure what you want me to do, but I will do my best."

More back and forth, and the boy shook his head. "It is not about doing anything, but merely witnessing that which few will ever see." He shrugged and I knew the next words were his own. "I'm not sure I understand it, either, but he says you will, when the time comes."

The old man had already gone back to staring into the fire, but as his grandson waved me to my feet, I gave the other man a nod. The only people I'd met who could see the ghosts I brought with me were other Crows. Either the old man was hiding his madness better than most, or he was something altogether different.

I guessed I'd find out which it was later that night.

CHAPTER 33

Sure enough, as afternoon turned into evening, we received word that the Mission had been invited to spend the night. Tents—what the nomads called tipis—were offered, but the weather was nice enough that most of us made do with blankets and bedded down under the star-filled sky. I had just figured out my sleeping arrangements—close enough to the fire to ward off the night's chill but still far enough from the others to be safe if I dreamed—when the same boy was back to escort me away.

"I never got your name," I told him, as we headed out of camp, past at least a half-dozen guards I saw and another dozen I could only sense. "Or your grandfather's, for that matter."

"My grandfather?" He laughed. "Grandfather is a term of respect. We share no blood. I have been recently named Charlie Runs with Water. Our *Wičasa Wakan*'s name translates into English as Seeks Peace in Clouds."

"I'm Walker," I told him.

"Then I should be faster than you." He laughed again.

Seeks Peace in Clouds was waiting for us, seated cross-legged on the crest of a low hill that overlooked the camp. He nodded as we arrived but said nothing. I sat next to him and waited again.

The plains stretched out before us in the darkness, a few clouds hiding the moon and constellations I'd never learned to name. A soft breeze blew in from the west, and the night was quiet except for the sounds coming from the camp below us.

Seeks Peace in Clouds didn't seem in any hurry to speak, leaving me to wonder why I was out there. I didn't press the old man for answers though. Our ride had been short enough, and the rest of the day devoid of chores or tasks, that I wasn't tired at all. And if there was one thing I was good at—besides pissing people off and surviving situations that should kill me—it was sitting and staring out into space for hours on end. We were a thousand-plus miles from the Pacific, but the plains were their own kind of ocean, especially when I let go of my purely human vision and looked with my power instead. I looked out into those grassy waters, felt the emptiness inside of me stir and shift, and waited.

Eventually, the old man stirred.

"Why have your spirits brought you here?" Charlie translated.

"I'm looking for someone," I told him, even though my own ghosts had had nothing to do with my search. "The person who caused the Break."

A slow nod, but those eyes never blinked. A staring contest between Alexa and Seeks Peace in Clouds would have been a thing of legend.

"We do not call it the Break. We call it the Renewal."

The old man continued speaking at length, and Charlie listened patiently. Finally, he turned to me, his words adopting the *Wičasa Wakan*'s cadence.

"In the history of our people, when our lands were taken and our lives spent like grass on the wind, we were taught that we would one day dance a new world into being, that the white man would be swept into the ocean and the land would be reborn. The Renewal was that ancient promise made real. Although," Charlie added, as Seeks Peace in Clouds shook his head, "not exactly as envisioned."

"In the Free States, we believe those changes were brought about by one man," I told them. "A man who dreamed our new reality into existence."

"And you are looking for this man?"

I started to reply, but something had changed out in the distance, something that called to the emptiness inside of me. I turned to see what it was.

There was a noise I heard with my power instead of my ears. A rumble like distant thunder. The clouds split and moonlight poured down onto the grassy plains. That soft breeze strengthened, bringing with it smells I couldn't recognize and the occasional word I couldn't understand.

And then I saw them.

Bison. A herd a thousand strong. Ten thousand. An impossible number of beasts running as one, passing through each other and the obstacles in front of them, glowing to my sight like the ghosts in my Crow dream.

I don't do things like awe very well. This story I've been recounting for all of you should tell you that much. The post-Break world is small and petty and mean and soaked with the blood that's been shed across the decades and all the blood that will be shed when we're just bones in the earth. But there was something majestic about that sight. Something special and almost sacred, that reminded me that life, for all its tragedy and conflict, had space for beauty too, for sunlight dancing across distant waves, for the warmth of a friend's hand in your own, for moments gone in a flash that nevertheless stick with you forever.

Charlie Runs with Water was looking from Seeks Peace in Clouds to me and back, clearly unable to share in that vision. For his part, the old man had looked at me once and then turned back to the plains, to the ghost bison who roamed their ancient territory, running free like water coming down the mountain.

"Before the Renewal," Charlie translated, when the old man began to speak, "when our father's fathers spoke of the *tatanka*, they meant the spirits before you, who upon occasion cross from the great hunting grounds to ours and back. These were all that remained of the herds who once provided us our way of life."

We watched the spectral herd stampede across the plains and disappear into the distance, leaving no grasses trampled in their wake, the rumble of their passage shaking my core long after they were gone.

"The Renewal brought back the *tatanka*," continued the old man. "It returned the land to us and us to the land. And if the white man did not disappear entirely, he at least found some measure of wisdom and came to us to learn our ways. Together, we endure."

His dark eyes were great chasms in the topography of his face.

"If this dreamer exists, if the Renewal was brought about by more than our dances and the spirits of the land and air, our ancestors and the mountains who touched the sky before people drew breath, you will find him?"

I nodded. "That's the plan."

Seeks Peace in Clouds turned back to the now-empty plains, his voice barely audible over the crackle of the fire and the murmur of the breeze through the grass.

"I ask that you give them our thanks when you do."

○○○

That night, I had the dream again.

This time, I was in the plains, a tipi at my back painted with scenes of desolation. The walkers arrayed in ranks around me were human and bison, spider and wolf, swaying in place, on foot and hoof and paw and barbed leg, eye sockets as empty as my soul. The grasslands stretched out behind them under a cloudless sky, and every shimmering star in that night was the soul of someone I once knew.

I was awake and up before anyone else in the Mission the next morning, cold despite the late-summer sun. I took a seat near the banked embers of our designated fire and tried to clear my mind. The dream came every night now, its setting always changing to reflect where I was, but familiarity hadn't lessened its impact. Jimmy Taylor, the murderous Crow I'd shared a father with, had dreamed that same dream. He'd said all Crows dreamed it... that it was just another aspect of the power that drove us mad.

And if there's one thing Jimmy had known, it was madness.

It had been more than a year since the dream had started though and I didn't *feel* crazy. Tired? Yeah. Angry? Always. Alone? Well, that's the weird thing about being a Crow. You're never truly alone, but the dead make for shitty company. And if me saying that offends you, you know where the exit is. At least one of us can leave this place.

I was a lot of things, but I didn't think crazy was one of them. But I couldn't forget that urge I'd had in Reno to wipe out the men and women I'd just saved. I couldn't ignore the way my powers kept growing, or the way death followed me around like a shadow growing ever more distorted in the setting sun. The Weaver had called me the heir to bone and said I was looking for a throne. Truthfully, the Weaver had said a lot of things that didn't make a damn bit of sense, but these last few months had felt like more than just a trip, like I was changing in ways I didn't yet understand.

So, as I sat by the fire pit in the early hours of the morning, I clung to the memory of the ghost bison I'd seen. I clung to thoughts of Tessa and Kayleigh, Paco and Lynn, and the lives awaiting Sofia and I when we finished our sojourn. Most of all, I tried to find a new balance with the emptiness that continued to swell inside of me, fueled by hundreds of spider deaths.

By the time the others began to wake around me, the dream was a distant thing again, packed away into the tiny kernel of fear and pain and grief that the emptiness had originally been summoned to hide, all those years ago.

Dirt might be an Earthshaker's element, but no Power buries things quite as well as a Crow.

CHAPTER 34

Mammoth and Denali were back with us by noon the next day, and we were on our way not long after that, an escort of nomads trailing us until we were well clear of their camp. The wagons meant we were never going to go very fast, but we traveled late into the night, as if trying to make up time.

When we finally stopped, Mammoth called for a meeting.

"Sorry for the unexpected break yesterday, but the nomad clan council wanted to share some information with us. They've been seeing an increase in the number of slavers coming into their lands out of the east."

"And they need us to put them down?" asked Supersonic.

"Hardly. But the last bunch *they* put down—"

"The clans show no mercy to outsiders," said Denali, "especially slavers."

"—broke under questioning. According to them, there's a new warlord east of the Mississippi and he's looking for manpower as he continues to expand. Men, women, children; he's paying for all of them, and the slaving companies are out in force because of it. The clan has asked us to spread the word as we travel, and to keep an eye out for his troops."

"We heard rumblings about a new empire last year," said Stark. "Wonder if this is it."

"We hear rumors every year," said Cagney, "and then those empires collapse just as quickly as some other asshole decides to start swinging his dick around. That whole region has been nothing but infighting since the Break."

"Well, it sounds like things are changing," said Mammoth. "And that spells trouble, both for us and the towns we're trying to help. We're going to be relying on our scouts more than ever before. Slaver trains are easy enough to recognize, the new warlord's forces march under the banner of a bloody skull and bones, and we'll have to be on the lookout for both as we head south. I let my guard down with the bandits up north, and that's not happening again. Those of you who haven't served on watch yet will need to learn. I'll pair you up with Lady so she can get you sorted."

"What happens if we do run into slavers?" demanded Silt. "We're not letting the fuckers ride away, are we?"

"The Mission is about peace—" began Mammoth.

"There's no *peace* when people can treat other lives as chattel," said Silt.

"Exactly what I was going to say." The big Power folded his arms across his barrel-like chest. "We're not going to leave our route to go hunting, but if we do encounter a slaver train, I'm going to stomp them out, and I invite you all to join me in that pursuit."

"I didn't sign up to become some kind of vigilante," said Cob, before shooting Silt, Supersonic, and I a look of contrition. "No offense."

"Capes aren't vigilantes, so none taken," said Supersonic.

"Those of you who prefer not to be in the thick of things will stay back and guard the wagons, as always," said Stark. "Like Mammoth said, the chance of us actually encountering anyone is low."

"It is," agreed the man himself, "and I'm not going to put any of us, including myself, in harm's way unless it's absolutely necessary. But we've never encountered incursions on this sort of scale before, and I thought it important that we talk about our potential response now. For now, just keep your eyes out as we travel. Emma and I will spread the word to the mayors or councils of the towns we visit."

"Wolves, birds, and the Weaver were already bad enough," groused Reese. "Now, we have slavers and maybe even scouting forces from the east?" He ran one hand over his shaved head and tattoos and nudged Cagney with the other. "I told you the Crow was bad news."

"We had cannibals your first year," said Lady. "Following that Summoner who Stark ended up taking down. You didn't hear any of us complaining *you* were a bad omen, did you?"

"Actually, I think I might have," mused Denali.

"That was totally different!" Reese sounded almost offended.

"Sure it was."

ooo

Despite the clan's warnings, we didn't see a soul as we crossed the plains, eventually meeting up with the Missouri river and following it south out of nomad territory. And the town we eventually stopped at, days later, hadn't been bothered by slavers, bandits, or even abnormally sized man-eating animals. I'd say it was almost a letdown, but I'd already seen more action than anyone could have anticipated on this trip. Helping Lady work on another failing generator was more like what I'd actually signed up for.

Things between Lady and I stayed friendly, and when she hooked up with some Nebraskan farm boy and left the town so relaxed that she practically slid right off her horse, I gave her shit about it like everyone else. Silt's power being almost as useful on watch as mine actually made Stark crack a smile, and we adjusted to our group's smaller size until the Mission was once again operating as a well-oiled machine.

We saw other nomads too, although none brought us into their camp, and each time, Denali and Mammoth rode out to spread the word and get whatever information they could in return. At one point, we veered wide to the west, using trails the wagons barely squeezed through, after the nomads informed us that a pack of howlers had moved into the region we'd been headed for.

Killing slavers was one thing. Taking on a dozen of some of the deadliest monsters in the Badlands? That was something even Mammoth wanted no part of.

I was probably the only person sad about that. A few dead howlers under my control sounded like my kind of party.

Still, even with those few exceptions, that stretch of the journey was almost idyllic. We were out in the middle of nowhere, seeing the world, and helping where we could. It was a hell of a lot closer to what Mammoth had sold us on at the Academy than what we'd actually been dealing with since Baker. It was also almost enough to make me forget about my dreams.

And then we came across the town of Wymore.

Or what was left of it.

ooo

We saw the smoke long before we saw the town itself, thick black plumes reaching to the sky. With the wagons slowly humping along, Mammoth sent a small group of us forward. Denali, Stark, Silt, Supersonic, and me.

Caleb was back before the rest of us were halfway there, his face streaked with sweat and ash. "Whole town's gone," he said, finding Silt and me. "I couldn't see anyone left alive, but there's still a lot of smoke and fire. Maybe one of you two can sense survivors?"

"Get up in the sky," said Stark. "Let us know if you see anyone coming or going." He turned to Denali. "Tell Mammoth we're going in."

Wymore was a hell of a lot smaller than Baker, but its wall had proven just as ineffective. We rode through the shattered gate, fragments of wood and iron spread across the town's main street for almost a dozen yards in front of us. The buildings inside were mostly shells, the remnants of wooden walls and what had probably been thatched roofs still smoking.

I wrapped a bandana around my face and tried not to inhale the death of an entire town.

"Fires look like they started in multiple locations," said Stark, his eyes hard behind his own bandana. "But even so, this has been burning a while."

Silt was off her horse, with one hand pressed to the earth. "I don't sense anyone, but I don't have your range, Damian."

"I don't sense anyone but us." I stopped and frowned. I didn't sense anything for me to raise either, but there was something...

I left Cloud at the gate, the demon horse already skittish from all that smoke and still-tangible heat, and headed down the main road, almost the town's only road. There couldn't have been more than thirty houses there when Wymore had been whole, and if the town was anything like the others we'd seen, there'd be a main square of sorts. Which was where my senses were picking up something. As we neared that square, I smelled something other than smoke on the air. Something nauseating and sweet.

We passed the remnants of one last house and saw just what it was.

At one point, there had been bodies there, the people of Wymore dumped into their town's center, corpses piled high like some sort of sick offering to the gods, but that was before the fire. My power found nothing to raise because there were no bodies left whole enough to qualify... just cooked flesh, burst skin, and bones that had cracked and split.

Outside the emptiness, I felt my nausea twist and writhe like a living thing, but I forced myself to ignore it, to ignore the smell of burnt hair and skin and the disturbingly barbeque-like smells lurking just beneath. I stepped closer, into the still-fierce heat and tried to make sense of what I was seeing.

If we were in the Free States, we'd have had access to forensic teams to tell us what exactly had happened and how. Out here, we just had our eyes.

"They started this fire first," said Stark, "and then worked their way outward, starting more fires as they left."

"They?" Silt was coughing, but her voice was hard.

I pointed to the dead bodies in the pile. "Someone gathered up these bodies. And I'm not an expert on this sort of thing, but at least some of those pieces look like they were severed before the fire."

"So, someone came in here, killed everyone, piled the bodies high, and set fire to the whole town? How? Why?"

"We'll see what kind of trail Denali and I can pick up outside," said Stark. "Assuming you two still don't sense any survivors?"

Silt shook her head, but I was frowning at the pile of human scraps. Something about it was bugging me—beyond the obvious, I mean—but I couldn't put my finger on it.

"You okay, Damian?" asked Silt.

"Yeah. Just—" I shook my head. "This wasn't a big town, but... shouldn't there have been more bodies?"

There was silence, as both Stark and Silt spent a few moments trying to put the pieces on the pile in enough of a mental order to give a rough guess at the number of bodies that had been burned.

"Shit," said Silt.

"If whoever did this took prisoners," said Stark, "they'll be moving slowly."

"Then let's fucking go."

CHAPTER 35

Supersonic spotted them first, as we knew he would.

We'd waited half an hour for the rest of the Mission to reach Wymore, then taken off, following the wagon tracks Stark had already identified. Stark, Cagney, Denali, Jacobs, and all three Academy students, leaving Mammoth as the lone Power to defend our own wagon train.

Caleb touched down, looking tired. It took a lot out of him to stay up in the air for more than a few minutes at a time.

"They're an hour or two ahead," he said. "They've got a wagon and a line of people walking behind it."

"Heading for Kansas," decided Denali.

"Numbers?" asked Stark.

"I counted twelve people on horses, at least two in the wagon, and a few dozen walking."

"That matches the trail we've been following. Did they see you?"

Supersonic smirked. "If they did, I'm sure I was just one more bird way high in the sky."

"If they are paying any attention at all, they'll see our travel dust long before we catch up to them," said Denali.

It was Silt's turn to smirk. "What travel dust?"

We looked down to see that the dirt and dust kicked up by our horses was settling immediately back to the ground, rather than rising into the air.

"I thought you couldn't do that," I told her.

"Turns out it's a hell of a lot easier than raising a wall. Although I'm not sure how much I'll have left in me by the time we reach them."

"Get us there with the element of surprise, and we'll take care of the rest." Cagney's voice was hard. She'd seen the pile at the center of Wymore.

"I'll do what I can."

By the time we'd closed within eyesight of the raiders, sweat was pouring down Silt's face, but she'd kept our passage hidden. As we rounded the bend and into view behind them, you could see the surprise and panic spread. Rifles poked out of the back of the wagon, and the men on horses wheeled about to face us.

Of course, by then we were already attacking.

The people walking were, as we'd assumed, prisoners, chained together in a line that left no doubt as to the raiders' primary occupation. That left at least fourteen slavers facing the five of us in sight.

Make that thirteen. A shot rang out from the woods on the side and one of the men on horseback sagged in his saddle. A blur from the opposite side was all we saw of Supersonic cutting through the air, but another two men fell from their horses, down if not entirely out.

And then we were on them.

I was low on Cloud, hugging his neck as errant shots flew over us. He brought me in close to the wagon, and then I was leaping from the saddle in the sort of maneuver that would have had me face planting in the dirt even a month earlier. As it was, I still almost missed my jump, and had to flail about to find a handhold to pull myself up and in.

One of the rifles was already turning in my direction, but if there was one thing Jessica Strich had taught us it was that long barrels were king in the open terrain, and unwieldy as fuck in an enclosed space. In two steps, I was inside the weapon's arc. I'd needed my hand free to pull myself into the wagon, so my mace was still sheathed; I reached instead for the knife the first slaver had at his belt and drove it into his lower back as I moved past him. There were three men in the back of that wagon, and another two up front, and for a moment, it was nothing but gunfire and smoke and limbs coming from every direction.

If I'd been a Stalwart, it might have felt like a ballet, something to dance through while emerging miraculously unharmed on the other side, but there were limits to what my power could do with a purely human body. I left the first man's dagger up under the chin of a second man and took a rifle butt to the jaw from the third man for my troubles. Something tore in my knee as I fought gravity to stay upright, knowing that the bottom of the pile was the last place I wanted to be, and then I was falling toward my attacker instead of away, my one hand reaching out.

If he'd known what I was, maybe he'd have been more focused on keeping me at arm's length than on stabbing his own knife into me as I fell, but nobody in the Badlands had ever heard of me or would recognize me if they had. I collapsed into him, feeling the hot flashes of pain I recognized from my mom's own murder, grabbed his wrist, and let the emptiness go.

It wasn't enough to heal everything—that seemed to be par for the course with most Normals—but it kept me on my feet even as he fell into dust. And by that time, the man I'd stabbed in the throat had finished dying and was now rising to his feet under my command.

One of the men who'd been driving the wagon threw down his gun as I came up front, two walkers already burying his friend.

"Mercy!" he cried, eyes wide above a face of sweat and stubble.

I had my mace out by then and felt nothing at all as the steel head arced through the air to bury itself in the man's temple.

"I don't fucking think so," I told him, pulling on the reins and bringing the wagon, and the train of prisoners behind it, to a halt.

Around me, the fight was still going on, a handful of horses running around riderless as Denali and Supersonic continued to attack from the flanks. Some of the smarter raiders had scattered to the sides and the cover those trees provided and were now putting up a more organized defense.

I raised both the man whose brains I'd splashed all over the dirt and the one my walkers had brought down and sent all four of my undead minions into the knot of resistance. If all went well, they'd kill the slavers and save us the trouble. If things instead went like I suspected—

Faced with the walking corpses of their own former companions, a few of the slavers screamed and fell back, but another man stepped past them. He swelled up, almost like a balloon, and then spat forth a stream of fire that tore right through my walkers, leaving three of the four as burning piles of flesh and bone beyond even my ability to command.

I fucking knew it.

The Pyromancer turned toward me, eyes all white as he began to suck in a second breath, only to stagger backwards, a hole appearing in his head as if by magic. He collapsed, looking almost befuddled, and then my last walker was on his companions.

Stark rode past me, guns blazing, but Cagney was twenty yards back, smoke curling from her rifle as she waited for any other Powers to make themselves known.

ooo

Thirty minutes earlier, we'd been working out our plan of attack, taking lessons from the bandits who'd ambushed us outside of Regent. Denali and Supersonic would come from the sides, while Stark and the rest of us would come in force from behind.

I would get in close, if possible, and Silt and Stark would play crowd control with their shotguns, taking down anyone who made it past the wagon.

And Cagney...

"Why do you think they have a Pyromancer?" she asked. "Beyond the obvious, I mean. It's not unheard of for raiders to burn towns when they leave, and this isn't the Free States. We've got our share of Powers, but not enough to find them everywhere we go."

"He killed Red Dragon," Stark reminded her.

Which, *again,* wasn't how things had gone down, but this wasn't the time to discuss things in depth.

"If he's anything like Red Dragon, we're fucked. But I can't imagine someone that powerful would be on slaver duty. I'm not saying they have a Pyromancer, but if they do, he's not going to be immune to bullets. Having someone ready to take him out as soon as he lights up could save a bunch of our lives."

ooo

And now, thirty minutes later, the Pyromancer's body still twitching as I raised it, the value of having Cagney held back to snipe was clear.

With their leader down, and one pocket of resistance crushed, the few remaining slavers turned and fled. Shots from Denali and

Cagney brought two of them down, Supersonic ran down the last horse like it was standing still, and then the crackle of gunfire gave way to the desperate moans of the dying.

None of those dead were ours, although Stark had taken some buckshot to one shoulder, and Denali had been peppered by tree shrapnel when the slavers first returned fire on his position in the woods. For my part, my jaw was swollen and bruised, and while my power had fixed up whatever organs had been punctured, the actual stab wound was still bleeding like a motherfucker.

As much as I'd trained to accommodate my loss of a hand, I felt its lack every damn time I went into battle. Before I left Reno, I should have raised Jimmy Taylor just so I could kill his ass all over again. As it was, I made myself a promise: as soon as I became a professional Cape, with money to burn, I was going to make damn sure Lynn had whatever she needed to create a prosthetic that could actually stand up to the stresses of combat.

While the prisoners were in bad shape, their wounds had been suffered when first captured or during the march. Not a one had been hit in our firefight, which was some kind of miracle, even with Silt standing by to provide protection. Some of the captives were thinner and weaker than the others, the wounds on their wrists and ankles too repetitive to have happened in just the day or so since Wymore.

Silt confirmed that, as she came back from cutting the rope bonds. A few prisoners were gathering in groups, tears and hugs as they clung to each other for comfort, but the others just lay where they'd fallen, unwilling to even move.

"Some of these people are from Wymore," she said, voice vibrating with a fury I could almost feel in the ground beneath us. "But they said the others were already captive when they were taken. These assholes hit more than one town."

"Why didn't we see the smoke of other towns burning?"

"Rain swept through here a few days ago," said Denali, joining us even as he picked shrapnel out of his arm. "Must have put out the fires, while the clouds hid the smoke."

"I've sent Supersonic back to let Mammoth know what happened," said Stark, "but it's unlikely the others will catch up before nightfall, and none of these people are ready to travel. We'll make camp here and do what we can to care for these people before Cob arrives. Denali, what are the chances of finding something to hunt?"

"With the racket we just made?" The other man shook his head, dark braids swinging. "Any large game will have made for the hills already, but there's water not too far from here that might bring some of them back."

"Do what you can. The slavers had supplies on them, but not enough to feed all the people we rescued."

"Most of them haven't had anything since they were taken," said Silt.

Stark spat to the side. "Alright. Let's get to work." He paused and gave me a look. "Why are you still injured?"

"Everyone's dead," I reminded him. "I ate the life of one of the bandits in the wagon, but figured I'd need the rest as walkers."

Denali shivered. Without a word, he slung his rifle over one shoulder and disappeared into the woods.

"We have *got* to come up with a better term for that than *eating a life*," said Silt. "What would your old public relations consultant say?"

"Ricky?" I shrugged. "He gave up on making me marketable before that first meeting was even over."

Stark's scowl had only deepened. "I don't care if you don't feel your wounds; get that cut bandaged and wrapped. Cob can give us both stitches when he arrives."

ooo

The worst thing about the Badlands wasn't the giant-sized animals... or the monsters that bore only limited resemblance to creatures we knew. It wasn't the Weaver, the bandits, or even the slavers, although I'd happily kill every damn one of the last two groups that I could find. It sure as hell wasn't the scenery, which had its own allure, from the mountains we'd crossed in Montana and Idaho to the woods in southern Nebraska and the arid, starkly beautiful plains in between. The worst thing about the Badlands wasn't even being so far from the ocean and the Net and home-cooked meals.

It was the absolute fucking lack of backup. Wherever we went, we were constrained by the supplies we carried with us. No access to hospitals. No doctors at all outside the larger towns. No support staff or emergency crews or even overzealous government presence.

Growing up in an orphanage, I'd thought I'd known what it meant to be self-sufficient, but I'd eaten government synth-rations, worn charity hand-me-downs, and lived—sometimes in terror, admittedly—with a roof over my head.

I'm not going to say I had it good, and any of you who want to tell me otherwise can fuck right off... but life out in the Badlands was something else entirely. Total freedom, sure, but only until someone stronger came and took that from you, put you in chains, and sold you like an old pair of shoes to the highest bidder. Was it worth it? *How* was it worth it?

I don't know. Didn't know then, as the sun went down on our campsite, as we waited for the wagon train to arrive, as Cob, who'd come back with Supersonic, tended to his dozens of patients. Didn't know then and don't know now, but there's a lot of shit like that, isn't there?

Maybe I'm just stalling, as we wait here for the inevitable. Maybe it's easier to think about philosophical bullshit—about choice and consequence, the cost of freedom, the price of safety—than why you're all down here with me.

Fuck it. Let's get on with the story.

And the dying?

Not yet. Still not yet.

But soon.

CHAPTER 36

It rained that night and for three days after, torrential downpours so heavy we had to brace the lightest wagon so it didn't wash away. Mammoth made the call to stay where we were until the rain had passed, and we took the opportunity to replenish water supplies never meant to accommodate so many people. Between the wagons themselves and some huts Silt built with her power, everyone had some kind of shelter, and the people we'd rescued looked better by the day.

Physically, anyway.

The rain was still pouring down as the sun came up on the third day. I was out in the woods that flanked the road, scanning for life sneaking up on us from that direction, even as I let the emptiness of my power drown out thought and emotion.

"I know you know I'm here, Boneboy," said Silt, now just a few feet away and drenched. "Unless you're asleep, you felt me coming. Hell, maybe even then."

"If I hadn't felt you coming, I'd have still heard you."

"Yeah. Denali says all the rain should make it easier to move through the woods in silence, but I'm starting to think sneaking just isn't my thing." She found a spot on the wet leaves next to me. "Wish we had a bench to sit on."

"There's always the trees."

"You only say that because you've never seen me try to climb a tree." I could hear the grin in her words. "Why are you out here?"

"I'm on watch."

"I thought you took first shift?"

"I did. Then I woke up early and decided I wanted to take last shift too."

"Dreams?"

I shrugged. "What else is new?"

"You tell me. You've been a bit spooky lately."

I didn't turn to look at her... just watched her torch of flame shift about in the ocean of darkness and light around us. "I thought I was always a bit spooky?"

"No, you were always more *scary* than spooky. Not in a bad way, of course. Just... is everything okay?"

"I'm tired. Tired of the rain. Tired of the Badlands. Tired of people being assholes. Tired of people in general, I guess."

I didn't tell her I'd woken from my dream that morning with that same feeling filling me, the inexplicable desire to extinguish the lights of the lives around me, to surround myself in darkness, quiet and deep. It had only been a moment, there and gone, but it had gotten me out of the wagon and into the woods. Whatever this was, it apparently wasn't a one-time, post-torture sort of thing, after all.

"Between the weather, all the people we rescued, and your walkers, our camp *is* kind of overstuffed," admitted Silt. "Hard to take a step without tripping over someone. Even harder to find time and space to be alone."

"Tell me about it."

"If you want me to go...?"

"Shit. That's not what I meant. You're always welcome, Sofia. Hell, I've barely even seen you in the past week."

"Yeah."

Something about her tone resonated, even through the emptiness. I let my power go, steeling myself against the emotions that came flooding back in, and turned to look at the Earthshaker for the first time.

"Are *you* okay?"

"When am I *not* okay, Skeletor? Actually… don't answer that."

"Trouble with Emma?"

"Kind of. We've passed the halfway trip of this year's Mission. This three-day halt has been a bit of an unexpected reprieve, but at this point, every step takes us closer to goodbye. We're trying to come to grips with that."

"It's not just a summer fling?"

"I don't do flings, regardless of the season. But we both recognize this relationship will end when the Mission does. Right now, I guess our time together is a mix of trying to ignore that and trying to accept it."

"I'm sorry."

"Shit happens and life moves on. All we can do is try to leave things better than they were when we arrived. I noticed Lady's been giving you space."

"Yeah. I talked to her after Regent. You were right."

"Duh."

"She *was* just looking for a summer fling," I said, "but I think we're okay now. I hope so anyway."

"You're a decent guy, you know. And not just because of all the slavers you killed the shit out of a few days ago."

"How are *you* doing with that?"

"Honestly? I'm kind of okay. I don't know if I'm just getting used to it—and even saying that makes me feel weird—or if it's just the difference between bandits and slavers. Seeing the people those assholes had killed and the ones they were dragging through the countryside... it's kind of hard to regret ending them."

"Was Texas like this?"

"Texas is a big place, and I came from a small town on the very southern tip of it... but yeah, kind of. Slavers and warlords and assholes, and in the middle of it all, some decent people trying to live their lives."

"And you really want to go back there?"

"You're not the only one with debts to pay."

I couldn't argue with that. "The old nomad I talked to—"

"Stares at the Clouds?"

"Seeks Peace in Clouds, but yeah. He said if I found Dr. Nowhere, I should *thank* him. First time I've ever heard that. As fucked up as the post-Break world is, I think the nomads' lives are better now."

"According to Denali, they've got land and autonomy. Those are great things to have, which is probably why everyone's trying to take them from everyone else. Twenty years from now? Who knows? The Weaver already moved south, some warlord's looking west, and Tezcatlipoca keeps pushing his border up into the Free States. I can't help but thinking our generation's going to see some serious changes."

"If we find Dr. Nowhere, maybe we'll convince him to do something about that. Although it's starting to feel like a pretty big if."

"Once Mammoth decides what to do with all the people we rescued, Emma says our next big stop will be Wichita. A place that size should have a lot of ghosts for you to chat with. And if you never find Dr. Nowhere, you still did your best. Your motorcycle mama's going to understand that."

"Motorcycle mama? Is that really what you want to call the Queen of Smiles?"

"Maybe not to her face, but otherwise? Shit, yeah! Where I'm from, we don't do royalty."

"So that's why you didn't like the Baron Boner name."

She shook her head in mock sorrow. "Keep telling yourself that, my friend. Whatever helps you sleep at night."

"I'll take any help I can get."

ooo

By mid-morning, the rain had finally broken, and by noon, the clouds were gone too. Mammoth gathered the members of the Mission together to talk. He had a woman with him, tall and slender, with dark hair in a braid almost to her waist.

"For those of you who haven't met her, this is Joyce. The people we rescued have elected her as their representative."

"Temporary representative," she corrected him, her voice quiet but firm. "Only until we get wherever it is we're going."

"And that's what I wanted to talk to all of you about," said Mammoth. "The people we rescued are from three different towns in Nebraska, but from what Joyce and Cob have gathered, those towns all met the same fate as Wymore. That means they have nowhere to return to. I'd like to bring them with us until we find a town that can handle the influx of new bodies."

"Wichita?" asked Cagney.

"Most likely, yeah. Obviously, that's going to slow our pace even further, and that means more work for all of you."

"What's the alternative, boss?" asked James. "Leaving them behind?"

"Fuck that," said Supersonic.

Mammoth scanned the faces around him, and a slow smile spread across his face, as warm as the sun we hadn't seen for days. "We're all in agreement then? Glad to hear it. I'd like ideas on how we can make the journey easier on everyone."

"Denali and I can take turns hunting," said Stark, "to help supplement our food. We don't have a lot of scouts though, other than us and Reese, and we won't be able to do both. Not well, at least."

"I can pick up a scout shift," said Lady. "Maybe Jacobs too?"

The soft-spoken security officer nodded.

"I can manage an hour or so up in the air every morning and afternoon," said Supersonic, "as long as I can eat and nap afterwards. There's a lot of stuff that's visible from above that might be harder to see from ground-level."

"And if anyone does attack," I added, "we've got my walkers here to soak up the bullets."

Joyce paled at the mention of the walking dead I'd parked around the camp, but I was done depriving myself of weapons.

"That works for security and food," said Mammoth. "What are we going to do for transport?"

"James and I have been working on that a bit already," said Emma. "We've got more space in our wagons than when we started, obviously, with donations going to the towns we've passed through, but I think we can expand on that a bit. Between that effort and the extra wagon we captured, we should be able to at least carry those townsfolk who aren't up to walking."

"We only have a few of those, after these past days of rest, food, and medical care," said Joyce. "But I could work out some sort of rotation for the rest, so everyone gets a break from walking?"

"We have the slavers' horses," added Denali, "as well as our string of remounts. If anyone knows how to ride, we can rotate them onto those horses. At the pace we'll be going, we could probably even have people double up on some of the horses, but I don't recommend it for more than a few hours a day."

"Emma and I have been talking," said Silt. "I don't have the power or the energy to make full buildings every night, but I could harden the earth around the wagons so people aren't sleeping in the mud."

"Like you did coming down out of the mountains in Montana?" asked Mammoth.

Silt nodded.

"If we get another storm—and it *is* that season—we could also use the wagons and some tarps to make lean-tos," said Stark. "It'll keep the rain off those who can't fit inside."

"We'll need fires to keep everyone warm," warned Cob, speaking up for the first time. "This trip is going to be hard enough on some people without them catching pneumonia at night. If we can keep everyone fed, dry, and warm, it will go a long way."

"Alright then." Mammoth had kept on smiling through the entire discussion. "Food, shelter, transport, and security. Unless anyone has something else to add, I think we're ready."

"Actually, I wanted to say something," said Joyce. "Thank you all. I know shepherding twenty-seven strangers wasn't something you expected to be doing, and I know it's costing you time that you don't have. We've all lost friends and family as well as our homes, and we've been mostly caught up in our own grief and pain because of it, but every person here knows we owe you our lives and our freedom. On behalf of them and myself, thank you."

It wasn't an endorsement deal or my own action figure, but it didn't suck. Made me forget all about briefly wanting to kill them all that morning too.

CHAPTER 37

Traveling with the people we'd rescued was every bit as slow as predicted, and the continued bad weather didn't help. By the time we reached Wichita, everyone was tired and irritable. The fact that we'd come across another burned out town on the way hadn't helped matters. Nor did the fact that its ruins were weeks old, and any trail had long since vanished. Even though it would have slowed us down even further, we'd all been ready to take our frustrations out on another group of slavers. And I wouldn't have minded adding to my collection of walkers.

Wichita may have started out as a city, but the decades since the Break had turned it into something of a fortress, buildings rising from behind the massive concrete wall that circled almost one hundred square miles of city.

"Jesus," said Silt, as that wall came into view. "That must have taken some work."

"Literal years," said Emma, for once on a horse instead of one of the wagons. "And a few Powers, too. Wichita calls itself a free city, and they may be, when compared to places further east, but make no mistake: the Millers can be hardline. Especially when it comes to your kind, and especially after what happened to Kansas City."

"The Millers?"

"The city has a sort of monarchy. The Millers have been in control since just after the Break."

"I didn't know we had any royalty on this continent," I said, remembering Silt's comment about Her Majesty.

"Apparently, people are okay with trading freedom for security," said the quartermaster. "It's not all that different from the people who moved to the Free States."

"Except we have a democracy. Everyone gets a vote."

"And how's that working out for you?"

"Emma—" began Silt.

"Sorry. I guess it's a sore subject for me," said the other woman. "Anyway, we won't have as much time in Wichita as originally planned, thanks to all the delays. We'll drop off Joyce and her people, and then most of us will get to distributing goods while Mammoth uses the call tower to get word to Arizona and the Red Flight."

"About the Weaver?"

"Yeah, and Derek and Presley, and everything else we've run into." Emma lowered her voice. "You don't think all those charitable donations the Mission gets every year come without strings, do you? Your government needs information, and spies embedded in the Badlands have a bad habit of dying."

"And you're okay with that being part of the Mission's work?" I asked her. "It's clear you don't love the Free States."

"We do a lot of good and being quartermaster is something I enjoy. If the Free States tried to expand east, maybe I'd have a bigger problem with it, but the current arrangement works. We get to help people and your government gets reassured that nothing bad is coming their way. Everyone wins."

"So," said Silt, bringing the subject back onto safer ground, "we're not going to have any time to sightsee?"

"We'll see what Mammoth and Stark have to say, but I can't imagine there will be more than a day of free time before we head back out. Honestly, that's probably a good thing. Like I said, the Millers rule with an iron fist, and they will drop the hammer on any Power that gets into trouble."

For some reason, both women turned to look at me.

"What? I've been a model fucking citizen this entire fucking trip," I told them. "Almost to a fault."

"True, but... Sofia's been telling me stories," said Emma.

"Then you should be warning Supersonic, not me."

"Did Supersonic sneak into a dorm room with a flamethrower?"

"That was *one time*, and it wasn't a real flamethrower. And I told you that in confidence, Silt."

"Oops," said the Earthshaker, not at all repentant.

"I'm just saying... all of you should keep your heads down. Even you, sweetie," said Emma, patting Silt's leg.

"Don't worry," replied her girlfriend. "I know to pick and choose my battles."

○○○

The wall around Wichita was at least thirty feet high and almost as thick, impregnable to anything that couldn't fly. And when it came to airborne threats, Wichita's standing military stood ready, patrolling that wall with rifles. Nearby oil fields and natural gas reservoirs even insured that Wichita's manufacturing arm had continued to some extent, despite the lack of the Sparks-powered grid we had in the Free States.

Can't say it did much for the air quality though.

With the wall strictly defining Wichita's dimensions, city planners had been forced to build up instead of out, and dozens of high towers loomed over the smaller buildings around them. Los Angeles had at least ten times the population, but it was spread over a significantly larger area. After three months out in the open countryside, the city felt overstuffed to the point of excess.

As a major hub of commerce in the region, the city had its own visitors' quarters, separated from the rest of the city by another, if smaller, wall. We made our way there, riding past city merchants eager to hawk their own goods to newcomers, and found an open stall with loading zones for our four wagons.

After that, it was mostly the same shit we'd done everywhere else. Mammoth, Joyce, and Emma went to meet with representatives from the ruling family's government, both to offload the people we'd rescued and to renew the Mission's annual permit for trading in the city. The uprooted townsfolk waited in small groups, some scared, some excited, as they discussed what the future held for them. And the rest of us? We were unloading our wagons yet again, following James' instructions this time, based on what he and Emma were anticipating would be in highest demand. In Wichita, most of those crates were earmarked for local charities, food banks, and orphanages. The rest would be traded for perishable goods that we could take with us to the towns we stopped at on the way back to Arizona.

I'd already talked James into letting me be on the crew that handled the orphanage deliveries—not that he was hard to convince—but one look at Mammoth's face on his return told me my hoped-for field trip might not be happening.

"We have a problem," he announced, once Silt, Supersonic, and I had been ushered inside to speak with him. Lady, Cagney, Denali, Reese, Jacobs, and Stark stood nearby, and between the ten of us, there wasn't anywhere near enough air flow in the small, windowless room.

"Red Flight can't make it up to grab Derek or Presley?" asked Lady.

"What? No. They can and they will. Three Flyboys are starting up tomorrow to see if they can spot whatever the Weaver told Damian about. They'll grab our two wounded on the way back."

"Assuming Derek wants to come back," murmured Cagney.

"If he doesn't, he doesn't. Regent could do with a man like him as they continue their rebuild."

"What's the problem then, boss?" asked Reese.

"Aftermath had a message of his own to pass on to us, from the Free States' Secretary of Defense."

"Well, shit," drawled Silt.

"That new warlord has the government worried," said Mammoth. "Worse, their eyes and ears in Kansas City were supposed to make their way here for a report almost two weeks ago, but nobody's seen or heard from them."

"What does state espionage have to do with the Mission?"

"You know how the game is played, Denali." Mammoth spared a glance for Jacobs and the three of us. "We're not a Cape team, but our existence depends upon support from the Free States. They've asked us to go on a fact-finding mission to the city."

"I'm in," said Supersonic. "I always wanted to see what that place was like."

"It's not a field trip," warned Mammoth, "but any of you Powers would be welcome. Especially since I won't be going myself."

"Why not?" I asked.

"Too recognizable," said Stark. "It would be like walking around the city with a giant sign over our heads."

"Stark will be heading things up in my place," said the big Power.

"If Walker goes, I'm going," said Silt.

"I figured. And Jacobs along with you?"

The other man nodded, and all eyes turned to me.

I frowned. "How does Kansas City feel about walkers?"

"The same as every other damn city," muttered Reese.

"Depending on which cartel is in control of the gates, you'll probably have to leave your walkers outside, like you did here."

"So, I'll just be One-Handed Death Touch Boy while we're there."

Lady snorted.

"Until the first enemy dies, at which point you'll be the focal point of the fastest-growing zombie apocalypse ever," said Silt. "You attacked a slaver wagon with nothing but a club and came away with how many new walkers? Eight?"

"Seven," I corrected, even as a part of me reached out to where I'd parked those walkers in the woods north of the city. We were at least three miles away, but the control issues Stark had been worried about had yet to materialize. Of course, I'd known that to be the case since before we'd even entered the Great Plains, all the way back since Regent.

Truth was, I'd never released the final three walkers I'd made from the Weaver's children. One of them had vanished as they crossed the Great Plains, but the other two were somewhere in Nebraska, steadily drawing closer.

"Alright," I decided. "I'm in."

The next morning, we were on the road to Kansas City.

CHAPTER 38

"Damian! Wake up! Please!"

I woke to emptiness filling my body, spilling out of me like a cup overflowing. For a moment, I didn't know where I was, didn't know if I was awake or asleep. Even with a cloud-streaked blue sky above me, and what looked like a hawk slowly wheeling about, there was a dreamlike quality to things.

The army of dead standing around me maybe had something to do with it.

"Damian?"

I shook my head and sat up. Around me, a half-dozen bedrolls had been abandoned and discarded, and past the bodies of my walkers, I saw Silt and the others gathered.

"What's going on?" I asked her, looking about me with a frown. "And where the fuck did all these walkers come from?"

My spiders were still a long way off, but there were more walkers around me than the seven I'd raised from dead slavers. The new ones were in worse shape too, little more than bone, dirt, and decayed scraps of flesh.

"Are you awake and in control?"

"I'm talking to you, aren't I?" At a mental command, my walkers broke ranks, falling into a loose huddle behind me. Sofia's eyes were worried. "What's going on, Silt?"

"That's what we want to know," said Reese, who had decided to be part of the group going to Kansas City. Because *of course* he had.

"Stark and Cagney were on watch," said Silt. "The rest of us were asleep when—"

"These things started digging their way out of the ground," finished the other woman, eyes wide in her dark-skinned face. "I woke the others and got them away, but you weren't responding, and Mammoth warned us months ago not to touch you when you were sleeping."

"Next time, try throwing something," I said, still waking up. I looked at the walkers behind me—seven dead slavers and what looked like a family of four, complete with a child-sized skeleton. "Shit."

"Now you're using your power in your sleep?" asked Supersonic. "What the fuck, man?"

"I've *been* using my power in my sleep," I told him irritably. "That's why nobody should touch me. The walkers are new though."

"There was a farm here," said Denali. "Decades ago, by the looks of it. I found remnants of an old house foundation in the field over there last night."

"So, we slept right on top of that family's graves?"

He shrugged at me. "There are bodies all over the Badlands."

"Fantastic."

"Can you... put them back?" asked Cagney.

"I can, but why?"

"One of them's a *kid*, Damian."

I blinked at Supersonic. Part of me wanted to tell him it was just meat and bone, and that there was nobody left from the family to care… but how would I have felt if someone raised Nyah or Unicorn or my mom?

With a sigh, I brought my four new walkers together and cut their strings, taking back the emptiness I'd unwittingly dumped into them. They clattered to the ground, and even Silt looked kind of green.

"Better?" I asked.

"It'll have to do," said Stark. "Let's try to avoid a repeat occurrence when we camp tonight."

As if I had any fucking control over what happened when I was asleep. "I'll do what I can," I told him.

"Yes fucking please," said Jacobs.

ooo

Without the wagons, we made considerably better time on our ride to Kansas City, but my walkers caught up every night after we made camp. There were eight of us on the fact-finding mission, a group large enough to ward most bandits off and yet small enough that we should be able to slip into the city without issue.

On the second day out of Wichita, we'd passed another walled enclave, this one built around the strange handful of working oil pumps that the city had managed to keep operational. Armored trucks, with combustion engines and everything, were parked at the oil fields' gate, ready to carry barrels of crude back to the city where they could be refined.

It was like riding past a museum, except this museum had guards watching us through the scopes on their rifles.

Then again, I'd never been to a real museum. Maybe they were all like that? After meeting the adult Paladin at my expulsion hearing, I'd come to the realization that what we saw in vids wasn't always accurate.

Once we left the oil fields behind, it was back to the mixture of forest and open land we'd gotten used to on the way down from Wymore.

"This all used to be farms," said Denali, "but it's too far from Wichita—and too close to Kansas City—to defend. The Millers keep their agriculture operations and their herds on the west side of the city."

According to the nomads, nature had a way of taking back its land as soon as humans left it behind, but we still saw occasional evidence that people had once lived out this way. Beyond just the family I'd accidentally raised in my sleep, I mean. Rusted and decaying shells of old water towers, crumbling stone walls, even the hollowed-out hulls of old vehicles that had long since become mere ornamentation for the grass or trees growing inside of them.

We passed a blackened stretch of former prairie where even the dirt had hardened into glass. I looked to Cagney. "Pyromancer?"

"Could be lightning," she said.

"From a Weather Witch?"

"Or just a normal storm." She shrugged slim shoulders, at ease on her horse in a way I still hadn't quite managed in three months. "Fewer people out here means fewer Powers too, especially with a lot of them killing themselves or each other during the Break."

I thought of my dead slaver walkers, several miles behind us, and the Pyromancer who marched at their front. "But there *are* still Powers."

"Sure. Every new child is a potential Power, just like in the Free States. We don't have our own Academics or Finders though, and what happens to those Powers depends on where they're raised." She nodded ahead of us, where Denali had disappeared on his usual scouting run. "The nomads integrate their Powers into society if they can and kill them if they can't. Wichita puts their Powers to work for the state."

"And Kansas City?"

"Most Powers get sold to the cartels as children. Even someone the Free States would categorize as a Two is worth enough for the selling family to live the good life for several years."

"The cartels are the closest thing to ruling powers in Kansas City," said Stark, riding closer. "They started out as gangs in the Break, but over the years, they've organized and expanded. They like the city existing in a near-perpetual state of chaos."

"Are we going to have any trouble?"

Stark shook his head. "Not unless we start it. We'll pay the entry fee for each of the districts we have to visit, keep our heads down, and the cartels should leave us alone."

"Should," muttered Cagney darkly.

"Pre-Break, there was an old saying: the only certainties in life are death and taxes. There aren't any fixed taxes in Kansas City, but death happens every damn day."

"Then I'd say it's a good thing Walker decided to come along."

○○○

Kansas City defied convenient labels. Think Los Angeles if that city had two rivers running through it and half of its buildings had been replaced by tents or pavilions. Think Wichita, if its wall had fallen, allowing buildings to spill haphazardly in every direction. Think Billings, if it was ten times larger and entirely devoted to trade, most of it illegal.

The city was a big, sprawling mess of humanity, feral cats chasing fist-sized rats through the decaying streets, wagons and horses blocking roads that twisted and turned around tents that had been raised with little care and looked liable to collapse at any moment.

"The Outskirts," Stark shouted over the general hubbub. "Keep an eye on your possessions. We'll push through to the Park as soon as we can and look for the inn we were told about."

Before we could do so, we were met by a trio of heavily armed men, red bandanas conspicuous around their right biceps.

"Colors," said the lead man, as the other two spread out, hands on the revolvers holstered at their waists.

"Just rode in," said Stark. "You're the first patrol we've encountered." He handed over a few coins. "We're headed to the Park though. Here's toll for the eight of us."

Hard eyes scanned us, taking note of the weapons we'd brought and the state of our horses. "What's the purpose of your visit?"

"Does it matter?" asked Reese, spitting in the dirt.

That got the attention of all three men. The one who had spoken sent Reese a killer's glare.

"It does if I say it does."

"Rest and probably a bit of whoring," said Stark. "My crew came across some fat targets back west. Figured we deserved some celebration. If I may?" At the other man's nod, he reached back into one of his saddlebags. Something shiny dangled from his hand.

"Platinum?"

"Just silver," said Stark, "but the stones are real and worth plenty. Consider it a show of respect and appreciation for all you and the Bloods do for the city."

"This here's a man who knows how things are done," the cartel member said to his fellows, slipping the piece of jewelry into a pouch that he then tucked away beneath his shirt. He passed eight small coils of rope to Stark, dyed in red and white stripes. "Show these to any of our people you see on the street, and they'll know you paid your toll. Lose it or have it stolen, and you'll be paying that toll again. Pattern changes on Saturday, and you'll all have to pay for a new one."

"Pretty sure we'll be out of money and headed out again long before then," said Stark.

"You're probably right." The other man grinned, showing a mouthful of ivory and gold. "Might want to keep a muzzle on Baldy over there. And an eye on your Indian too. Bracelets just mean you've paid the toll. They don't give you freedom to run your mouth."

We left the cartel members behind and rode another block before Stark turned on Reese with a scowl. "What was that about?"

"Punks like that?" Reese shook his tattooed head. "You know they're never happy unless they get to throw their weight around with newcomers. I figured better I end up in their crosshairs than Cagney or Silt."

"Please," snorted Cagney. "I'd have shoved that bandana right up his ass."

"Anyone touches me, and I start ripping off pieces," agreed Silt. "Starting with what's dangling between their legs."

"Which would attract exactly the sort of attention we don't want," said Stark, giving Reese a slow nod. "Fair enough. We've got our bracelets and that means we have passage through the Park district. If we have to cross into one of the other districts, we'll be dealing with other cartels. Let's head to the inn. If nobody acknowledges the callsign tonight, we'll move on to scoping out their home address tomorrow."

"And if we never find any of the people we've been sent for?" asked Jacobs.

Stark's scar twisted as he smiled. "Then we'll be seeing what sort of information we can find all by our lonesomes."

CHAPTER 39

The inn we'd been sent to find was called the Dying Bird, which sure as fuck didn't make me feel good about staying there. It had an attached stable, and Stark paid for our horses to be put up there before we went in to get a room for the night. I couldn't help but notice that Cloud was pretending to be meek and mild-mannered as the stableboy led him away.

That demon horse had everyone fooled but me.

Stark rented a single room for the eight of us, but the creaky wooden floor didn't look any less comfortable than the ground we'd been sleeping on for months. And we were on the third floor, high enough that we felt safe opening the one window and airing out the stench of whoever had stayed there last.

Supersonic was practically bouncing off the walls over the idea of getting a drink in the common room, so Stark and Reese took him below with Jacobs to look for our contact. According to Mammoth's information, the Free States had two spies in the Park district, posing together as man and wife. They were supposed to make regular appearances in this inn every Monday and Wednesday night, which was why we'd busted our asses to make sure we arrived on a Monday.

If they were still in town—if they hadn't been kidnapped or captured or even killed on the way to Wichita—the hope was that at least one of them would show up and respond to the signs we'd been told to give. If nobody made an appearance, we'd head to the house they'd been squatting at in the morning. I'd wanted to hit the house first, but apparently strangers showing up out of the blue at a residential property was the sort of thing that might blow their cover.

"You won't have any issues sleeping here tonight, right?" asked Silt. "Dead person issues?"

I rolled my eyes. I'd gotten some variant on that question every single damn time we'd stopped for the night over the past week. Accidentally raise *one* small family, and people get fucking paranoid. I set the emptiness free and let my senses spread with it, checking the inn and then the block around us.

"Yeah, I'll be fine. Weirdly, there's not a corpse anywhere nearby that I can feel."

"Weirdly?"

"How many people must have died when Kansas City fell?" I shook my head. "I'd think this city would have even more dead buried under it than Reno."

"There wasn't anyone to bury the bodies during the Break," said Denali, taking off his moccasins and lying back on the bed he'd just shaken free of bugs. "They just piled up. Even before the city fell, there was some sort of epidemic that killed a bunch of the survivors. When the cartels took over, they paid local crematoriums to have all the bodies burned. Then, one of those crematoriums got greedy, and started digging up old graves and burning those bodies too, to keep their profits going."

"How'd that work out for them?"

"When the cartels found out, the business' owner and staff joined the bodies they'd exhumed in the cremator." Denali shrugged. "Even so, the *burn-don't-bury* policy stuck."

"It would've been nice to know that before I came here," I said.

Cagney shrugged as she pulled a deck of playing cards from her bag. "It's like Silt said back in Wichita. This is a whole city of potential walkers; they just happen to still be alive. If things go sideways, I'm sure you'll have your pick of soon-to-be-undead minions."

She smiled as she said it but didn't quite make eye contact with me. Hadn't in a long time, come to think of it… not since she'd been there to watch me take down the slavers. I glanced at Denali, but he had his hat over his face, and was now already either passed out or studiously ignoring the conversation.

Silt grinned. "Don't be lazy, Skeletor."

"Lazy?"

"What would *you* call relying on someone else to provide you with corpses to raise? At least take some pride in your power, damn it! You're supposed to be a one-stop necromancy shop!"

The Earthshaker's grin was wide as she needled me, but out of the corner of my eye, I saw Cagney shudder.

ooo

A few hours later, Supersonic brought up food for the rest of us, some sort of meat sandwiches on something flat and practically tasteless called pita bread. I could smell the alcohol on Caleb's breath as soon as he opened the door, but he seemed steady enough on his feet.

"News?" asked Cagney, tossing down the cards I'd dealt her.

"No sign of either one," said Caleb. "Reese asked the bartender if he'd seen the guy, but the description and alias didn't seem to ring any bells."

"How is *talking to the bartender* keeping a low profile?" asked Silt. "I thought the whole point of signs and countersigns was so that nobody but our contacts would realize we were looking for them?"

"He's a *bartender*, Silt." Supersonic rolled his eyes. "Not talking to him would've been even weirder. Anyway, Stark says we're going to stay down there for another hour and then call it a night. If we're still here on Wednesday, you all can take a table instead."

"Fantastic." Cagney polished off her sandwich and passed the tray back to Supersonic. "In that case, I think Denali has the right idea. Wake me when it's my time to keep watch."

As Supersonic left, she sacked out next to the Mission scout, her own hat a mirror to his.

"*Go to Kansas City*, they said," muttered Silt. "*It'll be fun!*"

"At least the sandwich isn't bad," I said.

"I'm pretty sure it's rat."

I thought about that a bit and shrugged. "I like the sauce."

She shook her head, the corners of her mouth twitching up. "Never change, Boneboy. If you and Tessa don't work out, I'm pretty sure some good Texas girl will snatch you up when we hit Brownsville."

"If I'd known it would be that easy, I'd have suggested we go there as first-years. How do you think everyone's doing, anyway?"

"Vibe and Paladin are fine, I'm sure. Only the best for the two future Defenders. I've got no worries about Evie either. I just hope she's found a new arch-nemesis by the time we're back. Having to run interference between you two gets old."

"I doubt me dragging you into the Badlands made her any happier with me." I rolled my eyes, then snickered. "Any bets on how long it took Winter to read *her* temporary team the riot act?"

"I'm sure she was on her best behavior. So… maybe two days?"

My snicker turned into an outright laugh that had the sleeping Cagney twitching on her bed. "I never thought I'd miss any of them."

"Romance has made you soft," Silt joked. "And even though you've very carefully avoided bringing her up, I'm sure Tessa is doing fine too."

"I'm sure she is. She has Dominion watching her back, after all. It's just going to be weird seeing her again… being together again after all of this."

"Tell her about the Weaver and she'll be all over you like you never even left," Silt suggested. "Chicks dig acts of suicidal heroism. The fact that you saved the coolest person she'll probably ever know in the process is just a bonus. Or is it not her that you're worried about?"

I swallowed. "Who said I was worried?"

"I get it. You were together for like a month and then you got kidnapped and taken to Reno. Five months together as third-years, and now you're apart again for even longer. It would fuck with my head too. That's why I broke up with Anita before we left."

"Yeah, but you can find a new girlfriend just turning around," I told her. "Hell, look at you and Emma."

"Fuck you very much," she replied, genuine heat in her words. "It's not easy for me."

I raised my hands in silent apology. "I wasn't saying it was. I'm just saying you're better at it than I am, with way less potentially fatal baggage. Tessa feels like a once-in-a-lifetime chance for me."

"Don't invite trouble when there's none to be had." Silt gathered up the playing cards and shuffled them. "She'll be changed by her internship, just like you're being changed by this shit-ride we've been on, but that's how life goes. I bet she's missing you every bit as much as you're missing her."

I sure fucking hoped so. "And if not, you've got hot friends in Brownsville to hook me up with?"

"Did I say they'd be *hot?*" Silt pondered the question as she dealt our hands. "I'm pretty sure I only said they'd be *good.*"

CHAPTER 40

I remember two things from that first night in Kansas City. One was waking up when Stark and the others came back to the room, supporting Supersonic as he told them some nonsensical story from his childhood. The second was some hours later in the dead of the night; voices raised in anger beneath us, the roar of people in the common room, and then what my senses told me were two fresh corpses hitting the inn's wooden floor. It was all I could do not to raise them then and there, but moments later, they were dragged away, out of the inn, down the street, and eventually out of the ever-increasing range of my awareness.

When I woke the next morning, everyone but Supersonic was already stirring. Denali and Stark had even made a trip to the bath house and were pulling on their boots.

"I take it neither of our contacts showed up last night?" asked Silt over a yawn.

"Afraid not," said Stark. "We're going to have a few of you check out their house today, while the rest of us move on to the next set of contacts. We'll be back tomorrow either way."

"Are you sure you want to split us up?" asked Cagney.

"I'd prefer not to, but the next district's not the sort of place where you or Silt can walk freely, Cagney. Not without a lot more people than we have to guard you anyway."

"It's worse than this place?" I asked. "Two people died last night after you all went to sleep… and everyone just went right back to drinking."

"The Bloods keep the peace here. For the most part, anyway. The district we're going to, the one the locals call the Zoo, is contested. That means no security or law at all. I want us in and out as quickly and as unobtrusively as possible." He licked his lips, the first nervous gesture I'd seen from Stark since he'd tried to keep me from entering the Weaver's woods. "You up for coming along, Walker?"

Silt scowled.

"Sure," I said, "but if you want quick, isn't Supersonic your guy?"

"If he wasn't hungover, maybe. If we get into the shit though, I want a heavy hitter along with us. I'm thinking you, Jacobs, Reese, and me."

Got to be honest… having someone call me a heavy hitter gave me a rosy glow inside. You'd think knowing you were a Full-Five would make that sort of offhand compliment less meaningful, but it really, really didn't.

"Leaving Cagney, Denali, and I to look after Caleb," growled Silt. "While Boneboy gets his ass in trouble. Again."

"I'll watch his back," said Jacobs. "Nobody wants him dying on the streets of Kansas City."

"I'm not big on dying on the streets of *any* city," I said. "Sorry, Sofia. You know I wouldn't—"

"It's fine. None of you are responsible for your gender's general bullshit. Besides, I bet we'll have found this district's missing contacts before you all even make it to the next meeting place."

"I hope you do," said Stark. "While you're out and about, keep your ears open for news on this new warlord. If the informants *are* all dead, we'll need whatever information we can gather ourselves before we leave."

∘∘∘

Like the Park, the Zoo was named after a landmark that had existed long before the Break. The animals that had been held captive there for unknown reasons were all long dead, of course, and it now served as the center for the black market that the district was known for. Drugs, slaves, weapons, human organs, and exotic pets could all be had for some of the coins Stark had in his bag or the equivalent in trade.

"Who makes the money here?" asked Jacobs, as the scar-faced man paid our entry into the Zoo, handing out black and white striped bracelets to the rest of us.

"There's a mint up north, across the river," said Stark, "run jointly by the cartels. The Zoo is contested territory, but the mint is truly neutral. Even if the cartels are warring, their members work side by side in peace there. When the federal government collapsed, paper money lost all value, but coins are still worth the metals they're made from, and having currency makes trade within the city a lot more viable. Traveling merchants, from tinkers to slavers to full trading consortiums, spend the proceeds of their sales on goods here that they can take back with them. Very little money ever leaves circulation."

"How do you know all this?" I asked.

"I was born here," said Stark. "Father was a trapper, and my mother was his favorite whore. She died when I was a teenager, and Dad took me out on the road to teach me how the world works. Biggest lesson came when he took a bullet to the head after getting into an argument in the old Texas panhandle. Ran with a crew down there for a bit, then encountered Mammoth in New Mexico a decade or so later. I've been with the Mission ever since."

Jacobs and I exchanged glances. We'd just learned more about Stark in one conversation than in months on the road. As far as origin stories went, Stark's wasn't going to win any contests, but I have to admit, it made me warm up to him just a bit.

ooo

Kansas City had a dozen different flavors of violence. The Outskirts had been all hard edges and suspicious glances. In the Park, the violence had been more overt; hands on holsters, dead eyes daring the world to draw, a palpable tension buried just beneath the surface and primed to explode.

The Zoo didn't bother with the pretense of civility. In that first half hour, we saw three people shot in the streets and a fourth beaten to death by two men half again his size. The district had an odor to it: part piss, part blood, part despair. The men and women loping through the trash-stricken streets, slinking between shadowed shells of broken buildings as they kept pace with our group, barely seemed human at all, moving with animalistic grace, staring eyes, and teeth that, if they had any, were almost inevitably filed down to sharp points.

"Scavengers. This is worse than I remember," muttered Stark. "Stay ready. Even with our entry passes, someone is going to test us to see if we're easy meat. If we'd brought Cagney or Silt, we'd already have been attacked." He turned to me. "Don't raise anyone unless you absolutely have to. Walkers in the Zoo would be a great way to piss off every cartel in Kansas City, and we can't afford that."

"How far to the Unwanted Bastard?" asked Reese, naming the inn that was supposed to be our next place of contact.

Got to be honest... I didn't like that inn's name any more than the one our horses were still stabled at. I had a bone to pick with the business owners of Kansas City.

"Shouldn't be more than another twenty minutes if the roads haven't changed too much. Once we get there, we'll be fine. Every inn's going to have their own security. It's bad business otherwise."

I wondered to myself where the Dying Bird's security had been that night when people died... but for all I knew, it had been the security doing the killing.

And then two men stepped into our path, and the time for wondering was over.

"Your money or your lives," said the smaller man wearing a white motorcycle helmet that was considerably more scuffed up than Her Majesty's. His visor was up, and his grin was wide, showing us every one of the handful of pointed teeth he had in his mouth. The man behind him was Normal, given the dimness of his spark, but tall enough to be a Titan and wide enough to eat Cloud for dinner.

"We're not looking for—" began Stark.

"Oh hell, who am I kidding?" The little man's grin turned vicious. "We're taking both."

With wild screams, a dozen of his fellows charged us from all sides.

The boom of Stark's pistol sounded, followed closely by a similar shot from Reese and the staccato dance of Jacobs' rifle. Just like that, four scavengers were down, leaking fluids onto the dirt road. We'd known they were out there, of course, known that when an attack came, there was every chance it would be preceded by a distraction. But the streets were tight and narrow and after that first volley, the scavengers were on us, wielding everything from nomad hatchets to clubs to shards of glass that cut the wielder even as they stabbed.

Our close combat professor, Nikolai Tsarnaev, had always told us to watch out for amateurs because you never knew just what they were going to do, but it didn't take a genius to step out of a charging scavenger's path, and there was nothing unpredictable about the way my mace shattered his skull. I was out of position to block the next scavenger's attack, so I side-stepped instead and kicked out and down at the knee of his planted leg. And then, as he fell, I caught his face with my knee.

That should have been enough to give the third man pause, but whatever he was high on had supplanted higher brain functions. I ducked under the wild swing of his hatchet and drove my mace up into his elbow like I was planting a tent spike into the ground. Somewhere outside the emptiness, I felt a sense of grim satisfaction, as his arm snapped, but I was already rising from my crouch, stepping inside that flopping arm to introduce my weapon to his face. His screams ended in a shower of blood and teeth, and then he was down in the dirt with his friends.

I risked a glance at the others. Reese had a bowie knife in his hand and was dancing with a scavenger who didn't know how to take advantage of the reach his short spear gave him. Jacobs and Stark had cleared some space and were back-to-back, shooting as scavengers continue to pour out of the buildings around us. I couldn't help but notice that Jacobs was taking single shots now, preserving his ammo in the face of unknown numbers.

The shadow that fell on me was my first warning that I'd stupidly let myself get distracted in the middle of battle. It was also almost my last mistake. I dropped to the ground, letting the bodies beneath me break my fall, and then rolled to avoid the steel mallet that made soup of the men I'd just taken down.

Or maybe it was stew. I'd never been entirely sure what distinguished the two.

I blinked gore out of my eyes and was back on my feet, the wound I'd taken a week earlier against the slavers now torn back open and bleeding freely. The two scavengers who had initially greeted us had joined the battle, the big one with the mallet that had almost ended me, the smaller with a long knife in each hand.

I dodged the mallet again, accepting a knife slice across my leg as the price of survival, and tossed my club into the little man's face. He dodged like a fucking monkey, taking the projectile on the side of his motorcycle helmet, but I'd been expecting that.

Really, I just needed my hand free.

I waited for a third, thunderous swing of the mallet—the Viking could have shown this asshole a thing or two about how to *effectively* use an oversized hammer—and darted in to tap the big man on the hand.

The little man's eyes went wide as I stepped through the cloud of dust that had been his muscle, and he scrambled to his feet.

"Power!" he screamed, the noise piercing enough that it was audible even over the sounds of gunfire.

I took a step toward him, but he was already running, weaving through the detritus and rubble like it was an obstacle course and he the city champion. His fellow scavengers… the ones still alive at least… did the same, and twenty seconds later, the street around us was clear of attackers.

Reese was panting like he'd just run a marathon, and Stark had picked up yet another wound that would no doubt scar, but none of us were seriously injured. In fact, the energy I'd gotten from the big scavenger had been enough to heal both my week-old stab wound and the slice I'd just taken from the scavengers' leader.

"It's too bad your power doesn't clean you when it heals you," said Reese, face slightly green as blood and brain matter dripped off my body.

"You're one to talk. Did you just stand there while the last guy bled all over you?"

"You both can clean up when we reach the Bastard," said Stark. "In the meantime, let the Zoo see what became of the last street gang to step in our path."

CHAPTER 41

We got a few looks as we made our way through the Zoo, but not nearly as many as I would've expected, and none of these people looked a second time. We reached the Unwanted Bastard sometime in the late afternoon, and although the armed guards out front gave Reese and I dead-eyed stares, they didn't stop us from going in. The place was only one story, and more tavern than inn, with a common room up front, and a kitchen and bar splitting the back half of the building with several small private rooms.

The bartender was a small man with a face that reminded me of Paco's pet rats, but his hands were steady as he directed Reese and I past the bouncer and the private rooms he was guarding to a bathroom. Given the noises we heard from the rooms as we walked past, I was pretty sure they weren't for eating. Or sleeping.

To my amazement, the bathroom both had a shower and looked like it might have been cleaned sometime in the past week. Reese and I took our turns in that shower, still fully clothed, as the cold water washed blood and gore down a drain that had probably seen a lot worse. There were no towels, of course, but the Unwanted Bastard's only ventilation was a single partially opened window in the street-facing wall, and the interior was so warm that we'd be dry in no time. The whole place also smelled like Muse after a bender, but I figured the bartender and his armed guards already knew that.

Stark and Jacobs were sitting at a table when we came back, four mugs in front of them. I couldn't decide what was cloudier... the beer or the glasses holding that beer. Either way, Stark's warning not to drink it was entirely unnecessary.

"Doesn't look like there's any place to stay here," Reese told the older man. "Are we headed back to the Park if nobody shows?"

"The second address we were given is about five minutes away," said Stark. "If nobody shows, we'll head there. We'll find our contacts, or we won't, but either way, we'll have a roof over our heads. Walking all the way back through the Zoo at night is just going to get us all killed." He spared me a glance, that scar twisting his smile into its own breed of scowl. "Most of us, anyway."

"We could always keep our table for the night, if it came to that," said Jacobs, eyes scanning the interior. "This doesn't seem like the kind of place that ever shuts its doors."

"If we have to, we will," agreed Stark, "but house policy is every table has a minimum spend of one round of beer an hour. And we don't have so much money I want to throw it away on alcohol we can't even drink."

"Is that... meat in my beer?" asked Reese, nose wrinkling.

"If you're lucky. However this place makes its money, it's not because of its drink menu."

"It's a brothel," I told him. "One for the really, really desperate, I think."

Stark nodded. "Prostitution's a good side gig in Kansas City. But those few rooms wouldn't bring in enough to pay for all these guards. I'm guessing they have something else going on too. Maybe an arrangement with one of the cartels."

"Glad we've got these then," said Reese, rolling up his wet shirt sleeve so that both bracelets were showing. "So, what do you think, boss? Two hours until we go scope out the house instead?"

"Sounds about right."

With a grin and a wink, Reese nodded to the deck of worn playing cards in Stark's front shirt pocket. "Guess we'd better get some hands going then."

ooo

As the day turned to night, the common room gradually filled up, but it remained a far cry from the Dying Bird's level of business. A handful of people who looked even worse than we did settled down at different tables, drowning their sorrows in beer that was chewed as much as sipped, but the majority of customers made a beeline for the back rooms, returning five, ten, or twenty minutes later, their scowls just a little bit less prominent.

We'd paid for two rounds of drinks, untouched glasses collecting on the table in front of us, before Stark decided our contacts weren't going to show here either. As we left the inn, a brief brawl broke out as drunk men fought over the beer we'd left behind.

The sun had long since set and the violent squalor of the Zoo took on even more malevolent tones under the waning moon. Working establishments had kerosene lanterns hanging out front, and the flames kept the surrounding shadows in perpetual motion.

"Weapons out," murmured Stark, once we'd left the Unwanted Bastard's guards behind. "There's a lot worse than scavengers out at night."

Despite that feeling of impending doom, the sparks of life I sensed—the rats outnumbering the cats and humans by a factor of ten to one—steered clear of our party. Six minutes later, we were at the address we'd been given, and Stark's curses, whispered but heartfelt, split the silence.

We'll find our contacts, or we won't, but either way, we'll have a roof over our heads. That's what the man had said.

Problem was, the address we'd been given didn't *have* a roof. In fact, it only had one wall, and even that was partially collapsed. Where a house had once squatted between its neighbors, like a fat rich kid squeezing his way onto an already-full bench, there was now only rubble.

"Fire?" asked Reese.

"Not unless it was from a Pyro," I said. "Those other buildings are untouched."

"It collapsed inward," said Jacobs, "so it wasn't a bomb."

"Either way, the Zoo is a bust," said Stark. "Back to the Bastard. We can figure out what to do there and then return to the Park and the Dying Bird tomorrow morning."

"Think there's any chance we can get something that *doesn't* have things growing in it to drink?" Reese sounded as irritated as I felt.

"We'll see," came the reply. "If we're spending the night, we might be able to work out some sort of arrangement."

I sure fucking hoped so. Two days in Kansas City now and all we'd found were dead ends. If the Free State's spies were dead or gone—and that shell of a house made the first one more likely than the second—what exactly were we supposed to do?

Something that sounded an awful lot like a howler brought down a victim in the street, but we made it back to the Unwanted Bastard without issue. The door guards had their guns out and ready. One of them turned in our direction even before we entered the tavern's circle of light, goggles turning his face into something alien.

"Night vision," said Stark. "Must have been stolen from a nearby base, decades ago. I'm surprised they're still working; the Bastard *definitely* has cartel ties."

The common room was fuller than when we had left, but we found a new table without issue. A party of three was singing drunkenly by the bar, empty mugs in front of them. Women in leather collars and not much else had draped themselves over the laps of two men and one woman in fatigues at a far table, and the bartender had been joined by a waitress wearing only marginally more clothing than the prostitutes.

Sex work was a thing in the Free States, and if it wasn't a particularly well-regarded profession, it wasn't all that taboo either. But brothels were inspected and licensed by the government, ensuring that the people involved—clients and professionals—were healthy and treated appropriately. The Badlands didn't have that, as far as I knew, and even if they did, the Zoo sure as fuck didn't, judging by the bruise across the face of one of the three prostitutes.

I'd never be a Dominion or even a Mammoth... someone who put everyone else first. I'd spent most of second-year talking to Alexa about that very concern, about the insanity of choosing to put your life on the line for assholes you didn't even know. Maybe doing just that in Reno meant I'd turned a corner on that debate, but I wasn't so sure. Seemed to me it was a decision I'd have to make again and again... to keep making throughout my professional career.

The one thing that I've always known though?

I fucking hate bullies.

"What's going on?" asked Jacobs.

Stark and Reese were having a talk with the bartender, but my eyes were fixed on that far table. The battered prostitute had her stringy hair down to try to cover that bruise, but I could see her wincing every time her john stole a kiss.

"If you're trying to attract attention, sending death glares across the room is a great way to do it."

"I don't like assholes who slap around the powerless," I said, teeth gritted as one of the two men at that table laughed and tossed back a shot of something clear.

"How do you know she didn't ask for it?" Jacobs shook his head as I turned my glare on him. "Not in that way. Some people are actually into the rough stuff, whether it's giving or receiving."

"And if she's not?"

"That's my question to you. Are you going to kill everyone who's ever mistreated a whore in the Badlands?"

"Not everyone," I said, eyes drawn back to the table in question. "Just the ones I come across."

"And then what? You kill this man and his two friends and the guards who respond, play the knight in shining armor for a woman who's looking at payday... and then? Assuming the bartender doesn't throw her out on her ass for costing him business, and all the people you kill don't have friends that come looking for revenge... do you really think this won't happen again to her next week?"

"So, we should just pretend we didn't see a fucking thing?"

"Yes," said Stark, putting a dusty bottle of something clear on the table between us. "You keep your head down and your nose out of other people's business, so you don't get the rest of us mere mortals killed."

"I thought the Mission was all about helping people?"

"Some cities are beyond help. Some people too." The scar-faced man shook his head and poured measures of liquid into the four glasses—glasses that were almost clean—Reese had brought from the bar. "Look around you; the guards are here to keep the peace *and* to protect the merchandise. Let them do their job and save this hero shit for when you graduate from your school."

I didn't like it. I *really* didn't like it. But this time, I was pretty sure Stark was right. I sent the table one last dead-eyed glare and turned to the drink in front of me. "Vodka?"

"Gin. The owner makes it himself, apparently."

Reese tossed back his shot and shook his head like he was trying to clear it. "Damn, that hits hard."

"Which is why you shouldn't drink it all at once," said Stark. "We're going to be here all night, and I'm not paying for another bottle. Or carrying any of you back to the Dying Bird."

ooo

Sometime later, I made my way to the bathroom at the end of the hall. The table I'd been watching had picked up a third prostitute, this one male, and then all headed off to the private rooms, and I ignored the sounds emanating from those rooms as I walked past. I wasn't drunk—only Supersonic was dumb enough to get sloshed in the middle of a hostile city—but I was definitely feeling the effects of the gin we'd had, my thoughts a bit muddled, my bladder filled to the point of bursting.

I pushed open the bathroom door, stopped, and blinked. In addition to the shower Reese and I had used earlier, there was a sink, a urinal, and a stall with a toilet. The stall was occupied; the fatigues-clad woman from the table I'd been glaring at earlier in the night had her pants and underwear down around one ankle. The camo shirt was still on, but lifted enough to expose one small breast, and she was riding the male prostitute seated on the toilet behind her like he was a horse and they were both being chased by howlers. Her legs were skinny and pale, a counterpoint to the man's red, sweat-streaked face.

One more item successfully crossed off my *never fucking wanted to see that* list. And I'd thought listening to El Bosque and Ember as first-years had been bad.

I ignored the kiss the woman blew in my direction and went to do my business. As always, taking a piss at a urinal with only one hand was an adventure. By the time I was done and washing that hand at the sink, they were finished too, the woman cursing loudly as she came. Moments later, she stepped out of the stall, pants back on, and flashed me a humorless grin. Unlike most of the Zoo residents I'd seen so far, she had all her teeth.

"Hope you enjoyed the show, kid." She pulled her naked man whore to her side and gave him a casual grope. "If you feel like joining us in the shower, I might see fit to toss a few coins your way too."

I shook my hand dry, as dry as it would get without a towel, and turned to go. "I'm not interested, but thanks."

"You sure? Guy eye-fucks a group as much as you were earlier, I figure he's either really horny or he has himself a problem."

I let the emptiness fill me, chasing away the anger that might have had me saying something stupid in response. "No problem at all," I said instead. "I'll leave you two to your fun."

"Really? You're just going to walk away from all *this?* And here I thought Powers had balls."

I was reaching for the door handle when the fact that she somehow knew I was a Power sank in through my partially inebriated brain. As I turned back, the bathroom door blew open behind me, catching me right between the shoulder blades and sending me stumbling forward. My power did its best to fight gravity, but the woman shoved her boytoy into my path and we both fell to the side. I smacked into the sink with an impact I felt in my kidneys.

I pushed the prostitute roughly away, but he dropped to the floor like he'd been shot, tangling my legs even further. The woman now had a sap in her hands and lunged forward. Even with my feet tangled, I twisted enough to take the blow on my shoulder instead of my head, but I was trapped between the sink and the urinal with nowhere to go. I reached out to grab her wrist, but she was already pulling back out of range.

Which was when the man who'd kicked in the bathroom door finally came through, a nightstick swinging for my temple.

Off balance and overextended, reeling from the blow to my shoulder and with my feet still tangled by a prostitute clearly doing his best to hamper my movements, I couldn't dodge that strike. Light exploded behind my eyes, and I dropped like I'd been sucker punched by a Titan, my head bouncing off that same piece of shit sink on the way down.

And then everything was darkness.

I blame the fucking gin.

CHAPTER 42

I opened my eyes on a war-torn sky, clouds bleeding across monochromatic grey, the sun a wan and distant thing, as if desperately trying to avoid attention. Birds the size of cars swooped through the air, feathers falling away from wings of bleached bone.

The city spread around me like a rat's nest, trash and ruin left behind by those who once lived there. Walls reached drunkenly to the sky from a carpet of destruction; fallen rooftops and fire-scorched pathways.

I came to my feet, shook a dozen bracelets from arms that had no need for adornment, and stepped outside the wreckage of a building I didn't recognize.

The dead were waiting, like I knew they'd be, rotting flesh hanging from bone, walkers in buckskin and camo and nothing at all, lined up through the streets of a fallen city, heeding my call, here to watch my ascension, here to pay tribute to my reign.

Behind them were the spirits: Sally and my parents, Nyah and Mama Rawlins, the bandits outside Regent, the slavers of Wymore. And so many more. Thousands more. Hundreds of thousands, their glow washing away that tired and dying sun.

I looked upon what I had wrought, upon the dead and the risen, and knew contentment.

○○○

"Howard? What the fuck?!"

"What happened?"

"That's what I want to fucking know! We were just carrying him and now Howard's a fucking pile of dust on the fucking street!"

"We told you both he's a Power. Maybe in his next life, Howard will listen. Don't let him touch you and you'll be fine."

"Are you kidding me? I'm not getting anywhere near this asshole again!"

"Are you sure that's a choice you want to make?"

"Hey… hey now… there's no need for that. I was just playing. Honest. I said I'll help move him and I will."

"That's what we like to hear."

"It's just…"

"What?"

"I think his eyes just moved."

"Shit, so they did. Hey Bones, hand me your nightstick?"

○○○

The next time I woke, I was kneeling and shackled, manacles around my ankles and one wrist. For an awful, haunting minute, I thought I was still in Tyrant's lab, the past months nothing but the fancies of a shattered mind. Then, I realized I was chained to the wall instead of the floor, and there was a level of noise I never remembered from Reno. Voices murmuring. People crying. Doors slamming shut somewhere in the distance.

I opened my eyes to a world that swam about me. If I'd death touched someone in my sleep—if any of that had actually happened—I hadn't gotten nearly enough energy back to heal the damage I'd taken.

Or my captors had undone all that healing in their haste to send me back to unconsciousness.

I'd had enough concussions during my time at the Academy to recognize this one. This time, there wasn't a kind-hearted Healer waiting nearby to make it all better, but that was okay.

I was in the mood to kill some assholes.

My eyes were struggling, but my nose worked just fine, informing me that I reeked, that someone had vomited nearby, and that there were too many unwashed people all squeezed into too small a space. But honestly, that summed up my entire Kansas City experience so far. I needed more detail to go on.

I tried my eyes again, and this time they stayed open. The room I was in was about half the size of one of the Academy's classrooms but looked smaller thanks to the sheer number of people that had been stuffed inside. It looked like it had been days since their last meal and even longer since their last shower. And every damn person was in chains, either shackled to the wall, like me, or to hooks in the ceiling that seemed to have been installed for just that purpose.

The man nearest me snarled and snapped his teeth, saliva dripping off his unshaven chin. He wasn't the only prisoner in that room who seemed feral, but none of them could reach me, so I ignored them and kept scanning the room. A barred door in the far wall again brought unpleasant Reno flashbacks, but I ignored those too, focused on figuring out where I was and how I was going to get out of here.

Ten minutes later, I still didn't have answers to either of those questions, but I *had* solved one mystery. Apparently, *I* was the person who had vomited... I could feel the disgusting mess—mostly gin— soaking through my jeans.

Fucking hell.

The good news was that there were no dampeners running. The bad news was that apparently my captors had known not to let me touch them. Given that I'd only used my power once since entering the city, that meant there had to be some sort of connection between the surviving scavengers and the camo-clad goons that had captured me. And given that Stark and the others hadn't prevented that capture, I was guessing they were dead. That or they somehow hadn't heard the noise of me getting my ass kicked.

Then again, given Stark's attitude when Silt was taken, maybe the scar-faced asshole had just chosen discretion over valor. Again. Silt would move heaven and earth—literally, in the latter case—to get me back, but I couldn't wait on her or anyone else to save my ass.

Luckily, I didn't have to.

I fought off another wave of nausea and closed my eyes, setting the emptiness loose. Wherever the crematoriums were, they were a long way away from me, and there were no nearby dead to raise. Instead, I reached to the walkers I already had. My spiders were still several days away, but I'd parked the dead slavers just outside of town. I reached out to them, six dead Normals and a Pyromancer, and called them to me.

Stark had said walkers would piss off the cartels.

I was okay with that.

It must have been night, because my walkers traveled a good distance before one of them crumbled. Bullets or fire or a Titan with a maul... whatever had caused it, I was already down a walker, and my minions were still a hell of a long way from where I was being held.

I ordered two of them to fight back against whatever was attacking them, and the other four to keep on going. Not sure if I killed any innocents on the way. Not sure Kansas City even *had* innocents but instructing the walkers to only attack those who attacked them was the best I could do, chained up in this room with twenty-five other prospective slaves.

Whoever it was that paid the price for my walkers' steady parade, I was confident I'd see their ghosts soon enough.

ooo

It had taken us a half-day to reach the Park and another to reach the Zoo, and wherever I'd been stashed, I was at least that far. Even running at full tilt for hours, my walkers were still multiple blocks away when the door to our pen cracked open.

I recognized the woman who stepped through from our unfortunate encounter in the bathroom. Now, she was fully clothed and standing ramrod stiff, a beret in deep red sitting jauntily on her head. The man next to her was new; whipcord thin, with a face like a hatchet and a mustache that did nothing at all to soften his features. He too was in fatigues, but was missing the beret, steel-grey hair buzzed short atop his head.

They made straight for me, the corners of the woman's mouth turning up slightly when she noticed the puddle of vomit I'd found myself in.

"This is him?" asked the older man. "Are you sure?"

"Yes, sir. Slive said he was a Power, so we backtracked their path to the Bastard and waited."

"Slive is a notorious coward, thief, and liar." The man's voice was sharp and every bit as thin as his moustache. "Has there been any confirmation?"

"He ashed one of the men who was carrying him in," she said, raising her hands at the other man's sudden raised eyebrows. "A local, sir. Not one of ours."

"Excellent." He was studying me, beady eyes bright. "When you say *ashed*, what exactly do you mean?"

"The day laborer made the mistake of touching this kid's hand, and the next thing you know, he was gone. Just a pile of ash and dust in the street."

"A fire bringer of some sort?"

"Or possibly an energy user, sir. He doesn't seem to be able to project that energy, whatever it is, but if he lays a hand on someone…"

"Interesting. The fact that he has only the one hand hampers his usefulness," mused the man, "but it is still something. Well done." Finally, he squatted down and spoke to me instead of over me, carefully out of reach of my one free arm. "Do you know who we are?"

"Corpses," I told him.

"Charming. In fact, we are the vanguard of the Crimson Queen." He tapped a patch on his shoulder, a bloody skull sitting on a pile of equally bloody bones. "She seeks men and women for her legion. A Power like you could have an exalted position in that army."

"And if I tell you *and* her to fuck off?"

"Then we will break you and eventually you will serve anyway. If you were a Power of real significance, maybe I would grant you more than this one chance, but a one-handed energy user is of limited value. By the time our technicians are done, you will only be fit for the front lines. A tool, just like these other sad people, to be used and quickly discarded. Or you can make something of yourself. Join a cause greater than your own and maybe you too will find yourself commanding a company someday. The choice, of course, is yours."

I locked eyes with him and smiled. "This continent only has one queen. I bet she's dying to meet your pretender."

"Fascinating," he said, words dry, before turning to the woman. "Who do we have available? Carlos?"

"You gave him a prisoner yesterday, Major," she reminded him. "I believe Edmund will be free this afternoon though."

"Very well. He'll have this one sorted in no time. Inform him of his new assignment and make sure he is aware of the prisoner's abilities." He rose to his feet and shook his head pityingly at me. "The next time we meet, young man, you won't even remember your name.

As the agony begins, however, I do ask you to remember one thing: you chose this."

He turned and left, the heels of his shiny black boots slapping against the concrete floors. The woman stayed behind for just a moment, her bright smile never touching her eyes.

"You should have taken my shower offer, kid," she said. "A little bit of pleasantness before the pain."

"Torture is a hell of a lot more appealing."

I grunted as she drove her own boot into my unprotected side, but as she stalked from the room, suddenly stone faced, the smile she'd lost made its way onto my face.

CHAPTER 43

There's nothing convenient or easy about remotely piloting zombies. If I'd had to do more than call them to me, I'm not sure it would have been possible, but even with the major issue of direction taken care of, my walkers *still* hadn't reached me when more camo-wearing goons arrived to drag me to a meeting with my so-called technician.

I waited for them to remove the chains, but instead, they just unhooked them from the wall, shoved some sort of prod in my back, and forced me to walk, chains and all. Encumbered as I was, I didn't give myself much chance against two armed guards with advantages in reach, weaponry, and usable limbs, so I let them march me out of the slave pen and down a long hall to a small room with a steel recliner, an overhead light, and nothing else.

"Get in the chair," said the first guard.

"Only because you asked so nicely." The floor was angled down towards a wide drain in the center, and I tried not to trip as they pushed me to the chair.

"The mouthy ones always scream the loudest, don't they?" he asked his fellow guard.

The other man just grunted, waiting until I was seated to wrap thick leather straps about my wrists and ankles. He was careful to stay away from my left hand, even though he had gloves on to prevent skin-to-skin contact. Once the straps were in place, the guards removed my chains, and waited.

I was waiting too, but my walkers were at least a quarter mile away, and had run into some resistance. The original seven were now down to four, and I felt another one disappear from my senses. This time, they were close enough, however, that I could feel new corpses appearing around them. I sent the emptiness into those distant receptacles, and three became six again, and then five, and then seven, as my power warred with the attrition caused by whatever battle was raging.

When the door opened again to admit a short, slim man in glasses and a smile that didn't belong on anyone with a soul, I knew my time was up.

"I'll take things from here, gentlemen," he said, eyes bright under thick black eyebrows.

"Be careful, sir," said the first guard, his tone now respectful. "This one's got some fight still in him."

"I have been apprised of both the subject's abilities and his defiant nature," said the man I assumed to be Edmund, that shark's smile still locked on his face. "If you could bring in the cart before you depart?"

"Sure thing." The two armed guards headed out, like I'd been hoping they would, but not before doing as requested. The cart was all steel, like the recliner I was strapped onto, and one of its four wheels screeched as it rotated, a high-pitched sound that sent ice down my spine. The fact that I hadn't heard it until now told me this room was heavily insulated for sound.

"You should get that oiled," I told him.

"I find it sets the ambience rather well, as is," he told me, bringing the cart closer. "Man has five senses, after all. It would be shortsighted to ignore any of them in my work."

I probably should have had some sort of defiant comeback ready, but the cart was close enough now that I could see what was on top of it. Some of the implements were new, but I recognized others from my time in Reno. Blades, mallets, spikes… even something that looked like a tiny guillotine… the chills down my spine spread and I felt the emptiness shiver.

Just that quickly, my walkers paused, and another one went down.

I breathed out, a long slow exhale that took my sudden panic and fear with it, and felt the emptiness solidify, my walkers moving again to answer the renewed call.

Edmund nodded as he watched my face. "When they told me you were already missing a hand, I suspected this might not be your first time under a torturer's tender mercies. Rest assured, I am not as crudely barbaric as whoever cut that off. It will be my privilege to show you the subtler side of this great and ancient art."

He reached for a scalpel, but even as I tensed to try in vain to avoid the blade, he drew it down my body in quick strokes, avoiding flesh as he cut away what remained of my shirt. Given that that shirt was stained with both day-old blood and recent vomit, I didn't even regret its loss. If I got out of this alive, the Academy could damn well pay for another one.

"So many scars," said Edmund, eyes glistening wetly. "And in such odd locations, too. I take back what I said about whoever did this to you. Not a technician, of course, but they were at least a truly gifted amateur."

"I'll tell him you said so," I managed through gritted teeth. Truth was, only some of those scars were from Tyrant. The rest were a result of my power-given healing. Gladys might be able to use her power to stitch a person back up without scars, but mine wasn't nearly as concerned with aesthetics. The past few months on the road had given me my share of new scars, bright and shiny across my flesh, and I'd spared more than a few minutes to worry what Tessa would think of them.

Now, I just hoped I'd make it back to her in one piece.

My walkers were *still* distant. They were making more headway now that I could reinforce their numbers every time one of their attackers died, but I had no idea how deep we were in this building, or how many guards they'd have to fight through once they reached it.

I was pretty sure I'd be a bloody pile of flesh before they did.

I breathed out again as Edmund went to work, grateful for the lack of dampeners and the emptiness that muffled the pain, and let my power drift out around me again. There were no human corpses within a block of the building, but I already knew that. I looked for smaller receptacles this time. An undead cat had saved my life once, after all.

Instead, I found two dead rats in the alley outside, which gave me fresh minions and a better idea of the dimensions of my prison. They scurried about looking for a way in, but I was digging deeper already, looking for anything else that could help.

Edmund took a careful step back, shaking his head, his shark's smile giving way to a look of confusion. "I am not used to being ignored, even in these early stages. Perhaps you learned something from your talented amateur after all? Let's try electricity instead."

I paid him no attention, my conscious mind accepting and dismissing his words as so much noise. I was focused instead on what I'd found; tiny pinpricks of emptiness in the dark-watered ocean surrounding us. Smaller than humans, or cats, or even rats... something the cartels would never be able to burn, even if they thought to do so.

If there was one thing a trash-strewn city like this one had, it was bugs. Flies, gnats, mosquitoes, even regular sized spiders, wasps, and bees. They all decayed quickly if exposed to the elements, when they weren't consumed entirely, but there were still dozens of tiny bodies in the rooms around me. Hundreds, as I let my senses spread even further.

I sent the emptiness into their willing receptacles, absorbing the strain with an ease that came from controlling hundreds of walkers in the Weaver's web-strewn forest, and ordered my insect army to attack.

The first burst of electrical current, flashing through my body, almost ruined everything, but I managed to ride that wave, stepping even further outside my body until it felt like I was looking down on a stranger's disfigured form, the emptiness spreading across turbulent waters, as limbs quaked and shook and the smell of charred flesh wafted up to someone else's nose.

Edmund took a step back and waved away a mosquito that had flown into his face, smacking it out of the air. "All I ask for is a modicum of peace and cleanliness to perfect my art, but this city's filth is everywhere."

A second mosquito divebombed him and he scowled, but as he went to give it the same fate as the first one, a half-dozen small spiders dropped from the ceiling onto his head, and a column of ants spiraled up and under his pants leg.

A distant part of me was delighted that Edmund had ended up being the first of us to scream.

The torturer staggered back, slapping at the insects that were swarming him in ever-increasing numbers. Given sufficient time and quantities, fire ants could eat a person alive, but that was with people who were asleep and unable to fight back. Every slap killed some of my walkers, and it was anyone's bet whether I'd have enough to finish the job.

Then one of my rats fell out of the air vent above us and onto Edmund's shoulder. He staggered back, his scream going up by at least two octaves, and fell into me.

Despite what the Crimson Queen's soldiers thought, I didn't need my hand to ash someone. Any skin-to-skin contact would do, and there was plenty of that with the torturer fallen on top of me. But as much as I wanted Edmund gone and my wounds healed, I needed a human-sized shield, and someone with actual hands to undo my straps.

I squirmed about in my restraints as Edmund tried to fight off both the rat and my insect horde, but couldn't quite get into the position I needed. Not unless he moved his head—there! My rat leaped at the man's face and he shrank back again with another shriek, putting his throat just within reach.

I surged forward, pulling something in my neck and shoulders to get the necessary reach while still bound, and sank my teeth into his throat.

King Rex had called cars *meals on wheels* because he would scoop them up and dump the passengers into his mouth, consuming entire families in one fell swoop, but I wasn't King Rex. I wasn't a Beast Shifter or even a scavenger with needle-sharp teeth.

But I was desperate, and I was oh so angry, and I had a power that let me operate my body beyond normal human limits. My jaws clamped down on human tissue and tore through Edmund's throat as if I was a walker in truth instead of just a baby Crow named after them. I spat out flesh and took another deeper bite, and this time, I got something important. Blood spurted everywhere; into my mouth, making me choke; into my eyes, blinding me. I heard a strangled cry, as the torturer ripped himself free, heard the thump as he dropped to the floor moments later, but those five senses Edmund had been so keen on abusing were distant things. All that mattered was my sixth sense and what it told me.

Within ten seconds, I had a human-sized body to raise, and not long after that, my arms and legs were free again. I spat out blood and bits of flesh, ignored the nausea twisting in upon itself and the tiny voice screaming on the periphery of my consciousness, and crept to the door, opening it up a crack.

Apparently, the sound insulation worked both ways. A siren was blaring in the hall and yet neither Edmund nor I had heard a thing.

"What's going on?" asked another technician, sticking his head out his own torture room to interrogate a passing soldier.

"Some sort of attack," said the other man, not breaking his stride. "Stay put until the major gives the all-clear."

I waited until that soldier was gone and then sent Edmund after the inquisitive technician. Turns out torture implements are great against helpless humans and do shit-all against walkers. As I raised my newest minion, I checked the room, finding it empty of victims.

I could feel my other walkers, twelve strong now, and clearly the source of the disturbance that had the entire building on lockdown. I headed their way, picking off isolated soldiers from behind as I went. I ashed the first, healing my concussion and some of the cuts Edmund had left, but raised the rest. By the time I reached the series of barricades that turned the entry hall into a killing field, I had five human walkers, both rats, and a thick, buzzing cloud of death flying above us.

There were maybe twenty-eight soldiers crouched behind those barricades, sending a hailstorm of lead that cut down my walkers as they tried to force their way through the front doorway. Most of those walkers were in camo too, but at least one of the slavers I'd killed almost a week earlier was still up and shambling about in back.

I sent my new walkers forward and hit the guards from behind. Minutes later, I was fully healed, and my combined army was up to almost twenty-five.

Not counting my remaining rat, the flies, the mosquitoes, and a single, solitary hornet.

The doorway beckoned to me, but I turned away from its promise of escape. Neither the woman who had captured me nor the major who accompanied her into the pen was among the dead. I'd like to say it was civic duty that had me going back into the building I'd almost escaped... that I was focused on finding the information the Free States had been seeking on this warlord that thought herself royalty. I'd even like to say the idea of rescuing the prisoners who had been penned in with me had been a big part of that decision making process.

Really, I just wanted revenge.

CHAPTER 44

The facility was huge, capable of supporting up to several hundred people, but most of the halls were empty as we passed through. I had no idea where I was going and had yet to find a sign that read "Major Asshole this way." In fact, the walls were bare of anything but the occasional wall hangings with the Crimson Queen's banner.

I sent walkers down each hallway but kept a core of ten or so with me, the zombie rat riding my shoulder, and my cloud swarming ahead. Without any signs or arrows—and who had ever heard of an army that wasn't in love with labels?—I was relying instead on my power, seeking out the sparks of life my senses pointed out to me, and dispatching walkers to kill them as we went.

There's no such thing as a subtle zombie apocalypse, but throw in the right Crow, and it can at least be downright orderly.

I perked up as we reached the end of another hall, and I felt a dozen or more sparks in that direction. Two of those lights were even brighter than normal, which made them Powers. And if *I* was the commanding asshole of a company of assholes, and my base was under attack, wouldn't I keep my pet Powers nearby to guard me?

Actually, you already know the answer to that: fuck no. I'd charge right into the thick of things with one hand and a death wish, because apparently that's just the way I'm wired.

But I was willing to bet the major was different.

I pushed on the door, found it locked, and stepped aside to let a walker beat it down as the rest of us took cover. Maybe these soldiers were used to real army bases, with inch-thick steel doors and cybernetic guard dogs cobbled together on a remote Technomancer's orders, but here in Kansas City, they'd had to work with the materials available, and that meant the locked door was just wood. And a two-hundred-pound walker in camo with no brain or functional nerves makes surprisingly short work of wooden doors.

That same walker was absolutely shredded as the soldiers inside opened fire. Wherever the Crimson Queen had gotten her troops, they were a hell of a lot better trained than the bandits or slavers we'd encountered. As soon as the walker dropped, the gunfire stopped, and I could hear someone—a woman by the sound of it—ordering two of the men forward to scope out the hall.

Before they could get close enough to the doorway to see the rest of us, I sent my rat walker in with the bug swarm. And then, when Woodrow II had their attention, I let the rest of my walkers rush in after him.

Walkers aren't much stronger than living humans, and they're not a whole lot tougher either, but they do have one serious advantage over the living. While massed gunfire can tear them apart past even my ability to keep them moving, individual bullets aren't all that effective. Between my rat's distraction and the sheer number of walkers I poured into the room, the soldiers didn't have a chance to concentrate their fire. I felt new bodies hitting the floor and raised them up right after, turning the numbers even more in my favor.

And then one of the bright lights moved and walkers started disappearing from my senses.

I rushed inside, pushing past the last walker in the hall—that same dead Pyromancer, who was either the luckiest little zombie ever or somehow had kept a sense of self-preservation—and found what must have been a control room... central table now turned on its side to provide cover, monitors showing footage from the few still-working cameras inside and outside the facility, and chairs scattered in every direction.

There was also a hell of a lot of blood, but I was getting used to that. Four soldiers were still on their feet, including both the major and the woman who had ruined the fantasy of shower sex forever. They and one of the men with them all had guns out, but the last person, facing off against the remainder of my walker horde, was wielding a sword. It looked kind of ridiculous with his camo uniform... right up until that sword literally glowed as it bisected the walker reaching out for him.

Lightbringer or Stalwart or some shitty fusion of both? Hell if I knew.

I had four walkers left with me, including the Pyromancer, and I sent two of them forth to try to bury the asshole. He was way too quick for that, which *definitely* made me think Stalwart, but as he murdered another zombie and dodged to the side of the second, I was on him. I ignored the bullet that caught me in my shoulder—my right shoulder, because apparently we were back to that bullshit—and threw myself under a blade that sizzled as it swung. Then I was back on my feet, my hand going for the Stalwart's eyes.

I don't care how well someone is trained... there's an instinctive response to getting punched in the groin or having your eyes gouged. The man forgot his sword for just a moment as he smoothly tucked his chin into his chest, protecting his face and presenting me with the hard bone of his forehead instead.

Asshole apparently hadn't read the briefing report.

The rest of my aches and pains vanished as a sword clattered to the ground in a swiftly gathering pile of dust. I took a moment to savor the terror in the two remaining enemy's eyes.

Wait. Two? Weren't there—

Something hit me from the side… hit me and actually lifted me up and over the table to smash me into the far wall. I landed with a squelch instead of a thud and that, more than anything, told me what the second Power was, the one I'd stupidly ignored because he just had a gun. I was on my feet again, freshly broken arm dangling to the side, when the Hydromancer switched from a battering stream of water to something more subtle, a bubble of liquid around my head, forcing watery tendrils into my ears, my nose, and down my throat.

Makara had suffocated Stonewall like this in the Training Grounds and the big man had had nightmares about it for weeks after.

A flick of the Power's other hand sent a wave of water to pin my last few walkers against the opposite wall, but his pale eyes never left mine, watching me struggle for air that didn't exist. I used my power to lift myself back upright, to make my body sprint forward even as muscles screamed for oxygen, but another bullet caught me in the side, and I went slipping and sliding back to the ground.

The major said something, and the only thing that made this shitshow of a death better was that the bubble of water kept me from hearing his words. I reached out to my walkers, all of them, but most of those in the building were too far away, and the only ones nearby were still pinned against the wall by the Hydromancer's self-powered water cannon.

Kill them when I die, I ordered instead, using the emptiness still roiling inside of me, the emptiness that was doing fuck-all to keep me from effectively drowning in a puddle of water, to embed that message into their undead brains. Once I was gone, that order would remain. Maybe one of them would get lucky.

It wasn't much, but it was all I had.

And then the slaver corpse, the body of the Pyromancer I'd brought with me all the way from Wymore, raised its head and spat a torrent of superheated fire out of his long-dead mouth.

ooo

Water trumps fire. That's the simplistic elemental calculus every child grows up knowing. Something's on fire? Pour water on it to put it out.

Reality is just a bit different. As my Pyromancer walker impossibly called upon the powers it had had as a living asshole, those flames met the Hydromancer's water and what resulted was not the defeat of fire or the triumph of water, but something in between. Fire embraced water, and that marriage gave birth to steam.

There were four people standing on their feet in that small room. Three were alive, one was dead. I'll give you one guess at which one weathered the storm of superheated steam better. The screams as those three people started to scald was my first sign that the bubble around my head was gone. I sucked in a breath, and dragged myself along the carpet, ignoring the water droplets that fell onto me still hot enough to burn.

Something gave out in the Hydromancer soon after I'd made my way out of the room, and where there had been steam, there was now nothing but fire, devouring the people who had tried to make me a slave. I called the walker back to me, and climbed to my feet, looking back at the raging inferno in the room behind us. Flames were already spreading, licking the walls as the fire took on a life of its own.

One of the pre-Break books I'd read at Mama Rawlins' had said revenge was a dish best served cold, but honestly?

Hot seemed to work every bit as well.

○○○

With the fire spreading and smoke starting to fill the halls, I finally thought of the prisoners I'd been held with. I spread my senses out, felt the one cluster of sparks that *wasn't* moving, and looked for a hallway that would take me there. As I hurried, lungs still burning, the walkers I'd dispatched around the facility finally made it back to my side. One of them even emerged from a door as we passed it, and I was already ten steps down the hall when what I'd seen through that doorway finally caught up to me.

I turned and rushed back into what was a small, neat office, distinguished only by a framed picture of the commanding officer I'd just killed, in dress uniform and saluting the camera.

No; I didn't want a keepsake or a trophy from my latest kill. I'm not Black-tongue Karl, for fuck's sake. But I couldn't imagine a soldier hanging a framed picture of their boss on the wall, and that meant this was the major's office. And *that* meant there might be information on the Crimson Queen.

I pulled open the only file cabinet, grabbed the handful of folders that seemed almost lost within all that unused space, and passed them off to a walker. *Not* the Pyromancer. And then, as the building started to shake, fire eating away at a distant support, we headed back into the hall, running now to reach the prisoners before they suffocated from smoke or burned alive.

It wasn't until I reached that room that I remembered the shackles. Either my walkers weren't great at precise movement or I wasn't great at control, but after the first walker nearly ripped an arm off trying to get a prisoner free, it was up to me to run from person to person, unhooking their chains from the wall or ceiling.

I left the three feral ones chained up. Yeah, it sucked, and they probably didn't deserve to die, but I was going to have a hard enough time getting all these fucking people out as it was, without worrying about being attacked from behind. I'd learned my lesson in Reno, when a Beast Shifter I'd just freed turned around and immediately ate another former prisoner.

You can't save everyone.

And sometimes, you can't save *anyone*. In the handful of minutes it had taken to free seventeen people, the whole hall had filled with smoke. I wasn't sure how *I* would make it to the entrance, and between the chains, the torture, and the lack of food, the people around me were significantly worse off.

"Keep low," I told the lead woman, a scrawny girl maybe five years younger than me, with blonde hair that stuck to her scalp like straw. "Try not to breathe in too much smoke and follow the walker in front of you."

She nodded and took off, and I repeated the message to each prisoner as they passed me in a slow-moving parade of coughs and clinking iron. Finally, I followed my own advice and hunched down to follow them, as my walkers led the way to where I remembered the entrance being.

The smoke only thickened as we went. I tripped over a body, started to pick myself up, and then realized it was one of the prisoners, and not some soldier's corpse I'd forgotten to raise. The ragged rise and fall of his chest told me he was still alive, but either the smoke had gotten to be too much for him or he'd just run out of energy and was content to wait for death.

Fuck that.

My walkers were all up front, so I grabbed the man by his arm and dragged him behind me, my power doing more to keep me pushing forward than muscles that were nearing exhaustion.

Where was the fucking door?

Another body hit the ground, somewhere in front of me, and hacking coughs merged with the hungry roar of a fire growing closer. I wiped soot from my eyes, ignoring the sweat that burned in its place, and looked desperately for an exit, but there was nothing but smoke and the silhouettes of the people I'd tried to save, seventeen dim sparks of light to my power, preceded by the six of my walkers still on their feet.

And beyond that? Nothing.

Except... from one second to the next, that stopped being true. A cluster of sparks was moving our way, and at the front were two lights that glowed like lanterns, far brighter than the Stalwart with his glowing sword. We had nowhere to run, so I pushed my walkers forward, one coughing body over my right shoulder, with the other man now a dead weight—if not actually dead—behind me. If I could kill the newcomers, I'd heal whatever damage I had from smoke inhalation. I could raise the others as walkers, and maybe between my minions and I, we could get these people out after all.

And then we were close enough that I could hear voices even over the fire. Voices I knew. One voice that I even loved.

"This way!" shouted Silt. "I sense people this way!"

CHAPTER 45

So, it turned out Stark hadn't abandoned me, after all. Not long after I'd gone into the bathroom, a platoon of the Crimson Queen's soldiers had entered the tavern, trailed by the needle-toothed scavenger who had survived his ambush the day earlier. Outmanned and outgunned, Stark and the others had been forced to watch as I was taken away, but once the last soldiers were gone, they'd left the Bastard in pursuit.

Unfortunately, I was long gone by then, and nobody knew where I'd been taken. They'd gone back to the Park district to collect the others from the Dying Bird and figure out a plan. Not long after that, my walkers had started stirring up some trouble of their own, marching in from the city's southwestern gate, and *that* trail had made finding me relatively easy. They'd even held onto the backpack I'd left behind at the Unwanted Bastard and returned it to me as soon as we were safe.

Of course, safe was a bit of a reach in Kansas City, especially after I'd marched the undead right through two districts. Turned out there was a price to be paid for the things I had done.

Stark and Jacobs were away, meeting in an undisclosed location with the leaders of every cartel in the city. The rest of us were back at the Bastard, and this time, the common room was filled to the rafters. We were at the center, the six other members of the Mission gathered around a single table. Nearby were the prisoners we'd rescued, currently being seen to by some sort of midwife and witch doctor combo that had cost the last of Stark's Kansas City currency. With the help of the bar's three prostitutes, who wouldn't be seeing any business until ours was over, she bandaged and treated their injuries, occasionally tossing a scared glance at the walkers ringed around us, shoulder to shoulder and facing outward.

Or maybe the midwife was looking past my walkers at the armed men and women that currently had us surrounded. Bloods, Crips, Skulls, Aztecs, and at least two other groups that neither Denali nor Reese could identify watched us with stone-cold eyes, hands on pistol grips or axe handles or even what I recognized from Muse's time in the Training Grounds as an actual fucking flamethrower.

Tensions were high, and not just because my walkers had fought and killed some of the cartels' people in that march through the city. There was a shit ton of angry young hardasses staring us down, and testosterone filled the room, like gas just waiting for someone to light a match.

No, I didn't start anything. I wasn't eighteen anymore, it had been another long fucking day, and I'd seen shit most of those teenage killers never would. I ignored the eyes drilling into me from all sides, ate the terrible food the Bastard's staff had prepared for us, and waited to find out just how badly we were fucked.

An hour later, as the witch doctor finally finished her ministrations, Stark and Jacobs came back to tell us.

Actually, Stark started with a question:

"Can you pass off control of your walkers to someone else? A non-Crow, I mean?"

"What?"

"He means tell them to obey someone else's verbal orders," elaborated Jacobs. In the absence of Mammoth, he'd stepped up and taken on a co-leadership role with Stark.

"Oh." I shook my head. "I mean, I could, but—" I pointed to the nearest walker, whose head was partly caved in by the blow that had initially killed it. Only one of its ears was still attached, and that was hanging on by a thread of tissue. "Walkers don't really hear. Or see, for that matter. I'm pretty sure they sense life, just like I do. When I order them about, I have to implant the commands with my power. So yeah, I probably *could* order them to follow someone's orders... but that other person would still have to be a Crow to make those orders understood."

"Shit. That's what I figured." Stark traded glances with Jacobs. "Plan B, I guess?"

"I think we're up to Plan G by now," said the other man.

"What's going on, boss?" asked Reese.

"We're trying to negotiate our exit from the city," said Stark. "I informed the leaders that the facility Walker just destroyed was a foothold for this Crimson Queen. Given that they don't want her taking over the city any more than we do, that helped. A bit. The fact that most of the destruction happened in the Zoo instead of one of their home districts helped more, but we effectively invaded Kansas City with the undead and killed some of their men in the process."

"Fucking fantastic," muttered Supersonic. "So, what were their demands?"

"They wanted the information we'd gotten from the major's office, and I handed it over. They're making copies now and will give us back the originals when we leave." Stark cleared his throat. "They also wanted Walker. A year of service with his minions to pay for the lives he'd taken."

"Fuck that," said Silt.

"Yeah, Jacobs said the same thing, if in slightly more diplomatic terms. So then, they wanted to know if we could leave his walkers behind instead as free, tireless labor."

"And now that that idea is out the window?" I asked.

He shook his head. "Plan G, like Jacobs said."

The other man nodded. "I've been authorized to make some concessions on behalf of the Free States government. I don't think this was quite what the Secretary of State meant when Presley and I were granted those privileges, but here we are."

"Concessions?"

"Yeah. I'm thinking diplomatic relations and a return to trade with the Free States would give Kansas City a legitimacy that no other city in the Badlands can claim," said Stark. "Even Wichita."

"That's nuts," said Reese. "Why would the Free States do that?"

Jacobs shrugged. "Our orders were to do everything in our power to make sure Walker makes it back to the Free States. I'm just taking the Secretary at his word." He met my eyes. "I sure hope you're worth it."

"Me too." I shook my head,

"What makes you so special?" Reese asked me. "I mean, you're fucking terrifying, I guess... but most Powers are. No offense," he added to Silt and Supersonic. "Why is the government offering *reparations* on your behalf?"

"I have no idea," I said, glancing at Silt. As far as I knew, there were only a handful of people who even knew I was a Full-Five, and none of them were in politics, let alone the current presidential administration.

"I thought you and Presley were sent along to protect *all* of us," said Supersonic.

"Walker's my primary, but Mammoth agreed that adding our guns to the Mission would help make all of you safer."

"This is bullshit," muttered the Jitterbug to me. "Even when we're out in the field together, you still find ways to sneak out and make a name for yourself!"

"Yeah, because that's definitely what this has been all about." I rolled my eyes and waved at one of the prisoners at the table next to us. "Johanna over there can tell you just how much fun it was being kidnapped by the Crimson Queen's army. One moment, she's a schoolteacher, the next she's a potential conscript for some power-hungry woman's army? Read the fucking room, Caleb. This isn't about glory… it's about saving lives."

Supersonic had the decency to look almost ashamed.

Stark rose to his feet, Jacobs a heartbeat behind. "We're going back into the meeting to give them the bad news and then the good news. Hopefully, there's enough of the latter to keep you from having to kill half of Kansas City on our way out. Stay out of trouble while we're gone. Please."

Silt waited until conversations had started back up and then leaned over to me, voice quiet. "Her name is Claire."

"What?"

"The woman you pointed to. Her name is Claire, not Johanna, and she was a cashier not a schoolteacher."

"Oh." I nodded. "Fair enough."

"You just made all that up?"

I gave her a shrug. "Only a handful of the people we saved will even *look* at me. I'm not going to make things worse by trying to start a conversation."

ooo

This time, Stark and Jacobs were gone for less than an hour… or five full hands once Cagney dug out her deck of cards. As usual, Denali hadn't said more than three or four sentences in that time, and also as usual, he'd won almost every hand. His poker face would have given Alexa's a run for its money, but I was pretty sure he was also cheating. I just couldn't figure out how.

"One last thing and then we're good to go," announced Stark.

"Finally!" Reese threw down his cards in disgust. "I've been here long enough to see exactly why this bastard is unwanted."

I was *pretty sure* he was talking about the bar.

"What one last thing?" asked Cagney, eyes narrowed.

"They want them," he said, pointing at my ring of walkers.

I frowned. "Like I told you, it takes a Crow to—"

"Not your walkers. Just their bodies."

Oh, for fuck's sake. "Why?"

"They don't want a repeat of what just happened."

"As long as we're not attacked, there won't be." Every single fucking time I put together even the seeds of an army someone was insisting I set them free. It was starting to piss me off.

"Maybe so, but they say all the people you killed were citizens of the city, and therefore the bodies are their property," said Jacobs.

"Even the Crimson Queen's troops?" At this point, the vast majority of my walkers were dead soldiers.

"Even them."

"Just let them rest in peace, Walker," said Cagney. If anything, she was more skittish around me than she'd been at the Dying Bird. "Some of these dead people have families and loved ones. Give them some closure."

Having been to my mother's funeral, I wanted to tell her that *closure* was a myth, that nothing healed those wounds but time, and sometimes not even then… but I doubted she'd understand or agree.

And really, what was the point in arguing? I was more than ready to leave this fucking city behind, and like Mammoth had said, the Badlands had plenty of bodies.

But I had a condition of my own.

"Fair enough." I cut the links to my walkers and all their bodies hit the dirt like sacks of flesh and bone. Which they were, technically speaking.

All of their bodies except one.

I pointed to the only walker still on its feet, the dead Pyromancer who had saved my life by doing something impossible. "But this one died outside of Kansas City, and I'm fucking keeping him."

○○○

On our way out of the city, I had one more request. Can't say Stark liked it. Can't say the guards sent as our 'escorts' did either, but we made a detour anyway to a cemetery on the east side of the Park.

"There shouldn't be any bodies buried here," said Stark. "After the Break—"

"Yeah, Cagney told us. Bodies were exhumed and cremated."

"Right. But if there *are* any bodies—"

"I'm not here to raise anything," I told him. "I'm just here to have a chat."

"With who?"

I nodded to the spirits that only I and maybe a nomad shaman could see. "With them."

○○○

"Can all ex-Powers use their abilities as walkers, or is there something special about that guy?"

Silt's voice was low, so as to not disturb the sleeping members of our party. We were a day out of Kansas City, with several days more of hard riding before we met back up with the others in Wichita to let the Free States know that we couldn't find their spies but had dug up information on the Crimson Queen ourselves.

"I don't know," I admitted. "I figured raising someone who had been a Titan or a Stalwart would be valuable because a lot of their abilities are just kind of baked into their bodies, you know? Stronger bones, tougher skin, greater strength or agility even when not actively using their powers. All the shit that made fighting Orca, Paladin, or Erik a pain in the ass even when the dampeners were on. But a walker actively using their powers?"

"You've never read anything about that? And Sally never—"

"No and no. If I'd known, I would have used Fallout's powers to make our escape from Reno a shitload less painful."

"Assuming you could even manage it back then."

"What do you mean?"

"Damian, I'm not an idiot. What you're doing now, even what you did against the Weaver, it's beyond anything you were doing at the Academy."

"I couldn't go all out there. Didn't need to either, but... you're right. It's like I've told you in the past: Crows are different. Full-Five is my potential, but getting there takes—"

"Death."

"Yeah. And there's been a ton of it on this fucking trip."

She swallowed, the silence between us broken only by the snap and crackle of the low fire. "How much stronger do you think you're going to get?"

"I don't know. Two and a half years at the Academy and I still don't know. I'm mostly going off things I was told by a long-dead serial killer and whatever I've been able to puzzle out on my own."

"And you're still you, right? No mad desires to drive up and down the coast killing random strangers?"

"I'm not convinced there *was* anything random about Sally's victims," I said quietly. "But yeah, I'm still me. As far as I can tell anyway. If I do go crazy, I'll probably be the last person to realize it."

"Now *there's* a thought to keep us all up at night," said Silt with a shiver. "Well, if you *do* take over the world, just remember who your friends are, okay?"

I nodded. "Tessa, Kayleigh, Alexa, Jeremiah… Hell, if I didn't include Matthew, Vibe would give me no end of grief. Am I missing anyone?"

A clod of dirt hit me in the shoulder. "Not funny, Skeletor."

"Nothing's going to change what you and I have, Sofia. Not ever."

"Damn straight it won't." I could barely see her shake her head in the darkness. "And to think… if it hadn't been for Evie being terrified of being by herself in that Pre-Break History group project, we might never have gotten to know each other."

"I draw the line at gratitude towards Wormhole."

"Even so. Unicorn, Vibe, Wormhole, Silt, and Walker. All hail the Fearsome Five, am I right?"

"All hail."

She sighed. "Now, I'm just getting maudlin. I'm going to crash, since this is technically your watch. Well, yours and the dead man's, I guess."

"Sleep tight," I told her.

"On the subject of that dead man… maybe keep what you and he can do to yourself, even after we get back to the Academy?"

"How come?"

"I can't imagine there'll be a lot of Capes out there comfortable with the idea of you building an army of dead Powers. Especially if they might end up being one of them."

CHAPTER 46

Wichita was every bit as foreboding as it had been on our first visit, and I didn't get to see any more of it this time around. In fact, we were only there long enough to wash up, do laundry, and start to fill in the others on what they had missed before Mammoth was back from passing on our information to the Free States.

The big Shifter came with news of his own, and to what will no doubt be your vast shock and surprise, that news was all fucking bad.

Well, not *all* bad. The Secretary of State had apparently agreed to send an ambassador to Kansas City, and a second one to Wichita. For the first time in decades, the Free States would have relations with foreign countries… even if those countries were just small island cities in the Badlands.

No, the bad news had nothing to do with our trip, me, or how far Jacobs had apparently overextended the diplomatic powers he'd been granted.

"The boundary shifted *how much?*"

Supersonic was speaking for all of us, as we gathered around Mammoth.

"A full quarter of a mile, as near as they could tell. After yearly averages of just a few feet."

"Fucking hell," breathed Silt.

"Most of the people had long since been relocated north, but this pushed the boundary right past San Diego's border defenses in one swoop. Which means all of those people on the Border Patrol are now his."

His meaning the Free States' greatest bogeyman, the creature to our south who called himself Tezcatlipoca.

"The government is scrambling to set up a new perimeter," concluded Mammoth, "but there are a lot of people in southern San Diego that had resisted moving until now. Getting them out while moving more military in is making for a mess. Especially since they don't know why the boundary expanded so far or so rapidly."

"Is it possible it's like what Walker ran into with the Weaver?" asked Lady. As a former citizen of the Free States, she was a lot more invested in what happened to the country than people like Cagney.

"I don't think so," I said. "From what I understand, Tezcatlipoca's domain has been growing in proportion to his power."

That killed the conversation for a long moment.

"Well, that's a scary thought," said Silt. "Especially with my old hometown just across the river from his territory in Texas."

"There's nothing we can do about it that the government's not already doing," said Jacobs, who had gone with Mammoth and Stark, "but the Crimson Queen is no longer on their list of priorities. Protecting existing citizens is a lot more important than worrying about some distant warlord out east."

"It probably scores higher with their constituency too," said Cagney.

"Probably," said Mammoth. "Anyway, Aftermath said he was still waiting for word from the Flyboys he sent north, but we're not going to wait around Wichita. For the rest of our route, we'll have semi-regular access to communication towers, so I'm sure we'll get updates along the way."

"We're leaving already, boss?" That was Reese.

"Yeah, as soon as Emma and James give the okay. Between Regent, Wymore, and now Kansas City, we're way behind schedule. Leaving as soon as we can means more time to spend in towns that actually need us." He scanned the eight of us who had gone to Kansas City and turned to Stark. "You and the others are excused from watch duty for the first few days. It's not vacation in the big city, but it's the best I can do."

"We'll take it," said the other man.

"Okay," said Emma. "Everyone that didn't nearly start a war with Kansas City, come with me. We've got some work to do before we can leave."

ooo

Mammoth caught up with me as I was headed back to the warehouse the Mission had been using as a dorm in our absence. He waved an aluminum thermos and two matching mugs. "Any chance I could interest you in some coffee, Walker? I wanted to have a quick check-in."

"Coffee sounds good."

We found a spot in the shade and leaned back against the warehouse's worn siding.

"Stark has told me a bit about what happened in Kansas City, and I heard more as part of Jacobs' debrief to the Secretary. Who asked about you specifically and by name, by the way."

"Seriously?"

"Seriously. I had no idea you knew people in the president's cabinet."

"I don't."

"Well, they know you, somehow."

I took a sip of bitter, bitter coffee. "If Jacobs' authority came straight from the Secretary, I guess it would make sense they'd have been told all about me. Honestly, I had no idea the decision to send them had gone that high up the chain." I'd mostly assumed the duo were from Alexa's agency, which I was pretty sure I still wasn't supposed to talk about.

"There are a lot of eyes on you, but I guess that makes sense, given all that you have to offer the Free States. But the best part of being out here is that we can mostly ignore politics. That's not what I came over to talk about."

"Okay?" The coffee was either less bitter this sip or I was just getting used to the taste. "What do you need?"

"How are you doing? Kansas City didn't sound like a picnic."

I shrugged. "It's not the first time I've been kidnapped, although having it go down in the bathroom of a part-time whorehouse was a new touch."

"Stark said when they tracked you down to the Crimson Queen's facility, you were rescuing prisoners?"

"The ones I'd been temporarily housed with, yeah. By the time I'd cleared the building of the enemy, the whole place was on fire. I decided it was time to get us all out. Not sure we would have made it though if Silt hadn't found us."

"Temporarily housed with?"

"Yeah." I coughed. "Like the papers we found said, the Crimson Queen has been seeking conscripts for her army. If those conscripts are Powers, they either swear allegiance and beg for the scraps from her table or they're sent to what they call *technicians* to be broken and used as disposable shock-and-awe types on the front line.

I'm not a dog, so I guess we all thought the second option was a better fit."

"They were going to throw away a Crow of your abilities?"

"They didn't know what I was. Thought I was a Pyromancer or... something else, I guess. They weren't using the Free States' classifications. Anyway, they sent me off to my assigned technician. His name was Edmund."

Mammoth's eyes were wide. I shrugged.

"It's not the first time I've been tortured either. And honestly, he barely got started before I was breaking free. His walker went down in a hail of bullets when I attacked the guards at the front gate."

"Stark said you were shirtless, covered in blood, and had scars all over your chest when they found you."

"My power heals me when I kill someone with it. It doesn't clothe me or make me pretty. Or clean, for that matter," I added, remembering Reese's comment on our trip into the Zoo.

"But you're okay now?"

"Yeah."

"You're sure?"

I scowled. First Silt, now Mammoth? "I'm not going to snap and kill everyone. Cape's fucking honor."

"That wasn't what I was asking."

"Then I don't know what you're digging for."

He took a sip of coffee and sighed. "From what I've heard... from what I was told... you'd already been through a lot of things before we met. Situations that could very easily break even the strongest of people. And then came this year's Mission. This region is called the Badlands for a reason, but we've seen more action and death than I'd expect in a three-year period, let alone a single summer and fall."

"Maybe Reese is right. Maybe I'm a bad omen."

"Reese is a steady hand in a fight and a good enough man, but if he had his way, we'd be stuck back at home camp eleven months out of the year."

"And the twelfth month?"

"Drinking and whoring in your hometown. Reese loves that place."

"Bakersfield?" *That* was something I hadn't seen coming.

"No, Los Angeles. I didn't realize you'd grown up elsewhere. Anyway, we've gone off on a tangent. My point was that these past few months have been hard, and you've been in the thick of all of it. I was never a Cape, but I know how important downtime is for recovery, both mental and physical."

"You sound like Alexa," I murmured.

"Attractive woman all in black? Never blinks? Quietly terrifying?" At my nod, Mammoth gave one of his own. "We met. And she's not wrong. We've still got a few months left in our journey, but the worst of it should be over, and every day will take you closer to the Free States. So, just… try to relax. Enjoy the fall weather, don't work too hard, and if there's anything I can do, let me know."

"Honestly, I'd rather work than be bored, but… okay. Don't worry; I'm a survivor."

"Glad to hear it." Mammoth shook his head. "If I bring you back broken, that might very well be the end of the Mission."

"Seriously?"

"The Secretary was *very* interested in you."

Apparently, my secret was out.

○○○

True to Mammoth's word, our wagon train headed out of Wichita just a few hours later. It was already afternoon, and we didn't go far before making camp, the city's great wall still visible in the distance. Caleb bitched about that, but honestly, I was glad to be back on the road. Maybe Wichita was a great place, but that wall and the sheer number of guards kind of weighed on my mind after a while, in a way that the squalor of Kansas City never had.

Maybe I was just more comfortable in shitholes.

CHAPTER 47

The next few weeks were every bit as idyllic as Mammoth had promised. No slavers. No demons. No building-sized spiders or vanguards of power-hungry warlords. Just the open road and a scattering of towns that seemed thrilled to see us.

And Cloud only tried to bite me once.

Once a day, that is. When the Mission was over, when we were all back at the organization's southernmost camp, that horse and I were going to have ourselves a talk.

The biggest development during that stretch of time had nothing do with our charitable work, or international politics, or even my persistent—and persistently futile—communion with the dead. In fact, it was a development that kind of snuck up on me without any fanfare or explosions; one morning, I realized that Silt had been sleeping by the fire with the rest of us, instead of in the wagon with Emma. And that I hadn't seen the two spending nearly as much time together as usual.

My first instinct was to let it be. Safety in ignorance and all that. If Silt wanted to talk about it, she would. Otherwise, we could just hang out and ignore the elephant in the room.

That's a metaphor I learned from Winter. There haven't been any elephants in the Free States since the Break. Closest you can get is probably Pachyderm, and he's been down in the Hole since before I was born.

And even if he wasn't, you sure as hell wouldn't want him in a room with you.

Unfortunately, for me and maybe for Sofia, I'd spent all of second-year living with the Weather Witch and her *we are having a team meeting right now to talk about this or so help me God nobody is sleeping tonight* attitude. And I'd spent another few months sharing a studio apartment with Tessa, where the silence when I'd somehow fucked up could damn near kill a person all on its own.

In short, I'd learned that it wasn't always a good idea to just pretend everything was okay.

When we broke camp that day, I nudged Cloud up into his usual spot next to Silt and her horse, Whinny.

Quick aside on that front: who the hell names a horse Whinny? For those of you who've never been around the four-hooved hell spawns, a whinny is just the noise they make sometimes. It's like calling a dog Bark, or a rat Squeak instead of Woodrow.

Anyway, I rode in silence next to Silt and her absurdly named horse for a few minutes, and then leaned over. "Did you and Emma break up?"

"Jesus, Boneboy. Don't they teach subtlety at the Academy?"

"If so, you and I would have both failed the class. It just occurred to me that you'd been spending your nights out with the rest of us recently. And that you've been grumpier than usual when your friend asks totally innocent questions."

"Like when, exactly?"

"Like about twenty seconds ago."

"Ugh." She sighed. "I liked it better when you just stared at the ocean all day."

"I can still do that, if you'd rather." Truth was, I was wrapped in the emptiness pretty much every hour of the day, and that meant the Crow part of me saw ocean where my boring old eyes saw hills, red rock, and gathering clouds.

"Shit, I really *am* being grumpier than normal, aren't I?"

"By your standards, anyway. If you were Alan-Fucking-Jackson, I'd think you had just started taking antidepressants."

"Like I keep telling you, Alan's not all bad, once you get to know him."

"It's the getting to know him part that nobody wants to attempt. I'm pretty sure he considers small talk a murdering offense."

"So do you!"

"I never said I wasn't an asshole. But we were talking about you and Emma."

"Yeah."

I waited, nudging Cloud with a knee when he decided it would be a good idea to wander off the path. Eventually, Silt spoke again.

"Eight weeks, give or take a few days, until this year's Mission is over, Skeletor. And then the three of us will be back at the Academy."

"And Emma will still be out here in the Badlands."

"Yeah."

"Wasn't that the point? You both knew this was a short-term thing from the start."

"Obviously, but…" She sighed. "Things don't always work out as planned. A summer romance becomes something more and then everything gets serious, you know? There's no switch for turning off emotions."

There was if you were a Crow, but I got what she was saying.

"You guys still have time though. Why let the future fuck with your present?"

"I asked her the same thing."

"And?"

"She thinks it would be easier to end things now; that it will give us time to get used to being apart even when we're still together."

"That's the dumbest thing I've ever heard. *Out of sight, out of mind* wasn't just the Specter's motto."

"A shitty motto, at that. *Hey everyone, I can basically go invisible, so you should all just forget me!* And the Free States happily did just that. I don't think he ever starred in a single vid. No wonder he ended up going Black Hat in the end."

"That's kind of my point. It seems like it would be easier to get over each other if you guys weren't literally sharing space every damn day."

Silt shrugged. "It takes two to have a relationship. Emma wants to end things now, so we will. And in two months, we'll just be memories to each other anyway."

I sighed as she rode up to join Cagney and James, who were busy with some sort of a spirited debate about squirrels being tree rats. Next time, I was going to listen to my instincts and leave the meddling to Winter.

ooo

The days kept rolling and our wagons did too, and if Emma and Silt mostly stayed away from each other, they both handled it better than I probably would have. Especially when Caleb, James, and Lady all kept getting lucky at town after town after town.

We came across a few other caravans of merchants—actual merchants, not bandits masquerading as such—and the occasional bit of wildlife, but the bears and mountain lions Denali found sign of were of the perfectly ordinary variety. The closest we came to Badlands weirdness was a herd of deer led by a stag whose antlers were made of fire.

I wasn't sure how that worked, but from what Lady had said, spiders the size of people were biologically impossible too, so I didn't waste brainpower worrying about it. In the post-Break world, some things just were. Figuring out how to fit our new reality into the framework of science was an ongoing effort for people a whole lot smarter than me.

Still, those weeks were just what the Mission needed after everything we'd gone through. As we moved deeper into fall, you could almost see people remembering to breathe, see the tension draining out of people around us. Not everyone, of course. The few who'd been through the shit in Kansas City still held onto some of that post-battle strain. Especially when they were in my vicinity. Reese had joined Cagney in steering clear of me while doing their best not to make it obvious.

I'm here to tell you all: it was very fucking obvious.

Supersonic and Silt hadn't changed a bit, but they'd also both known me for three years and seen some of what I was capable of in the Training Grounds. Stark, Denali, and Jacobs were... somewhere in the middle, I guess. They didn't treat me any differently than they had, but there were times I looked up to find one of them watching me, kind of the same way they'd watched that stag with the burning antlers.

Not precisely wary, but... *aware*.

I took Mammoth at his word and started making more time for myself. Meditation became a daily thing again—an hour of communing with the emptiness inside and around me every night before dinner. The number of bodies I'd left behind me in Kansas City was barely a fraction of the spiders I'd killed in the Weaver's forest, but every death was still changing me. I was so far beyond where I'd been when we started out in Idaho, four months earlier, that it sometimes scared even me.

Other times, I just felt grim satisfaction, nibbling away at the fringes of the emptiness. The country was focused on Tezcatlipoca's latest incursion, and rightly so, but the so-called god wasn't the only threat that needed solving. Tyrant had kept hidden since Reno, but this was one instance where that Shadecaster motto was just a lie, because I hadn't forgotten him at all. And once Tessa and I had graduated... once we had a Cape team of our own...

We were going hunting, and that sister-killing motherfucker was going to regret ever having paired my mom and dad together as part of his breeding experiments.

○○○

Three weeks, then four. We crossed into the Texas panhandle, where Stark's father had died, and back out of it and the worst thing we saw was a kettle of buzzards circling over something dead far to our south. We stopped at towns along the way, leaving each one better than we'd found it, but not one of those towns' ghosts had anything to say when I reached out to them.

The Mission was doing its job, but as for Her Majesty's favor? Me finding Dr. Nowhere so she could ask him her questions?

I was coming up empty on all fronts.

And then one morning, I woke up to a sky with two suns instead of one.

CHAPTER 48

The first sun—the expected one—was rising in the east, barely peeking through the storm system that had just soaked our campsite. The second sun was to the west and maybe a bit south, visible only to my Crow's eye, overpowering any of the other sources of light that might have dotted the dark-watered ocean of my power's sight.

Normals were sparks of light. Silt and Supersonic were lanterns. The Weaver had been a damn forest fire. But this... this was something on a whole different scale.

There's only one Cat Six Power in the world, and something told me I had just found him.

Or... sort of found him. We were at least a few days ride away, as far as I could tell. Maybe more. It was way beyond my range to sense things normally, but I guess you don't need a magnifying glass to spot a skyscraper.

"What's down that way?" I asked Stark, trying not to squint into a light that nobody else could see.

"Our next stop," he said. "Place called Deming."

"Is there anything south of there?"

"A few towns, I think. Mammoth would know for sure, although it's getting pretty close to Tezcatlipoca's domain. We were originally supposed to go to Albuquerque, but the government called in yet another favor and asked us to check with Deming on whether the border's shifted this far east." He rolled something around in his mouth and spat to the side of the road. "Hopefully, this bit of recon goes better than the last. How come?"

"Just curious," I told him. "I thought I saw something in the sky. We're starting to reach parts of the Badlands I might need to know about, if I get recruited by Red Flight or the Thunderbirds."

"Unless you've learned to fly like an actual crow, I doubt Red Flight would recruit you," said Supersonic, inviting himself into the conversation.

"The Thunderbirds then. They're closer anyway."

"We'll be in Deming for a few days," said Stark. "If you and some others want to drop off supplies with the southern satellite towns, I'm sure they'd appreciate it."

ooo

Deming was bigger than I'd expected, and prettier too, thanks to the river that cut through just to the north. It was also cold. We'd finally hit late-October, and even though the locals swore the weather was usually mild this time of year, fall was making itself known. For the first time in months, I made use of my jacket for something other than the rain. Denali said there was even a small chance we'd see overnight snow if a storm came through.

I wasn't sure how I felt about that. It got cold in Bakersfield too, but not *frozen water falling from the sky* cold.

Apparently, Deming had served as something of a port of entry back when the United States of America—and what a mouthful *that* must have been to say all the time—was still a thing. With Mexico and everything south of it now home to Tezcatlipoca and his drones, the town didn't get much traffic anymore, and the people who had stayed had turned back to agriculture as a means of survival, relying on the river just like populations must have for hundreds of years before the country was even born.

A town the size of Deming almost definitely had some Powers of its own—probably Ones and Twos, or a Finder would have already tracked them down and recruited them—but for once, my power was going to be of no help in identifying them. Dr. Nowhere's light was now so bright that it overpowered everything else, from the sparks of light that were Normals to the lanterns of the two Powers in our own caravan. As we'd come closer over the past few days, I'd had to turn off my extra sense, closed my Crow's eye, just to keep from blinding myself.

Can't say I loved being reliant on purely human vision after months of supplementing it with my power, but life had never given a fuck about what I thought and was clearly determined to keep that streak going. If Bard had been with us instead of living the sweet life back in Los Angeles, he'd probably have told me it was an opportunity for self-reflection and to be reminded how the Normals lived.

Got to be honest, one of my favorite things about Mammoth was that his focus was on the Mission itself and not the *continued personal growth* of the Cape students he'd brought along for the ride.

Deming was thirty or so miles north of the border, or what we hoped was still the border. The town's mayor seemed happy to see us and even happier for the supplies in our now mostly empty wagons. Cob and I dragged two full crates of medicine over to the town's hospital, and the two doctors and three nurses there welcomed us like we were the second coming of Lincoln and Jesus combined.

Cob stayed behind to assist the doctors, at least one of whom had once made the trek into Arizona to study medicine, so I wandered back on my own. The streets were empty except for members of the Mission, the town's welcoming committee, and a handful of children too small to work but too big for their parents to keep an eye on. I dodged some of the last group as they barreled around a corner, chasing a child with a ball.

Mama Rawlins' House for Unwanted Brats hadn't been big on sports. Too likely that the older kids would see it as an excuse to do some damage to the rest of us... on the rare occasion that they needed an excuse. But the kids that ran past me all seemed to be laughing, even the one being chased, so I ignored it and kept going.

Lady was setting up our last pair of solar panels at the town center and had asked for my help later that afternoon. Turns out using my power to control my own body gave me one hell of a steady hand. If this whole Cape thing didn't pan out long-term, I figured I could always be a repairman instead. Maybe even if the Cape thing *did* work out. Having a fallback option or a second source of income was never a bad idea. Hell, Winter was planning to moonlight as a baker even while serving on an active team.

I stopped in the middle of the street as a thought struck me. As professional Capes, we would have our own support staff, from public relations reps to accountants to nutritionists to personal trainers and (in some rare occasions) even masseuses and acupuncturists. Maybe I could get a baker added to that list?

I'd bring it up with Tessa when we finally saw each other again.

But before that, and before I went to help Lady with the solar panels, I had a job of my own to do. I turned off the gravel road onto an empty side street, found a spot out of sight, and dug through my backpack. Beneath the clothes—some dirty, some clean, and fuck if I could tell you which were which—and the razor, the underwear and one of the fresh bars of soap Emma had traded for in Wichita, at the very bottom of the pack was something the length of my forearm that looked like nothing so much as a random scrap of leather.

Provided you didn't touch it. I tried not to grimace at the feel of the thing, warm and moist, pulsing to my touch just like the gun I'd smuggled into the Hole to shoot my father with. There was a reason for that similarity, of course. Both the gun and this device had been provided by Her Majesty, and both were Legion tech, creations of the tyrannical Technomancer who ruled Old Baltimore way out east.

Even in the sunlight, the device looked harmless, strange patterns on what appeared to be a thick, roughly scraped hide. It was heavier than it looked, but the mechanical portions were hidden somewhere inside the leather exterior. Thankfully, Her Majesty had told me what to do.

I took a seat in the dirt and laid the strip of leather across my lap. I then drew my knife and made a small slice along the inside of my right arm, careful to avoid the veins and arteries. It would have been a hell of a lot easier if I could've just poked one of the fingers on my right hand instead, but those fingers and that hand were ash in the Red Dragon's funeral pyre, and I had to make do with what I had. Carving up my arm seemed a hell of a lot safer than trying to hold the knife between my knees and stabbing my left hand with it instead.

That's my story anyway. Truth was, with only one working hand, I was more than a little bit protective of it.

As for why I didn't just get Silt to cut me, considering she already knew about Her Majesty and my real mission?

Okay... so maybe I didn't fucking think of that until *after* the cut was already made. There's a reason Alexa called me a hammer instead of a scalpel... and a reason I'd never seen myself as team leader material.

We all play the roles we're given.

Sometimes, even when we don't realize it.

I angled my arm so the blood that beaded to my skin's surface dripped onto the piece of Legion tech. Instead of splashing, each droplet disappeared like it had never even existed, like water spilled in the desert. Three drops, then four, then the dripping became a steady stream and I had to wonder both if I'd made the cut too deep and if this whole setup was just a practical joke by Her Majesty to see if I'd willingly bleed myself out.

And then the device cracked down the middle and the leather shell unfolded to reveal a metal and flesh creature with over a dozen sets of paper-thin wings. Five of its eight legs were some kind of metal, but the other three looked like misshapen, nailless fingers, and it had cameras instead of eyes, mounted in bulbous arrays.

It trained those cameras on me, and I tried not to shiver. According to Her Majesty, I had only fifteen seconds before this little monstrosity would leave in search of its bonded pair. I could be grossed out on my own time.

"I've found him," I told the cyborg bug thing. "Dr. Nowhere is just south of Deming, New Mexico. Based on the map I've seen of towns still around, I think it's a place named Columbus. I'm headed down there in a day or so to check it out, but we'll probably be gone before you arrive."

I had barely finished before the creature took to the air. Its many wings created an audible buzz as it streaked off into the sky. Going down to Columbus wasn't strictly necessary, of course. Given how small the town was supposed to be, I didn't think the mercenary would need my help to identify Dr. Nowhere... but hell if I was going to pass up the chance to lay eyes on the man who had destroyed the world.

Besides, Seeks Peace in Clouds had given me a message to pass along. And maybe I had a message or two of my own.

I was putting pressure on the incision I'd made, a small scrap of bandage doing its best to soak up the blood that continued to spill, when I heard a sound from the street behind me. Gravel crunching. I was on my feet in an eyeblink, but by the time I made it to the main road, there was nobody there. Worse, that cosmic fucking event that was Dr. Nowhere continued to make my Crow senses useless.

Just a street kid, I told myself. *Some little shit wanting to see why one of the Mission was off sitting by himself.*

I wished I could believe that. Wished I knew how much whoever it was had heard or seen. All I knew for sure was that heading down to Columbus was now no longer just a matter of curiosity. Dr. Nowhere's existence, let alone his or her location, was the sort of information people would kill for, and there was no telling what Black Hats, the Crimson Queen, or even my own government would do with that knowledge.

Her Majesty's favor had been to find Dr. Nowhere, and if he left to escape unwanted entanglements, all I'd have done was give her a location Dr. Nowhere had abandoned. Like it or not, that meant staying in Columbus—staying near Dr. Nowhere—until she arrived.

As for how I was going to sell *that* to Mammoth?

Fuck if I knew.

CHAPTER 49

Turned out getting permission to go down to Columbus was easy. As Stark had said, Deming had a handful of satellite towns and if we wanted to distribute supplies to those towns ourselves, the mayor and his people were more than happy to let us do so.

The number of people who signed up for the trip, however, rang all sorts of alarm bells in my head. Supersonic and Silt were a given—the former because he didn't want to miss out any action where I was concerned, and the latter because she was tired of me getting kidnapped and tortured. Jacobs made sense too, given that I was his whole reason for being there.

But Mammoth? I couldn't remember a time he'd ever joined us on one of these side trips. And Cob? Shouldn't he have been helping the doctors still? Throw in Reese, who'd been dead set on hanging out in Deming's one remaining bar when we first arrived, and there were suddenly seven of us going to a small town of barely two hundred people.

To say I was suspicious of their motives was a massive understatement. I had yet to figure out who it was that had spied on me, but I was pretty damn sure they'd included themselves in our little group.

I really hoped it wasn't Mammoth.

It took a day before we were ready to head down. Lady and I finished getting the town's second solar installation working, and then, once the shortwave radio we'd brought from Wichita was juiced up, Jacobs tested it out. Unlike the microwave relay technology used to communicate previously, this was more of a full-on broadcast that anyone might be able to pick up. If someone did try to listen in though, they were no doubt disappointed; Jacobs' message was a long string of gibberish that he said only the government would be able to decipher.

It wasn't a secure-but-disgusting human/robot/bug hybrid messenger, but I guess we couldn't all have access to Legion tech.

Once we confirmed that both the solar array and radio were working, it was time to head south. Five of us had been on that ill-fated Kansas City visit. You'd think someone would have done the math, remembered how that last trip had gone, and bowed the fuck out.

Don't know if it would have changed anything.

Don't know if anything could have, honestly. Fate is an asshole just waiting to fuck you sideways.

But you don't need someone telling you that. Me, least of all.

ooo

It took us three days to reach Columbus. If we'd ridden hard, we might have made it in two, but that was a great way for one or more of our horses to come up lame, and none of them deserved that.

Even Cloud.

As we got closer, Mammoth went into the wagon and pulled out a stick twice as tall as he was. At the end of it was a cage and in that cage were a pair of birds, one brown and white, the other brown and white with a bit of red around the head and chest.

"House finches," said Mammoth, extending the cage out in front of him as the birds chirped to each other, "courtesy of the people of Deming. We'll ride in single file until we see signs of other people."

"What are the birds for?" I asked.

"Tezcatlipoca affects more than just humans," said Jacobs. "Any animals that come into his range become his puppets as well."

"If the finches stop behaving like finches, we'll know we've hit the edge of Tezcatlipoca's domain," said Silt. "That's brilliant."

"Mayor Green said they'd heard from Columbus as recently as last month," said Mammoth, "and I'm pretty sure the border remains a long way south of our destination, but until we see people acting like people, I'm not taking any chances."

I sighed. "You should probably have me ride up front with the birds, just in case."

Six pairs of eyes turned to me, but only Silt already knew what I meant.

"You're my responsibility," said Mammoth, "despite all evidence to the contrary over the past five months. I'm not going to put you in harm's way here."

"Or give Tezcatlipoca a potential weapon," agreed Jacobs.

"I have it on good authority that Crows are immune to the whole brainwashing thing," I told them. "The same way I can shrug off a Siren's song."

"That last part is true," volunteered Supersonic. "It used to drive Prince nuts at the Academy."

"Johannes is *still* dating Orca," I grumbled. "He's got nothing at all to bitch about."

"You're sure?" asked Mammoth.

"Definitely. I'm a taken man, but if you ever met Nadia, you'd—" I coughed. "You're asking if I'm sure about taking the lead, aren't you?"

Mammoth's grin was as big as the rest of him.

And that's how Cloud and I became the vanguard of our mission down to Columbus. Me, a demon horse, and two finches who had no idea their little bird brains were on the line.

Another hour passed, and my arm ached no matter how I tried to position the pole across Cloud's back, but eventually, our destination came into view.

Columbus was nothing like I'd expected. Which had kind of been the unofficial motto for this whole journey, if I was being honest. In place of stone fortifications or the earth tones of a typical desert city, we got an explosion of color and form: blues and reds and greens, spindly towers reaching into the sky from behind a fence that seemed more like an art installation than a defense.

Apparently, long before the Break, there'd been two towns here, instead of just one. The first was called the City of the Sun, a planned community for creatives, set just north of the larger town of Columbus. In the years since the Break, both populations had dwindled, and the people of Columbus, conscious of the expanding empire to their south, had moved north to mix in with the artists' community.

There's no such thing as traveling quietly when you have a wagon, and we were still a hundred feet or more from the gate when heads started popping up over the fence. A little boy's cheery hello told me the border hadn't shifted this far yet, and our two finches evidently agreed. My opinion of the town's defenses didn't improve any as we drove through its ramshackle gate. The fence was creative as hell, sure, but I didn't think it would do much to stop a group of determined Normals, let alone a Power or two.

Dr. Nowhere had picked an odd damn place to hide himself.

Columbus didn't have a mayor, but they did have an elected council, and those people—two old men and a middle-aged woman—

met us just inside the gate, their smiles more for the wagon we'd brought down than any of us as individuals.

I sent a look to Supersonic and Silt, but they'd already noticed the handful of men who had kept to the shadows, armed with guns as they moved to encircle us. If this went bad, I knew they'd be ready.

The Council exchanged words with Mammoth and then the woman's smile turned genuine. She waved her hands in the air. "It's okay! This is the Mission! They're here to help!"

"The Mission doesn't come this far south." One of the armed men we'd spotted came out, and while his rifle was no longer pointed in our direction, his tone suggested that could be a temporary thing.

"Normally, that's true," said Mammoth, his voice carrying easily. "In fact, we were headed to Albuquerque before we got diverted to Deming instead."

"You're coming from Albuquerque?" A woman popped her head out of a nearby window, eyes wide. "Tell me you've got some goods to trade!"

"They said they *were going* to Albuquerque," shouted back another man. "Sounds like they never made it there."

"That's right," said Mammoth. "But we do have supplies from Deming and Wichita with us, and your town is welcome to them. A few of us are skilled laborers too, and Cob over there is a trained medic. We're here to help."

○○○

We'd arrived in Columbus in mid-afternoon, and by the time night rolled around, the list of requests had grown instead of shrunk. This, despite the seven of us working our asses off the whole time. Aside from the artists—easily identified by both their outfits and their wildly imaginative homes—the people of Columbus felt kind of like people everywhere. Some were dicks, some were bullies, some were kind or generous, and some gave no fucks about anything. In other words, Columbus, New Mexico wasn't all that different from Los Angeles, California.

People-wise, at least. Not having an ocean nearby was a pretty big strike against the city itself from my point of view.

Still, I'd come to the Badlands expecting mutants and cannibals and monsters, and while we'd gotten some of that, I'd also realized there were a lot of people out here just living their lives. As far as I knew, none of them even called this place the Badlands. I didn't know why they'd choose this sort of existence over one where they could be protected by Capes and a well-trained military, but they seemed happy with that decision.

We ate a feast out under the stars: foods they had grown locally, supplemented by both a wild turkey one of the farmers had come across and the salted jerky we'd packed in Deming. The low murmur of conversations surrounded us, and for a moment, it was like being on the so-called Beach at the Academy. Full bellies, lazy conversation, and the ache of tired muscles put to good use.

Appreciate those moments when you find them in life. They're rare, they're precious, and they're gone before you know it.

CHAPTER 50

"Any luck?" asked Sofia.

It was the next morning, and we'd just finished adding a supporting wall to a home that had been near collapse. Honestly, Mammoth had done most of the work, but Silt and I had held the things he told us to hold and hammered in a few nails.

If my second career as a repairman didn't work out, maybe I could be an apprentice carpenter? The Mission was teaching me all kinds of employable skills.

With the wall up, Silt and I had wandered off on our own to get some water before tackling whatever was next on the to-do list.

I shook my head. "I'm pretty sure he's here—"

"Or she."

"The Weaver said Dr. Nowhere is a male."

"The Weaver is a batshit crazy spider as big as a house."

"Fair. I'm pretty sure he *or she* is here. But it's like standing in a fire and trying to tell exactly where the heat is coming from."

"Given that I'm right next to you, I'm not sure I love that analogy, Boneboy."

"You know what I mean. With only a few hundred people here, I thought he—or she—would stand out visually instead. Like Mammoth does."

"Dr. Nowhere's not a Titan though, right?"

"As far as we know." I shook my head. "Come to think of it, without his costume, Dominion doesn't look all that impressive either. And Tyrant is the definition of unremarkable, except for his eyes. This could be harder than I thought."

"Have you tried asking the ghosts? If this is Dr. Nowhere's town, maybe the dead would know something?"

I frowned. The spirits of the dead had heeded my call in every town we'd visited over the last five months, but they'd never had anything to say. Still, she was right. Cob had been seeing patients all day, but I scanned the streets behind us for Mammoth and Reese and found them both hard at work on another house a few blocks away. For the moment, none of them were in position to spy on us.

"Watch my back?"

"Always."

I took a seat in the dirt, closed my eyes, and let the emptiness flood out of me. These days, stepping aside to let my power take over required no effort at all, like I was pulling open a door that already had someone pushing from the other side. The biggest challenge was not letting my vision lapse into that other perspective, where Dr. Nowhere's presence would drown the world in blinding light.

Come, I told the ghosts of Columbus. *Hear me and come.*

I felt that call go out, like a vibration along one of the Weaver's massive webs, and waited another few breaths, in and out, my detached mind as quiet and still as the air about me. Then, I opened my mind on the crowd of ghosts I had summoned.

Only... they weren't there.

"What the fuck?"

"What's wrong?" asked Silt.

"This town doesn't have any—" *Ghosts*, I'd been meaning to say, but as I stood and looked around, I realized that wasn't true either. There were ghosts everywhere now, snapping into existence like Wormhole had dropped them off after a trip through her private little outer space dimension, but none of those ghosts were moving to answer my call.

In fact, none of them were moving at all.

"Skeletor?"

"One second." I approached the nearest ghost, the faint image of a woman with holes where her eyes should have been, a toothless mouth open as if she was caught in mid-scream. There was no sign of what had killed her, but that was true of every ghost I'd known. Most ghosts, however, were in constant motion, swaying back and forth, mouths flapping soundlessly to form little nonsense words.

But this ghost, and every other ghost in the street, was still.

"What does that mean?" asked Silt when I told her.

"I have no idea." I crossed over to a second ghost, who was huddled in the middle of the road, the suggestion of arms wrapped around an impression of knees. Like the woman, his eyes were vacant holes, but his mouth was set in what had probably been a grimace.

Neither ghost had anything to say to me, and when I brushed my hand through their form, they didn't so much as flicker.

"It's like their spirits are trapped in amber or something," I finally said. "And if they can't move, they can't talk."

"Or point out where we need to go," agreed the Earthshaker. "Well, shit. I guess we'd better—Damian?"

I didn't answer, scanning the street to look at the other ghosts in view. Like I'd told Silt, they were all frozen, and that meant they couldn't speak to me, couldn't share a vision of their deaths. But as for pointing out where we needed to go?

Every ghost on my street was facing the exact same direction.

"Come on," I told her, crossing into a side street to look at the ghost there, shells of people frozen in time, from infants to the very old. These ghosts were also looking in one direction... but whereas the first set of ghosts had been staring directly down their street, these ghosts were facing just a little bit to the left of theirs.

I checked three more streets, Silt getting ever more impatient and irritated in my wake, before I was certain.

Every ghost was positioned slightly differently, the angle changing the further I went in either direction from the starting street. And if I drew an imaginary line from each spirit's gaze, they would intersect somewhere in town.

And there was only one thing—one person, even—that I could think of who could keep the undivided attention of an entire town's dead, beyond even the ability of a Full-Five Crow to disturb.

Dr.-Fucking-Nowhere.

"You're a genius," I told Silt. "Let's go."

We walked the dusty streets of Columbus, New Mexico, ignoring the brilliantly colored doors and the art that covered almost every wall, following the sightless gazes of the town's dead to a house on the north side of town, butted up against the exterior fence and not far from the gate we'd first come through. Like many of the buildings that had been originally part of the City of the Sun, this one leaned toward the fanciful, an earthen dome whose top and sides were decorated with shards of stained glass that sparkled in the mid-morning sun.

Unlike those other buildings, this one had a sign.

"Is that a tooth?" asked Silt.

It was. A smiling cartoon bicuspid, which was already a weird enough fucking sight even before you added the sunglasses drawn over the tooth's own toothy grin or the arms that reached out to the sides of the sign before ending in two oversized thumbs up.

"What the actual fuck?" muttered my friend. "Is this a dentist's office?"

"There's only one way to know for sure."

We tried the door, found it unlocked, and went in.

Silt made sure I took the lead.

It was *definitely* a dentist's office. Inside, there was a small receptionist desk and two chairs along the wall. The side table between those chairs didn't have available Glasses like you'd find in the Free States, but since the Badlands didn't have a Net to stream vids from, that made sense. Instead, there were two well-worn books, both hardcover, their dustjackets long since lost.

Past the receptionist desk was an open doorway leading into a single room with a raised, plastic-covered chair. Next to the chair was a tall, floor-mounted device with arms and attachments, including a light and what looked like a vacuum hose. And next to that primitive tool was a small man in a white coat, already turning to greet us with a smile.

"Hello there!" he said, leaving the operating room to extend his hand across the receptionist desk. "You folks must be with the Mission everyone's been talking about? I'm Peter Goodwind, but everyone around here just calls me Dentist Pete. Are you dealing with some sort of toothache? Bleeding gums? Our resources are limited here, but I'll be happy to take a look!"

I just stood there, frozen like a first-year in his very first sparring match. Silt nudged me aside and shook the dentist's hand. "Nice to meet you, Dentist Pete," she said, her drawl thicker than ever. "We're all good on dental care, but were stopping by to see if there was anything *you* needed?"

While she talked, I studied the little man. Behind the professional smile, he looked tired, dark circles under his mild brown eyes. His hairline had skipped right past a careful retreat in favor of abandoning the field entirely, leaving only a small fringe around his ears and the base of his skull.

"I can't think of anything I need," he was telling Silt. "How long are you folks here for? Give me enough time and I'm sure I'll come up with something!"

A minute later, we were back out on the street.

"That was interesting," said Silt. "Don't think I've ever seen you so quiet before. I take it we should have gone one street further over?"

"No." I shook my head, remembering the handful of ghosts that I'd seen in the dentist's office. Every one of them had been caught in mid-motion, just like those in the street, and yet every one of them had still somehow pivoted to track Dentist Pete as he left his operating room to greet us.

I was pretty damn sure that we'd just met Dr. Nowhere.

I turned to tell Silt just that and paused. On the other side of the town's shaky wall, I could just barely hear a sound. It was the hum of an electric motor, quickly drowned out by excited shouts.

Columbus had just gotten its second visitor in two days, and I knew exactly who it was.

oOo

Her Majesty stood in front of the bike she was so proud of, facing down a handful of the town's people with nothing but the smiley-face decal on her visor. As always, she wore black leather, from a thick riding jacket and gloves to the pants that had been practically painted on her mile-long legs and boots that looked like they'd been designed as much for ass kicking as for riding.

"That's her?" murmured Silt, as we pushed our way through the growing crowd. "Your motorcycle mama?"

"In the flesh," I told her.

Despite how close we'd been to the gate, we weren't the first members of the Mission to reach it. Mammoth's long strides chewed up the empty space as he interposed himself between Her Majesty and the people of Columbus, and Jacobs appeared, as if by magic, out of a nearby alley.

"Why hello there, Mammoth." Her Majesty's voice hadn't changed a bit, throaty and harsh, with the discordant clash of metal lurking just underneath. "It's been a while."

"It has."

Silt and I traded confused glances. Since when did those two know each other?

That motorcycle helmet cocked to one side, and for a moment, the smiley face decal across its visor looked almost sad. "You've gotten old."

"And you look exactly the same." Mammoth shook his head. "What brings you to Columbus? If it's a job—"

"This once," she said, voice quiet but carrying, "it's personal. I'm here to see one of your charges."

From behind, we could see Mammoth stiffen. "You know I can't let you hurt them."

"And we both know you couldn't stop me if you tried." Her Majesty shrugged. "Luckily for us, a fight's not in the cards today." She spotted me in the crowd and raised a leather-clad hand. "Bakersfield! I was starting to think you'd forgotten all about me!"

ooo

"What the hell is going on, Walker?"

Ten minutes later, the four of us—Silt, Her Majesty, Mammoth, and I—were meeting in one of the council member's houses, a three-story affair and the closest we would come to true privacy.

I hesitated to reply, torn between competing impulses.

On the one hand, Mammoth's reason for coming down here—to see if the border had moved the five-plus miles from its last location, seemed flimsy as hell, the sort of excuse someone who'd overheard my message back in Deming would manufacture.

On the other hand, he'd brought that birdcage contraption with him and treated the whole thing with the level of seriousness of someone who really was worried about what he might find. And Mammoth had been nothing but solid since I'd first met him in Los Angeles. If anyone was the real deal, it would seem to be him.

On the third hand—because in a world with Body Shifters, only having two (let alone one) was considered *passé*—the best lies were the ones nobody saw coming... and I'd gone a whole fucking school year thinking Tyrant was just an asshole Finder. Maybe my judgment wasn't the best where possible sociopaths were concerned.

And on the fourth hand—the one that finally decided me—I wasn't sure it mattered. I'd found Dr. Nowhere. He was here, and so was Her Majesty, and I'd lay odds on her carving Mammoth up like roadkill if he tried something.

"I owed Her Majesty a favor," I told Mammoth. "She called it in before I volunteered for the Mission."

"Which explains why a Full-Five would volunteer instead of taking one of the cushy internships waiting for him," muttered the older Power. "I should have known."

"You're a Five?" Her Majesty looked me up and down. "Damn, Bakersfield. And here when we first met, I thought you were just a foul-mouthed, chicken-legged orphan."

"I was." I shrugged. "Things changed."

"Only some of those things changed," said Silt, eyes still trained on Her Majesty.

"And who is this?" asked the other woman, turning her helmet on Silt instead. "Don't tell me you brought your little missy with you on the trip?"

"I'm Silt," said Sofia, squaring her shoulders. "I'm not his girlfriend, but she sent me along to keep his ass safe."

"And what a sweet little ass it is. Bakersfield and I go way back. Glad to see he's gotten himself a new protector. And some actual friends." The metal snarl in Her Majesty's voice vanished for just a moment. "I'm the Queen of Smiles."

"I thought you'd be taller."

"Says the girl-child who barely comes up to my chest."

Silt's smile grew to match the one on Her Majesty's visor, and the earth beneath us trembled, just a bit. "Size isn't everything."

The Queen of Smile's laughter sounded like a thousand buzzing bees.

"I don't know what the fuck's going on between you two," I said, breaking up what was looking suspiciously like either flirtation or the prelude to a fight, "but this isn't the time for it."

"I'm still waiting to hear what this favor is," said Mammoth, "how it will affect me and mine, and why this is the first I've heard about it."

"It's nothing bad," I told him. "She just wanted me to find someone."

"That's right. And? Have you?" asked Her Majesty.

"Yeah," I said. "Right before you showed up, in fact."

"Who?" asked Mammoth.

"Come with us and see for yourself, Gerald." She turned back to me. "Let's go."

I traded glances with Silt. *Gerald?* No wonder he went exclusively by Mammoth.

Not that I was one to talk.

Dentist Pete's smile had a bit of confusion lurking behind it when we reentered his office, his eyes drawn naturally to the giant-sized Mammoth just behind Silt and me.

"You're back already? Does your boss need cavities filled?"

"You can give up the act," I told him. "We know who you are."

"I don't understand."

"Me neither," rumbled Mammoth.

"Mammoth? Your Majesty?" The latter of the two was still hidden behind Mammoth's bulk, but I addressed her anyway. "Meet Peter Goodwind. A dentist instead of a doctor—"

"Dentists *are* doctors," muttered the small man.

"—but very much the man who broke the world."

"I beg your pardon?" said Pete, but I could see the sudden fear under his façade.

"Wait. You think *this* is Dr. Nowhere?" said Mammoth. "Seriously?"

I looked at the frozen ghosts around us, each still fixated on Pete, and nodded. "Remember how I can see life energy?"

"Yeah."

"Well, the Weaver was a forest fire." I cracked open my Crow's eye for just a bit and flinched from the energy filling that small office. "This guy is the sun."

"Now, hold on just a second," said Pete. "I don't know what you're talking about, young man, but I can assure you I have nothing to do with this Weaver or forest fires or anything else!"

"We're not here for blood," growled Her Majesty, stepping around Mammoth, "but I have questions that need answering."

The color had drained out of Pete's already pale face. His brown eyes were riveted to Her Majesty's helmet.

"You?!?"

"Me."

"I didn't think you were real!"

"I wasn't," she snarled, crossing the space between them with one long stride to put her helmet right in his face, "until you fucking made me! Now, talk!"

Mammoth went to interpose himself between Her Majesty and Dr. Nowhere, but the dentist waved him off.

"It's okay. She has the right to be angry." The circles under his eyes seemed to darken. "Assuming you do go by *she?* I heard the young man call you Her Majesty, I think?"

"What the hell is going on?" Silt asked me in a whisper.

"Fuck if I know," I whispered back.

"You have my word that I will not let her hurt you," said Mammoth. "We're not all Capes here, but I won't just stand by and be party to that."

Pete sighed. "That's not a concern. I wish it was, honestly. You might as well all come back to my living quarters. If one of you could close the door and flip my sign about?"

The sign in question was a placard I'd missed. On one side, it said "The doctor is in." On the other: "The doctor is out."

I turned it so the "out" side was showing through the window, closed the door, and followed the others to a living room in the back with an easy chair, a couch, and two wooden chairs that looked like they'd originally been part of a dining table set. A second door led to a bedroom. Apparently, Dentist Pete didn't keep his home and work lives all that separate.

"Does anyone want some lemonade? Iced tea?" asked Pete. After a moment of silence, he sank into the easy chair with another sigh. "I guess not. To be honest, I always suspected this day would come. I just didn't think it would be today."

"So, you're not going to deny it?" asked Mammoth, leaning forward on a couch that struggled to bear his weight. "That you're Dr. Nowhere?"

"I'm *not* Dr. Nowhere," said the other man. "That was a ridiculous title coined by some Pulitzer-hunting journalist hack in lower Manhattan. May God have mercy on his soul."

"But you did cause the Break," I said.

Tired eyes met mine. "That's right; I did."

"Why?"

He ran a hand over his bald pate. "I'm sorry?"

I couldn't keep the growl from my voice. "Millions of people died. Maybe billions. And for the rest of us, we're all forced to live in this shithole you created. Why would you do that to the world? Why would you do that to *us?*"

I'd seen Tyrant's smile: alien and remote as the surface of the moon, devoid of anything approaching human emotion. I'd seen Sally's smile, a cold, painful sliver beneath the bleakness of her graveyard eyes. I'd seen people smile as they laughed, smile as they cried, smile as they gave of themselves or took from others, or drove their fists or feet into defenseless flesh… but I had never, ever seen a smile as sad as the one Peter Goodwind gave me just then.

"Dear boy," he said, that smile a match for the half-moons under his eyes, "what makes you think I did it on purpose?"

CHAPTER 51

"I went to bed on an unseasonably cold night in April," said the man we all knew as Dr. Nowhere. "That night, I had a dream. Or, rather, a collection of dreams. No different really than any other nights; a kaleidoscope of subconscious fantasies and fears. But when I woke up, everything was different. Every network channel in the country was sharing footage of people doing incredible things, of creatures and weather phenomenon that had seemingly sprung into existence overnight."

"How did it happen?" asked Silt. "That's the one thing I've never understood. If your dream was the start of people having superpowers, then what gave you the ability to change reality? What was the chicken and what was the egg?"

"The prevailing theory," added Mammoth, "was that you were either the subject or the lead for a government-funded science experiment."

"I'm a dentist. I've *always* been a dentist." Pete shook his head and shrugged. "I have no answers for you. It wasn't the first dream I had, or even the most vivid, but it was the first time a dream of mine became reality."

"That's it? Shit happened and nobody knows why?"

"My belief," he said, smile crooked and sad, "is that God was punishing me for the sins of my youth. Even if I can barely remember that youth these days."

"In the Free States, some people think *you* are God."

"What about her?" asked Silt, pointing to where Her Majesty stood in the doorway.

Dr. Nowhere sighed. "A fragment of an idea, like a thought between dreams. A solitary rider alone on the highway, tumbleweeds dancing across the asphalt, random chaos given form and direction." He looked to the mercenary. "Until you showed up just now, I didn't think you were real."

Ever since Reno, I'd suspected Her Majesty wasn't fully human, but this... this was something else.

"You created her? From nothing?"

"That explains her body," muttered Silt. *"Men."*

"My first memory is standing in the middle of a highway in what used to be Utah," said Her Majesty, the grinding of metal loud in her voice. "My second memory is the eighteen-wheeler that ran me over... and my body, this shell, flying apart, setting the storm free."

"The storm?" asked Dr. Nowhere.

"Chaos and energy, like you said." She was suddenly standing over Dr. Nowhere, that smiley face decal on her visor more maniacal than ever. "Given form and direction through bullshit rules and impossible restrictions, that every action taken maintains a balance between what I get and what I give. It took me twelve years to figure that shit out, another decade to test the parameters, and ever since, I've been doing jobs across this continent, never helping because I can or because I want to, but always because the client can *pay* enough to satisfy your inane requirements."

"That wasn't…" Pete looked down at the hands he'd folded in his lap, unwilling to meet Her Majesty's unseen gaze. "It's not how it was supposed to be. But that's true for all of this, isn't it? I'm sorry."

"Fuck your apologies," she said. "I haven't spent all this time looking for apologies. I want you to *fix* it."

"Maybe fix the rest of the fucking world, while you're at it?" I suggested. Pete's sob story was all well and good, but the fact remained he was the only damn Cat Six in the world, and he'd been sitting on his ass treating cavities all this time.

"I can't," he said.

"You will," replied the mercenary, the tiny living room filled with the sounds of the storm lurking just beneath her surface.

"No; I *literally* can't!" He growled back. "Do you think I watched all those news reports before the networks went down, realized *I* was somehow responsible, and just sat back and did *nothing*?"

"That's kind of what it looks like," I said.

"I went to bed the night after what the world called the Break and I tried to fix it," he said. "Tried to undo everything my dream had done before—"

"And nothing happened," finished Mammoth. "Whatever power had moved you was gone."

"I wish. Something happened alright, but I had no control over its effects."

"What do you mean?" asked Silt.

"Have you ever tried to control your dreams?" he asked her. "Did it work?"

"No…"

"Exactly. I went to bed thinking I could save the world, undo whatever harm I had done, maybe even leave it better than when I had started. And Australia paid the price."

"What's Australia?"

"One of the world's seven continents."

I frowned. "There are only six continents."

"So everyone believes. Even my contemporaries who knew better. One day, Australia was a place, filled with great people, better food, and terrifying wildlife. The next, I was the only one who remembered it had ever existed. The difference was, I *felt* it disappear this time. Felt all those lives vanish like they'd never been. Felt the tidal wave caused by its disappearance hit neighboring countries—Indonesia, New Guinea, New Zealand—killing even more millions. And as I was waking up, shaking with the horror of what I had done, I made sure it would never happen again." That same sad smile flickered and died on his face. "Although not even that worked out the way it was supposed to."

"Meaning?" demanded Her Majesty.

"Meaning I don't dream anymore. I don't sleep. I don't age. I don't eat unless I feel like it. I tried to fix myself, to remove this terrible curse, and instead I'm simply—"

"Frozen," I said, thinking of the town's immobile ghosts.

"Right. Stuck as who I was at that moment, for more than eighty years now." He turned back to Her Majesty and this time he met her gaze, unseen beneath the visor and its decal. "If I could fix you, I would, whether that meant returning you to nothingness or freeing you from whatever rules I inadvertently set, but I can't. I couldn't even fix myself."

"So, you're useless. Maybe I *should* just kill you then." That motorcycle helmet shook from side to side. "The life of a dentist in a nothing town would barely require any recompense at all."

"Queen—" warned Mammoth.

"Do what you must," said Pete. "Maybe this time, it will take."

"This time?" asked Silt.

"I ate a bullet five years after the Break, once it was clear that the damage from my dreams would exceed even the toll of Australia. By the time the bullet penetrated the back of my skull to embed itself in the wall, I was whole again." He waved to the wall behind the couch Mammoth was sitting on. "I left it there as a reminder but as decades pass, I've found hope springs eternal. I've tried pills and poison. I've tried stabbing myself and having someone else do it, and the results are always the same. Maybe this storm of yours will fare better."

"Nobody's killing anyone," said Mammoth. "Even if you can't use your powers anymore, there's a lot you could offer the scientific community."

"As tired as I am of life, I have no interest in serving as a lab rat," said Dr. Nowhere. "Not if it leads to someone unraveling the secrets of my former abilities. I broke the world. I will not be party to another such event."

"Let's get back to the part where I shred the flesh from your bones, grind those bones into powder, and—"

I never got to hear whatever else Her Majesty was threatening to do, because a sudden pounding on the building's front door interrupted her.

"Boss, you need to get out here. We've got trouble!"

∘∘∘

We left Dr. Nowhere behind and followed Reese to the town's main gate, collecting our weapons as we went. The crowd that had been there for Her Majesty was nowhere to be seen, and the gate was currently manned by Cob, Supersonic, and a few armed guards.

We climbed one of the two ladders that flanked the gate on the inside and looked out at the people arrayed in front of us.

There were four of them out in the open, three in costumes, the last one bare chested like he hoped to one day star in a romance vid. A fifth figure was a substantial distance behind the others, lurking on the fringe of the desert scrub to our north.

Thanks to Dr. Nowhere's blinding light, I couldn't see shit with my Crow's eye, but the costumes alone told me that these were Powers. Even worse, I recognized two of them.

"The half-naked asshole up front is a Beast Shifter named Jaws," I told the others. "One of the escapees from the prison break at the Hole. The woman in back is Wysteria Appleton, a Teleporter." Both worked for Tyrant, which made me think the grey-suited bastard was somewhere nearby as well.

"And the others?" asked Silt, shotgun at the ready.

I shook my head. "No idea."

"Thank God Emma's not here," she muttered. "I told her you were an expert on Powers."

"The guy in silver is a Lightbringer named Prism," said Supersonic. "He fought Rocket once. No idea about the woman in white, but I'm betting the big guy in green is a Titan."

"The real question is what they want," said Mammoth.

"I can answer that for you." Jaws yawned, showing teeth that were every bit as pointed as when he was in his beast form. "Our boss finds himself missing the company of your one-handed little bird over there. We've come to retrieve him. Whether we kill the rest of you or not is entirely up to you."

"Their boss?" asked Mammoth.

"Tyrant. Major league asshole and the reason I only have one hand," I told him. "We're not sure exactly how many powers he has, so if he shows up, leave him to me."

"Never gonna happen, Boneboy."

"I'm giving you all this one chance," said Mammoth, voice raised so that even those without beast senses would hear it. "Walk away. You'll be empty-handed, but you'll be alive."

I frowned as they postured back and forth. Real battle wasn't like it was portrayed in the vids, Capes and Black Hats making speeches and pausing mid-combat to pose. Victory was a matter of numbers and power, yeah, but it was also a matter of striking hard and fast before the enemy was ready. Why had Tyrant's forces willingly given up that advantage?

As Jaws, Prism, and the unnamed Titan charged the gate, and the woman in white took to the sky, something told me the answer to that question was every bit as important as the battle that had just begun.

CHAPTER 52

"Supersonic! She's yours," said Silt, in full team leader mode.

"On it." The Flyboy took to the sky like a bullet, streaking up to attack the enemy flyer, but a crackle of thunder was accompanied by a wind that came from nowhere, slapping him off course.

"Weather Witch, Lightbringer, Titan, and Beast Shifter," said Mammoth, "but we have numbers as long as the Teleporter stays out of the fight."

Which, of course, raised more questions. From what Alexa had told me, Wysteria wasn't a combatant, but she had the ability to transport a lot more than just five people. Why would Tyrant send so few Powers to get me, when I'd killed more than that just breaking out of Reno? He wouldn't have expected Her Majesty to be with me again, but if he'd known to track the Mission somehow, he'd also known I wouldn't be alone.

Jaws transformed fully and leapt onto the wall with a howl, as the Titan crashed into the gate below us. Behind them, the Lightbringer came to a halt, mid-charge, and fanned his hands out, palms up, as if dealing an entire deck of cards at once. I squeezed my eyes shut just in time, but even then, the aftereffects of the light burst, brighter than anything but Dr. Nowhere's bullshit energy signature, had me blinking away tears and seeing triple.

My Crow's eye blinded by Dr. Nowhere, the human eyes by Prism… I guess it was no surprise that I didn't spot the mercenaries appearing out of the thick scrub behind Wysteria. Not until they started shooting anyway.

Mammoth had caught Jaws in mid-leap, hurling the smaller Shifter right back off the wall, when the first bullet hit, followed closely by another and then another. The Mission's leader was so big that he merely took a step back with the impacts, but that was enough to send him crashing down to the ground below, where a tremendous boom had just marked the quick end of Columbus' shabby gate.

And then the whine of bullets tearing through the air, the pounding of thunder, and even the trumpeting of a now-transformed Mammoth were drowned out by another sound, the grinding of metal on metal, as Her Majesty's shell fell away, and the storm that lived inside of her poured forth.

I heard the screams from below and wasn't sure if they came from Jaws or the Titan. Either way, Mammoth and the Queen of Smiles had the gate fully covered.

"I've got the shooters," I shouted to Silt, who was crouched low on the wall with Reese and Cob, doing her best to keep the Normals alive.

"I'll take Prism!" she replied.

Out in the field, a construct of dirt and mud took shape, but even as its earthen appendage hit the Lightbringer from behind, the soldiers by Wysteria adjusted their aim, bullets tearing through the packed earth.

"I thought you had the shooters?!"

I didn't reply, but two of the enemy guns went silent, brought down by walkers they never saw coming. With Dr. Nowhere's energy still drowning out everything else, I couldn't feel the new corpses as they appeared. Instead, I just threw emptiness in that direction, like an old man swinging a newspaper at a bothersome fly. Guns sounded again, but this time, some were under my control, firing at Tyrant's mercenaries from the unprotected flank. Toss in the flames that toasted another two shooters on the opposite end of their line, and it was suddenly a bad fucking day to have sold your services to the Black Hat.

The sky above us had gone black, then green, and Supersonic *still* wasn't making any headway against the Weather Witch. I turned my newly acquired guns against the woman in white, but the winds surrounding her were already strong enough to make marksmanship all but impossible.

So I had them shoot Wysteria instead.

That was the plan anyway. Instead, bullets tore through the air where the Teleporter had been, as her form collapsed into fractal patterns and then disappeared entirely.

A second later, lightning forked out of the sky, and the connection I had with over half of my new minions disappeared. Whoever this Weather Witch was, she was a shitload stronger than Winter.

I'd have to tell her that when we got back to the Academy.

For the second time in as many minutes, I tried to regain my vision while the battle raged around us. I still had a handful of walkers out there in the desert, including the three I'd started with, but they wouldn't last long against the Weather Witch and remaining mercenaries. And if Wysteria had left to get more reinforcements...

Wait. She hadn't left at all. I spotted the Teleporter a hundred yards away from her original position, arms folded across her narrow chest.

Why would she stick around once the bullets started flying? Especially once Her Majesty had made her presence known? This fight

was a long way from settled, but she had to see we had the upper
hand... right? Even with me half-blind?

And that's when it hit me.

What if they weren't here for me at all?

What if this whole damn fight was just a distraction?

ooo

There was no time to tell Silt what I was doing. I pushed past
the townsfolk only now climbing the ladder, and leapt to the ground,
tucking into a roll the dead Macy Jackson had taught us as first-years.
Then I was on my feet again, running through the streets to the
dentist's office.

By the time I reached it, a black-clad figure was emerging from
the house with a squirming Dentist Pete over one shoulder. I didn't
break stride as I charged toward the pair, but was tossed aside by a blur
that hurled itself into my path.

I came up with my mace in hand, lightning-fast as my power
pushed my body to its limits, but every strike was parried neatly by the
opponent who had appeared out of nowhere.

A Stalwart, all in black, just like the person kidnapping Dr.
Nowhere, but armed with the weapons Jessica Strich had called sai—
two long daggers with curved side prongs.

I still didn't know the name of the Weather Witch who was
wreaking havoc, but these two... them I recognized. They'd once called
themselves Triplicate, a group of triplets all born as Stalwarts. They'd
lost one brother to the adult Paladin almost five years earlier, and the
two survivors had gone underground.

Or joined Tyrant's crew, by the looks of it.

Neither Stalwart was on the level of someone like Carnage, but
they didn't have to be either. One could hold me off with a wall of steel
while his brother escaped with the prize they'd been sent for.

Fuck that.

I didn't have the time to get around the first man, so I went straight at him instead. I ducked under a strike and lashed out with my mace, but the other sai was already in position, catching my wrist between blade and prong. Triplicate twisted sharply, and something tore in my forearm, sending the mace flying.

Exactly as I'd planned.

Even as he used his leverage to push my arm out wide, I took another step forward. The second sai was already back in position. I couldn't see the man's face beneath the mask, but something told me he was smiling as he drove that sai into my chest.

He wasn't the only one smiling.

I twisted as the anticipated strike came, felt the blade slip between my ribs and puncture a lung, turning what might have been an instantly fatal blow into something that would take a few seconds to kill me.

And a few seconds was all I needed.

Both of the Stalwart's sais were trapped, one locked around my left wrist, the other thrust deep into my chest. Even second-rate ninjas had to see, and that meant their masks had eye holes. I reached out with my right arm, the handless arm, and thrust my stump into his face.

Triplicate dropped his sais and tried to dodge, but not even a Stalwart is that fast.

"I learned that move from Carnage, asshole."

I stepped through the cloud of dust that had once been a man. His brother, the last of three siblings, had stopped, letting out a cry that sounded more animal than man. With a visible effort, he turned back and headed for the wall.

I could already feel the energy from the brother I'd just killed, going to work on my injuries. I felt my smile widen. Stalwarts are fast and strong, but it's hard enough to climb a tall fence with dead weight on one shoulder. Doing so when the person you're carrying is struggling like a madman? There was no way he was getting over the wall before I caught him.

And then something hard pressed up against the back of my head and I heard the cold, metal sound of a gun cocking.

"I'm afraid I can't let you stop him, Walker," said a voice I knew, even as a hand relieved me of the knife sheathed at my waist.

"Are you going to shoot me here in the streets, Jacobs?"

"Not unless you make me," said the man who'd supposedly been sent along to fucking protect me, tossing something metal into the street by my feet. "Boss still has plans for you, and that means you're going to put those ankle cuffs on, we're going to lock you in the former dentist's office, and then I'm going to go join Wysteria and the last third of Triplicate in getting the hell out of here."

"You overheard my message to Her Majesty."

"Maybe don't say names like Dr. Nowhere where anyone can listen, idiot. I was originally just supposed to keep you alive so the boss could harvest you later," he admitted, "but that little conversation was an unexpected bonus. If anyone knows what to do with the only Cat Six in the world, it'll be Tyrant." His voice lost all its color. "Now, put the damn cuffs on or I'll blow a fist-sized hole through that deviant brain of yours and the hell with the consequences."

"You got it." My left hand now fully healed, I reached down to the cuffs he'd thrown in the dirt.

"Steady…" said Jacobs.

I sighed as the last Stalwart made it to the top of the wall.

"I only have one hand, asshole. How am I supposed to put these on?" I tossed the cuffs back down in the dirt.

"It's not that fucking—"

I was already spinning, taking advantage of that tiny window of distraction. I brushed the gun barrel to the side with my right arm and completed the turn, my left hand stabbing out with the sai Triplicate had left in my chest.

I didn't wait for Jacobs to fall before I raised him, didn't even spare him a moment's thought to wonder if he'd always been a traitor or if Tyrant had turned the man using the minor mind control gift he'd stolen from his own sister.

I just snatched the gun from his undead hand, shoved it into the belt of my jeans in a manner Jessica Strich would have outright flunked me for, and ran for the gate.

CHAPTER 53

Jaws was in pieces, but Her Majesty was engaged with the person we'd assumed was a Titan, now shifted into a form of black iron and looking like the world's ugliest fucking statue come to life. The massive bulk of Mammoth had squeezed through the gate and was charging the Lightbringer, elephantine hair lit ablaze by the other Power's energy blasts. Supersonic was *still* fucking around in the sky, unable to close the distance on the Weather Witch. Nobody had noticed the Stalwart making his way down the exterior of the fence with Dr. Nowhere.

My lung wound hadn't healed yet, delayed by the foot of steel that had been shoved through it for most of Jacobs' speech, and even with the handicap of carrying Pete, there was no way I would catch a Stalwart with that kind of lead.

Not on foot anyway.

Our horses were corralled outside the gate and in the opposite direction, but I was there in seconds, moving as fast as my power and purely human body would allow. Most of the horses were terrified, bucking and screaming as the weather went from shit to apocalyptic, but one horse stood in the middle, as calm as the fucking day he'd been born, tail swishing about, one equine eye coming to focus on me as I rushed in.

Cloud.

I didn't have time to saddle him or even say hi. I just ducked under his half-hearted bite attempt, vaulted onto his back, and turned him towards the now-open corral.

And then we were in motion. I bent over the horse's neck, kept him pointed toward the fleeing Stalwart, now halfway toward Wysteria, and held on for dear life.

Another blast of pure light lit up the field, but when it ended, Mammoth had trampled right over the Lightbringer and was wheeling about to grind the Power's remains into powder. I called up to Supersonic but between the thunder and the gunfire, there was no way in hell the Flyboy would hear me. Jacobs' walker didn't make it out the gate past the Mineral Shifter, and my other walkers were still engaged with the soldiers in the woods.

In other words, it was all up to me.

To be honest, I didn't give a damn about Pete Goodwind, the person. He seemed like a nice enough guy, but the world continually spawns nice guys just so it will have someone to shit all over. His history as Dr. Nowhere, before he'd locked his power away forever, was interesting, but it mostly mattered to the scientists and the government.

But there was a reason Tyrant wanted him.

Pete had changed himself so he couldn't use his power anymore, but that didn't mean his power wasn't still there. And there was one person in the world that had a track record of stealing other people's powers.

Tyrant as a Cat Six wasn't something any of us would survive.

The problem was, even with Cloud running like the demon horse he was, Dr. Nowhere's kidnapper would reach Wysteria long before I caught up. I pulled Jacobs' gun from my belt and extended it in front of me, trying to keep my hand steady as Cloud charged.

There was no fucking way. Even with two hands and a stable position, I couldn't have made a shot from that distance. With one hand and Cloud jerking every time I pulled the trigger, it was a lesson in futility.

Until the ground around the Stalwart pitched and shook and Triplicate was tossed off his feet.

Silt. It had to be. She'd seen me on Cloud, figured out my target, and used her powers to give me a chance to catch up.

The Black Hat's usual grace was again hampered by his need to both restrain Dr. Nowhere and keep the little man from harm, and by the time he was back on his feet, I'd closed the distance even more. I squeezed the trigger, missed every bit as badly as the first few shots, then fired again and again.

Through the grace of the God I don't believe in, the God Dr. Nowhere blamed for his own mistakes, one of those bullets finally hit something other than dirt. The Stalwart spun about and fell to the ground. This time, when he came back up, he left Dr. Nowhere behind, hands darting to the black sash of his outfit.

I pulled the trigger again, but Jacobs must have killed some of the townsfolk on the way to ambushing me outside Pete's office, because his gun was already out of ammo. I didn't even see the weapons Triplicate threw—some kind of shuriken, given his theme—but Cloud faltered under me, his great chest heaving as his legs abandoned their drumbeat rhythm.

I pulled my feet up onto Cloud's back, and as the horse went down, I leapt forward, launching myself into the air. Maybe if I'd been a Stalwart, I'd have stuck the landing. As it was, the best I could do was extend my arms in front of me to break my fall, trying to turn it into a roll instead of a swan dive in the dirt.

Thank fuck there was one of those ugly desert bushes there to sort of break my fall. Something gave in my shoulder—my right shoulder because that joke was apparently still playing itself out—and I had spines and scratches in places I didn't even want to think about, but I was alive.

My power got me back to my feet... just in time for a kick to the liver that crumpled me like I was made of paper. It didn't launch me into the air, like one of Carnage's hits, but that just meant I was still in range. A line of fire across my belly was the first indication of a near-miss from my attacker, and by the time my power had me upright, he'd stabbed me twice more.

My knife and mace were back where I'd left them, my stolen gun was somewhere out of reach (and empty, besides), and this asshole was coming for blood.

Apparently, Tyrant's instructions not to kill me were being treated more as general guidelines.

I slapped one knife strike aside, barely dodged the follow-up, and took another bloody line across my forearm as I deflected the third, but Triplicate was every bit as good as Paladin, if not Orca, and I had fuck-all to work with. I couldn't feel my Pyromancer walker out in the field anymore, there wasn't enough of Jaws or Prism to raise, and the few walkers I *did* have were too far away to help me.

I feinted to the left and threw myself to the right, onto the Stalwart's second sai, but he'd seen what I'd done to his brother. He pulled his weapon back before I could pin it and all the maneuver gained me was more of my blood splashing into the desert. I dumped emptiness into the dirt at our feet, but if there were any bodies buried down there, they'd arrive far too late to save me.

Fucking Stalwarts. Swarm them with numbers or send in a Titan to overpower them, but don't ever fucking try to fight them hand-to-hand. And especially don't do it when you only have one hand

and they've got weapons as long as your forearm. The only thing I had going for me was that Triplicate couldn't fully commit to a blow, knowing I'd use it to reach out and show him how much I cared. My power was keeping me upright, keeping me moving, ignoring muscles rapidly filling with lactic acid, but it was anyone's guess whether I'd tire Triplicate out before he finished bleeding me dry.

Given the stained earth around me, I was betting on the latter.

Another tremble of the earth came, but we were too far from Silt for her to do much else and Earthshakers were never known for their precision... both Triplicate and I ended up on the ground. This time, I was back up to my feet almost as quickly as he was. I accepted another two hits, all glancing blows again, and tried to bullrush the other man, but he stepped backwards and to the side, neatly dodging my charge.

Which put him right where I wanted him.

Where someone else needed him to be.

Peter Goodwind, dentist and one-time breaker of the world, wrapped his arms around Triplicate's leg and pulled.

One of the first things you learn about fighting is balance. All the agility in the world won't count for much if you don't have control of your own body. As the Stalwart's leg buckled under him, I reversed course. Triplicate was better than Paladin but I'm not sure he was quite as fast, and this time, he couldn't avoid my tackle. I caught his wrist as he twisted to stab me *again*, found the seam between sleeve and glove, and the rest was sweet victory.

Dr. Nowhere gaped up at me through the dust of the last of the triplets known as Triplicate.

"What are you?"

"One of the horrors you made possible," I told him.

Which is when Wysteria Appleton shot me in the back.

So much for her not being a combatant.

I watched my blood spatter across Pete's face and chest, felt my body twitch as a second bullet tore through something vital—like anything in your chest and abdomen *isn't* vital. One more bullet, this time to my spine, and my legs gave out under me as my control shattered.

I watched Wysteria's feet, small as my hand and wearing brightly colored, child-sized Chucks, move past me to stand over Dr. Nowhere.

With enough time, maybe my power would have gotten me back on my feet, taking the rein to my body's strings once again, but time was something I didn't have. I crawled toward the two, incapable of muffling the pain tearing through my body with every motion. If I could just get a hand on the Teleporter…

It was no use. She was too far away and I was too late. Her body started going two-dimensional, dissolving into fractal patterns, and I grabbed instead for the only thing that was in reach.

Dr. Nowhere's leg.

Through a veil of blood and other fluids, I met his eyes, and as he too started to fade away, I gave him back the emptiness he'd given my kind.

○○○

Time stopped.

Wysteria was caught, still in mid-teleportation, half three-dimensional, half slivers of an artist's shattered stained-glass window. The blood pouring from my open wounds paused in mid-flow, like when Polar Vortex had frozen Los Angeles' William Mulholland Memorial Fountain. Even the dust that had once been a Stalwart, tossed into the air with my collapse, was now static and refusing to fall.

In that endless second, when the universe itself ground to a halt, Peter Goodwind turned to see my hand on his leg, looked further to where I lay, hand outstretched. I couldn't read the expression on his face, eyes ancient with exhaustion and the years, but I thought for just a moment, there was something like hope.

And then the sun that was his power, inaccessible but ever-present, went nova in a burst of heat and incandescence, and the emptiness I'd poured into him started to recede.

I pushed back, but the power I carried with me, the emptiness I'd been born with, that I'd first wrapped around a little boy's pain and grief, that I'd unknowingly nurtured with fifteen years of suffering and all too knowingly fed with over four hundred deaths...

It wasn't enough.

I read that knowledge in his eyes, as time started to creep forward again, every millisecond a minute, but the end already a foregone conclusion.

Wysteria escaping.

Dr. Nowhere a captive in Tyrant's latest lair.

The man responsible for my birth, my parents' death, and so many other atrocities gaining the power to change the world with a single dream.

I'd made a promise as an eighteen-year-old out in the Mojave.

Fuck going out easy.

Fuck just letting things happen.

Fuck my own limitations.

I tightened my grip on Pete's ankle, and then with my other arm and the hand I still sometimes forgot was missing, I reached out to the world and *pulled*.

The ghosts of the City of the Sun, of post-Break and pre-Break Columbus, were the first to answer my call, tearing free of the stasis they'd been locked in all this time, but whatever aid they could lend me wasn't enough.

I pulled harder, feeling something tear inside of me, deeper than any place mere bullets could reach. Other ghosts began to appear around us, faceless, shapeless, glowing like they always did in my dream, but they weren't enough either, the emptiness still being pushed away, millimeter by painful millimeter.

This time, I focused inward instead of outward, reaching with my mind's eye, my Crow's eye, for the tear I'd felt, digging at it with my dead hand, peeling back whatever metaphysical barrier I had found, tearing away at the edges of the hole that had once let emptiness in as a trickle, then a stream, then a flood. The bucket of my power wasn't enough, so I opened myself up to that black-watered ocean.

And the tides of emptiness stopped receding from Peter Goodwind's body.

We lay there like that, time frozen again, eyes still locked as the empty ocean of my power battled the superheated plasma of his very being, caught in a stalemate that showed no signs of stopping.

Until a figure appeared, the shadow of a woman all in black, with bits of lace at her wrists and the hem of an old-fashioned dress buttoned all the way up to the beginning of her long, pale neck.

Mud brown eyes like bottomless graves looked from Dr. Nowhere to me, and Sally Cemetery smiled that quiet, vacant smile. The ghosts I'd only seen once before, in a dungeon in Reno, manifested about her, each of them monstrous, misshapen, and disfigured even as they cast shadows that looked almost human.

And then, an ugly light crept into those endless eyes. Her doll's mouth twisted into something savage, and she reached out with a lace-covered hand and stabbed her spectral fingers into Pete's chest.

The resistance I'd been facing gave way all at once, like a dam bursting before a single crack, and the emptiness I'd brought forth, the death I'd summoned from every place my power could reach and beyond, flooded his body, drowning the plasma, extinguishing the sun.

And in the arid desert of New Mexico, under the second sun neither of us could see, Dr. Nowhere died.

CHAPTER 54

I wish I could stop there. The death of a legend. Tyrant foiled yet again. The world saved from a threat it didn't even know was coming. I wish that was the end.

God, I wish that was the end.

But that's not how the post-Break world works. You know that as well as I do. Better, maybe. Even with its creator finally gone, this fucking world keeps on grinding, and wishes, like Dr. Nowhere himself, are just dust on a cold October wind.

Peter Goodwind died and I ate his death, felt the power that had fueled him tear through my body, healing every wound I'd taken on that too-long day before it overflowed my shell, flooding into the earth beneath us, like lava seeking to return to its home. The tidal wave of heat that had once been a life poured into me and out of me just as quickly, but the black ocean I'd opened myself to still remained.

Time caught up with itself, Wysteria completing her teleport, the storm above Columbus renewing its depthless fury, my two remaining walkers pouncing on the last of Tyrant's mercenary soldiers. My eyes told me that the unnamed Weather Witch had summoned a tornado to Columbus, the funnel touching down right at the fence, tearing it and the buildings beyond apart and sending shrapnel and bodies flying. My eyes told me that Her Majesty's storm had been broken by that same tornado, pieces sucked up and scattered across the surrounding acreage, that Silt had been thrown clear of the wall and lay still and unmoving in a heap in the dirt far to the side, that Mammoth was now fighting the mineral Shifter out in the devastation, the two Powers heavy enough to withstand even nature's latest horror. My eyes told me Supersonic was streaking through the air, aimed like a bullet at the Weather Witch's back and that the chances of her turning in time to defend herself were less than good.

But with Dr. Nowhere's sun finally extinguished, all my power saw were vibrant, antagonizing sparks of life, organisms polluting the ocean whose waters licked at my soul. All my power saw were intruders, invaders in my domain. Uninvited, unwanted, unacceptable.

And my power wanted them gone.

My power.

This whole time, since this long, strange story started, I've talked about it like it was a separate thing, something that merely shared real estate with the rest of me, acting independently of my wants or desires. But that's just bullshit, isn't it? That's finding refuge in disassociation. That's running from the truth.

I am my power. My power is me. We are the same.

And we killed every living person in that town.

I didn't even have to reach out to the people the nameless Weather Witch had killed, or the guards on the fence who had been taken down by gunfire. I didn't have to find the receptacles that were their corpses, because everything around me was ocean, and those bodies were already part of my domain.

With barely a thought, I set them hunting, set the older corpses in the graveyard to Columbus' south to digging themselves out of the ground to join in.

Lights flickered out like candles being snuffed and I raised their bodies too, a mass of walkers pouring out of the town to dogpile the torch that was a Mineral Shifter. The torch next to him—the figure my purely mundane eyes told me was a rust-colored mammoth—shook off the walkers that came for him and barreled my way, but the trumpeting of his charge was a distant thing, like the pain I no longer felt, like the voice in the back of my head babbling in foreign tongues.

I met him in the field, ducked under those curved, thrusting tusks, and slapped my palm against that massive, wooly chest.

The tornado at the gate guttered out and died, and I caught the Weather Witch as she fell... sent power into a body broken by a Flyboy charging at Jitterbug speeds. My newest walker flew back into the air, lightning filling the sky around a wannabe Cape suddenly on the defensive.

That Cape breaking and running, streaking north toward Deming or maybe even beyond that to Albuquerque, was the only thing that saved his life. Part of me watched him go, even as I slipped my left hand down through the still squirming pile of walkers and snuffed the life of the iron man buried beneath.

I could sense fragments of a being, spread across the town, like a hivemind broken down into disparate components, but those fragments were cool and dim, not alive, but not dead either... just will and chaos made flesh, and my power and I moved on, unbothered by their presence.

The lights of Columbus died, one after the other, as I walked across the field to the one spark left outside those broken walls, a lantern's glow that seemed like it should somehow be familiar. She stirred as I approached, rising onto unsteady legs, brown eyes in a brown face beneath brown hair, her mouth moving, speaking words that drowned in the ocean of my kingdom. She held a shotgun in her hands, fingers shaking so badly that the shells she tried to load ended up in the dirt at her feet.

I tilted my head as I approached, stepping around a horse's corpse, studying this light that kept shining when all I required was darkness.

Why was this one *so familiar?*

Against my own better judgment, I stopped. I engaged my other senses, my useless, purely human senses, and listened.

"—don't know if you're still in there. I don't know if you care or if any of this matters, but please, Damian. Please stop this before everyone is dead."

I wanted to tell her that she was too late, that she was the only one left, but when I opened my mouth, my voice betrayed me, even more hoarse than usual, as if I'd been screaming since the battle first began.

"Silt?"

And that's when the earth at my feet went liquid, swallowing me to my chest, and the butt of that unloaded shotgun sent me crashing into unconsciousness.

Just like she'd threatened when we were first-years.

For the second time in my life, I heard Sally Cemetery laugh.

○○○

Two hundred and twenty-nine people were living in Columbus, New Mexico when our supply wagon arrived. Men. Women. Children. Some of them had been assholes. Some had been saints. The vast majority had probably fallen somewhere in between.

None had deserved to be killed in their houses, to then be raised and sent after their neighbors.

In the span of twenty minutes, I'd ended a town, more than tripled Sally's kill count, and proven every one of my doubters right… but those are just words, faint approximations of true meaning.

Some moments change everything. There is what came before and what came after and the only thing that connects those two realities is the person at the center. The Break was Dr. Nowhere's moment. Whatever happened to make Sally Jenkins into Sally Cemetery was her moment, and the City of the Sun massacre was mine.

I'm sorry, Columbus.

I'm sorry, Mammoth.

I'm sorry, Alexa and Bard.

I tried. Believe me, I did. I tried so hard, only to end up right where people said I would, in the middle of blood-soaked carnage wrought by my own hand.

I'm sorry, Tessa.

I'm sorry, Vibe.

I'm sorry, Silt.

I couldn't be what you wanted me to be.

ooo

I came to slowly, still buried in the earth, my arms and legs pinned by dirt that had been compacted around me until it was almost stone. I'd swallowed some of that dirt at some point, and my first breath was a cough, spitting out soil as I struggled for oxygen.

"Are you… you?" I couldn't see Silt, but her voice was ragged.

"I'm not sure I would know if I wasn't," I said. "Why didn't you kill me?"

"I didn't know what would happen to your walkers if I did." She dropped the words like hammer blows, hard and cold. "Enough damage has been done without unleashing a town's worth of zombies on Deming."

"Smart." I reached out and snipped the strings of the one-hundred-and-eighty-eight walkers still in existence. The sound of that many bodies collapsing, all at once, was grotesque. "That's all of them. Go ahead."

I felt her raise her shotgun, the barrel close enough behind me that it stirred the hair on the back of my neck, and then she lowered it again.

"What the fuck happened, Damian?"

"I killed Dr. Nowhere."

"I saw that part. Hell, that part makes sense. Giving Tyrant access to a reality-shaping power would be the end of everything. I'm talking about after that."

I shook my head as best as I could. "I don't know. I didn't have enough power to finish the job at first. I had to break something inside of me, rip out the barriers between me and my power. And then..."

"And then?"

"I fucking lost it. Like everyone alive around me was an invader or an insult that needed to be answered." I sighed, blinking eyes that still remained dry despite fucking everything. "I have no excuses, and no guarantees it won't happen again. So please, just end this. Better you, here and now, than a lifetime in the Hole where my father died."

Another noise, and this time the barrel of the shotgun pressed against the back of my skull. I held my head steady, closed my eyes, and then—

"Fuck!" The barrel pulled away, and Silt screamed up at the sky. "Fuck fuck fuck fuck! *You killed fucking everyone!* A whole fucking town! Why can't I do this?"

"I don't know. But you should. Or get Her Majesty to do it."

"She took off as soon as she saw what you had done. Seemed pissed as hell about Dr. Nowhere, but I guess she didn't have what it takes to kill you."

"Then you're my only hope. Pull the trigger, Sofia."

"Stop fucking telling me what to do!"

"Or what? You'll shoot me?"

Okay, so maybe I was *trying* to piss her off at that point. Push her past that sentimentality she normally hid so she could do what needed to be done.

Unfortunately, the universe chose not to give us that time.

"Silt."

"What?!"

"Someone just appeared and then disappeared again in that direction." Unable to turn or point, I waggled my head to the right. "Given how they blinked in and out, I'm betting it was a Teleporter."

"Appleton?"

I tried and failed to shrug. "I couldn't feel her energy when Dr. Nowhere was alive, but it seems likely. Maybe she was just checking back in for survivors, and that'll be the end of things, or maybe—"

"Maybe with Tyrant's main prize taken off the board, he's going to focus on the consolation reward of a not-so-Baby Crow?"

"Yeah. I'm not asking for your help—in fact, you should get the fuck out of town while you can—but if you won't shoot me, I'd really appreciate you freeing me. I'd like to kill that penny-eyed asshole on my way out."

CHAPTER 55

Twenty-five minutes later, I felt almost two dozen people blink into existence on the far edge of town. Five minutes after that, a man walked down what had once been Columbus' main street to meet me. He was unremarkable in appearance—grey in hair, clothing, and personality—except for two eyes that gleamed like copper pennies.

"Mr. Banach." His voice was as colorless as the rest of him, somehow masking a soul that had never been truly human.

"Tyrant," I replied. "Did you run out of Powers to throw at me?"

"In a sense. My forces are occupied elsewhere, and unnecessary for this one task."

"So, you came instead with Wysteria and a bunch of mercenaries?"

He cocked his head. "I'd heard you could sense the living. Another new wrinkle of your gift?"

"It seems so. Good luck trying to take it from me." Above us, the sky boomed with thunder, black clouds swollen with a rain that had yet to fall.

"We have moved past such considerations, Mr. Banach. I've seen what you did to this town. You are damaged goods and of no use to me."

"You sacrificed an entire town to Tezcatlipoca two years ago!"

"Because it was necessary. Because I willed it so. This was you succumbing to the madness of your power. Not so different from your poor, broken half-brother, it seems." He shrugged. "Thankfully, I have nothing but time. I can wait for your replacement."

"Then why come here at all?" Truth was, I didn't give a fuck what his reasons were. I was using my power to watch the dim light of his mercenaries creeping closer, setting up their perimeter, establishing their fire lines.

Walking into my trap.

"You no longer represent a viable tool, and that means you must be removed from the board. I cannot allow you to become a threat to my plans."

"Fuck your plans," I said. "I'm a threat to your existence."

In an alley three houses away, someone screamed. Gunfire erupted in the opposite direction, and sparks of light extinguished around me as the walkers of Columbus did my bidding. And then, what I'd been waiting for; the heavy boom of a shotgun going off on the northern fringe of town, a lantern of light fading to be replaced by a corpse.

Thank you, Silt.

"So much for your mercenaries," I said, "and Wysteria Appleton. If you survive this, have fun walking back to the Free States."

"Why walk," said Tyrant, the coins of his eyes slipping aside to expose the white-hot hunger lurking beneath, "when you can fly?" He rose into the air, a nimbus of darkness gathering around both hands.

Which is when I had my nameless Weather Witch walker bring the thunder.

Or, in this case, the lightning.

The sky split, and even with my eyes closed and my head turned, the near strike was momentarily blinding. This time, however, there was no Dr. Nowhere to render my other vision useless. I watched the multi-colored conflagration that was Tyrant reel back and then correct himself in mid-air. More gunfire sounded as the mercenaries I'd just killed and raised took their shots at the hovering villain, but their bullets had even less effect than the lightning.

"I see Mr. Jacobs' reports were not the fanciful exaggerations I had taken them for. For what scant good it does you. The second Power whose gift became mine," said Tyrant, his voice carrying despite the storm, "was a Titan. Obviously, I didn't gain Behemoth's stature in the process, but the procedure was otherwise quite successful."

My vision returned just in time to see him turn to the sky, copper eyes now actively glowing with their own light. Beams of energy lanced into the sky, piercing the clouds to find the Weather Witch at their heart. What was left of my walker plummeted from the sky.

"The third Power," he continued in that same mild tone, "was a Lightbringer. A Cape, this time, although Starburst had not made much of a name for herself before her end."

One thing hadn't changed since Reno; asshole still loved to talk.

"I'm guessing flight was one of your more recent acquisitions?"

"How did you know?"

"You're a long way from graceful in the air." More gunfire, but this time, I was able to *see* the bullets bouncing off him. His ill-fitting suit shredded under the onslaught, but the man beneath remained whole. "Like a pregnant fucking turkey."

"Charming as ever." He waved a hand, and the houses behind him burst into flame, consuming the walkers that had been sneaking in. Another wave of the hand, and this time, twisting spears of darkness shredded another dozen walkers, mercenaries and townsfolk both. "But now it is time to die."

You better believe I turned and ran.

One of the few powers Tyrant *didn't* seem to have—besides mine, of course—was Jitterbug, because I made it to my fallback position without him catching up. Or maybe he was just having too much fun wiping out my walkers as he followed. By the time I ducked into the blind alley, two blocks away, most of my minions were dead. Again.

Luckily, the one I needed was waiting for me in that alley.

Silt's shotgun had made a mess of Wysteria's skinny chest, but her head was still intact, as I'd requested, and she had one hand left to grip mine with. As soon as we clasped hands, the world was sliding sideways, the dirt and the darkness of the alleyway giving way to smoke-filled air.

Maybe I should have had Wysteria teleport us out of Columbus, but where would we have gone? Fuck finding another town that I'd only destroy in my sleep or my dreams or when the power moved me. Fuck hiding from the Capes who'd come to bring me to justice or the Black Hats wanting to remove my threat.

Fuck letting Tyrant win.

Instead, I had Wysteria teleport us forty feet back the way I'd just come and roughly twelve feet in the air.

Right above that floating motherfucker.

○○○

I don't know what tipped Tyrant off. Maybe he heard the air being displaced by our arrival, or maybe the part of him that was a Stalwart was every bit as quick as Paladin. Whatever the reason, he spun as I fell toward him. One hand—gloved, because of course it would be—caught me by my throat, and the other pulled back for a punch that would decapitate me.

I reached for the arm that held me, past the elbow-length glove, to the tears my borrowed mercenaries had made in his wardrobe, but he reacted before I could make contact, hurling me away, straight through the wall of a nearby building.

Not the *right* building, goddamn it.

Wysteria Appleton died a second time, before I could command her to teleport away, and I gave up counting the number of my own bones I'd just broken at six. Not because there were only six... I just didn't have the time to count further. My power got me to my feet right before a burst of energy tore where I'd been lying, and I limped through the wreckage of the building, looking for my second fallback position... the one I hadn't thought I would really need.

Truth be told, I would still lay odds on Dominion in a battle against Tyrant, but it was feeling like it would be a hell of a lot closer fight than I'd originally believed. The only reason I was still alive was because the Black Hat used his powers like someone who'd stolen them instead of growing up with them.

Honestly, enrollment at the Academy would have done him a world of good. Too bad he was a murderous, cold-blooded, sociopathic asshole instead.

The next attack was fire instead of light, and I didn't dodge it nearly as well, flames scorching a hole in my side. The pain was distant, the smell of my own cooked flesh only slightly less so, and I kept moving forward, looking for—

There! It was a door I wasn't likely to forget: lime green with a purple sun. The council member's house where we'd met with Her Majesty was across the street, one of the few multi-story houses still mostly intact, but this other place, squat and unlovely, had been built like a makeshift bunker, its walls thick enough to deflect small artillery shells, with an expansive basement dug out beneath.

I stopped in that reinforced entryway, turned, and waited.

"I am disappointed, Mr. Banach." Tyrant shook his head, still hovering a good eight feet off the ground. "I sent you to the Academy so you could learn to both utilize your power and control it. And here you are, a mass murderer whose concept of strategy is to simply punch your obstacles until they give way."

"I've been told I'm a hammer."

"You are a neanderthal," he corrected. "Like most Capes."

"A neanderthal," I agreed. "And also a distraction."

Two pony-sized spiders, the walkers I'd brought all the way from the Weaver's forest, leaped from the second story balcony of the building across the street, pouncing onto the floating Black Hat and driving him closer to the ground. One spider disappeared in an immediate explosion of blood and guts, but the other brought its great fangs to bear on Tyrant's unprotected head. Before the man could react, the Weaver's child bit down—

—only to have its fangs scrape against the Black Hat's armored skin, every bit as ineffective as the small caliber bullets he'd been shot with earlier.

But that was okay... because my spiders were distractions too.

The building they'd leaped from, the building that had once housed one of Columbus' dead council members, pitched forward as the ground beneath it went soft, upending pilings and foundation, sending one-hundred-and-forty tons of rubble falling across the street.

The plan—what little plan Silt and I had come up with—was to lure Tyrant here, use the spiders to distract him, and then drop a building on his head while I hid out in the bunker. Problem was, we'd made that plan before I knew just what he could do. I was no longer sure the building would kill him. Hell, I wasn't sure one of Los Angeles' skyscrapers would be enough to finish the job.

Worse, he wasn't Jitterbug fast, but he *was* Stalwart quick. Even as he killed my second spider, he reacted to the trap we'd unleashed. In that space between moments, both of us flush with our respective powers, I saw his eyes turn to the bunker I was standing in, saw the recognition of a possible escape route, saw the clench of his jaw as he summoned his flight powers to rocket towards the bunker's open door.

I could have shut that door... prayed it was strong enough to stop a Titan flying at desperation speeds, prayed the falling building was enough to kill Tyrant or that it would at least stun him long enough for me to find my way back out of the bunker to end him the only way I knew how. Could've prayed for a lot of things, really, but whatever Pete had believed, I knew God was dead. And I'd killed the next best thing, forty minutes earlier.

I rushed from my bunker to meet the charging Power.

If Tyrant had been a Jitterbug, he could have juked past me. If he'd been a true Lightbringer, using his abilities to blast me aside would've been second nature. If he'd trained at the Academy, maybe he would have learned enough not to be lured into a trap by a Mid-Three Earthshaker and a baby-fucking-Crow. But none of those things were true, and when faced with the one thing he didn't expect, that same mad Crow rushing toward him, killing hand extended, he did what amateurs always do.

He flinched.

What had started as a straight shot to the door became an arc as he tried to pull up to avoid me.

I had the brief satisfaction of watching that arc abruptly aborted by the falling building, all those thousands of pounds of mass swatting him from the sky.

Sometimes, you just need a bigger hammer.

Unfortunately, before I could reach out and touch his flailing form, all that stone and rock buried us both.

CHAPTER 56

I came to again, sometime later.

Still alive somehow, although the pain even my power could no longer suppress told me I didn't have much time. Still alive, even though I couldn't feel my limbs.

All of that mass should have crushed me into human paste.

So, *how* was I alive?

Only one of my eyes was working, and all it saw was darkness, so I reached out with a Crow's senses. The bonfire of Tyrant's power was nearby, still fucking alive, as I'd feared, but there were other shreds of life spread around me, smaller than Her Majesty's fragments had been and complete on their own, mixed in with pockets of death of similar sizes.

Bugs. Worms. Beetles. All the things that crawled through the earth beneath us, living and dying under our very feet, only now they were above and around us.

Maybe you think I should have figured it out earlier. But then, you've got the advantage of having lived here all your lives, of having been down here with me since I called you, since I started this story. You know the bunker's basement extended just a little bit further than the building's walls, that Silt weakening the soil beneath our makeshift trap also weakened the exterior of that basement, and that the subsequent collapse kept the falling building from killing us outright.

Or killing *me* outright anyway. My other senses were coming back online, and I could hear movement from Tyrant's direction; earth groaning, broken beams shifting as he sought to bring a Titan's strength to bear.

A weight across my back told me I had been partially pinned by another beam. It was probably the other reason I was dying instead of dead, but I was too busy trying to get free to feel kindly disposed toward it for that fact. There were pockets of air down here, spaces where the reinforced walls had done their job, and that meant Tyrant would likely survive long enough to free himself.

And that was something I just wasn't willing to die knowing.

I don't know how many of the bugs I raised were actual termites, and how many just played the part because my power told them to, but I heard them swarm over my dead limbs, felt them swarm over my torso, as they dug into the beam that had shattered my spine. I didn't know exactly what that beam was now holding up, but I was pretty sure I didn't want it collapsing on top of me, so my bugs took off just enough from it to clear some space without further damaging its structural integrity.

Didn't do a damn thing to help me breathe better, but it turns out breathing's a challenge with a broken spine, broken ribs, and the all-too-fucking-familiar punctured lung. The *other* lung this time because the world loves its pretense of fairness.

Still, the beam was no longer directly pinning me and arms and legs that couldn't respond to a nervous system with more leaks than the Hoover dam moved just fine under the instruction of my power. Things tore, broken bones grinded, breath went in and out in tiny gasps that didn't bring me even half the oxygen my body needed, but I moved... out from under the beam and into the first open space on the path to the copper-eyed bastard down here in the darkness with me.

Ten minutes. That's how long it took to crawl the twelve feet to where Tyrant lay. Ten minutes, leaving pieces of myself behind, following a path through the rubble that my minions told me was clear, if not precisely direct. By the time I reached him, I could barely feel the non-paralyzed parts of my body, the chest slick and raw with my own blood, the working eye I'd stopped trying to see anything out of halfway through my journey.

"Is that you, Mr. Banach? Still alive, after all of this?"

Tyrant's voice was hoarse, but I could hear him working to free himself. Down here, he couldn't use his fire without burning out what little oxygen we had. He couldn't use his laser-fucking-eyes to do more than bring additional rubble down on top of us. He couldn't fly, with all that stone on top of him, and he couldn't teleport because for some reason he'd let Wysteria Appleton keep her power.

Down here, he was just a Titan, a Stalwart, and a Shadecaster, and I'd had plenty of experience killing all three.

I tried to say something back, but when even breathing is a struggle, speech is a downright impossibility. Instead, I just reached through the gap my bugs had found, reached for the leg pinned there, bare except for a few remaining scraps of what had once been an awfully shitty suit.

It was my right arm—turning around enough to use my left would have taken me ten minutes all on its own, and I'd have been dead by then—and without the extra reach of a hand and its fingers, I don't know if I'd have touched Tyrant's legs at all. Luckily, I didn't have to. Tyrant reacted like a true Shadecaster would and sent a tendril of darkness to pin my reaching arm to the ground.

Guess Fallout never told him that some things transmit *through* a Shadecaster's shadows.

ooo

I'd love to tell you that it took all I had… that killing Tyrant was a repeat of that silent, unseen battle with Dr. Nowhere, darkness against light, death against life, two fundamental powers of the universe clashing in their endless conflict made flesh.

It wasn't like that all.

Tyrant may have been a Full-Five, like he claimed, but he'd been born an empty shell, and the powers he'd stolen from other people burned as their own flames, each a different color in the conflagration that was his soul.

I extinguished them, one by one, and those powers deserted him. I left the Shadecaster for last, leaving that connection alive until the end. By the time he died, he was just a pale shred of light, outshined by even the worms that had led me to him.

Then that too was gone, and I ate it just like the rest of him.

ooo

And that brings us to here and to now and to the end of my story. A story that began before I was born and ended the only way it could… in blood and pain and misery.

Truth was, I hadn't expected to outlive Tyrant, but my power did what it did, and made my body mostly whole, which meant I got to lie here in the darkness, buried under the building of a town I destroyed, waiting for my oxygen to run out.

And that's where I've been ever since. Down in the dirt with the dead, with new spirits showing up all the time, as if I'm an attraction, like the Bay's old bridge or the Sequoia National Forest before it burned down.

I don't know what you want from me. A happy ending? You don't need me to tell you those are bullshit. You're all dead, after all.

You know as well as I do that the light at the end of the tunnel is just an asshole with a flashlight, giving us the finger.

You want closure? I can't give it to you. Tyrant is dead, but Dominion is dying… just like me, if hopefully somewhat slower. I don't know what will happen to the Free States, to Tessa and Kayleigh, to Matthew and Jeremiah, Alexa and Bard, even Paco and Lynn. All I know is I won't be there to see it, and unless some other Crow gives you a call, you won't be there either.

You want peace? I wish I had any to offer. I don't understand what you are any more than I did at the beginning. I don't know if you're souls waiting to move on, or empty fragments like Sally claimed. I don't even know if you're real, or if you're just something my mind's conjured up to keep me entertained.

The only thing I had to give you was my story and that's finally done. Can't say you earned it, can't say you were all that great at listening, but what the fuck, right? I had all this oxygen left to kill, and you helped me do it.

So, thank you.

Thank you, fuck you, and goodbye.

CHAPTER 57

The first sign that something had changed was air. Sweet air, sucked into my healed lungs by the mouthful. Then there was sunlight, bright even against my closed eyelids, and the sounds of a familiar figure making her way toward me.

Damn it, Silt. Can't even let a guy suffocate in peace.

"Are you alive?" Her voice called down, as tired as I felt.

"The plan was for you to get the hell out of town as soon as you triggered the building."

"The plan changed. Besides, I did pretty much all the work while you ran away. I figured I might as well just keep that rolling." I opened my eyes to find Silt ten feet above me and slowly climbing down. Some of the collapsed basement had been buttressed by pilings of compacted dirt, and she'd cleared away the rubble of the building that had been on top.

"Then what took you so long?"

"Like I've told you a hundred times, I work with dirt, not stone. Moving all this shit took hours." She was as dirty as her namesake, but her eyes were bright. "When I sensed you moving about underground, I figured it was worth a shot."

There was a lot I could have said to that, but I swallowed the words. However long I may have been buried, it had been less than a day since I'd torn the town apart, person by person. There was no way in hell we'd moved past that yet, and honestly, little chance we ever would.

"What if I'd been Tyrant?"

"Then I'd have been fucked, I guess. But you've still got a few walkers up here and none of them tried to kill me, so I figured it was a good bet you were the person I sensed moving down there." She scowled. "Please tell me the asshole is dead?"

"Dust in the earth," I told her. "Hell, you probably used part of him to build these supports."

"Thank God. Now, are you just going to lie there, or are you going to get your ass up here to thank me?"

○○○

"Have you thought any about what comes next?"

Five minutes later, we weren't far from the giant hole Silt had dug to get me out. I had my pack again and was no longer mostly naked or quite so covered in gore. It shouldn't have made much of a difference, but it did.

"Given that I fully expected to die? Not really."

"It's been about three hours since Supersonic left—"

"Seriously?" I shook my head. "I thought it was longer."

"Three hours, give or take. Which means even with his limited flight time, he'll be reaching Albuquerque soon. Assuming he flew straight there instead of stopping in Deming. Either way, Capes will be coming for you."

"Yeah."

Her voice was soft. "You could surrender. Take it to trial."

"And end up in the Hole, like my dad? Like every other Power who's ever used their abilities to kill civilians?"

"These were extenuating circumstances."

"Circumstances that might happen all over again and at any moment." I frowned. "When Tyrant took me from Mama Rawlins' and sent me to the Academy, it wasn't becoming a Cape that mattered most to me. It was *not* becoming my dad. Fuck if I'm going to die down in that prison like just another asshole."

"What then?"

I shrugged as if I didn't know, but the truth was, I'd already figured it out. A way to maybe atone for the people I'd killed, to maybe give what was left of my life, or at least my death, some shred of meaning.

"I can't go west because of all the people there. I can't go north because the Red Flight and Thunderbirds will be mobilizing to hunt me down."

"East then? Texas could stand to see a little bit of death and destruction."

"Is there still anyone you love in Texas?" I read the answer in her face even before she nodded. "Then east is out too."

She frowned. "That only leaves—"

"Yeah. Honestly, it feels like fate. We're just a few miles north of the border, and there isn't a Cape in the world who can follow me into Tezcatlipoca's domain."

"But that's a death sentence. Even if you *are* immune to his mind control, Tezcatlipoca has hundreds of thousands, maybe millions, of drones."

"I'm pretty sure they'll still be outnumbered by the dead."

"And Tezcatlipoca himself? You have a plan for him?"

I tried to keep the emotion off my face, but I didn't dare call on the emptiness, and I'm pretty sure she saw right through me.

"Maybe I won't be able to kill him. Maybe I won't even reach him, but he calls himself a god, right? Maybe killing a few thousand of his worshippers will slow him down, keep his domain from expanding for at least a while. The Free States could use the breathing space, and I'm pretty sure your hometown could too."

She chewed that over for a bit, and then her sigh echoed mine. "Fuck."

That seemed as good a word as any to end on. I climbed to my feet and slung my pack over one shoulder.

"I put our extra rations in there," she said. "Figured wherever you were going, you could use them more than me. Assuming you do still need to eat?"

"As far as I know. And thanks."

Okay, *that* was as good a word as any to end on.

Except Silt just kept on talking.

"Is there anything you want me to tell folks back at the Academy? Poltergeist? Vibe?"

"Tell Tessa I love her—" I stopped myself, mid-sentence. "Actually, don't tell her that. Tell her goodbye, that I'm sorry, and that I tried. Hell, tell them all that."

She swallowed. "Anything else?"

"Yeah. Lynn was going to be working on a new kind of prosthetic while we were gone..."

"I don't think she'll be able to take it down to you in Mexico."

"No, but there's a little girl up in Baker who lost her leg. Maybe Lynn could repurpose some of that tech to help her out?"

"Damn it, Damian." Her eyes had gone past bright, tears carving tiny channels through the layers of dirt on her face.

Against all odds, despite the shadows I saw in her brown eyes and the fear barely masked in her voice, Sofia Black sent me on my way with a hug.

I squeezed her tight and then I stepped away, called on the emptiness, and sent it north of the city, to one of the few corpses I hadn't thought to raise in my battle with Tyrant.

A minute later, Cloud trotted into view, followed by the handful of still-whole walkers whose inactivity had told Silt I was still alive. For the first time ever, the demon horse didn't try to bite me as I mounted.

"Goodbye, Sofia. Thank you for being my friend."

I rode Cloud out of town, headed south, headed for redemption, headed for a reckoning, emptiness spreading out from me like the tides of the ocean I'd never see again.

And the dead followed with me.

EPILOGUE

"Lady Protector, you have a visitor. Your friend from the Free States." The woman who enters the small office is slim and cute, eyes sparkling above a mischievous smile.

"Again? Has it already been six months?"

"Six months on the day, ma'am."

"Well, shit. Time flies, I guess." Sofia Black takes her feet off the desk she spends way too much of her time behind and stands, twisting to relieve the tension in her spine. "Thank you, Lily. Please, take the rest of the day off. I'm pretty sure we'll spend the next few hours drinking, as usual."

"I'll make sure some food is sent up to the wall as well," says Lily, curtseying on her way out.

"You should seriously ask that girl out," says Poltergeist, coming through the door in her familiar green and black costume, her curly hair long and hanging past her shoulders.

"Don't I know it." Sofia shakes her head. "I'm her direct supervisor though. It wouldn't be right."

"Does *she* know that? I swear, the sexual tension every time I come here is enough to make even a straight woman swoon."

"Wouldn't that be a story for the people back west? The leader of Stormwatch fainting like a vid actress over a little bit of romance."

"You heard the news then?"

"Yeah. Sorry I couldn't make it to the funeral. From what you've told me, Dominion was a great man."

"A hero in every sense of the word. I don't know what we'll do without him. But," she adds, voice teasing, "we were talking about you and Lily."

Silt shrugs. "She's not dumb. In fact, she gave notice just a few weeks ago. Said she's enjoyed being my assistant but always wanted to try her hand at cooking instead. Her last day is this coming Friday and if I know Lily, she'll give Winter's bakery a run for its money in no time at all."

"And once she's not your subordinate...?"

"I really, really want to hear her call me Sofia."

ooo

An hour later, the two of them are up on the wall that encircles Brownsville. To the south, the Rio Grande winds its way east, and a trail of tall poles leads from its riverbank to the town. Every pole has a birdcage hanging from it.

"Still no movement out here either?"

"Not as far as we can tell," says Sofia. "Lots of bird crap to clean up, lots of songbirds to feed and take care of, but it's been twenty months since graduation, nineteen since you all helped me take back Brownsville, and the border hasn't budged."

"You don't think—"

"I think he did exactly what he said he would. He rode into Tezcatlipoca's domain and bought us almost two years of safety." The Earthshaker studies the other woman, her voice gentle. "It was a good death, Tessa, but he's gone."

"I know."

"Then why do you keep coming here? Not that I'm complaining, of course; it's always lovely to see you, but I also know you have responsibilities."

"It's good practice for our new Teleporter," argues Tessa, stopping with a wince. "That sounded like a better argument in my head. I just... I never got to say goodbye."

"You didn't see him in Columbus when he lost it. I feel like that's a fair trade. He was still Damian at the end, but for how much longer? Besides, I heard you were dating someone now. A Cape called Kismet?"

"That's a long story, and it's not at all what you think."

Sofia waves to their plates of fresh tamales, rice, and beans. "I'd say we have nothing but time."

ooo

They're almost done with their beer, and only halfway through dinner, when the perimeter alarm goes off.

"Motion sensors?" asks Tessa. "Those are new."

"Evie brought them out on her last visit," says Silt, climbing to her feet even as the on-duty members of the town militia grab their weapons and take positions along the wall. "That Technomancer Damian mentored is a damn treasure. They don't do shit for tracking the border of Tezcatlipoca's power, but they at least let us know when his drones cross the river."

"Do you get them often?"

"This is the first one in well over a year." She shakes her head, glancing over at the Telekinetic. "I guess that time he bought us just ran out. I'm sorry, Tessa."

"In my heart, I knew. I really did. It's just—" She trails off again, but this time, she's not trying to find the proper words. Instead, she's staring across the field, at the drone just making its way past the first birdcage. "In the Free States, whenever Tezcatlipoca's drones cross over, they come in bunches. Is it different out here?"

"No. They swarm across like they were cosplaying as the Weaver's children. Why?"

"Because that one is all by itself. And it's limping."

The two Powers trade glances, and then Sofia is up on her feet and yelling to her guards. "Don't shoot!"

ooo

With Poltergeist present, they don't even bother with the gate; waves of telekinetic force pick them both off the wall and lower them to the ground. Sofia waves a hand and the earth rumbles, surface layers of dirt sliding forward beneath their feet like a conveyor belt.

They stop about fifty yards out from the wall, still within reach of the guns in the unlikely event that this one intruder is something a Low Four Telekinetic and a Mid-Three Earthshaker can't handle on their own.

The figure limps its way toward them, coming to a halt a good ten yards away. This close, it's clearly a man, clothed in black, shirt and tattered pants dripping wet from the river crossing and plastered to a gaunt form. His flesh is bronzed by the sun and covered in burn scars, and his left eye appears permanently shut. His right ankle is visibly swollen and his right hand... his right hand is missing at the wrist.

"Damian?" Tessa's voice is a whisper that barely even makes it to Sofia's ears.

"Are you still, you know, *you*, Boneboy?"

He raises his head, as if surprised to hear anyone speak, and then flinches as his eyes drift past Sofia to fall on Poltergeist. A moment later, that emotion is gone like it never existed, but it's enough.

"It's done," he says in a voice hoarse from disuse, worn and thin even beyond the way it was when he escaped Reno, almost three years earlier. "Tezcatlipoca is dead. I rule to the south. Tell them… tell them they have nothing to fear from me."

He turns to go, but Tessa finally finds her voice.

"Damian, wait!"

The look on his face stops both women in their tracks.

"I can't stay," he says. "The Weaver was right. I claimed my throne and there is peace there, but it's a kingdom of the dead. I don't know if being around the living again will—" He shrugs. "I could have sent a walker, but I wanted you to hear the news directly from me. I'm glad you finished your business here in Brownsville." His eyes linger on Tessa. "I'm sorry; I can't stay."

He's made it three slow, limping strides when a wall of dirt rises in front of him. At the same time, telekinetic bonds lift him into the air.

"If you think you're just walking away from me like that, Damian Banach, you've got another damn thought coming," shouts Tessa, rotating one of the continent's last Full-Fives in the air like he's a doll.

"We'll talk about it over dinner," agrees Sofia, waving to where Lily stands on the wall, having once again disregarded her orders to go home. "Just the three of us, down by the river. It'll be nice to finally see the Rio Grande up close again."

For the first time ever, the smile that twists its way across his face doesn't make Sofia shiver.

THE END

AUTHOR'S NOTE

Five years ago, I wrote what would become the first line of *See These Bones*. I was drinking at the time. I had just finished the first draft of *The Italian Screwjob* (The Many Travails of John Smith, book 4) and was in the mood to write something with a different voice and a more free-flowing style. Doing so with a glass of whisky in one hand seemed like a brilliant idea.

That practice didn't last very long: Hemingway, I am not! Loose outlines demand a clear head when writing, especially when the plot keeps snowballing all on its own, and alcohol and clear heads don't mix. Still, it's fun to look back at how this whole thing started: a dram of Scotch, an empty screen, and a whole boatload of expletives waiting to be used indiscriminately.

And now, five years later, the story is done.

Damian's tale has always been one of battle against terrible odds. His childhood, his power, his peers, and the conspiracies he was born into. He's a flawed character, obviously, but I think he grew up significantly over these three books, moving from the angry young teenager whose own pride was responsible for half the problems he encountered to someone who entered *One Tin Soldier* with real friendships, hopes for the future, and (unbeknownst to him) a growing circle of admirers.

But of course, there's always been a subtext to Damian's journey. It's not just about who he is as a person... it's also about who he is as a Power. As he has grown and matured, his abilities have too, and each step has taken him a little bit further down that road to his inevitable fate.

This was always going to be a tragedy. Damian said it in the very first chapter of *See These Bones*.

We all go mad. That's just how it is. The weaker among us— the Ones, the Twos—end up in asylums with the everyday lunatics, one more flavor of crazy for the nuthouse. But the true Crows, the Threes and Fours who somehow survive to adulthood?

Villains. Black Hats. Murderers.

Every. Damn. One of us.

The challenge for me as an author was in staying true to that reality, to the bleakness of the setting and situation, while still giving you all a satisfying series-long arc and conclusion. How do you keep something tragic, the loss of everything the character has been working for, from being the ultimate bummer?

I found my answer in the roots of who Damian has always been: a survivor and a fighter. He loses as often as he wins, but he never, ever stops. So, when Silt dug him up from what he thought would be his grave, when he realized he had three possible futures— surrender and become a prisoner; run and become a fugitive who will potentially murder again; or die fighting the so-called Aztec god to their south in a bid for redemption...

Well, obviously, he's going to choose to go down swinging. And Damian being Damian, he's somehow going to survive even that. In a strange twist of fate, he accomplished exactly what Tyrant bred him to do... if not, perhaps, in the manner the Black Hat imagined. Tragedy and triumph? Damian can live with that, and so can I.

I am happy to say that this will *not* be the last book in the post-Break world. You may have noticed quite a few dangling character threads. Her Majesty. Vibe, Paladin, and all the other Cape students. The sickness that drove the Weaver out of her long-time habitat. And, of course, the Crimson Queen, who has her sights set on the Badlands. Dr. Nowhere, Dominion, Tezcatlipoca, and Tyrant are all dead, but the world keeps on spinning, and there are more than a few stories still to tell in new trilogies and short stories and even stand-alone novels.

As for Damian Banach, one-time Baby Crow of the Academy? This *is* goodbye. For now, at least.

Thank you all for coming on his journey with me.

ABOUT THE AUTHOR

Chris began life as a gleam in someone's eye, but birth and childhood were quick to follow. He's been fortunate enough to live in Spain, Germany, and all over the United States of America, and is busy planning a tour of the distilleries of Scotland.

A graduate of the Johns Hopkins University's Writing Seminars program, he put that degree to ill use for twenty years as a software engineer but has finally circled back around to the idea of writing for a living.

Chris currently lives in Nevada with his angelic wife and ever-expanding whisky collection and occasionally ventures outside to peer upwards, mutter to himself about 'day stars', and then scurry back into the house.

One Tin Soldier is his sixth novel and the final book in his trilogy, The Murder of Crows. Chris frequently shares updates and new content on his author website at https://christullbane.com.

Made in the USA
Columbia, SC
06 January 2025

49357398R00262